"Don't worry, sweetie. She just wants to watch. This time, at least."

There's a pause and Liam doesn't want to ask. He really doesn't. But he doesn't have a choice, and from the look on her face, Della knows it.

"What does she want to watch?"

"You're booked with another employee for this appointment. Jacen, to be specific. Jacen's her pet. She just loves him to death, but she's gotten this idea that she'd *really* like to see Jacen take control and have his way with another, very pretty, man, while she watches. And she's willing to pay *handsomely* for it." Della gives him a Cheshire cat grin at the thought of the cash rolling in, without even having to go fishing for a new client. It saves her work, time, expense, effort.

"No," Liam says tightly, almost swallowing the word. "No. I won't. No."

Standing from the table, his legs don't quite feel like they'll support him. There are no windows overlooking the back yard in the dining room and he's grateful for it. The cold pit in his gut grows huge and races upwards, lodging in his throat.

"Sweetie, you can't say no," she says soothingly to him, like the words aren't laced with bile and threat.

Also recommended...

If you enjoy this story, you may also like these other ForbiddenFiction works:

Deliver Us by Lynn Kelling
Darrek thinks he is just a straight, hard-working but lonely guy. When he decides to try a session at a private BDSM club, Darrek is unprepared for a life-changing encounter with beautiful, powerful and very male Dominant, Gabriel. Once they cross the line, nothing is off limits and nothing is enough as they crave ever more: more trust, more pleasure, more pain, and more devotion. As Darrek and Gabriel negotiate their relationships with each other and their coworkers, carefully-buried secrets and abusive pasts come to light. (M/M)
http://forbiddenfiction.com/library/story/LK1-1.000004

The Charming by J.A. Jaken
Clayton MacAllister had it all, but the shadow of a past love blinded him until life was slipping through his fingers. Just as Clay is ready to give up on the idea that he might ever be happy, a charming stranger steps into his life like a blessing — or a curse. (M/M+)
http://forbidden-fiction.com/library/story/JAJ-1.000046

Whatever the Cost

Lynn Kelling

ForbiddenFiction
www.forbiddenfiction.com

an imprint of

Fantastic Fiction Publishing
www.fantasticfictionpublishing.com

WHATEVER THE COST
A Forbidden Fiction book

Fantastic Fiction Publishing
Hayward, California

CREDITS
Editor: Rylan Hunter
Cover Design: DM Atkins
Cover Photos: konradbak at Pixmac; Rich Niewiroski Jr.
Production Editor: Erika L Firanc
Proofreading: JhP323

SKU: LK1-000005-02
ISBN: 978-1-62234-074-3

Published in the United States of America

DISCLAIMER

This book is a work of fiction which contains explicit erotic content; it is intended for mature readers. Do not read this if it's not legal for you.

All the characters, locations and events herein are fictional. While elements of existing locations or historical characters or events may be used fictitiously, any resemblance to actual people, places or events is coincidental.

This story may contain descriptions of erotic acts that are immoral, illegal, or unsafe. Do not take the events in this story as proof of the plausibility or safety of any particular practice.

This story depicts fictional BDSM. The characters are not models for the Safe, Sane and Consensual forms embraced by most current practitioners of BDSM. The author takes license with the use of BDSM for dramatic effect. It is not recommended as a manual for how to practice BDSM.

To Terry, Ang, Leyanne, Eli, and Kitty, for believing in me.

Contents

Chapter 1
Cowboy's Seduction

"Hey. Damn. Um, you must be William." Standing in the doorway to his suite, Tucker stares unabashedly at his guest standing in the hallway while wondering what he's gotten himself into.

Men aren't supposed to be this pretty, he finds himself thinking of the stranger waiting patiently to be allowed inside, with almost femininely expressive, thickly-lashed eyes that contrast curiously with a strong jaw and distinctly masculine presence. It's a little overwhelming to have the reality be so much better than the fantasy. Life isn't supposed to work that way. William has short, just-rolled-out-of-bed-tousled, golden blond hair and irises so vibrantly jewel-like and emerald-hued that they don't seem real; eyes that seem to drink in everything they fix on with intelligence and ample, unhurried confidence. Rosy, succulent lips curl in a natural pout. Broad, thickly muscled shoulders stretch out the fabric of a perfectly tailored plaid flannel shirt that highlights the man's lean, toned build. From slim hips hangs a chunky leather belt laced through the belt loops of obscenely snug jeans, showing off every bulge, line and curve. A glimpsed necklace's cord is tucked almost out of sight, under the shirt, lying delicately against the bare, suntanned skin of William's chest, visible only because the top two buttons are undone. It inspires a nearly unquenchable need to reach out and touch — to pull gently on the cord like a leash or maybe just brush fingertips against tantalizingly exposed, warm skin.

It's overwhelming already and they haven't even started. He got himself into this — this 'date' — and now it's officially too late to turn back without making an ass of himself. Heat rises, baking under his skin, thickening the air; his clothes are far too constricting, his body too awkward.

Why did William have to turn out to be so dizzyingly sexy?

And then he smiles.

"Tucker?"

Somehow, Tucker manages to form his lips into a polite grin of acknowledgement that's too strained and anxious.

"Nice to meet you," William says in a buttery-smooth baritone, extending a well-manicured hand.

Touching. The touching has started already, Tucker thinks as they shake. William's grip is firm and his palm dry.

Feeling like a pitiful, helpless animal caught in a predator's trap, Tucker ushers William inside the suite, muttering, "She said you were attractive, but... wow. You're really...." *Why am I saying this? This is the shit that's supposed to stay safely locked inside my damn head.* "Uh, anyway. Come in."

As Tucker shuts the door, he glances up and down the hall for any onlookers. There aren't any. Sighing in relief, he turns back around to find William checking out the space. It's not the most impressive hotel room in the world, but it serves its purpose. The bedroom and sitting area adjoin. A fully stocked wet bar located on the far wall beckons, drawing them farther inside. Two glasses are set out, as well as a bottle of Jack Daniels. One glass has been used, is still half-full, and the other is clean. Crossing to the bar, Tucker downs the rest of his whiskey before filling both glasses.

"Care for a drink?"

"Sure. Thanks. You a big whiskey drinker?"

"Today I am," Tucker chuckles nervously, passing William his glass. Their fingers graze each other and goosebumps race up Tucker's arm. Sinful little dimples pop at the corners of William's mouth, framing it as his smile twists wickedly.

"Nervous?" William hooks a finger behind Tucker's belt buckle, drawing him forward while taking a sip of the amber liquid swirling in the tumbler. Setting the glass down on a side table, he sits down on the edge of the foot of the bed, ignoring the sofas completely.

Too fast. It's happening too fast. Tucker's heart leaps up into his throat and if he wasn't nervous before, he sure as hell is now.

He nods. Vaguely, at the back of his mind, he's aware of some of the psychologies at play, the reasons behind the decisions his guest is making. With the taller William sitting on the edge of the mattress, he is positioned at a higher level—kissing range—than he would be if seated on the couch. Tucker is shorter than the average guy, unlike William, but now, seated in front of where Tucker is standing, William is perched at a height that makes him much less threatening, letting Tucker feel like the one in charge, even if he's not.

"Tell me about yourself," William invites with a hint of a Southern drawl that acts like a light tickle over Tucker's balls. Thickening inside his jeans due to the mind-numbingly alluring vision before him, Tucker watches William suck his bottom lip wet with half-lidded eyes, slowly easing his thighs apart, shifting a few inches forward. Tucker is conversely drawn closer by William's continued hold on his buckle. They migrate together, the heat from both their bodies colliding.

Tucker's sizeable apprehension is quickly overtaken with the even larger tide of his raging lust. He hasn't gotten laid in months. Screw the formalities and small talk. If the hot guy perched with spread thighs on his bed wants to get right to the good part of their evening, Tucker is more than all right with that plan.

Looking right into Tucker's alert, denim-blue eyes, William smiles provocatively. The hand that was holding Tucker by the buckle rubs downward over the swelling in Tucker's jeans. A hot, determined palm rolls over Tucker's dick, kneading the flesh. It jumps eagerly at the touch. Eyes closing over, Tucker exhales sharply through his nose.

William asks casually, "Is this okay?"

"Yeah," Tucker replies hoarsely. It's difficult to form sentences while he's being fondled, but he tries. "I'm in L.A. 'cause I'm on tour with my band. I have some friends here too. Old friends. I sing, play guitar."

"I know," William smiles. "I was listening to your stuff on the way over here. Your voice is really sexy. I like it. You're good."

Is that true or is he blowing smoke up my ass? Eh, you know what?

Doesn't matter. It's a good thing either way.

William's hand splays wide, grabbing all of Tucker, closing gently around his balls then stroking repeatedly along his shaft. A tense chuckle erupts from Tucker. For a second he tries opening his eyes, but when he does William is still watching him like a hawk fixated on its prey. Tucker blinks and becomes hypnotized by the particular shape of William's lips, and imagining what they'd look like stretched wide around his cock.

What the hell am I doing? What would people say if they knew I was doing this? What the fuck was I thinking?

He grunts, blushing a deep red when he realizes how hard he is. William keeps manipulating him through his jeans. The friction and heat from his fingers and palm, the particular rolling press of them is too good. But Tucker can't really contain the evidence of his enjoyment anyway, given that he hasn't let anyone touch him like this in so very long.

"Don't get the wrong idea here," Tucker says before his brain can completely leak down into his dick. "I don't do this. I'm not that guy. Hell, I'm not into guys at *all*. I was just… curious." *Liar. Why are you lying to him? You really think he cares?* "Being on the road with the band, there's always these women just throwing themselves at us. God, that sounds really arrogant, doesn't it? The fuck is wrong with me?"

"It's okay. Keep going," William coaxes, his nimble fingers working to loosen Tucker's belt now. "Tell me about them. They're your groupies?"

"I guess. They're as sweet as could be. Some of them are really hot, you know. But they just don't—don't interest me as much anymore. And then, when I talked to Della…."

"She thought you and I would get along?" William supplies.

"Yeah, she sure did. Are you from Louisiana, because I'd swear I can hear a hint of a—"

"Yep. You?"

"Yeah," Tucker sighs, then shivers as William finally gets his pants opened and pulls Tucker's dick out. Stroking silky skin stretched tight over thickening, pulsing flesh with one hand, he plays gently with Tucker's balls with the other.

Eyes rolling up into his head with delirious pleasure, Tucker fights not to thrust into the touch. He tries to maintain some control of what's happening, but it's so tempting, feels so exquisite.

In a low and seductive purr, William asks, "So, Tucker, what *does* interest you? What do you *want*?"

He doesn't even need to think about it. "Your mouth."

William chuckles darkly. Sliding backward up farther onto the bed, he wraps both hands behind Tucker's thick, clenched thighs and guides him forward so that he's kneeling on the mattress between William's spread legs. Discreetly, William slips a condom from his pocket and tears the wrapper open, rolling the latex sheath onto Tucker, who barely notices.

"Is that all?" William asks with a cocked eyebrow, biting his lip almost eagerly, wanting more.

Yes. That's all. But those fuckin' jeans.... That perfect, round butt encased in that smooth, worn denim, and the way he'd buck and moan if I peeled those jeans down, stuffed my fat cock up his pink pucker, and fucked him rough, as deep as I could get.

"No. It's not." Knowing he shouldn't feel guilty for saying it, Tucker does anyway.

"Good," William smirks, seeming pleased.

Steadying Tucker's erection in the junction of his thumb and index finger, William opens his mouth, his tongue pushing forward. He licks a few times, repeatedly, greedily, up through the divot on the underside of the head, making Tucker shudder, then feeds Tucker into his mouth, closes his lips behind the ridge and hums. With the straining flesh cradled on his tongue, William makes a tight seal around it with his lips and sucks lightly at first, hollowing his cheeks. Applying pressure to the bundle of nerves under the ridge, William guides Tucker back, inch-by-inch; sucking harder the deeper he goes. With eyes upturned to Tucker's face, William sees Tucker's expression—shyness overcome with wrenching need and a desperate fight for composure. Unwilling to let that hint of bashfulness win out, William holds Tucker by the hipbones and urges his hesitant partner gently into movement. Tucker swallows back a moan, but complies, and starts to thrust at a gradually building pace. The total stranger latched on to him allows Tucker to slide as deeply as he wants without complaint or anything but hungry moans.

Once he's buried, hugged tightly by the hot, wet, velvety vice of William's throat, Tucker's nervousness miraculously disappears and he's only driven, wanting more and ready to take it, pushing again and again. Each thrust is harder than the last. Tucker threads his fingers through William's soft, tousled, short hair, hooking his hands around William's ears as he rides his mouth, watching with pleasure as he takes the brutal treatment. William blinks as his eyes tear up, his lips and chin shiny wet with saliva.

When Tucker happens to slip free for a brief moment, William licks and suckles just the head of his dick for a long, unending moment, moaning wantonly like there's nothing he wants more than a mouthful of Tucker. The low-pitched sound tickles up Tucker's shaft, making him shiver and pulse, dribbling pre-come inside the sheath of the condom. No longer able to hold in his cries, Tucker gasps and moans, and just when he thinks William can't possibly suck harder, he does. It almost hurts. With one hand still closed up carefully around Tucker's sac, William tugs on it when he feels the testicles draw up, getting ready to shoot.

With a small shout, Tucker trembles and bucks. His orgasm is so close that when William pulls off with a wet slurp, Tucker growls in complaint.

Unashamed, flushed and horny, his lips darker now and swollen, William rasps, "Wanna fuck?"

Jesus.

Focused on William's used and abused lips, how filthy and debauched he looks, all Tucker wants is to get his fingers up William's hole, to fuck his tight little knot until it's just as swollen and wet as his lips are.

"Hell yeah, I wanna fuck."

"You or me? Whad'ya say, cowboy? Want me to take you for a ride? Nothing better in the world than a thick cock fucking your brains out."

Breathless, aching, Tucker frowns as he debates the offer. William is greedily palming his ass, squeezing the muscle, and Tucker has never wanted that, to be the one that receives. But in that moment, hearing William suggest it, it sounds like it would be the best thing in the whole goddamned world. Tucker believes completely that it could be. There's still something he wants more, though. This time. Next time is a whole other story.

Is there going to be a next time? I guess maybe there is.

"You. It has to be you. I fucking have to be inside you."

"You sure?"

He knows. How does he know? Am I that obvious?

"I'll make it so good for you," William promises darkly, so very temptingly, trailing a single finger down Tucker's ass crack. Deliberately stroking over his opening, feeling it clench, making sparks of sensation rocket up Tucker's spine, William sees Tucker frown more deeply and sigh.

"I can't," he barely whispers. "Not yet. I'm not ready."

"Okay. That's okay. We've got time. As much time as you need."

Fuck.

"It's just, you're so hot, as soon as I saw you," William confides softly, his eyes sparkling, "wanted to bend your ass over the damn bed and just fucking bury myself in it."

Swaying a little on his knees, too hard, too worked-up, some of Tucker's apprehension crawls back into his gut. Sensing it, William turns swiftly, getting up onto his knees, facing away from Tucker. He twists his shirt free and slides his pants off before Tucker even sees him undo a single button. All slim, tan, chiselled muscle, William's body is breathtaking. Now he's only wearing some skimpy, low-slung, pristinely white boxer briefs that don't even completely cover his cheeks, the cotton stark against the caramel color of his skin.

Like it has a mind of its own, Tucker's hand darts out, pushing the briefs down in the back, exposing William's perfect ass and inserting two fingers into him without asking permission or giving warning.

"Sweet merciful Christ," Tucker sighs.

William moans softly as Tucker fingers him, corkscrewing the digits up and around, into his heat. He's already stretched and wet. Tucker slips in a third finger without any trouble, but it gets William to tilt his hips, pushing back onto the fingers. Reaching an arm behind himself to grab on to Tucker for purchase, William's hungry hole swallows the three thick fingers, clenching up in flutters around them. "It's... mm... ch-cherry flavored lube, by the way. If you're into it... *fuck* ."

Primal need drowns out all rational thought. Tucker pulls out, grabs his cock by the root and fits the head against William's hole. Caressing the sexy-as-sin pair of dimples in William's lower back, right above his ass, with the pads of his thumbs, Tucker groans loudly as William pushes himself back onto Tucker's dick, impaling himself on it with a guttural moan of his own.

"So fucking good... *ahh*, god, you're big...." William gasps a little as Tucker bottoms out and immediately starts fucking him with abandon. Latching onto a spot at the base of William's neck, Tucker sucks a mark there and muffles his cries against the overheated skin. William is so snug around him, gripping mercilessly. Hard as a steel ramrod, Tucker slams into him, knocking small grunts from his conquest. Wanting it to last forever, but knowing it's not going to, Tucker rides it right up to the edge, then pulls out, stripping off the rubber and squeezing up his dick. He comes hot and messy over the pert swell of his lover's bottom, painting it milky white. The viscous fluid drips down the tan muscle, through his crack, as Tucker keeps tugging, keeps coming.

Tingling and sated, he does what he deems the logical thing and reaches around William, finding his long prick fully hard and jutting up between his legs. It sends another thrill through him, the proof that William got off on getting fucked.

"You don't have to," William tells him, sounding like he's trying to catch his breath and hold it together.

"Shut up," Tucker growls, wrapping the sensitive flesh in a tight fist and pumping. William's hips stutter as he pushes frantically into Tucker's hand, chasing the provided, much-needed relief. Glancing at William's face, Tucker sees his long, sweeping eyelashes flutter closed, his mouth going soft, his lips parting. Sinking the points of his teeth into William's shoulder, Tucker bites him, then sucks at the shallow dents. Hissing and groaning, William draws his hips back, then ruts forward. "Come, damn it. Fucking come."

His head falling forward, turning his face slightly away from

Tucker almost timidly, William cries out low and long. Every muscle in his body goes tense and he exhales a shaky breath as he spurts, jetting semen over Tucker's fingers, the bed and his own abdomen. With one last fervent push of his hips, William trembles and relaxes, going boneless. But he's careful not to lean back against Tucker, keeping his weight on his own knees.

Once Tucker has released him, and they've shared a long, serene moment, enjoying the afterglow, William says, "I'm gonna jump in the shower, if that's okay. You don't have to stick around if you don't want to. I can show myself out. It's your call."

Too bewildered to reply, Tucker lies down on the bed, stretching out as William gathers up his clothes and disappears with them into the bathroom. Twenty minutes later, he re-emerges. Tucker hasn't moved. William, clothed, clean and fresh, is immaculate once more. Self-consciousness creeps into the edges of Tucker's tranquility. Naked, dirty and tangled in the bed sheet, he asks, "Can I see you again?"

"Of course. Whenever you want, I'm yours. Just call Della. She'll set it up."

"She, um, said she would wire your fee from my account directly. Is that okay?"

Giving his client a sweet, deferential smile, William nods and murmurs, "Yeah, that's okay."

"I had a great time. Hell of a lot better than I thought I would. Thank you."

"No problem. Call me," William smiles, backing toward the door and slipping his phone from his pocket to call the office and check in with Della. The electronic payment is typical. It means William doesn't have to deal with the money at all apart from getting paid. But he does want to let her know the job has been completed before he takes off for home.

"I will," Tucker agrees. "Next time I'm in town."

"Good."

As soon as the door closes with a soft click, Tucker rolls over, burying his face in a pillow and releasing a yell full of the last remnants of his pent-up anxiousness into it, needing to be purged of it as much as he needed to be purged of his spunk.

"Oh my *god*," he bellows into the down. "That was fucking *awesome!*" Rolling again and letting his arms fall widely outward, he bursts into carefree, weightless laughter. "I need to get my ass to L.A. more often. Yeehaw."

Chapter 2
Domestic Bliss

"Hi honey, I'm home!" The door slams and keys jingle as they drop into the porcelain dish sitting atop the narrow table in the foyer. The house is neat and tidy as always – the furnishings sparse but elegant with dark colors and clean lines. It almost borders on being sterile, perhaps in allusion to the fact that it's not nor will it ever truly be home to the inhabitants. It's merely a temporary resting place on much longer, as-yet-unfinished journeys. In the meantime, the cleanliness comforts those with lives that take them, regularly, to very unclean places. The careful order of things soothes when so much else is amiss.

Footsteps click-clack over smoothly polished hardwood as, from the kitchen at the back of the house, Jacen Pruski calls, "Come and give us a kiss. Hard day at the office?"

"Oh, *yeah*," William Taye, known to his good friends as Liam, groans dramatically. He makes his entrance in brown leather boots, tight-fitting designer jeans and one of many carefully tailored shirts, this one ivory and blue. The ensemble perfectly complements his diligently toned physique; his short, mussed, sun-kissed hair catches the overhead light like spun silk. Liam gets a heartfelt, welcoming smile from Jacen, who is impressively tall and classically handsome. Jacen's hair hangs past his chin in richly dark, messy waves, obscuring eyes that are a bright aqua blue. The air smells of Jacen's famous tomato sauce. One of Mozart's operas plays quietly from speakers in strategic, discreet places in the walls around the room. Liam feels his phone vibrate as he gets a new message and he glances over it before tucking the phone hastily back away. It's the details of his next assignment, messaged over from the head office.

"After one look at my, uh, presentation," Liam tells him with a heavy look, "the boss really stuck it to me good; really had my balls in a vise."

Jacen lets his stirring spoon drop against the side of the pot, his absurd red and white gingham apron, complete with frilly ruffle at the bottom, sagging just like his expression. The apron was a gag gift—a Christmas present from Liam, since out of the two of them, Jacen is the one that really knows how to cook. Liam never actually expected him to ever wear it, but it has improbably become Jacen's favorite cooking attire. Splattered, as usual, with runny drips of red sauce, Liam knows he'll have to scrub them out himself before he goes to bed if they don't want the stains to set and Jacen to get a hang-dog expression like the one he had the last time he accidentally ruined one of Liam's presents. As if Jacen was already anticipating this, all levity drains from his face as he asks, "You're kidding, right?"

Cocking an eyebrow, Liam purses his lips around a repressed grin at his best friend, co-worker and roommate, and assures him, "Yes, Jacen. I made a funny."

Jacen smiles; his deep dimples denting his cheeks, framing his recently whitened teeth. Pushing a stray tendril behind one ear and picking up where they left off in their typical banter, before Jacen's usual over-protectiveness of Liam derailed them, he says, "So the big man really reamed you out, huh?"

"Pretty much," Liam smirks, flipping through the small pile of mail, mostly bills and junk, though there is one coupon for his favorite Moroccan restaurant. He holds it up, waving it.

"Ooh! Stick it on the fridge. Maybe we can go there Thursday night," Jacen says eagerly.

Walking to the refrigerator, Liam puts a whale magnet that he'd bought at the Vancouver Aquarium on his last vacation, taken too many years ago, on top of the slip of paper and heads over for a taste of the simmering sauce.

"Mm, wow. That smells incredible," he hums, inhaling deeply and favoring the chef with a chaste peck on the cheek. Since Liam never kisses *anybody*, ever, getting even that much from him is like a precious gift. It brightens Jacen's expression until he's beaming. Warm affection for his dear friend temporarily makes him shy. Dropping his gaze to the sauce, Jacen stirs it diligently.

Leaning back against the counter beside Jacen's workstation and folding his arms, Liam happens to look down at himself. Seeing that two of his shirt buttons are still open, revealing a small triangle of bare skin, he closes them quickly up, teasing his lip between his teeth as memories from his day come back to him.

Jacen watches Liam fiddle with the buttons and, while Liam is distracted by the task, uses the opportunity to scan all of his visible skin for any bruises or marks. There aren't any and for this Jacen is incredibly grateful.

"You're smiling. What's with the smiling?" The question has the same teasing tone to it that Jacen's previous comments had too, but in a subtly different way. It's just a hair softer, a smidge more earnest.

Chuckling softly, Liam represses an even wider grin, his eyes alight.

"What?"

Liam's only response is to rub a hand restlessly over the back of his neck.

"What?" Jacen gapes. "Oh, well, now you have to tell me."

With a sly upward glance, Liam murmurs, "Client was a cowboy."

"A cowboy?!" The spoon clatters on the counter, spraying another drop of sauce on Jacen's gingham. He wipes his hands on a rag, then plants them on his hips, waiting.

Though Liam admittedly is dressed in full-on cowboy-mode himself, complete with one of many oversized silver belt buckles the roommates share whenever their attire seems to warrant it, that doesn't mean anything really. Jacen is still completely surprised. "I shit you not. Country singer and everything. The real deal. Southern gentleman."

"How did you get a cowboy?" Honestly jealous, Jacen stares and shifts his weight to the other foot, "Well? Spill. Was he hot? Please, at least tell me he was a pig."

"No, he was hot," Liam chuckles, blushing. "Gorgeous, thick, wavy long hair that he had tied back. Longer than yours. Soft blue eyes, really nice smile. Sweet as hell."

"Liam!" Jacen swats him with the dish towel.

"What can I say? God loves me. He was bashful, too. First time. Closet case."

His brow furrowing, but still retaining a semblance of a smirk, Jacen shakes his head with astonishment. Turning back to his pot, he grabs one of the fresh dinner rolls from the basket already laid out along with the vinaigrette for the salad. Jacen bites a chunk out of the bread and flings the rest at Liam's head.

Ducking out of the way and laughing, Liam scoops up the roll and overhands it into the trashcan.

"So not fair," Jacen complains quietly around his mouthful. He shakes some more oregano into the pot's bubbling concoction and asks without turning around, his tone light on the surface but deadly serious underneath, "He was nice?"

There's a pause, and it's long enough to cause Jacen the beginnings of real concern. When Liam grunts and nods, Jacen sees it out of the corner of his eye. "Yeah."

"Good. That's awesome, Lee," Jacen says, using the nickname he alone uses for Liam. It's become a way for Jacen to punctuate their closeness. He calls Liam 'Lee' because everyone who likes to act like they know William, but doesn't—because, in this case, sexual closeness does not necessarily imply *actual* closeness—calls him 'Will' for short. And more and more, when Liam hears *that* particular nickname, it sours his mood and makes him close off. Being called Will is just another way that people try to get close, to get a piece of him, to claim and mark him. So then he just pushes them all away, receding inside himself, putting up walls. Liam has the opposite reaction when being called 'Lee' by Jacen. It reminds him that there is more to who he is than what the world sees. It gives him hope. "Maybe he'll be a new regular."

"I don't know. He's from out of town." Liam shrugs, as if, with a raise of his shoulders, he can push away any and all lingering hopes on the matter. "So, how 'bout you? Didn't see you last night, but I had a late one. Couldn't be sure."

"Oh. I had an overnight. With Spencer. Got back this afternoon after food shopping."

Other than the soft aria floating from the stereo, absolute, brittle, tense silence descends on the kitchen. Jacen's clipped, abrupt way of answering sends a clear message to Liam, but it's one Liam doesn't like at all. Spencer is a bad guy, maybe even an evil guy. But he's also Jacen's highest-paying client. Glowering at Jacen, even walking around to the end of the counter for a better look at his face, Liam clenches his jaw and fumes.

"Don't look at me like that. It doesn't help," Jacen laughs bitterly, unable to hold Liam's stare for more than a second.

"Sorry. I can't help it."

"Try."

Knowing not to ask if Jacen is okay, to trust him to say so if he wasn't, Liam needs something to quiet the unease in his heart, so he comes up to his much taller friend and wraps him in a loose hug from behind, resting his lips against the back of Jacen's impressively muscled shoulder. He wonders to himself what sort of ugly bruises hide under Jacen's ridiculous apron and old t-shirt, under his loose-fitting sweatpants, the ones he likes to wear when he's recovering from a particularly brutal appointment. After a long moment, Jacen softens slightly and nods once to Liam. It's both thanks and a white flag.

"What can I do?"

"Boil noodles."

"Wow, you're actually trusting me to boil the noodles?"

"Just don't fuck 'em up," Jacen retorts slyly, but without his usual vim. A cold tickle of foreboding burrows deeply into Liam, and, no matter how hard he tries to shake it off, it just won't go. Setting the water on the stove, sprinkling in some salt, Liam opens the pantry and looks for the right box.

"I'm flattered that you have such faith in me."

"As well you should."

The place Jacen and Liam spend the most time, other than at the downtown hotels and their house, located on the outskirts of L.A., is their local spa, Amé. Their employer, known only as The Company, has a running account at Amé and encourages them to go as frequently as once a day for massage, skin treatments, manicures and pedicures, acupuncture, or whatever else they need. The spa's employees know them personally, as Jacen has been using them since he started working as an escort for The Company a year ago. For Liam it has been over twice as long as that.

But even after long years working at his trade in different cities, for different people, Liam can still be surprised by the requests he gets from his handsomely paying clients.

At breakfast, wearing a knit hat, a well-worn t-shirt and sweats, Liam sits down across from Jacen and grumbles good morning.

"You headed to Amé?" Jacen asks, taking a big bite of cereal.

"Yeah," Liam sighs. "You?"

"Yeah, I'll tag along. Don't have much to do 'til late tonight."

Liam sips his coffee and eyes his roommate. "Who?"

"Claudia," Jacen mutters, scratching the side of his nose. Before he takes another bite he adds, "Tomorrow morning is Patrick."

"Why do women love you so much?" Liam complains.

"Why do men love *you* so much?" Jacen retorts.

"No, I'm serious. Half your regulars are women. No one else at The Company manages to draw male and female clients. It's bizarre."

"You could if you wanted to, which you don't, from what I can tell. Why, you wanna tag along?" Jacen smirks.

Liam grumbles and buries his face in his mug.

"How 'bout you? What's up?"

"Don't ask."

Jacen discreetly covers his mouth with a hand as he attempts to master his expression, his hair falling in his eyes. Tossing it back with a flick of his head, he asks gently, "That bad?"

"No," Liam whines. "Just, well, here." He takes out his phone, pulls up the message from Della, their booking agent, and slides it over to him to read.

Jacen huddles over the phone and, as he reads, his smile gets wider and wider, though he does successfully mask it before looking up and returning the gadget. Clearing his throat, he says, "Well.

Hm, that's, uh—"

"I know what it is. It's fine. I can handle it. I've done it plenty of times before; it's just been a while."

Liam's sweats take on new meaning as Jacen looks him over. "So, what," he lowers his voice, like anyone could overhear them anyway in their own home. "You're not getting completely waxed are you?"

"No," he scoffs, though it sounds like it might be a lie. "Just the usual. But, you know. I'll get... other stuff done."

The corners of Jacen's lips twitch up in a highly amused smirk before he forces them back down. "You need help?" he offers, trying not to sound too eager. "Wanna rehearse? Or something. You probably should."

"Jesus Christ. Yeah, probably. One thing at a time, though, okay? I'll worry about the rest once I get past having my balls waxed, thank you very much." He pushes away from the table and pauses. "Uh, I'm probably gonna be a while, like all morning, so a package might arrive while I'm gone. If you're here, just, you know, put it aside."

He shuffles to the door. Jacen bounces to his feet. Taking one last huge bite of Fruit Loops, he jogs to drop his dirty dishes by the sink and hurries down the hall to grab his car keys. "I'll drive! Just call me when you're done and I'll come pick you up."

"You could try to be less entertained by this," Liam frowns.

"Sorry, Lee. Not possible. This is gonna be the highlight of my week."

A few hours later, Liam is parked in the passenger seat beside Jacen, his hands carefully hidden from sight in the pockets of a baggy sweatshirt, just as they have been since he emerged from Amé. His skin glows, looking well-exfoliated and moisturized—touchably soft and smooth—so Jacen assumes he must have had a special kind of facial or something of the sort, along with the hot towel, straight razor shave treatment that the spa is known for. But he doesn't ask about it.

He does, however, find himself wondering if Liam is hiding his hands because he got colored polish painted onto his nails. Inexplicably, the idea of Liam wearing red, or, even better, *pink* nail polish starts to make Jacen hard. Biting down on his tongue to distract his libido with pain, Jacen forces away a sudden vivid fantasy of Liam, completely naked—all rippling, hard, bronzed muscles— stroking his fat cock with gleaming, pretty pink nails.

Liam murmurs, "Did my package arrive?"

"Um. Yeah. It's pretty big."

Accusatory and on-edge, he asks, "You didn't open it, did you?"

"Like I'm not gonna see it all anyway," Jacen says, rolling his eyes. "No, I didn't open it. So touchy."

"Don't you have things you need to be doing too?" Liam slumps down lower in the seat.

"Nope. I'm good. Had a shiatsu massage. Got my chest waxed...."

"Yeah, I heard you screaming like a little girl."

Jacen frowns heavily, and continues, "Did not. And now I'm just hanging out 'til I have to leave. Not like I have much prep to worry about. Claudia's not really into pegging or anything too kinky."

"Lucky bastard."

"Hey, don't even try to play it like you don't get off on it. There's a reason your clients are *yours* and not mine."

Liam won't even face him after that comment, staring out the side window, his newly buffed skin flushing.

"Liam, I didn't mean anything by it," Jacen sighs. "It's just that you... prepare... a lot more than I do. I show up, complete the transaction and go. I don't make it complicated."

"But I do?"

"Yeah, you kind of do. But there's nothing wrong with that."

"Whatever."

"Can you seriously try to pretend that this appointment with Chris isn't complicated? You see me trying to pull this off?"

Liam softens.

"It could be worse," Jacen warns. "It could be a *hell* of a lot worse."

"Yeah, you're right. It could be Spencer," Liam says, some of the bottled-up fury from the night before erupting in his words. He's been trying for months to get Jacen to complain to the higher-ups about Spencer's treatment of him, but the money is just too good, according to Jacen. And Liam resents the hell out of it.

Jacen swallows thickly, averting his eyes. He doesn't say another word for the rest of the drive.

Chapter 3
Crossing Lines

Jacen is hovering restlessly in the living room. It's been four hours since they returned home from the spa. The last text message Jacen sent Liam told him to come downstairs whenever he was ready, that he would be there, waiting. But that was almost an hour ago, and Jacen is starting to wonder if he should go up there and check on things.

It's five o'clock. Liam's appointment is at seven. There's plenty of time. It's Jacen's own impatience to see Liam's transformation that stirs him, though he doesn't quite realize it. It's easier to blame his eagerness on the schedule.

Part of their routine, built gradually over the course of their year together, has been for Jacen to assist Liam in creating the personas he uses on his dates. Whether it's a cowboy, a punk, a biker, a club twink, a perfect gentleman complete with three-piece suit, or something more extreme, something like what he's going to attempt today, everything has a label. It's always an act. Liam becomes whatever particular thing it is that the client is looking for — their fantasy come to life. That's what Liam has deduced his job to be — to provide a service of wish fulfilment. Of course, Jacen has observed that it makes it easier on Liam's psyche to take himself out of the equation entirely. Liam is never really there when someone is paying him to be there. His character is present, as is his body. But everything else stays buried away, under many hard-coated, protective layers.

When Jacen first met Liam, as bubbly and personable as Jacen is, it took them a while to warm up to each other. At first Liam was all overly-polite smiles, ready with concerned questions and inquiries into how Jacen was, or how his day was going. It had been Liam's attempt at a 'friend' persona. It wasn't him at all, and Jacen could tell. It had hurt his feelings, that Liam wasn't being honest or real with him. But they were stuck together. Liam needed a room-mate to help cover expenses, and Della had told Jacen discreetly that she also wanted someone else there, someone like Jacen, who was big — at six foot six, Jacen was plenty big — and could hold his own in a fight, to watch Liam's back when he was alone, to let her know if there was ever anything to be worried about and to maybe try to break through some of Liam's defenses. Because the longer Liam has been in the business, the further he has receded into him-self. It worries Della. She fears for Liam's sanity.

There were other factors that got them together, too. They both had similarly bizarre schedules and responsibilities, working in the same profession, for the same people. It made sense to be in each other's lives. Only after months of concerted effort did Jacen work his way past the first few outer layers, deeper into the heart of who Liam really is. And even still, after a whole year, Jacen is still discov-ering things about his friend. Secret, new facets are slowly revealed. Small, priceless moments sometimes happen between them that make Jacen step back and take in how lucky he is to have gained some of Liam's trust.

Lost in thoughts and memories, comparisons of the old Liam and the new, Jacen doesn't at first see the woman lingering in the doorway, leaning against the frame, her fingers curling a little around the trim. Wearing a silk, jewel-green dress that perfectly complements her similarly colored big, beautiful eyes and dainty silver high heels, her long red hair swept in a cascade over her right shoulder, she gazes up at him through long, dark, sweeping eye-lashes and bites shyly at her lip, waiting to be noticed.

"Oh *wow*," Jacen breathes. Heart jumping in his chest, at first he's too stunned to react, and just stares — taking in all the details; the French manicure, her shapely bare legs and the way the stilettos show them off, the way the delicate edge of her loose skirt skims her thighs, the fullness of her breasts heaving gently with every breath. Most of all though, it's her lips, the incredible ripeness of them and the way her tangerine-colored lipstick makes them shiny wet, a perfect, plump bow.

A small wordless plea, communicated only with her wide, beseeching eyes, is what gets Jacen to move. He has a job to do here and, so far, he's not doing it. If this is going to work the right way, there can't be discussion beforehand. It just has to happen naturally, like Jacen is just another John Doe. If they acknowledged each other first, it would break the spell and it's always nearly impossible to get Liam back to being comfortable enough to try again.

Before he's able to realize that he should let her cross to him and practice her walk, Jacen is surging toward her, his larger, towering, broad-shouldered form coming at her. She backs herself up to the doorframe, leaning against it with upturned eyes, breath catching on the inhale as Jacen invades her space. He slips a hand around her small waist, his other cups under her jaw, his thumb stroking the butter-smooth skin of her cheek and *god* but he wants to kiss her, especially when her lips part softly in what seems to be an invitation and her head tilts slightly into his touch.

"Leah?"

"Yeah," she whispers. It's barely a sound, a purr, and he has to lean in even closer to hear it.

Then he can't hold back any longer. Simply reacting to her, her beckoning stare, he leans in and his lips barely skim against the line of her jaw. It's the lightest of brushes of skin on skin, though it does make her shiver. She tastes faintly of peaches when he sucks the lingering taste of her from his lips, pulling back.

On instinct, he takes her hand and spins her out into the room, making her skirt flare out, her hips twisting as he reins her back into his arms, walking her slowly back to the couch. His eyes are all over her, peeking down the V of her neckline, groping over her hairless arms, knowing instinctively that she's waxed everywhere. When his hand skims down past her hip to her upper thigh, he feels the muscle bunch, working as she steps backward with his continued advance, trying not to topple over, anticipating the edge of the couch at any moment.

Just before she gets to it, he shifts around behind her, sinking down onto the cushion and caressing her legs as he goes, holding her there, not letting her get away.

Pushing the skirt up a few inches, Jacen gropes her bare thighs and catches a glimpse of the curve of her ass and her black lace thong as he pulls her down onto his lap, straddling his legs, facing away from him. She lands gracefully, legs clenched as she tries to keep her weight on them and not Jacen.

"Relax. It's okay. I've got you," he hushes. "Just relax."

He pulls her back even more and she leans against his firm, broad chest, her head falling to the side as his lips drag open-mouthed almost-kisses over her long neck, inhaling more of the scent of her.

"Damn, you smell good enough to eat," he murmurs, pulling her thighs apart, spreading her wide.

Leah's breath catches on a soft surprised sound when his big hands drag up her inner thighs, all the way to her crotch, lightly stroking the soft skin there, right beside the edge of her panties. Jacen tugs sharply again at her legs, pulling her ass flush against him, wanting her thighs even more spread, hiking her skirt up further. Watching her expression as she teases her lip between her teeth again, he fondles her breast through the dress. It gets her to push her chest out a little more, pressing into his touch, her back arching as he squeezes.

He is utterly astonished at how much this is turning him on.

Keenly aware that her firm, bare ass is rubbing against his growing hard-on, and wanting *much* more of that, needing it like air, wanting to grope between her legs, Jacen's hand twitches, ready to palm her crotch, rub and *thrust*.

He comes back to himself all at once, slamming back to reality. It's like a splash of cold water, waking Jacen right-the-fuck-up.

He takes his hands off of Liam, blushing a deep red and hissing a fervent, "Shit! Sorry. Fuck. Sorry. I don't—I don't know why I did that. Jesus."

Liam gets right up, wrapping his mouth with a hand and facing away from Jacen as he takes a second to compose himself. Smoothing out the dress, especially in back where Jacen had pulled it up to his waist, Liam braces a hand on his hip muttering very quietly to himself, but Jacen can't make the words out.

"I'm so fucking sorry," Jacen pleads to break some of the tension. "Can you forgive me? Please? I guess I just slipped into it, you know? I kind of forgot it was you. You're really, *really* convincing."

"No problem, that's the whole idea, right? To sell it," Liam says, his deep, gravelly voice shocking coming from such a demure-looking figure. "So I guess it was a success."

Liam is still facing the window, his back to Jacen. Controlling the pitch of his voice to keep his anger and hurt out of it, Liam is blinking and breathless, hating himself both for not putting a halt to the practice exercise earlier — too curious in a detached sort of way to see if he could keep Jacen going — but also mad at himself for getting upset at Jacen's abrupt halt, change of mood and apologies.

One more deep inhale and Liam is back to normal. He turns to Jacen, finding him still on the couch, but hunched forward (*probably to hide a hard-on*, Liam thinks distractedly) with his elbows braced on his knees, looking embarrassed.

"So what's the verdict?"

"Awesome? The verdict is awesome. Just generally... wow. Christ...." Jacen groans, putting his hands to his face in mortification. Liam grins, chuckling a little when Jacen tugs his shirt lower, to cover the protrusion in his pants. "Why are you laughing at this?"

"Because it's hilarious?" His eyes crinkle slightly at the corners as his amusement grows and he absent-mindedly bites at his lip again, tasting some of the peach-flavored lip-gloss he's wearing. "I still need some detailed feedback. Come on. Don't hold back."

"Okay. Well, the uh, lip biting thing is really good, and sexy. So stop it. Please. Because it's disturbing to be this turned on by you. And the red hair? With your ridiculously green eyes? Awesome."

"That was Della's idea. I think she's living vicariously or something. What else?"

"The whole outfit is perfect. And yeah, I understand why you were at the spa and in the bathroom all day. I hope this guy's worth it."

"He is," Liam smiles. "Top dollar. Any suggestions for improvement?"

"Hmm. Remember to keep your shoulders back and down. Don't forget, it's all tits and ass. Stick out the tits, push out the ass, downplay the muscles as much as possible. I guess the minimal speaking was intentional?"

"Yeah, it's not like there's much I can do about my voice. So less is more."

"Walk a little for me. I didn't really get to see you walk."

"Okay," Liam nods, pacing across the room. He walks into the kitchen, then back.

"Take your time. Keep your hips loose. Don't be afraid to move 'em. Walk like you're dancing," Jacen suggests. "Yeah, good. That's really good," he grins, as Liam exaggerates his movements a little more. "Just don't over-do it. You might give him a stroke. Or fall with those crazy heels. Did Della buy those too?"

"No, those are... mine," Liam mutters, eyes downcast. "Thanks, Jace. Really. You always give me great tips. It's really helpful."

"No problem," he nods.

"I'm gonna, um, get freshened up, so —"

"Yeah. Of course."

Jacen, still mortified, watches him go, staring helplessly at the way Liam's ass shifts and sways under the silk as he walks away toward the stairs. As soon as he hears the door close upstairs, Jacen inhales deeply of the air in the room, moaning softly on the exhale when he can still detect a faint whiff of peaches. Slumping down on the couch, he yanks open his fly. Pulling out his straining erection with the hand that had just been caressing the butter-smooth inside of Liam's bare thigh, Jacen jerks off furiously at the thought of what could have happened if he hadn't stopped, and had let Liam wriggle on his lap. Jacen fantasizes about getting a double handful of the firm muscle of Liam's ass, rubbing Liam's cock through the special black lace panties with the hidden panel designed to tuck away his genitals, feeling him get hot and wet and shoot inside them purely because of Jacen's touch.

Coming in hot splatters over himself thinking of his best friend, Jacen, who never feels guilty about anything he does, aches at the cold pit of shame that forms in his gut and heads to the bathroom to clean up some of his mess.

Chapter 4

Leah Unleashed

Liam doesn't realize that his client, 'Chris,' is *that* Chris until he arrives at the hotel room as Leah.

Chris is someone he knows, sort of. One of Liam's regulars is Adam Chance, a C-list actor on a network TV show. To Hollywood, the media and most of the world, Adam is straight, and married. But in reality, Adam's interests are more varied, so Liam obliges whenever he needs to. Sometimes Adam is interested in performing for an audience, just like he does at work, so he'll invite friends to watch when Liam is scheduled to visit. Chris, aka Christopher Morrow, another actor, is one of those friends. Chris has sipped scotch and watched from afar as Adam fucked Liam six ways from Sunday, or vice versa, depending on Adam's mood that day, but not once has Chris deigned to participate. Participation costs extra and requires prior warning. Liam wouldn't have been averse to it, it just never happened. It never even came up. So he's a little surprised when the door opens with Chris on the other side, 'Chris' who ordered *Leah* specifically.

It would have been easier for Liam to be Leah when the client didn't already know him as Liam, or, rather, one of Liam's characters. Rattled for a few seconds, he blinks at Chris, who is looking him up and down with dark lust in his eyes and evident satisfaction, practically drooling.

I can do this. Focus. Remember how it was with Jacen. Go with that. He's 'Chris' not Adam's friend. If I can be Leah, he can be someone else, too.

The dance begins; Liam embraces the persona of Leah entirely.

26

Just like that, he's not himself at all anymore. He's *her*.

"Hey, Leah," Chris croons, reaching out and circling Leah's wrist with his fingers, using the grip to guide her into the room.

Leah plays up the bashful act, working her false eyelashes for all they're worth and making sure to sway her hips when she walks. Taking her directly over to the back of the couch, Chris positions himself behind Leah and wraps his hands around her waist.

"You're not shy, are you? This your first time?"

"Yes," Leah says, letting her voice flutter and lilt, speaking hesitantly to convey timidity. "I don't—"

"Shh," Chris hushes, slipping his right hand around Leah's waist and down to her crotch, humming at the flat, smooth plane he finds at the junction of her legs. Rubbing lightly over it, he cups her left breast with his other hand and squeezes. She gasps, reacting to the intimate contact. He pins her against the back of the couch and fits his pelvis to the curve of her ass, letting her feel how hard he is. "Don't talk. You just stand there, lookin' pretty. Damn, the dirty things I'm gonna do to you. Gonna be dirty with me, baby? Are you a *bad girl*?"

Leah hums and bites her lip, even though doing so makes her think of Jacen, writhing for show when Chris's hand rubs harder between Leah's legs, like he's rubbing her clit. Breasts heaving, she presses into the shameless groping and fondling of her fake tits.

"Yeah, that's what I thought. That's why I had to have you."

Chris lifts her skirt, flipping it up in the back to expose her ass. Leah makes a soft sound of feigned surprise when Chris slips a leg between her thighs, spreading them open. Grabbing the back of the couch, Leah bends forward slightly, pushing out her ass, sticking out her tits too, like Jacen said to, but at the same time, tries to somehow remain demure and shocked.

"Fuck. Your ass in that thong," Chris groans. "Looks good enough to eat. You wear that just for me? You did, didn't you? Dirty girl. I'll show you what I do to dirty girls...."

Leah is glad she lubed up before coming over as she feels two dry fingers trace down the back of the thong, through her crack. They wriggle and rub over her pucker as Chris breathes roughly against her neck, squeezing her breast harder, stroking down her abs once in a while but always returning there, like he needs to have hold of the 'proof' of Leah's gender.

"Don't," Leah whimpers, only because she senses that Chris wants her to. It works. Chris growls back in his throat and forces the fingers through, impaling her on them. Fighting for show, Leah twists weakly in Chris's encircling hold, and on his fingers as they work, rotating and questing deeper into her body, grinding against her wet inner walls. "Please...."

"A dirty girl like you deserves to have her asshole fingered. Doesn't she? Know what else she deserves?"

Leah makes a small frightened sound as she glances back over her shoulder in order to make sure Chris is putting on a rubber. If Chris isn't doing so, he's going to have his little fantasy disrupted whether he likes it or not, because Leah won't let Chris's dick anywhere near her without it, helpless girl routine be damned. But she sees Chris rolling one on, so she relaxes and continues to pretend to be nervous.

The two fingers slide in and out of her, fucking her shallowly as she tenses up, clenching intentionally around them. Chris grabs her by the back of the neck, her red hair swept over one shoulder. He holds Leah still as he pulls free of her hole and uses the hand to steady his dick instead, slapping it against her slick knot, the thong now nudged to one side.

With gentle pressure, far gentler than Leah expected really, Chris presses inside, breaching her with just the head first, then feeding the rest of his length in gradually, being much easier on Leah than she's used to. Chris curses under his breath and groans. Once he's fully nestled in Leah's heat, Chris caresses over her curves, her hips and narrow waist, back up to her fake tits, holding on to them as he fucks Leah tenderly.

It doesn't last long before Chris is filling the condom with a gravelly moan and kissing along the back of Leah's neck, praising her for being such a good, sweet girl. Staring at the windows and fading daylight, Leah is detached from what's happening, merely waiting to be dismissed. Taking his time in pulling out, Chris fingers over Leah's panties, plucking at the lace and elastic. It goes on and on, and Leah wonders at what the hold-up is, if Chris is trying to psych himself up for round two, when Chris's hand suddenly pushes down inside the front of Leah's underwear, rubbing hard over smoothly-waxed skin. Almost violently, he pushes the panties down and tugs Leah's cock out. With a trembling hand, Chris strokes it, getting Leah hard.

Leah breathes out in a rush of air, taken completely by surprise. Every nervous touch Chris gives her evaporates any sort of intelligent reaction or protest, so Leah goes with it. It takes her a few moments to really get into it, but there is intensity to Chris's demeanor and evident desire, more so even than before.

When Chris pulls out a second cordom, Leah moans freely as it gets slowly rolled onto her. Her last coherent thought is, *Well, now, this is interesting....*

Jacen takes a hand from Liam's deck and isn't mentally there at all for his appointment with Claudia that night. When he bends her over and fucks her doggy style, he pretends she's Leah in the green dress and red wig, even though Jacen has never had to fantasize to enjoy sex before. The real thing has always been enjoyable enough on its own. It makes him feel bad for Claudia's sake, since he's been with her for months. It feels like he's cheating her out of the full experience of what she's paying him for. But Claudia doesn't seem to notice. In fact, she tells him some of her more secret fantasies as they screw, with Jacen pounding her wet pussy from behind, dreaming of being buried balls-deep in Liam's sweet ass. And when she mentions that she wants to see Jacen fuck another man while she watches, Jacen comes with a guttural moan, nearly passing out from the force of it as his vision whites out and he pumps into her, trying to maintain it until she comes too. He expertly fingers her clit, rubbing it until she orgasms and he's out of there twenty minutes later, showered and dressed.

When he gets home, Liam is already there, which is unsurprising since Jacen's appointment was at nine, two hours later than Liam's. What does surprise Jacen is that Liam is just starting to get undressed when he goes upstairs to check on how things went.

Standing at the door to Liam's bedroom suite, Jacen pushes his hands into his jeans' pockets in case there's a repeat of his Liam-in-duced boner. He feels his throat go dry at the sight of Liam in a bath-robe, golden hair dusting his tan forehead, the red wig laid carefully on a mannequin head on his dressing table. He's still painted with the elegant make-up, false eyelashes, lipstick and earrings. His bare, smooth legs protrude from the robe, his feet unclad as well, and Jacen secretly hopes that Liam is naked under the robe, or maybe wearing just the lace thong.

The cold pit of shame grows larger.

He can't speak at first, going suddenly self-conscious like he's some nervous kid, and Jacen is so totally unused to something like that happening to him that he's at a loss. Staring at Liam, his heart beating more strongly than it should, he apologizes with his eyes and lingers where he is as Liam removes the earrings from the holes in his earlobes, watching the reflection of Jacen's imposing form in the mirror.

"Hey. How was Claudia?"

Jacen grunts, shrugs, thinking, *Boring as hell until I started to pretend she was you, bent over, wet and willing, and begging for my cock.*

"That exciting, huh?" Liam chuckles. "Damn."

He grabs a jar and unscrews the lid, taking a swipe of some white cream and smearing it over his face.

"Y-yeah, uh. Nothing really to report," Jacen stumbles. "How was Leah received? Was she punished for being a bad girl or some-thing?" He regrets the tease even before it leaves his mouth.

Liam glances downward, away from Jacen, and Jacen opens his mouth to apologize when Liam says, "Funny you say that. It kind of did start like that." He stops there, letting the suggestion hang between them, floating invisible on the air currents.

Knowing he shouldn't ask, that he should just make sure Liam is all right and talk about something else, Jacen ignores logic and asks, "Did he spank you?"

Yanking out a few tissues from the box, Liam wipes away the cold cream and considers his reply. "No. Nothing like that. It was...." He pauses there, debating whether he is actually going to talk about this or not. They hardly ever seriously divulge the details of their appointments with clients with each other. Liam can count on one hand the number of times Jacen has explained to him anything specific about what transpired and it was always after a bad experience, to explain away injuries or why he had to stop at the clinic to get patched up before coming back home. Then, there was the one nightmarish time Jacen had had to call Liam to come pick him up because he couldn't even stand, let alone drive a car. Never have they talked about a good, successful exchange. It's uncharted territory for them. But Liam decides he's too boggled by his night to want to keep it to himself.

"It was weird. It started out like I thought it would. He acted as if I was just a girl. But, I *knew* him. He's watched me, as Will, with Adam a bunch of times. So that threw me. Didn't waste any time, though. While he was... um... going at it, he kept hold of my tits, like he needed to feel like I was a woman to go through with it. So I was a little surprised when he finished off by blowing me."

"What?!" Jacen exclaims before he can self-censor. "He *blew* you? Then what was the point of pretending you were a chick?"

"He was really nervous during that part. But he enjoyed it. Never seen a guy enjoy giving a hummer that much. I think he had to psych himself up for it."

"So you were completely made-up as Leah and he's sucking your dick." Jacen says with awe. "That's ..." *Hot.*

"And I had to shower, but it was part of the agreement that I come and go as Leah, so I had to get re-made-up after the shower, and I told him not to bother waiting 'cause it takes me so long. When I came out, not only was he still there, but he had this big spread set up. He had me stay for dinner, demanded it actually. Like, caviar and champagne and lobster. Waiters to serve us and everything. And he kissed my hand when we said goodbye."

Jacen can only stand there, mouth open, gaping, sputtering.

"I'm seeing him again on the twelfth. He was really sweet. He seemed grateful."

Bitter, seething jealousy comes out of nowhere and strangles Jacen. *No. You have to say no, Lee. I won't let him have you. I won't let him have Leah.* It's the happy smile on Liam's face at the memory of it all that hurts the most. *This is what Liam wants*, Jacen realizes. *He wants a client that appreciates him, pampers him, and enjoys him as his creation, and as Leah. He doesn't want me; he wants the fantasy just as much as his Johns do.*

"That's awesome," Jacen lies. "I'll, uh, let you get cleaned up. You need anything from the kitchen? I'm gonna grab a snack and go to bed since I've got an early call."

"Nah, I'm good. Thanks, Jace," Liam smiles with painted-peach lips and dark, smudged make-up ringed around his bright green eyes.

"I am really glad he was nice to you. You deserve that. If it was me, I'd bring you champagne and caviar every day, for breakfast and everything."

With that, he's gone, slipping back into the hall and out of sight. Liam is left blinking, reeling slightly at the comment. He stares at the doorway for a good five minutes, part of him wanting to call Jacen back to explain, part of him hating Jacen a little for saying something so sweet but inappropriate. *How dare you, Jacen? How dare you just fucking say that to me?* Liam resents the hell out of his friend telling him what he deserves and throwing out a comment so laden with sincere romantic innuendo that it makes Liam queasy. It paralyzes him and rips away his happiness over how the evening turned out. The fantasy is shattered. All that's left are Jacen's heart-broken words like knives slicing into Liam's heart.

Chapter 5
The Hard Way

Liam doesn't sleep well that night. His life has always been neatly compartmentalized. A big facet of it is his work, which includes everything sexual about himself. It's his emotional outlet, his chance to express himself and be whatever he wants or needs to be. The rest of his life is about simpler pleasures, like being able to buy nice things, to have a nice home and all of the comforts that come with it. The two compartments never mix. Liam doesn't date or have relationships or sex. He doesn't have feelings for anyone. He doesn't allow it to happen. He decided, long ago, that finding love is not something he requires to be happy. In fact, it makes him incredibly uncomfortable to even consider the idea. So, the mere implication that Jacen is even capable of seeing him in a romantic light, to have Jacen flirt with him with no purpose behind it, no character or charade, just himself, disturbs Liam. Sure, they joke around all the time about being a couple and their line of work. There is never anything behind it, Liam tells himself. It is just the nature of their senses of humor. And when Jacen got turned on by Liam when he was in drag and being Leah, that was just Jacen doing his job, getting aroused by his appointed mate in that situation. That's why he gets the big bucks; he can get into it with anyone he needs to, and enjoy it in the process.

The comment made in the doorway to Liam's room, about what Liam deserves, about what Jacen would do for him if he could, is something Liam can't get past. It bothers him. A lot.

The best recourse seems to be to get over it and pretend it never happened. It's what he decides to do. But it's easier decided than done.

The next morning, Jacen is gone before Liam is able to get up and makes his way downstairs. Without any appointments that day, Liam goes out for a round of golf, then comes home around lunchtime. He's in the kitchen making food when Jacen gets back from his meeting with Patrick.

Liam waits for it, for Jacen to call back to him from the hallway and say hi. Liam's truck is in the driveway, so it's obvious that he's home. It's what they do, they check in with each other after each gig. That's how they know they're all right. Jacen and Liam check in with each other just like they check in with Della. It's reflexive, they don't even think about it anymore.

Jacen doesn't say a word. The front door closes gently, barely audible, and then equally soft footsteps pad upstairs.

A sort of panic begins to suffocate Liam. It's shapeless, stifling, overpowering, and at first he doesn't even understand it. Then small voices begin to whisper in the back of his psyche.

Even when Spencer practically took Jacen apart, he still called. He still checked in. Hell, he called me as soon as he was sequestered in the bathroom of Spencer's rental house, before the job was even finished. Never has Jacen avoided me completely. It's never been that bad.

Maybe it went really well. Maybe it went so well that he's still in the afterglow, too high to remember where he is or what to do.

Liam is almost able to convince himself of this until he hears the water turn on in the upstairs bathroom.

He's running upstairs before he can even form a conscious thought about it, about how both of them make sure to wash up at the job site, and do a self-evaluation, health-wise, before even checking in with Della. The only times they shower at home, too, are when —

"Jacen?!" Liam screams, disturbed even more by how shrill and shaky his voice sounds in his own ears. "Jacen? Are you okay?! Jacen!"

Patrick's a good guy. Patrick's nice to Jacen. Jacen told me so. He told me how tender Patrick is, how caring...

And how possessive. He said that too. He said Patrick likes to think he owns Jacen, that he belongs only to him.

Liam ascends to the second floor. He bursts into Jacen's bedroom, going through it, following the trail of hastily discarded clothes — a pair of designer jeans, a thin white t-shirt, Jacen's black leather boots. They lead into the bathroom, the door of which is closed over, but not completely shut. Liam can hear the water pounding against the glass in the shower stall. Another step forward, a slight push against the bathroom door, and he can see Jacen.

Look at him. Jesus, look at him.

Gripping the doorframe hard enough to hurt, Liam berates himself. *What are you doing? Don't fucking look at him. You have no right to look at him.*

But he can't not look.

He's beautiful. My god, he's breathtaking.

The only time Liam saw Jacen without clothes, Jacen was bloody and beaten. It wasn't sexy. It was horrifying. Now, Jacen is standing nude behindglass. Every golden inch of his flesh, every stark, chiseled muscle, every curve, every line, every ridge is on display, highlighted by the soft light of the bathroom sconces. Jacen is facing the other way, so Liam is left staring, helplessly *staring*, at Jacen's bare ass.

Stop looking.

You have no right. Only his clients get to have this. You didn't pay for the privilege. What did you expect, anyway? For him to be disgusting? Of course he's gorgeous. Get over it. Get out. Back up and get the fuck out.

That's exactly how long it takes Liam to notice the subtler details. Like the fading welts on Jacen's backside, right across the thickest part of the muscle in thin, pink horizontal lines.

"He whipped you? That son of a bitch fucking *whipped* you?!" It comes out as a shout, uncensored, unfiltered.

Jacen jumps, startled, not having realized that Liam was there. "Jesus *Christ*," he hisses, glancing quickly over his shoulder and then receding back farther into the stall instinctively, like he could possibly hide himself that way. "Lee, come on. I'm taking a fucking shower here. You mind?"

"Look at me," Liam growls. He'd gotten a glimpse of Jacen's face. It was enough to convince him to stay, even if Jacen hates him for it.

"Why, you want the full show?" Jacen asks without turning, bowing his head and spitting out water as it fills his mouth. "You got a couple hundred on you? If you like what you see, maybe we can work something out."

"You're scaring me," Liam says in a more hushed tone, a cold tickle forming in his gut. "What happened? What's wrong? What the fuck did he do to you?"

"Doesn't matter," Jacen says hollowly. "I was properly compensated."

It takes only four steps for Liam to cross to the stall. The splayed fingers of Jacen's hand slip down the slick wall and he tenses visibly, turning his face further away from Liam, keeping his back to the door. Liam yanks the glass door open and frigid water begins to spray out, dampening his clothes, pooling on the floor, soaking into the rug. Jacen is trembling. It stokes the fire of Liam's fury.

"Don't," Jacen whimpers, broken. Liam reaches for him and Jacen flinches away like he's expecting Liam to manhandle him, or strike him, too. It's the last straw. All self-control drains from Liam, all of his pride, all of his guardedness. All that matters is getting to Jacen, and pulling him back out of whatever hell he's sunk into.

Liam's fingers graze Jacen's jaw and Jacen surrenders, throwing away whatever was left of his dignity. He looks at Liam from over a shoulder.

His eyes are bloodshot from crying. Water courses in rivers down the planes of his face, off the tip of his nose, from his chin, over his split lip.

"Patrick hit me," Jacen says. "Punched me square in the mouth when he saw the welts."

Liam shuts off the water. Grabbing a towel, he wraps it around Jacen. "Come on."

Making no move to get out of the stall, Jacen, shivering, mutters, "I don't want to talk about it."

"Tough shit," Liam says, frowning. "I'll give you a second to get dried off, but I'm gonna be right there."

He points to the bedroom.

When Liam leaves, Jacen sighs heavily, his head falling back on his shoulders. Moments from his morning come back to him in flashes. It had been going so well.

Being with Patrick is usually a walk in the park for Jacen. It's easy, not much effort or thought required. He just turns on the charm and pushes all of Patrick's buttons. They were no sweat to figure out. Patrick's a top. Cut and dry. He likes a flirt, but an understated flirt. That means lots of lip biting and sly looks from half-lidded eyes. He likes when Jacen touches his own hair, pushing it back over an ear or just combing his fingers through it.

The body language is essential, too. Jacen gets nice and close to Patrick, keeping his knees loose and head bowed so that he's in kissing range, should Patrick be in the mood for it, since Jacen is much taller than him. Shoulders back, movements fluid. He always wears some perfectly tailored jeans to show off his ass and short-sleeved, V-neck shirts to show off his arms and chest. Almost every time they meet for an appointment, it's at Patrick's rental house in town, usually in the morning. They have breakfast or maybe take a dip in the pool before he fucks Jacen up the ass. Jacen doesn't have many clients that ask that particular service of him. Because of his size and personality, he's mostly booked for either kinky women or guys looking to bottom, since Jacen is good at putting guys at ease, coaxing them into things without being scary about it. It's only Spencer and Patrick that, time and time again, expect him to give it up.

At first it did freak Jacen out a little. When he was a teenager he was completely straight. When he was in his early twenties, in college, he was gay for pay, blowjobs mostly. There was the occasional fuck, but it was always him doing the fucking. And hey, if he didn't focus on appearances too much, or the deep tones of his partners' voices, he could usually pretend they were chicks. Except for the dick sucking. That was more of a challenge to excuse away.

It was only when the price for his services got bumped up to professional levels, when he started working as an escort, that he started making everything available to his clientèle. He had to. There was no getting around it. If he wanted to make the big bucks, he had to put out once in a while. So he got used to it. It took some time, but he managed to. Then Spencer came along, looking for a submissive that wouldn't chicken out at the last minute and say his safeword. Bondage, sexual torture, whipping, spanking, all of it was on the table. It wasn't just anal, it was freaky shit. Logic told Jacen to say no, and at first he did. Until he saw what Spencer was willing to pay.

The money is convincing, and for one reason only. Jacen doesn't intend to be an escort forever. He wants to be able to live his life the way he wants to live it, without a nine-to-five job behind a desk, rotting away in an office chair, getting fat and lazy and not living life while he can. Willing to sacrifice a few years in the name of giving strangers pleasure, Jacen looks forward to many more years being free, living off his savings, being happy. That's what he wants. And if it takes some pain and discomfort to accomplish that, then hey, he's got the balls to handle it.

Patrick, though. Patrick complicates things. Sure, Jacen is taller than him, packed with more muscle than him, but Patrick's presence is commanding and intimidating to say the least. He makes Jacen feel small, weak, vulnerable, even when he's trying to keep his walls up and just be the persona that Patrick wants him to be, and not himself. Patrick wants Jacen to feel like he could take Jacen apart and turn him inside out if he wanted to, that he could reach inside to all of Jacen's hidden places and trigger him in ways that Jacen never dreamed possible. And it works. Jacen's kind of scared of Patrick. He's like a perverted father figure, telling Jacen what to do, to take what he's given and like it. Usually Jacen does. Patrick treats him well and Jacen reaps the benefits. Patrick always gets him off, makes it feel good, makes him happy. It lets Jacen walk away feeling proud of himself for a job well done.

Not today. Today, Patrick stripped Jacen, bent him over and saw the proof that Jacen had been messing around and letting other people touch Patrick's things.

Usually Jacen tries to fuck Patrick face-to-face when he thinks the cover-up make-up won't completely hide a bruise or welt. It's not typically an issue. Patrick likes to kiss while he fucks, anyway, and it's easier to do that if Jacen's on his back, legs in the air, totally accessible.

But Patrick had been riled that morning. He'd had a streak of bad luck with his acting career. It had soured his mood. He needed an outlet, so Jacen complied. It was too late to reposition or reformulate his plan when Patrick shoved Jacen against the edge of the table and yanked his pants down. There was no room for finesse there. When Jacen apologized and tried to make an excuse about having an accident that caused the marks, it just made it worse. Patrick yanked Jacen's head back by his hair almost hard enough to rip it right out by the roots. He'd spit in Jacen's face, called him trash, a pig, filth, a dirty whore. He spun Jacen around, punched him with enough force to split his lip and then fucked him brutally, dry and with no prep until Jacen was biting the inside of his cheek just to keep quiet, tears running in rivers down his face.

He'd been seeing Patrick nearly every week for the past nine months. They weren't strangers. It wasn't just like getting a bad call and having to put up with a shitty client until Della could collect their fee and tell them to try going somewhere else, thank you very much. It was Patrick. Familiar, protective but tender Patrick.

You can't have sex with someone regularly for that long without putting a little faith in how they see you, and getting hurt when they turn around and literally spit in your face. It doesn't matter if it's just a job, just money. Something like that leaves a mark that's even harder to heal than welts from a bad date with a Dominant.

Jacen wipes off his arms, torso and legs, then wraps the towel around himself, hovering in the middle of the bathroom. There's something about Liam's reaction that upsets Jacen even more, and he had been pretty upset to begin with. Wanting out of there, to do anything to avoid a 'talk,' Jacen grits his teeth and forces himself to walk into the bedroom.

"You have to tell Della. You have to cut these fuckers loose," Liam seethes as soon as Jacen is standing on carpet instead of tile. He moves to the bed and sits on it, hiding his face in his hands, mainly just so that he doesn't have to see the way that Liam keeps looking at him.

"First of all," Jacen argues tiredly, without much will left to fight this particular battle. "She knows already. Second, they're my highest paying clients, next to Claudia. It'd be bad for business."

"Fuck the business."

"Well, that'd be ironic, wouldn't it?"

"Don't you dare joke about this," Liam snaps. "If you'd told

Spencer to fuck off months ago, you wouldn't have had this problem with Patrick in the first place, but clearly Patrick is too unbalanced to be trusted any more. That," Liam growls, pointing at Jacen's lip, "is assault."

"...Of a whore. Assault of a whore, Lee. Finish the thought. Don't fool yourself into thinking what he did was uncalled for."

Liam reacts dramatically to Jacen's words, coming at him almost exactly like Patrick did, grabbing his jaw with one hand, forcing his head back to get a better look at his eyes. It makes Jacen flinch away instinctively.

But then Liam's face softens and he's too close, Jacen thinks. Liam is *way* too close, their lips inches apart. He holds Jacen there, not letting him pull away.

"Don't," Jacen pleads, ashamed, embarrassed, spent.

"Stop saying shit like that," Liam rasps at him, his large, improbably beautiful eyes searching Jacen's face in a way that gets Jacen's stomach to flip-flop.

"Make me. Go on, Lee. I dare you. Be like them. Tell me what to say, what not to say. Tell me where you wanna stick it, how you wanna hurt me, what you're gonna do to me. Go on."

Liam's lips press together in a tight line, his brow creases with anguish.

"Why do you care? You don't have to fight this battle for me. I'm dealing with it."

"Bullshit," Liam hisses, his voice wavering. "No you're not. You're letting them do whatever the hell they want and then falling apart as soon as you get home."

"That's what home is for, isn't it? To let things out and vent and move on? Am I not supposed to do that here?"

"It's not supposed to hurt like this. It's not supposed to be like this."

"Says who?"

"Says me. How far are you going to let this go? What if Patrick pulled a knife on you? What if Spencer decides it'd be sexy to try choking you?"

"How about you let *me* worry about that," Jacen says quietly, wishing that Liam would let him go, hating the scrutiny, the care painted across his features. He grabs Liam's arm in an attempt to pull his arm away from where it's grasping his jaw, but all it does is remind Jacen how thickly muscled Liam's forearms are, how good his warm skin feels under his palm, how much Jacen likes touching Liam. And then he can't let go either.

"No," Liam says simply, standing his ground.

"*No?*"

"No," he repeats.

"I never asked for you to protect me. I'm a big boy, you know. You don't owe me shit."

"I'm your friend, and if you won't stand up for yourself, I'll do it for you, whether you like it or not. And if Della knows about this and isn't doing something to correct the problem, I'm gonna be having some words with her, too."

"Okay, hard-ass. You've proved your point. I seriously don't know why you get so riled up about this when I just wanna forget it ever happened."

Liam's lips draw back and he growls through his teeth. Disturbingly, he even gets closer, so close that his lips almost brush against Jacen's when he says, "*That* is exactly why I get riled up, dumbass."

He lets Jacen go. Straightening, he takes a deep, rough breath and runs a hand over his face.

"No, c'mon. Keep comin'. Don't quit now. Get just a little angrier with me and I bet you'll be punching me in the mouth, too. And we all know what comes after that. Maybe you'll even do what Patrick didn't manage to and tear me up inside when you force-fuck me. Then I'll be out of commission for weeks. You'll get your wish."

Liam's hand claps over his mouth and he makes a small hurt sound. As if in slow motion, Jacen sees him move, but for some reason, can't react or protest, even when he sees Liam coming. He moves to stand between Jacen's legs, wraps him up in his arms, hugging Jacen to his body, his hands wind around behind Jacen's head, against Jacen's back. Liam's fingers tangle in Jacen's hair and graze over his bare skin. Breathing in Liam's scent, Jacen's lips press against Liam's abs as his mouth works around a soundless cry. His hands ball up into fists that curl around behind Liam's lower back.

It's an awkward embrace that goes on long after Jacen has started praying for Liam to release him, before his hands disobey him and relax enough to touch and take hold of what's right there for him, the definition of temptation.

"I don't wanna fight with you anymore," Liam says in a small voice.

Jacen turns his face, pressing it flat against Liam's stomach, a thin, damp shirt the only thing separating them. Liam's fingers slide against Jacen's scalp, through his long hair almost in a caress. It sends a hard shiver racing down Jacen's spine.

"This doesn't feel like fighting," Jacen observes.

"Good. Let's keep it that way."

Chapter 6

Damned If You Do

That sunny afternoon after Liam and Jacen's confrontation in the bedroom, Liam leaves to give the CFO of a prominent healthcare organization a wicked blowjob in the back of a stretch limo, dressed as a punk. He slicks his naturally blond hair up into a faux-hawk, spray paints it blue. From his collection of magnetic jewelry he puts on a few pairs of earrings and facial piercings, goes heavy on the eyeliner. For clothes he chooses a tight black tank top, some cargos, steel-toed boots, and lots of accessories like a dog collar, leather cuffs, and chunky silver rings. His nipples and penis are already pierced, and for some clients he takes that jewelry out, but for this one they stay in, though he replaces the plain titanium studs with more decorative ones.

When Liam heads out, he texts Jacen to let him know. Jacen is in a meeting with Della down at the main office over what happened, so Liam doesn't see him or talk to him between their 'fight' and when he goes out on his call.

Liam is back within the hour and, since there was no way to clean up in the limo, he plans to head right for the bathroom. The messenger bag that he brought with him contains a bottle of mouthwash, which he has already used and spit out into the gutter. The pitiful hand release the client gave him left Liam scrounging up some sort of clean-up with baby wipes. All of this adds up to Liam feeling intensely gross. Jacen's car is in the driveway, so Liam knows he's home. He doesn't see the motorcycle that is pulled around back until he gets through the front door, shouts for Jacen, gets no response and then finds him in the backyard. Yasha, an old friend of Jacen's is there, with the motorcycle he rode in on. The two men are in heavy conversation, so Liam pops his head out to say, "Hey. I'm home. Hittin' the showers."

"Liam. Wow. That's a good look for you," Yasha says, giving Liam the full head-to-toe once-over but fixating on Liam's lips when Liam's hand goes, self-consciously, to his mouth, rubbing it like there might be evidence of what he did staining them.

Liam clams up, like he always does around Yasha. Yasha is one of Jacen's best friends but Liam constantly feels like the outsider in his company. It's not really due to any one thing, more a clash of personalities, one headstrong, one reserved. Some of it might also have to do with Yasha and Jacen's past, that they've known each other — intimately — since before Liam and Jacen were ever introduced. At first, Liam couldn't quite get a handle on what it was about Yasha and Jacen together that gave him a weird vibe, especially since Jacen told him that they've never dated or anything, since, well, Jacen doesn't date guys and Yasha is married to a woman named Valery.

Slowly, though, facts began to slip out. Yasha used to work for The Company. He was an escort for ten years — the typical length of a contract with them — and met Jacen a little over two years earlier, through a mutual friend who was also a sex worker, before an overdose killed him. Jacen and Yasha met at the funeral.

Now Yasha is a private contractor, so to speak, picking and choosing his clients himself, mostly old regulars, and any new people are heavily screened before being considered. He also runs a counseling service specializing in sexual disorders out of his lush house down by the beach. Knowing all of this, things make more sense to Liam, like Yasha's intense proclivity to flirt with anything that stands on two legs. It doesn't explain everything, though. Jacen acts differently with Yasha than with anyone else, like Yasha has some sort of power over him, or holds some secret that Jacen doesn't dare tell anyone else.

Only a few months ago, Liam found out why. When Jacen got into the business professionally and was preparing to sign on with The Company after learning of Yasha's experience with them, he had gone to Yasha to 'break him in.' Jacen admitted that he hadn't wanted his first experience on the receiving end of anal sex to be with a stranger. So he'd gone to someone trusted, someone who understood — Yasha. They spent a whole weekend together, alone, in Yasha's house. Yasha had fucked Jacen every way he knew how, over and over again, for days, until some of the novelty had worn off and Jacen discovered how to really enjoy it. Just one friend to another, fucking his brains out.

In the doorway leading to the back patio, in a yard enclosed with tall trees and an abundant, well-tended garden, Liam balls his hands up into fists inside his cargo pants pockets and bites his tongue, ignoring the lingering looks he's getting from Yasha. Conversely, the ones he's also getting from Jacen don't bother Liam at all, but he doesn't quite consciously realize that.

"Yeah, well, he'd look good in a paper bag," Jacen mumbles, being coy in a way that suggests whatever talk Liam just walked in on is one that might raise some eyebrows if the details became known.

"He isn't grotesque, that's for sure," Yasha adds in agreement.

"Whatever. I'm, um —" He thumbs back over his shoulder before leaving; nearly jogging through the house and taking the steps two at a time just to get away that much faster.

Brushing his teeth five times in a row, washing the crap out of his hair, scrubbing his body with a loofah for twenty minutes before moisturizing and redressing in normal clothes, Liam takes his time in what he thinks of as the detox phase of his job. An hour and a half after leaving Yasha and Jacen, Liam descends the stairs once more in search of food and a comfortable chair.

Aggravatingly, Yasha is still there, talking quietly outside with Jacen, though now there are drinks in front of them both and a bowl of fresh cut vegetables. Trying to ignore them, Liam throws together a half-assed dinner out of leftovers and claims the recliner in the living room, turning on the news and zoning out.

Every now and then, he finds himself trying to make sense of the low murmuring filtering through the windowpane. Sometimes, when he turns to glance out back, he sees one of the two men nodding or otherwise gesturing toward the house, like they're talking about Liam. It's unsettling to say the least. *Probably your imagination,*

Liam tells himself. *Or your arrogance. Thinking everything's always gotta be about you.*

He wonders how the meeting with Della went, and why exactly Yasha is there. Wanting to ask Jacen what's going on, Liam tries to be patient. Not for the first time he laments the fact that he doesn't have more good friends that aren't in his line of work, to talk to about normal things, like the weather, sports, and politics. Even with as long as Liam has been in the service industry, he is sure that he'll never get completely used to it, how everything becomes a lie, a game, a mind-fuck, a charade. It makes honesty, purity, directness become that much more cherished.

And there's so little of that going around, it makes Liam nauseous.

His phone rings. Grumbling, he digs it out, sends up a little prayer that it's nothing urgent, because fuck it, he's tired and not in the mood.

It's Della.

"Son of a *bitch*," he complains, whining. Clearing his throat and letting his head fall back against the cushions, he answers. "Dee. What's up, darlin'?"

"William, I'm going to be stopping by your place for an impromptu meeting with you. We've got some things to discuss and I'd rather handle it now than wait 'til tomorrow when I'll be in the office again. You around? Will you be there?"

"Sure, I'll be here," he says cheerfully, rolling his eyes and making a face. *Not good. This does not bode well at all.*

"Cool. Gimme twenty minutes."

"No problem."

Jacen picks up a carrot stick and drums it against the tabletop. Through one of the windows, mottled with shifting shadows from the palm trees and high bushes, he sees Liam, or at least the back of Liam's head. Liam is sitting in front of the television, relaxing, as he should be.

Yasha, sipping spring water, follows Jacen's gaze to the object of his thoughts. "You're right that he's not me. But he's not so different either."

Jacen frowns. The tap-tap-tapping begins to drive Yasha insane. The carrot stops beating its irregular rhythm when Jacen viciously snaps it in half.

"No one's like you," Jacen says. "Your perspective is... unique."

"Thank you."

"I mean, you and Val are like the definition of open-mindedness. This was a bad idea. Maybe there's still time to call it off."

"You're not really naïve enough to believe that? That you can stop this now? Not even Liam can stop it. The arrangements have been made. Money is at stake. A lot of money. And guess who the collateral is?"

"Wow, Yash, you're really making me feel better," Jacen grumbles sourly.

"Oh, was that my job here? Sorry, I wasn't clear on that. You want me to spit-shine your ass while we're at it? Here I was, thinking we were having an actual exchange of thoughts and ideas."

"You know what I mean," Jacen sighs, biting the end off of a sprig of broccoli.

"Okay. You want me to tickle your balls for you? Here you go. What's with your fucking attitude problem? You got your wish. You got a few of your wishes, if I'm not correct. Stop acting like a child."

"This — " Jacen laughs maliciously, jabbing a finger at the house. "*This* is not my wish. This was never my *wish*."

"It's not exactly a punishment though, is it?" Yasha counters with a leading, crooked smile and a quick raise of his eyebrows, grabbing a cherry tomato and popping it in his mouth.

"Depends how you look at it," Jacen says darkly, his eyes clouding over.

"Please," Yasha scoffs. "There is no down-side here. This is the best possible outcome."

"No," Jacen argues, his voice getting lower, more resigned and forlorn. "No, it's not."

They sit in the dining room, directly across from each other in two of six chairs.

"You want a drink? We've got a bottle of vintage merlot open."

"No, thanks," Della smiles. "This'll be quick. I have to be at Fourth and Main by six with a bright smile firmly in place and all of my wits intact."

"New client?"

"Hopefully. If all goes as planned."

"Great," Liam says, settling into his chair. "So, to what do I owe the pleasure?"

"Well, Jacen and I spoke this morning and some things were brought to my attention," she starts. Immediately Liam sits up straighter, focusing with laser-like precision on his boss.

"What did he say?"

"I'd rather not get into specifics. Confidentiality and all that. You understand. But it all boils down to this. You convinced Jacen that he needed to get himself out of what could become a dangerous situation. Jacen was able to persuade us that there were lingering... risks. The problem is, we're talking about losing a major account. That needs to be compensated for."

"So...."

"So, Spencer has been informed that The Company will no longer be able to service his particular needs," Della says slowly, trailing some of the syllables out.

"Spencer." Liam echoes. "What about Patrick?"

"Patrick was a one-time incident and he was very apologetic for what happened. We have been assured that it won't happen again, that Jacen is very important to him, and the last thing he wants is for Jacen to be hurt."

"Bullshit." He sits forward, hands splayed on the polished oak, and roars, "That's fucking *bullshit*!"

Della's heart-shaped face is the picture of composure, framed with perfectly styled, thick, recently-dyed auburn curls, her hands primly folded in front of her. Clearing her throat, she waits to see if

Liam has anything else to scream at her; when it seems he doesn't, she continues. "I'm going to let that go, only because I know it's out of concern for Jacen's well-being that you are so disturbed. But that's your only free pass, Will. Got it?"

His jaw clenching, Liam grits his teeth together to keep from letting out a tirade of obscenities and possibly face some seriously unpleasant repercussions.

"As I was saying, Spencer was a major account, but luckily we have found a way to balance the scales and, you know... fill the gap. Everyone walks away happy."

"What the hell does this have to do with me? Are you just telling me this because I'm the one that told him to speak to you, or — "

"You have a new job. New client, for *you* anyway," she says with a pristine, gleaming smile. A cold, hard, weight of dread settles in Liam's gut. "Tomorrow night. I'll message the location to you."

"What are we talking about here? What kind of client? What's the request?"

"The request is for a pretty boy. Nervous. Shy. Jock. Straight-acting."

"And the client?"

"Not really important. Her name is Claudia. She's been with us for a while, as you probably know."

"What?" Fumbling for speech and a valid arguement, he can't disguise the tremor in his voice. "You're sending me to a... I don't have female clients."

"Don't worry, sweetie. She just wants to watch. This time, at least."

There's a pause and Liam doesn't want to ask. He really doesn't. But he doesn't have a choice, and from the look on her face, Della knows it.

"What does she want to watch?"

"You're booked with another employee for this appointment. Jacen, to be specific. Jacen's her pet. She just loves him to death, but she's gotten this idea that she'd *really* like to see Jacen take control and have his way with another, very pretty, man, while she watches. And she's willing to pay *handsomely* for it." Della gives him a Cheshire cat grin at the thought of the cash rolling in, without even having to go fishing for a new client. It saves her work, time, expense, effort.

"No," Liam says tightly, almost swallowing the word. "No. I won't. No."

Standing from the table, his legs don't quite feel like they'll support him. There are no windows overlooking the backyard in the dining room and he's grateful for it. The cold pit in his gut grows huge and races upwards, lodging in his throat.

"Sweetie, you can't say no," she says soothingly to him, like the words aren't laced with bile and threat.

"R-ryan. Get Ryan to do it." Liam stammers. "Or—"

"Ryan's on an overnight all weekend. He's unavailable. Blake's too gay. David's too old. That leaves you. Claudia was very specific about what she wants. I intend to give it to her. Really, this should be a piece of cake. The character isn't too much of a stretch for you, and there is no possibly unsavory client to service. You get to just lie there and let a hot guy—who's not going to go all psycho on you—get you off. Not so bad, huh? A lot of people would *love* to be paid for something like that."

Arguments, legitimate reasons why this is a horrendous idea hover at the edges of Liam's mind, in sight but out of reach. He can feel in his bones, in his heart, that this is bad. It's bad and nothing good will come of it. There's not a single part of him that wants it. *Not this way, at least,* the small, secret voice of his conscience whispers. Sure, Della's right in that there's almost no work here, no real risk, except to his and Jacen's friendship, which, of course, is of no concern at all to The Company.

It counts for nothing that he simply doesn't want to do it. They have ways to make him comply if they have to—withholding payment; loading him up with more frequent appointments with clients that might not be to his liking at all, physically, sexually, psychologically; or even less pleasant recourses, things that veer further outside the law than they already are.

Some of this can already be seen in the way Jacen has been handled. The reason why Jacen has gotten more of the less savory clientele is because he's the newbie. He gets to scrape the bottom of the barrel for the sludge that no one else wants. There could be another

Spencer waiting in the wings, who doesn't care what character Liam plays, just how brightly he screams. If Liam says no to this—sex with Jacen for Claudia's pleasure—not only will he be faced with possibly nightmarish encounters for less pay than he's used to, but Jacen will too. Liam's efforts to get Jacen into a safer arrangement would be for nothing. They'd both suffer for it.

Della's right. He can't say no. It doesn't matter if he doesn't want to do it. He has no choice.

Without waiting for a reply, seeing the resignation on Liam's face, Della stands and slides her purse strap higher on her shoulder. "I'll send you the details in a few. And if it goes well, hopefully it'll become a regular thing."

"Yeah," Liam murmurs.

He walks Della to the door. They pause when she turns to him and says, "You made the right call, Will. Just think of who you'd rather Jacen be with, Spencer or you."

Nodding, wearing a hollow expression, he holds the door open for her, watching as she gets in the backseat of the Lincoln and her driver slowly pulls away.

Chapter 7
Damned If You Don't

Once alone, Liam goes online to check the balances on his accounts, not thinking too hard about why he's taking stock of his available funds and, in the recesses of his mind, debating his options concerning the future, only that it makes him feel better to see over three hundred thousand dollars there, and even more in investments. Possibilities spin out before him, taking vaporous form, then dematerializing before becoming too tangible.

This doesn't have to be forever. It can just be for right now. He'll make the most of it, keep saving and bide his time. And then, one day, he'll be free, whether The Company likes it or not. He'll just gather his things and vanish. There one day, gone the next. Nothing but a memory. He's done it before, countless times. In some ways, it's who Liam is—someone temporary, changeable, someone who knows how to slip through fingers for a quick escape. It has never been as tempting as it is right in that moment. Liam has always been mostly happy doing what he does. It defines him. It's his outlet. So he's not sure why it suddenly feels nothing but toxic and wrong.

Sure you do, a ghost whispers in his ear, a very young voice both desperately welcome and grotesquely bitter; one he knows very well; one that haunts him day and night, and will do so until the end of his days—Timothy's voice. *I don't even recognize you anymore. How did you let yourself become this? How did you stand by this long, letting Jacen whore himself out to monsters? There is no good reason, is there? Greed? Fear? Hmm. Maybe a little. Maybe something else, too.*

"You. It's your fault," he spits into the air, knowing his own bitterness, his own hurt, is the cause of the words. He wants to take them back as soon as they're spoken, but it's too late. It's been too late for years.

Meanwhile, outside and standing by the motorcycle, Yasha and Jacen are inches apart. Yasha is getting ready to go. He's stayed longer than he planned, but Jacen needed it. There is still a sense of heavy foreboding and dread around the big lug. Only one thing will dispel it, and it's nothing Yasha can give him.

"So, in conclusion," Yasha says, laying a hand flat on the center of Jacen's chest. "It's fully possible for you and Liam to fuck like bunnies and still stay friends. If you want it that badly, make it happen."

"He's one of the best things in my life," Jacen admits sadly, hanging his head, making cascades of shaggy, dark hair fall in his eyes. "I don't want to lose him over a shitty job."

"Then don't. Keep hold of him. You can do that much."

Jacen thinks this over, then nods.

"What's the first thing I ever told you about The Company? Huh? Day one?"

"You don't get a say," Jacen responds with resignation. It was Yasha's biggest argument against Jacen signing a ten-year contract of his own, but Jacen was absolutely confident that he could handle it.

"That's right," Yasha agrees. "The client, the request, the gender, the fetish — it's their call, not yours. You don't get a say. Liam doesn't get a say. If they think you're capable of delivering with a moderate degree of success, it's a go. *This* is a go. It has nothing to do with feelings or your preferences, it's a fucking *job*. Do your job. Then get paid and walk away."

Yasha reaches up and wraps his hand around the side of Jacen's face, his thumb dragging in a slow arc over Jacen's cheekbone, his fingertips sliding back over his jaw. Jacen leans in and down, his lips losing their tension, going soft as Yasha reaches up to kiss them tenderly. There's a slow series of light brushes of lips on lips as they take the moment to enjoy each other, remembering vividly what they've shared and how much they trust one another. They were strangers, then friends, then suddenly, almost inexplicably, lovers — for a time. They went back to being friends after that, but the intimacy never left, and probably never will. The force and passion of the kiss deepens. Yasha's fingers slide farther back, around Jacen's head, bringing him in closer so that he can get more, licking over his tongue, sucking on it, mapping out his mouth, his taste, remembering how it felt to be wrapped in the soft, pulsing heat of him, how Jacen had given over to him completely, how good it had been.

They break apart, dizzy, and Yasha's fingertip traces over the healing wound on Jacen's lower lip where Patrick hit him, drying the silken skin, feeling heat emanate from it.

"It'd be his loss, you know," Yasha tells him with more affection than Jacen can bear.

"I don't want to do this anymore," Jacen hisses.

"Well, that's your decision. You might never see money like this again, though. Remember that. Give it a try. Make it work for *you*."

"You're so smart," Jacen smiles, his cheeks dimpling.

"Oh, no you don't. Your charms have no power over me," Yasha says sternly, even as his fingers tighten in Jacen's wavy hair, which tickles over his face when Yasha dives in for another, dirtier kiss.

"Liar."

Jacen licks the taste of Yasha from his lips and pushes his hands down into his pants pockets as Yasha straddles the bike and pulls his helmet down over his clipped-short, spiky, light brown hair. Warm brown eyes shot through with amber gaze out from the shadows the helmet casts over his angular features.

"You know where we are if you need us," he says with a pointed look. "Let me know how it goes."

"Yeah," Jacen nods. "Thanks, man. Give Val my love."

Yasha laughs and revs the engine. When he's gone, all that's left is the urgent pull at the core of Jacen's being, telling him to go inside, to find Liam and face him.

"I don't want to do this any more," Jacen moans again, telling no one, telling himself. It's no use; he doesn't heed his own words. His feet carry him back through the yard, into the house, up the stairs.

Liam is in the spare bedroom, at the desk they share, their home office. Jacen lingers in the doorway, hands still in his pockets, scuffing his toe on the carpet, hang-dog expression on his face. "Lee...."

"I don't want to talk about it. That's my one condition. I can't. I *can't* talk about this with you," Liam says. There's a strained roughness to his voice that Jacen doesn't like at all.

"I'm not your client, Liam," Jacen says softly, hurt by the standoffishness, if not entirely surprised by it.

"You are. Now you are."

"Look at me," Jacen pleads.

Liam shakes his head, keeping it turned away. After a moment, though, he caves and sighs heavily when he sees Jacen's wet, shining eyes.

"I'm glad Spencer's gone," Liam allows. "It's worth it, to get rid of that asshole."

"You can trust me, you know. I'd never hurt you." Jacen pledges urgently.

"*I don't want to talk about it,*" Liam interjects forcefully.

"So, you're going to punish me for this? By shutting me out? That's not fair. This isn't my fault!"

"I'm not," Liam starts, then closes his eyes and takes a breath, lowering his volume with effort. "I'm not punishing you. I just don't know how to do this as your friend."

"It needs to be a game, doesn't it? Or an act? Like with Leah?"

Tugging absent-mindedly at the edge of his shirt, shoulders hunched, Liam seems to try to get smaller, to shrink in on himself.

"Okay," Jacen says slowly. "I'll be your client. For this, I'll be your client. But you're my best friend, Liam. I refuse to give you up over this. You hear me?"

Liam turns his face away, covering his mouth with a hand, the elbow braced on the desk.

"Will you come downstairs and have some dinner with me? There's a small chance I'll even let you toss my salad."

Laughter is surprised out of Liam at this, but it quickly turns into a shaky, pained whimper.

"Liam...."

"No. I'm sorry. I can't. I just... I can't." Liam pushes past him, almost running to his room and slamming the door violently shut behind him.

Jacen reels, fists balled up at his sides. He pounds them against the wall and presses his forehead against the drywall, letting out a wrenching cry of frustration and anguish. Not once for the rest of the night does he see Liam. Dinner is made quietly, on his own. The house is still and the air eerily thick around him as he sits by himself at the table, picking at his food, listening to the clink and clatter of his fork against the china.

The two friends remain close in proximity but separate all that night and the next day, too. In the morning, Liam slips out, headed to Amé and Jacen's stomach flips at the realization that he's going partially to get ready for him, that in only a few hours, Jacen will have Liam, naked, willing, begging, underneath him, to be touched, sucked and tasted, explored and adored. Jittery with his own nervous energy, Jacen goes out for a run after doing his daily exercise routine in the small gym set up in their garage with his set of weights and weight bench. He runs for miles, coming back purged, feeling better for it, steadier, ready. Liam is back in his room, closeted away. Time ticks by, sometimes fast, sometimes slow, but ever forward, carrying them both toward the inevitable — the moment that will change everything for them, forever.

Jacen and Liam drive to their job separately, in their own vehicles, leaving the house at different times. The messages received from Della directed Jacen to be there a half-hour before Liam, at eight in the evening rather than eight-thirty. But they wouldn't have driven over together anyway. Liam's psyche wouldn't be able to bear it, driving to a strange house with his friend, knowing they were only going there to fuck for someone else's amusement and about a grand extra in their bank accounts.

Or maybe it won't have to go that far. The text from Della implied that Claudia was expecting oral, and not more than that, but Liam knows that things can go any which way once they start. It's best to be prepared for everything. That's a lesson learned the hard way for him, after a number of overly eccentric paying clients with decidedly kinky tastes. Say they want one thing over the phone, ask for another in person, promising more money, *lots* more money, if only —

At about seven o'clock Liam stops being 'Liam'. He shifts into the character of a shy, straight-acting jock, who's meeting a hot guy for sex. All he knows about the hot guy is that he's the favorite of a rich woman on the east side of town; that she pampers him and spoils him with gifts and favors. Wanting to be with this guy, he's also freaked about it, about what it'll feel like to have a man's mouth busy between his legs, licking, kissing, sucking, while *she* is there, seeing everything, maybe instructing the man to do this or try that, anything to get a louder moan, a sharper cry.

He tells himself it's as much of a far-fetched fantasy as Tucker's request for a cowboy, that it's make-believe, a play where the only audience is the people in the room. It's secret, private. Anything can happen with no consequences, because as soon as the play is over, and the night is through, they stop being their characters and go back to being the boring, normal, unexciting people they are.

The saddest thing is that a part of him truly believes that.

Nervousness and shyness are not hard for Liam to muster. He's got both of them in spades as he gets ready, going into the bathroom, washing his cock and balls, douching, scrubbing every inch of his skin and doing absolutely everything he can to not remember that he's doing it all for Jacen.

When Liam grabs one of his small, tapered butt plugs, lubing it up, pressing it into himself with one leg braced on the edge on his bathtub, coaxing the muscle loose, his stomach ties up in knots. He works it in and out, tugging and pressing until the toy moves easily, rotating it around inside for a greater stretch as dull memories of what Jacen looked like naked flash in his mind. Remembering the size of Jacen's cock, Liam tries to adjust the amount of prep accordingly to be ready for that. The plug gets withdrawn and Liam squirts more lube all over his fingers, inserting three of them into himself, smearing it around his inner walls, wondering if someone else's fingers will be in there instead in a little over an hour.

Since he's mentally stoking the fires of his own paranoia for the character's sake, he manages to make himself so worked up that he has to sit by the toilet bowl for a good fifteen minutes, hugging the porcelain and praying that his lunch doesn't come chasing up his gullet like it wants to.

Without a drop of product in his hair or bronzer on his skin, he slips on a pair of crisp, white briefs, some snug-fitting khakis and a grass green, short-sleeved polo shirt. Jacen has never seen Liam naked. As far as Liam knows, Jacen has never even seen him without a shirt on, since Liam likes to keep covered when he's not on the job. This causes Liam to take an extra few seconds in front of the mirror, obsessing over each little detail. The body jewelry is a toss-up. He decides to leave it in. Jacen doesn't know about the piercings either.

At eight-fifteen, he's in the driver's seat in the driveway when bile rises in his throat. Forcing it back down, without time to go back inside and clean up, brush his teeth, use mouthwash, the whole deal, he tempers his panic and wills himself a little calmer. The drive is a short one, and thankfully he doesn't run into any traffic. Grabbing some breath spray, he squirts two pumps onto his tongue and sets the gearshift in park in the long, winding driveway that curves in front of a grand estate.

A push of the bell at the main entrance brings a butler in a non-descript grey suit.

"William. For Claudia. She's expecting me," he says curtly, his hands folded neatly in front of him.

"Of course," is the polite reply. The servant steps back, opening the door widely. "Please, right this way."

With a deep breath, terrified, Liam lives the fantasy and steps inside.

Chapter 8
The Unthinkable

They walk through a wing of the house, up a set of curving stairs to the second floor, down another wide hall to a door that is shut tight. Liam's heart hammers in his chest. Taking a deep, shaky breath when he feels his skin get too hot, then too cold, then too tight, and sweat threatens to break out over his body, he stands back as the butler knocks softly and calls, "Your second guest is here, Ma'am."

"Show him in, Teddy. Thank you," a pleasant, lilting female voice answers from beyond the closed door. She giggles and then Liam catches the sound of a deep, male voice murmuring. Jacen. The bones in Liam's legs nearly turn to jelly.

The door swings open and the butler gestures for him to enter. It's a large room with dark, fabric-covered walls, some of it hanging in elegant drapes from the ceiling, framing a huge bed with crimson silk sheets. The light is more substantial than Liam would like, atmospheric with candles, but recessed overheads and a few sconces brighten the space considerably.

Liam becomes his character, rubbing the back of his neck, lowering his eyes, flushing pink. Jacen is standing with the woman, who must be Claudia, his long fingers dancing over her fair skin and her pink silk negligee. Focused entirely on her, her cupid's bow-shaped lips when she giggles, the long sweeping line of her neck, the soft swell of her ample cleavage, Jacen presses close to her, one arm circled around her back, his hand resting at the small of her back, hunching forward ever so slightly so that his lips are in kissing distance. Jacen is barefoot and shirtless, wearing only a pair of worn-soft jeans that Liam has laundered for him countless times.

Sweet Jesus, he's gorgeous, Liam moans inwardly. Jacen is sex — his suntanned skin, oiled muscles bulging, veins popping, hair twisted back at the nape of his neck in a leather tie but a few tendrils slipping free, and curling around his face. Liam can't stop staring at the ridges of his friend's washboard abdominal muscles, his small, dark nipples, the perfection of Jacen's belly button, the cut of his hips descending in a V under the jeans, pointing toward his groin.

Claudia appears to be about forty years old, with long strawberry blond hair and a round, doll-like face. Wearing her age well, in amazing physical shape, with creamy skin, her eyes sparkling with her laughter, she quickly puts Liam at ease with only a smile.

"William. Come in. Welcome," she purrs. "Jacen, look at him. He's beautiful. This is going to be fantastic, I know it. Now, you'll be nice to him, won't you? Look how bashful he's being. We mustn't scare him off."

She leaves Jacen and glides over to Liam instead, slipping a small, delicate hand inside his and guiding him to be closer to the bed. It takes only a few steps and then she's kissing his cheek, soft as a butterfly's touch.

"Don't be scared. We won't bite. Much."

"Okay," he murmurs, catching his lower lip between the points of his teeth.

"Is this your first time?"

There's a hopeful note to the question, so, with a quick glance to Jacen's towering form a few feet away, Liam ducks his head and answers, "Maybe, ma'am. Depends what you're asking, I guess."

"Call me Claudia. Please." Liam gives her a vulnerable, shy grin and holds her hand a little tighter. "What I would *love,* William, is to introduce you to my good friend Jacen. Would that be okay? He's a big teddy bear, I promise, don't let the hard body fool you."

"Yeah, that's okay," he says with another nervous glance to his intended. Jacen is staring right at him, like he's seeing Liam for the first time, like he's absolutely starving for him. There's a wicked, heady, naked lust in his cool blue eyes as they grope over Liam's form, one that Liam's never quite been at the receiving end of before, not even when he was Leah, not in all the many times they rehearsed in the downstairs of their home.

Stomach swooping, breath catching, Liam turns his attention back to Claudia when she asks, "William, have you ever been with a man before?"

"B-been with —" After a sharp exhale, his blood rushing under his skin, roaring in his ears, making him dizzy, he sees from the corner of his eye as Jacen makes his way over.

"Guess I have my answer," she smiles wickedly, completely enthralled.

"Hi, William," Jacen says, his hands slipping easily around Liam, one around his waist, the other around the junction of his neck and shoulder. Never before in all of the thousands of times that Jacen has said Liam's name has it ever sounded as filthy as it does then. A hard shiver races through Liam's body. Jacen feels it. His thumb skims over Liam's skin at his neck, making the spot tingle.

"H-hi," Liam echoes, not knowing what to do with his hands, or at least pretending he doesn't.

"I'll let you two get acquainted. Don't mind me," she giggles, lounging on a chaise with a tall glass of champagne, watching with rapt attention.

Jacen's hand slides up under Liam's green polo shirt, caressing over the skin above his hip at his waist. It tickles a little, causing Liam to reflexively suck in his stomach. Blood rushes to his head, making it swim, making him feel overheated. His heart is beating so hard and fast that it's louder than everything else by far, knocking against his ribs.

Jacen moves them to the edge of the bed, backing Liam up to it. Taking hold of the hem of his shirt, Jacen tugs at it and says, "Let's take this off, okay?"

"Okay," Liam murmurs very softly, blushing a fierce red as Jacen tugs it up over his head for him, letting it fall to the ground at their feet. At first Liam can't look at Jacen at all, staring out into a point in mid-space instead, because Jacen is staring right at Liam's pierced nipples, a lot of Jacen's 'character' falling away purely from shock.

Jacen's hand comes up. The pad of his thumb rolls over the titanium bar embedded in the small, dark, sensitive nub of flesh that hardens instantly at the touch. Brushing again over the impaled nipple, Jacen's fingers close up around the bar, pulling gently. A surge of blood shoots down to Liam's cock. Tensing, pressing ever so slightly into Jacen's hand, Liam exhales an audible breath.

"Mm, seems William's a naughtier boy than we thought, Jacen," Claudia observes from her seat. "I'll bet you want to suck on those piercings...."

"Yeah," Jacen moans softly, honestly, twisting the nipple slightly, getting hard at the way it makes Liam react, his breath roughening.

"Why don't you take his pants off, then get onto the bed," Claudia instructs, taking a deep sip and then chuckling, drawing one leg up onto the chaise, exposing the creamy skin of her thighs all the way up to her matching pink panties.

"Just relax," Jacen tells him as he pops open Liam's fly and tugs down the zipper. Bringing the khakis down over Liam's hips, easing them over the pert swell of his ass, Jacen pushes them down Liam's legs, helping him step out and tossing them aside. He runs his fingers over the waxed-smooth skin of Liam's legs, usually covered in golden blond hair, as he stands. It's perfectly clear to Jacen how very much Liam is truly overwhelmed, that most of it is not for the sake of the character anymore, it's all him. So Jacen takes control, deciding to do what he needs to in order to make this as quick and as good for Liam as he possibly can.

Easing Liam down to the bed, getting him seated first, and then manhandling him back further up the bed, Jacen lays him out, bringing him down with a hand behind Liam's neck, rubbing over Liam's stomach. Jacen plants a knee between Liam's legs to ease them apart and leans down over him, bracing a hand on the bed. Claudia stands and walks around for a better view, leaning against a wall at Jacen's side. Caressing down Liam's taut stomach, Jacen rubs over the stark white cotton of Liam's briefs, rolling his palm and fingers over Liam's genitals. Liam is barely half-hard. Glancing up, Jacen sees Liam squeeze his eyes closed, a small, delicate frown line appearing between his eyebrows at the intimate touch. The real anguish in the expression, not pleasurable, just heartbreaking, knots Jacen's gut.

Grabbing lightly at Liam's flesh, manipulating him to get him hard, Jacen realizes he needs to distract and move this along faster when Liam lets out a broken half-whimper, half-sob that makes Jacen feel nauseous, like he's molesting Liam against his will.

Surging downward, Jacen seals his lips around Liam's right nipple, suckling both the metal bar and the erect flesh while he begins stroking in a steady rhythm along Liam's shaft through the cotton of his briefs, coaxing him stiff with gentle, constant stimulation. His fingers catch on a hard but small protrusion under the head and Jacen moans against Liam's skin as he realizes what it is.

Liam arches into the touch of Jacen's lips to his chest, shivers of pleasure rippling out from the spot. The tip of Jacen's tongue flicks the nipple over and over again. His lips kiss around it, his tongue drags over it. He closes his teeth behind the titanium bar and tugs. Then he shifts to the other side and gives it the same treatment. His hand begins to ease the underwear down, inch-by-inch, over Liam's hips. Breaking away from Liam's nipples, leaving both wet, erect and pinker from the attention, Jacen uses both hands to slide the briefs down just enough to expose him, letting the elastic pull tight around Liam's upper thighs.

Panting, turning his cheek into the bedding, eyes still tightly closed over, Liam makes a small, helpless sound back in his throat as Jacen touches him for the first time, fingertips skittering up his swelling shaft to the glinting jewelry fed through the tip of Liam's cock and out through the piercing in his frenulum, just under the divot in the crown on the underside. Jacen's index finger and thumb pinch around the tiny silver ball nestled snugly against Liam's slit and play with it, tugging gently on it, rubbing around the edge of the metal.

Liam grunts and hums, biting the side of his lip and canting his hips, chasing up into the touch to relieve the intense tickle it sends shivering down through his dick, but Jacen doesn't ease up, fingering at him.

"Good. Play with it. He wants you to. Just look at him," Claudia marvels.

Jacen stares down at his fingers for a long moment, trying to memorize the gorgeous sight of Liam's body, every inch, every vein. But he still has to hurry, and not torment Liam longer than he has to, so he goes back to his left nipple, teasing it with the tip of his tongue, stroking very slowly up and down Liam's shaft. Circling his fingers loosely around it, Jacen squeezes up and down, feeling Liam thicken. Leaving Liam's nipple dark pinkish purple and oversensitive, Jacen begins to suck little kisses in a trail down the center line of Liam's body, over his sternum, down through his six-pack abs, over his navel, across to the side and covering the velvety smooth skin of Liam's pelvis, inside his hip, around the root of his cock.

Groaning softly, Liam rocks gently into Jacen's loose fist, riding it. Jacen squeezes tighter up to the tip and milks a few drops of pre-come that dribble downward from the slit. All Jacen wants in the whole world in that moment is to taste that, to lick Liam's cock and suck his flesh and his piercing clean. Somehow he restrains himself and slips a hand into his pocket for the rubber.

Nuzzling between Liam's legs, placing tender, open-mouthed kisses to the inside of his thigh and hip, Jacen moans and breathes in the heavenly, heady scent of him. He fills his nostrils with it, his lungs, his every pore. Discreetly, he tears open the foil and extracts the condom, rolling it onto Liam.

On the bed, Liam's eyes shoot open, feeling Jacen sheath him in latex. "Jace-Jacen?"

"Just gonna taste, you, okay? I'm dying for a taste of you. I'll make it good. Suck you so fucking good, William...."

A few ragged breaths rip from Liam's chest and he makes a slight, shocked sound as Jacen opens his mouth and cradles Liam's dick on his tongue, tapping it lightly against it, the ball on the end of the stud smacking against the wet muscle. Liam shudders and bucks. Jacen goes with it, closing his lips around the girth, behind the ridge, and feeds Liam back into the eager heat of his mouth.

"Fuck. *Fuck*," Liam moans. Curling his arms up over his head, he grabs at the bedding, twisting his hands in it, hips coming up off the bed and undulating into Jacen's mouth. His reddened length slides back between Jacen's stretched lips, gliding over his tongue, and then draws back. Jacen hollows his cheeks and Liam moans more deeply, bucking quickly back inside, needing to be closed up in Jacen's mouth. Turning his face into the side of his arm, Liam lets out every whimper, every gasp.

"Hold him down, suck him 'til he comes," Claudia says to Jacen, her voice lust-roughened.

Bearing down on Liam, locking his hands around his hips, pinning them to the bed, Jacen works his mouth on him, sucking him raw through the condom, bobbing his head. Hungry for it, maddened by the stark, visceral reality of being stuffed full of Liam's cock, and being instructed to take him completely apart, Jacen obeys. He hums and sucks even harder, moaning around Liam's flesh, working and curling his tongue when he can, giving Liam such intense sensation that, for Liam, all rational thought seems to funnel out through his dick and down Jacen's throat. Lips drawn back over gritted teeth, Liam whimpers and hisses, so erect it hurts, right on the knife's edge of oblivion.

Jacen pulls off with a slurp, strips off the condom and corkscrews a tight fist up Liam, root to tip. He erupts. Semen shoots in a wide arc from his slit, pulsing with the beat of his heart, spattering in thick drops over the whole length of his gloriously naked body.

Slowly, Liam comes to himself again, feeling emptier, drained. Staring up at the ceiling for a long moment, aware of his nakedness, of the come drying on his skin, he listens but doesn't dare look as Jacen gets off the bed and Claudia goes to her knees in front of him. There's the zip of Jacen's pants coming open, the crinkle of foil, a thunderous, rolling groan from Jacen as he buries himself in her throat, finally getting some much-needed relief for his own raging passion.

Liam waits to be summoned, keeping his eyes averted, knowing he'll be haunted later by the wild sounds of Jacen's pleasure at her rosy lips. But they leave him be. A few minutes later, Jacen is pushed unceremoniously down onto the bed and Claudia climbs on top of him. Knowing he isn't needed anymore, Liam slips away, unnoticed. He rolls off the bed and escapes to an adjoining bathroom.

In a fog, he cleans himself off, not wanting to bother with a shower, just wanting to leave. Dimly aware that he's still whimpering like a kicked dog and that tears are streaming down his cheeks, he uses a wet cloth to clean up. Tugging his underwear back up, he waits at the door, cringing inwardly as Jacen groans loudly with his climax, Claudia's higher-pitched cries burning like a scar into Liam's brain.

There's a soft knock at the other side of the door, so Liam opens it, eyes trained on his feet as Jacen slips through into the bathroom. Not saying a word, nor waiting to see what Jacen might say, Liam goes back into the bedroom, gathering his discarded clothes and pulling them hastily on.

"Thank you for joining us," Claudia says somewhat deliriously from where she is curled up like a cat on the bed. "You were spectacular, my darling. I enjoyed it immensely. Will you consider doing this again? I'd like that."

"Yeah, that'd be great. Just let me know," he says with a smile that is completely convincing in its sincerity. If nothing else, Liam is at least well-trained.

"I will. Excuse me if I don't show you out. Shall I summon Teddy for you?"

"No, thank you. I can manage it," he says.

She smiles kindly at him. "Okay then. Goodnight, William."

"'Night, Claudia," Liam returns.

As soon as he's got the door shut behind him, he's running blindly through the hall, down the curving staircase, out of the wing to the main foyer, bursting out into the fresh air and fumbling for his keys. Moments later, he's racing down the streets in his truck, coming up fast on home, pulling into the driveway and slamming the gearshift into park.

Then he loses track completely. It all goes grey and formless.

Jacen finds him a short time later, sitting in the dark a few steps inside the house, his knees curled up to his chest, hugging them like a scared little kid. Boots clicking on the hardwood, Jacen walks up to him, stands there over him for a long moment, and then sinks down beside Liam with a groan.

They sit side-by-side, their backs to the wall, cocooned in the darkness, Jacen a little bit taller, Liam a little bit smaller. With a sigh, Liam's head tilts sideways, leaning against Jacen's shoulder. Eyes fluttering closed, heart lightening, Jacen kisses the top of his friend's head.

"You smell. Like mouthwash."

"Mm," Jacen hums. "Thanks for clarifying."

Liam smiles, just a little. "Welcome."

"I keep an economy sized bottle in the car. Emergencies. You know."

"Yeah. Totally."

From the living room, a clock chimes ten o'clock. They listen as it bongs, the sound echoing and fading away.

"Couch'd be more comfy," Jacen observes.

"Yeah," Liam agrees, slipping a hand around Jacen's bicep, resting it there. The natural scent of him, richer now, fills Jacen's senses. He gets a little high off of it, sighing softly.

"What?" Liam grunts.

Jacen buries his nose against Liam's head, his short hair tickling. "You smell too."

Frowning, Liam admits, "Didn't shower yet. Sorry."

"Mm, no. It's a good smell. *Your* smell. I like it."

This makes Liam frown even more, until he hears Jacen take another deep inhale.

"Stop smelling me."

"Make me."

Liam sighs, "Too tired."

"We should go to bed."

Liam's head snaps around. Looking incredulously at Jacen, Liam struggles to his feet, groaning as his knees pop, smoothing out his polo shirt and fidgeting. Jacen follows suit, standing as well.

"I mean, you know. *Separately* go to bed."

"Yeah, I know," Liam scoffs, looking like he knows no such thing.

"Hey," Jacen says gently, getting face to face with Liam. Weariness overpowers Liam again, so he leans back against the wall, unable to protest as Jacen invades his personal space yet again that evening, hooking a finger under his chin to gently tilt it up.

"Jace...." Liam aches, letting Jacen move him, letting him press up close, their bodies flush from chest to thigh. Shifting his legs slightly apart, Liam's suckable, plump lips go soft and pliant, ready to be kissed. It gets under Jacen's skin, just like Liam's unique perfume.

Jacen's lips drag in a light, open-mouth kiss to the faint wrinkle by the corner of Liam's mouth where shallow dimples sometimes dent his cheeks. "Why don't you kiss? You never—you said you never kiss, and I never asked why, so, why don't you kiss?"

Tangling the fingers of both hands in Jacen's touchable, soft hair, Liam nuzzles Jacen, the tip of his nose dragging over his cheek as Jacen continues to pepper kisses around Liam's mouth, skirting the edges of it.

"Is it... like a boundaries thing, or keeping something sacred?"

"I get off on it," Liam breathes, cupping the side of Jacen's face, feeling his jaw work as he applies the next kiss, this one to the small dent under Liam's lower lip. "I love to kiss. Fucking love it. And I don't, I don't want to give them that. I don't—"

Jacen's lips are right there, hovering. They've left a tingling, spearmint-scented trail over Liam's skin and the temptation is too great, his defenses too weak. Angling his head slightly to the side, Liam moans out a breathy little sound and catches Jacen's lips between his own.

Exhaling sharply through his nose, Jacen's brow furrows. He grunts and parts for Liam, the very tip of the sweet-tasting tongue licking lightly over the center crease of Jacen's lower lip, flicking over his top lip before it is swallowed up by Jacen. Sucking a hard kiss to the luscious fullness of Liam's mouth, Jacen fits his hips snugly against Liam's. For a second they break apart, with Jacen panting roughly as he discovers that Liam is hard. He's completely hard and as soon as Jacen inhales, Liam attacks his mouth again, tongue-fucking it. Simultaneously Liam's hips roll forward in a needy thrust, grinding against Jacen's body.

Jacen palms the curve of Liam's ass as his tongue delves back into Jacen's mouth, into the same hot cavern that his hardened cock had ridden to an exquisite climax not so very long ago, darting in and out of it, moaning when Jacen sucks on it, then pushes back for more of Liam's sweetness. They tangle together, teeth nipping lips that press tightly, joining them, binding them. Every sound they make gets lost and swallowed back, devoured. Counter to every kiss, surging in and out, back and forth, go Liam's hips, rocking desperately against Jacen's upper thigh when it draws up snugly to

Liam's balls, giving him more to move against. Jacen squeezes his handful of Liam's bottom, guiding him faster. The tempo increases. Liam's keening sharpens. Quivering, bucking against Jacen, held so tightly that Jacen feels every shiver, drinks down every exhale, Liam comes, wrapped in him.

The sterility of their earlier intimacy causes something to snap in Jacen's mental control center. He needs contact with the proof of Liam's passion, that raw, primal, sacred moment between them. Pushing a hand down, pivoting it at the wrist, Jacen yanks open Liam's pants and slides his fingers under the waistband of the white cotton briefs. His fingers drag through Liam's hot, dripping come and Jacen makes a small, wrecked sound, taking a big swipe of the fluid, gathering it up.

With his clean hand, Jacen hastily undoes his jeans, shoving them out of the way. He takes a quick lick off the tip of a come-coated finger, moaning with heady pleasure at the salty flavor. Liam's eyes fix on Jacen's mouth as he rolls the tiny drop of fluid back on his tongue, swallowing it, then he surges in and tries to lick his own flavor from Jacen's mouth.

Jacen's soiled hand wraps his straining cock. He jacks himself rough and fast, fingers sliding slickly with the lubricant of Liam's spend. Gasping and grunting, Jacen beats off feverishly as Liam kisses him dizzy.

Stars explode behind Jacen's eyes as he climaxes, painting Liam's polo shirt in streaks of pearly white.

"*Lee*...."

"It's okay... it's okay..." he promises between caresses of his perfect lips.

They take a shower together in the dark, washing each other off, letting the warm water soothe them as it cleanses. Turning on the light seems to equate returning to reality and neither of them can bear that yet, so after they've dried off, they find clothes to sleep in without turning on a single lamp or light switch.

"I don't wanna sleep alone," Jacen admits, when they are left wondering what comes next. "Can we just sleep? Please?"

"Yeah," Liam says, sliding in under the covers on the other side of Jacen's queen-sized bed.

"Lee?" Jacen asks, his voice hushed, his head nestled on the pillow, facing Liam who gazes back sleepily at him.

"Yeah?"

"Thanks for kissing me."

"Go to sleep," Liam whispers.

Jacen is out cold in minutes. He sleeps straight through until morning. When he next opens his eyes, the sun is out, the sheets rumpled, and the bed empty except for himself. Liam is gone.

Chapter 9

What's Mine is Yours

Right about the same time that Liam is in East Hollywood with a married, successful screenwriter perched between his spread thighs, getting fondled and receiving a slow, sloppy blowjob, Jacen is shuffling up to Yasha's front door. Bleary-eyed, Thermos of coffee in hand, and still wearing pajama pants, he rings the bell. The scent of jasmine is overpowering, as the front yard is littered with it. The perfume tickles his nose and he sniffs, rubbing the back of his hand over his upper lip as footsteps approach from within the house. Beneath the perfume he can smell the ocean, hidden behind the property.

A slender, petite brunette answers the door. Valery Savaria, Yasha's wife, gawks at Jacen, his plaid flannel pants, his flip-flops, his dazed, watery-eyed expression, and tsks, "Honey, you look fucking pathetic. Come on in. Yasha's just finishing his shower. Went for a run." Jacen follows her into the home like a lost puppy. "You need anything? Breakfast? Xanax?"

"Hug?"

"Yeah, okay. I can work with that. C'mere," she says, waving him on, opening her arms as Jacen folds himself around her much smaller form and groans, the coffee held carefully out of the way.

"Fuck my life," Jacen complains, grumbling into her hair, hanging loose and soft around her shoulders in dark tight curls.

"That bad, huh? Who is it? Man or woman?"

He grunts then admits, "Most of the time he's a man."

"Hmm. Well, that's new for you anyway," Valery observes, patting him on the back, trying not to get smothered, rolling her

71

eyes as Jacen starts unconsciously groping her left breast through her shirt. "Is it serious?"

"In every conceivable way. Why couldn't I just settle down with a good woman like you, and listen to what my momma always told me? That would have been so much easier. Shitty job. Shitty kids. Nice and boring."

"Gee, thanks, Jace," she scoffs, trying to untangle herself, but Jacen just wraps her up tighter, his busy, roaming hand now cupping the firm, healthy curve of her ass, the other playing with the ends of her hair.

"You know what I mean. I want a cool wife too, that lets me fuck guys sometimes and isn't a psychopath. But no. I'm in love with someone that might not even be real."

Shoving him away to arm's length, staring up at him, she smacks his chest.

"Ow," he pouts, rubbing the spot.

"You're in *love*?"

"I didn't say that."

"Yes you did! Who the fuck are you in love with?"

"Can I just talk to Yasha? There's less hitting when I tell him stuff. Though he's not as good a hugger as you. And you've got better tits."

She turns and leaves him there, calling over her shoulder as she slips into another room, "Go on. Check the bedroom. I'll be there in a sec. No way I'm missing this."

"Great," Jacen sighs, shuffling to the stairs leading to the second floor.

Yasha is there, getting dressed. Standing naked by the closet, he glances up when Jacen moves into view. "Oh. Hey," Yasha says conversationally. "So that was you molesting my wife?"

"Yeah." Jacen comes into the room and sits on the bed. Unscrewing his Thermos, he takes a sip and hopes it helps clear away the cobwebs in his brain. He's temporarily, happily distracted by the slight wood Valery gave him. A few minutes later, his belly is warmer for the coffee, Yasha has gotten pants on and Valery is leaning against the wall near the door. Yasha sits down next to Jacen. Holding out a hand palm up, resting it atop the duvet, Yasha waits until Jacen lays his hand over it and squeezes it lightly.

"All right, go. What happened?"

"I'm pretty sure it's just an obsession," Jacen prefaces. "In a few days, we'll have to fuck anyway and then the allure will be gone and I can go back to normal. Right?"

Valery shoots Yasha a questioning look, so he sighs, muttering quietly to her, "Liam."

Her shock is apparent, so Jacen tries to ignore it.

"What happened?" Yasha presses.

"Exactly what I thought would happen," Jacen says exhaustedly. "He was *beautiful*, and I just wanted to kiss him everywhere. Just kiss him. No more than that. But I couldn't. It doesn't work that way, so he was, like, upset that it was me that was touching him and I had to do it anyway. It was horrible. He was on the verge of tears and right after he came he shut off. Just—shut off, and disappeared into the bathroom when the client was distracted." Yasha stares expectantly at him, so Jacen clarifies, "Blowjob."

"And then what?"

Jacen bows his head, eyes fixed on his lap and the container of coffee nestled there between his legs. "I don't know."

"Jacen, you know that we can't help you if you don't talk to us," Yasha warns. "Clearly something happened. You wouldn't be this disturbed by a blowjob."

"He's in love," Valery says softly.

"No, I'm not," Jacen argues a little too forcefully. "I didn't mean it, okay? I just said it. I'm allowed to say things without them always meaning something. It was a figure of speech. It—"

"And you said he wasn't real," she continues.

Jacen stops, his expression blank, if subtly pained. "He's always different. He's always being something else. He's a liar. He's a professional liar, so how do I know? Hmm? How do I know it's not all bullshit? And why should I bother putting myself through that?"

Knowing from experience to be concerned about the hopeless tone in Jacen's voice, Yasha raises their joined hands to his lips, kissing the back of Jacen's. "I'm glad you recognize that much. It's good. It means you're learning. Tell us what happened," he urges.

His expression twisting as he tries to mask his terror with the ever-so-slightly more appealing options of anger and shame, Jacen bites viciously at his lower lip and closes his eyes. After a long moment, he shakes his head.

"He's out there. Right now. He was in *my bed* last night and even after what we did, he snuck out of it without even waking me, like he does every time he's *finished* his *job*, and now he's...." Jacen flaps a hand at the window.

"Working?" Yasha supplies.

Jacen's eyes squeeze shut. He winces, imagining it—a stranger touching Liam like only someone that loves him should, a stranger hurting him, a stranger stealing away another piece of Liam's soul.

"You can't be judgmental about this," Yasha says.

The words are truer than Jacen wants them to be. Yasha is right; Jacen can't be a hypocrite.

"What do you want here?" Yasha prods, "Think about it. What do you really want? What's the goal? Do you want to fuck him outside of work and have Liam be okay with that? Do you want him to tell you if he has any romantic feelings for you? Do you want to find a way to still be friends with him despite fucking him for money and leave it at that? You have to decide. Because if you get all sentimental and needy, it's only going to make Liam pull farther away from you."

Haltingly, Jacen argues, "But it *was* sentimental. It felt—"

"Was it?" Yasha asks doubtfully, "Was it really? Or did it only seem that way?"

Only more lost, Jacen turns to Valery. "What do you think I should do?"

"Give him time. Let him be the one to come to you. Have him be the one to decide what comes next. If it was what you think it was, Liam will show you that. If it wasn't? Well...."

"Yeah," Jacen sighs morosely. "God, I hate this."

Jacen doesn't cross paths with Liam at all that day, so Jacen sends him a text letting him know that in the morning Jacen has an appointment with Patrick, and that Della is sending him over with security, just in case. Instantly, Liam tries to call Jacen back, but he doesn't pick up. In Jacen's mind, there is no point in arguing about this with Liam over the phone. It'd only cause more heartache. Jacen spends the early evening at their local health clinic, getting a thorough check up, partially because it's part of his routine (and contract) to do so regularly, but also because Della thought it might be a good idea to document the fact that Jacen was perfectly healthy before going to see Patrick, should anything happen during the visit. The pessimism in that line of thinking makes Jacen slightly ill but he can't escape it. For the rest of the night he is left wondering what his fate will be and what state he'll be in once Patrick is done with him.

Liam is out late that night, and gets home well after Jacen has already gone to bed. In the morning, Jacen wakes alone once more, as he had expected, but the other side of his bed seems curiously slept in. When he reaches over to touch the sheets there, they feel warm.

He tries to imagine Liam lying next to him, watching him sleep, and can't. He can't manage it, even with the tangible evidence right there. Jacen thinks that maybe it's his head trying to forbid further hope, or maybe it's just because it's not true, but either way, he doesn't dwell on it. All that matters is that he's alone now, and that he has to get ready for his client.

Robotically, he goes through the motions, cleaning himself up, getting dressed in something expensive but casual. He stares at himself in the mirror in the bathroom for a long time, trying to put aside everything that happened with Liam, along with everything that happened with Patrick at their last meeting. Some of it recedes, but not all. His eyes remain haunted, wary. For a moment he considers calling Della and saying he can't do it, even with the knowledge that Patrick came in personally to see her to reassure her that things would be different, and even with the awareness that Patrick isn't expecting Jacen to be completely trusting after what Patrick had done.

Jacen is glad when Liam is nowhere to be seen as he climbs into the car sent from the main office, with his security in the form of a massive wall of a man named Duke wedged behind the wheel. Relaxing against the cushions and headrest, Jacen does some breathing exercises and tries to remain calm. He closes his eyes as they coast through the streets. All too soon, they're at Patrick's place.

The house is set close to the road but on a lot spaced far apart from its neighbors. Leading the way up the short path to the door, Jacen is hyper-aware of Duke's presence behind him, looming and threatening. When he knocks, Jacen can hear multiple voices, laughing and chatting within. The prospect of performing his services with Patrick in front of an audience stirs little reaction in Jacen, not much more than a dull queasiness and impatience to get it over with.

The door opens. Patrick is there in a black short-sleeved shirt, aviators and dark-wash Gucci jeans, a cigar perched between his fingers.

"Hey, baby," he smiles, "You brought a friend."

"Yeah," Jacen says with the smallest backward glance at Duke. "Not my idea."

"Oh, I understand. It's fine," Patrick assures him.

"I'll wait here," Duke tells them.

"We might be a while," Patrick warns.

"No problem."

Jacen pushes his hair back from his face as Patrick slips a firm hand around Jacen's narrow hips, ushering him around the side of the house instead of through it.

"Come on. Let's go out back."

Jacen murmurs an assent and lets Patrick lead him away.

Liam sits slouched down in the driver's seat of his truck until Jacen and Patrick walk around the side of the house just to make doubly sure Jacen doesn't see him. Quietly, Liam gets out of the truck and stands beside it, watching from where he's parked, up on the crest of the hill of the road, behind a large bush. Duke sees him and promptly recognizes him, giving Liam a nod. Liam nods back. There have been a handful of times when Duke's presence has been requested on one of Liam's jobs.

Pushing his sunglasses farther up the bridge of his nose, Liam tracks the pair of men making their way back to Patrick's pool.

Already Liam has noted the presence of a number of cars in the driveway, the faint sound of voices from inside the house on that quiet, peaceful morning. He has a good view as Patrick leads Jacen to a lavish spread of food set out decadently on an outdoor dining table. None of Patrick's other visitors join them as Patrick begins to eat breakfast and Jacen pretends to pick at some of the dishes, mostly eating from the platter of fresh fruit.

Liam doesn't have anywhere he needs to be that morning, and he fully intends to stay for the duration of Jacen's visit. If anything goes bad, Liam wants to personally get his hands on the creep mistreating his best friend. Earlier, Liam had come into Jacen's bedroom to lay beside him for a while, debating what to say to convince Jacen not to go to Patrick. Of course there was no rational argument to be made. This is Jacen's job. Things with Patrick have been arranged by The Company and Jacen needs to do as he's told, as they all do. The only thing Jacen could do is quit, and take off before they could track him down and make him fulfil the years left on his contract whether he likes it or not.

And then what?

Liam doesn't know. The sheer desperation in him to get Jacen away from those who would hurt him or take advantage of him moved Liam right up to the brink of waking Jacen up and suggesting they just go, just get in the car with some of their things and drive, maybe up the coast. It wouldn't matter, as long as it was away. They could use their savings to start a new life, one much more mundane than their current one but infinitely more *safe*. He lay there for hours, unable to speak, unable to do it, to go through with it. It would be too real, too hard. It's so much easier for Liam to stay quiet, to go along and not make a fuss. For all of his good intentions, a small thing like suggesting something he wants very much, deep down in his heart, is peculiarly impossible. So it stayed a fantasy and Liam crept back out of Jacen's room, hating himself for it.

That self-hatred only grows when Liam watches Jacen get up from the table and go to a large bed under a cabana, placed by the side of the pool. Patrick is speaking to him, helping him get undressed, pulling Jacen's shirt up and off, unbuttoning his pants. His fist balled up tight, Liam presses it to his lips and uses all of his will not to run down there and beat Patrick to a bloody pulp. His heart starts to hammer against his ribs; his throat constricts his air.

Jacen lies down on the bed and Patrick kisses him deeply, demandingly, as he pulls off Jacen's underwear.

Liam can feel Duke watching him, as panic crawls up his gut, bubbling and threatening to come out as a ragged scream of outrage. He can't see Jacen's face. All he can see is Jacen's body from the waist down as Patrick spreads Jacen's legs and inserts a few fingers into him.

Liam's fist unclenches and claps over his mouth instead as a sickly groan erupts.

It's because it's Patrick, not because it's Jacen. It's because he's a monster, not because I'm jealous.

Patrick yanks his jeans open and enters Jacen in a smooth, firm thrust. Jacen's low cry echoes back amongst the trees.

I'll kill him. I'll fucking kill him with my bare hands.

The curt shake of Duke's head, just once, side-to-side, is like a shout, warning Liam to stay back when he unconsciously takes a few steps forward before he even realizes it.

But, no matter whether he likes what he's seeing or not, Liam is there for Jacen's sake. He's there to make sure Jacen is okay, so that instinct triumphs, for the moment, over wild, possessive resentment. Walking back to his spot by his car, Liam forces himself to watch as closely as he can while Patrick fucks Jacen, looking for any warning signs, any roughness or violence, trying to be thankful that the deed is happening in plain view instead of inside the building, even though it also makes Liam sick to think of how Patrick is clearly getting off on making a show of his conquest.

Jacen's cries become sharper, more anguished when Patrick's hand begins to play between Jacen's legs, and Liam wants to break every finger of that hand when it grabs Jacen by the dick and manipulates him to orgasm.

Finish. Just finish. Please just finish, Liam prays.

But of course, it's not that easy. It never is.

Patrick inserts a small toy into Jacen. Once it's in place and

Patrick is walking away, Jacen shifts farther up the poolside bed and reclines on his stomach. Lighting another cigar, Patrick goes inside the house. He returns a short time later, bringing two friends with him. The three of them sit around the table laden with food, eating and indulging in conversation while Jacen lays naked and beautifully displayed a few feet away.

When Patrick fucks Jacen a second time, Liam simply can't bring himself to watch and further invade Jacen's privacy. It's disgusting enough that Patrick's buddies are getting a free show, without Liam personally increasing the size of Jacen's audience.

The whole party moves inside an hour later. Liam goes to sit in his truck, waiting for Jacen to come out.

Jacen's mind is blank, his body exhausted, as he follows Patrick through the house to the front door. The combination of nervous anticipation along with everything that had transpired after he had arrived weighs on him, leaving him nothing but spent.

Once they had been seated at the table, Jacen was too nervous to eat. He had also politely refused a suggestion that he go swimming to cool off, and then, once they had gotten into the real reason Jacen had been called there, with Patrick's friends clearly visible through the rear windows of the home, Jacen couldn't get it up. He just couldn't. Part of it was fear of Patrick, even though Patrick was back to being a sweetheart, but underneath that excuse, Jacen purely just didn't want to be there and be touched by that man.

He tried his best, though. Putting on a good show, moaning loudly, writhing in feigned pleasure, Jacen lost himself in one of his best fantasies, removing himself mentally from what was being done to his body. It worked well enough. Jacen was able to get hard and get off. It was nice to be able to lounge and enjoy the beautiful weather after that. Being naked in front of other people has never been a big deal to him. The thick butt plug Patrick put in him was like a promise, though, that they were nowhere near finished. And they weren't. First, Patrick got him on his hands and knees and fucked him with the toy for a while. Jacen, still mentally detached, always the professional, was sure to make lots of appreciative noise and react to everything Patrick gave him. The whole time Jacen felt keenly watched, like he was on a stage, and the nervous tickle in his gut never went away.

The second time Patrick entered him, pounding into his body like he had something to prove, there was plenty of shame there for Jacen.

I hate my life, he marveled hollowly to himself. *I truly hate it. And it's never going to get better than this. How fucking pathetic is that?*

Jacen couldn't look at Patrick's friends, but that wasn't part of the job, so he didn't sweat it. And now, so very close to leaving, just a few feet from the exit, Jacen doesn't care anymore. About anything. Getting away is all that matters.

Patrick stops at the door, turning to him. He pulls Jacen in for another kiss. It's sweeter than Jacen expects it to be. Some more of Patrick's long, drawn out apology slips into it, making it more tender and urgent.

"I don't know what the hell was wrong with me the other day. I promise to make it up to you. You're important to me, you know that, right?"

Jacen nods, turning into the touch of Patrick's hand on his cheek. Patrick's thumb drags over the place where Jacen's lip is almost completely healed after being split open by Patrick's knuckles and then falls away. After digging in a pocket, Patrick brings out a fat roll of bills. The one on the outside is a hundred. The whole thing gets slipped into Jacen's hand.

"Patrick," he starts.

"That's for you. I already paid your handlers. This is just for you."

If they're all hundreds, Jacen thinks distractedly, there must be a couple grand there. Enough for the first and last month's rent on a new apartment, maybe somewhere in Arizona, near the desert. Plenty of places to hide in the desert.

"You really don't have to do that," Jacen says instantly.

"I want to. Won't take no for an answer. Treat yourself. On me."

The money feels slimy in Jacen's hand, even though the paper is crisp and dry enough.

"Thanks. That's incredibly nice of you," he says.

As he walks past Duke toward the waiting car, Jacen can feel himself already burying the memory of the entire experience, dissolving it, breaking it apart and letting it blow away in the wind. Unseeing, unfeeling, he walks hunched over to his seat, folding himself into it and closing the door quickly once he's in the car. Wanting to toss the roll of bills away from him, onto the seat, and leave it there like a wadded up burger wrapper, just another piece of trash, Jacen instead slides it into his front pocket. Then he wipes his hands on his pants.

He has no idea that Liam is there, parked up the hill, nor that after the car Jacen sits in, driven by Duke, pulls out of Patrick's street, Liam follows closely behind them for the drive back home.

Chapter 10
Given Over

After the job with Patrick, Liam gives Jacen a few minutes to get inside their house and get situated before he pulls up to the garage door and follows him in.

Scanning what he can see of the place from just inside the front door, Liam shouts, "Jace! Hey, I'm home! You here?"

"Yeah!" Jacen hollers back from the second floor. "Be down in a few, okay?"

"Okay!"

Liam breathes out his relief that Jacen was all right enough mentally to answer and stalks through the house, flopping down on the couch with a groan. He had three appointments the previous day. Nothing complicated. One of them was a quickie with Adam at his office in the city. The other two Liam barely remembers. But after having such a packed schedule, he's been given a day to recuperate. All morning he's been expecting his phone to go off with the details for his next job, knowing his reprieve won't last long, but so far there's been zilch, not a peep. For an hour and a half Liam lies on the couch, listening to the clock on the wall tick away the time, waiting for Jacen to come down.

His phone vibrates. Liam digs it out. After barely glancing at the message from Della, Liam's panic slithers back up his belly, wrapping around his throat. He expects that Jacen is getting a very similar message on his own phone upstairs.

"Fuck. *Fuck*," Liam hisses.

His alarm is much more powerful than his desire to confront Jacen just yet. Grabbing a sweatshirt, Liam doesn't bother announcing that he's going, because Jacen will know why he's going anyway. Keys in hand, Liam just goes. He walks past his truck and moves in the direction of the beach.

Upstairs, sitting on the edge of his bed, Jacen holds his phone cradled in his hand.

This is it, he thinks. *This is everything.*

It's almost a relief, knowing that it's out of his hands. His entire life will change in one way or another a few nights from now, no matter what he does or says.

As Jacen hovers near the top of the stairs, dressed in comfortable, baggy clothes, he hears Liam slip away, the front door closing with a soft whoosh. Then Jacen heads downstairs, curling up on the couch in the same spot that Liam had been laying in, feeling the ghostly warmth of him for the second time that day, radiating from the cushions. It's soothing. Jacen nestles into it and clicks on the television, craving any sort of distraction.

It's not until late, the sun set and the crickets chirping, that Liam comes home. Jacen has eaten, paid some bills, checked his accounts, made a few calls, and is back relaxing by the television, reading the newspaper. The door opens and shuts. He waits for Liam to yell hello and skulk away upstairs to hide some more, so it puts Jacen slightly on-edge when Liam instead appears silently in the doorway, hands buried in his sweatshirt pocket, head bowed.

"Hey," Jacen says softly in greeting. "It went fine with Patrick, if you were wondering."

Liam's expression tightens at this, and Jacen isn't sure what that means. He tries not to feel hurt that Liam seems to not want to talk about it or inquire about Jacen's well-being. Sure, the message about their forthcoming appointment with Claudia is a big deal, but it's not the only thing going on.

For longer than is comfortable, Liam stays silent, just standing there.

"You wanna sit down? Or...."

A small shake of Liam's head.

"What's up?" Jacen asks.

Liam rubs a hand over his forehead, looking pale and miserable. "Um. Christ, I've been trying to figure shit out all day and what to say to you, and I really thought I finally had it all straight, but now...."

"We don't have to talk about it," Jacen tells him. "We can pretend it's not even happening if it makes it easier for you."

"I can't." Liam says adamantly, his voice jagged. He takes a breath and tries again, "I *can't* pretend this away."

"So what are you saying? Do you want to leave? Do you want *me* to leave? We've been doing a pretty damn good job avoiding each other so far. I don't see why we can't just keep doing that—"

"Jacen," Liam cuts in, exasperated. "I'm trying here. I really am, but this is difficult for me so can you please just let me...."

"Fine. Fine, I'll shut up. Go ahead."

"This is hard for me! Don't you see how hard this is for me?!"

"It's just sex, Lee. It's something we're both fairly good at. It's not that hard."

"That's *not what I'm talking about!*"

"Then tell me already! For fuck's sake! Just say it!"

Liam won't look at him. His eyes are fixed firmly on his feet. Then they close and when Liam starts speaking, his words are hushed and low, like he's talking to himself.

"I don't want it to be like that. It's all... out of control. It's all out of control. And I just need one thing. *One thing.* To be in control. If we go in there like this, I won't be able to do it. I just won't. Don't you know how hard it was for me to bear it, to be with you like that? To be paid to degrade myself with you just so that she could get off on it? It was empty. It was *fucking.* It wasn't a fantasy. It was real."

The words turn Jacen cold. They shatter all of his dreams that maybe, *maybe* Liam really cared about him, that he wanted them to be together as badly as Jacen wants to be with Liam. But clearly it's not true. Not if all it was to him was empty and degrading and unbearable. Suddenly, Jacen can't be there anymore, can't let Liam break his heart any more than it already is. He gets up off of the couch and drops the newspaper. Pushing past Liam, who is bodily blocking the exit, Jacen is stopped with a hand to his chest.

"I'm not finished."

"*I* am," Jacen says bitterly. "I'm done. If it was that horrible for you, I won't bother you anymore. Somehow we'll get through the job and then I'll—I'll move out. Find an apartment. Whatever."

"Jacen," Liam almost sobs, at the end of his rope. "Please, *let me finish.*"

Sighing tiredly, Jacen relents.

"I don't want our first time to be like that," Liam hisses. "I want it to be *ours.* Just ours."

Shocked, Jacen's head snaps around so fast he almost gets whiplash. Staring intensely at Liam, who still won't look at him, he demands, "What are you saying?"

"I'm saying, yeah, we have to go through with this. We have no choice. But...."

"But?"

Liam groans, "You're seriously going to make me say it, aren't you?"

"Yes! Because I'm pretty, you know, *confused,*" Jacen sputters. "What? You want a practice run?"

"No," Liam frowns, sighing a little. "I just want something that isn't empty or a fantasy. If we're going to be together and it's going to be real, I want it to be on our terms. For the first time, at least."

Jacen starts to understand. That's why his answer is a quick and deliberate, "No."

"What?" Liam blinks, startled. "No?"

Rolling his eyes at himself, Jacen folds his arms, and gathers up his pride. "Being with you means too much to me to do it just to get it out of the way, or prove that we can make our own decisions. I want it to happen only if you want it, too."

"Are you kidding? You are kidding me, right? You huge idiot, that's what I'm saying! You're my best friend, Jacen! It means a lot to me too!"

"Not like it does to me," Jacen argues.

Liam's lips purse in an angry little bow. "Are you fucking arguing with me over whether you care about me more than I care about you? I'm asking you to make love to me and you're saying no because you care about me too much to disrespect me like that? Seriously?"

Jacen is kissing Liam before the last raspy word gets past his lips. Liam resists at first, stiffening, but that's mostly instinct. As soon as Jacen's big hands frame his face, Liam melts into it, softening, savoring the soft brushes of Jacen's lips against his own. Then Jacen is wrapping Liam in a close hug, holding on to him as the rest of the tension seeps away.

"You suck sometimes," Liam grumbles. "You know that?"

"I just wonder, would this still be happening if we didn't have to because of current... circumstances?"

"I don't know, Jace," Liam admits weakly. "Can we stop analyzing it and go to bed?"

Feeling Liam's smaller, firm, warm body under his hands, hidden beneath the soft outer layer of his sweatshirt, Jacen grunts, "Yeah. I guess so. If you're sure."

"I'm sure."

Self-consciousness creeps into Jacen's expression. He drops his gaze and admits, "There's kind of one more thing that's been bothering me. I've never really... been with a guy. When I wasn't, you know, paid to be with a guy."

"Liar," Liam scoffs. "What about Yasha?"

"Yasha doesn't count. He was like practice."

"Three continuous days of practice?" Liam waves a hand to dismiss his own argument before it continues. "Never mind. Are you trying to tell me you're not gay?"

"I don't know. I've never really thought about it."

"Are you shitting me? You have to be shitting me. Okay, let's make this easier. You wanna?"

"Hell, yeah, I wanna."

"Then stop being difficult."

"Okay."

On the short walk upstairs, the gears start to turn in Liam's head, locking into place, spinning and spinning, picking up speed. Without knowing he's even doing it, he starts to rationalize everything, compartmentalizing the reasons, the whys and the hows. He knows keenly what Jacen endured earlier that very day at Patrick's hands. He knows, as well, what transpired between himself and

Jacen with Claudia. Thirdly, he recognizes that Jacen is aware of aspects of how Liam is with clients, his many characters, and has probably gotten a well-formulated preconception of what to expect of Liam in bed.

Liam wants what happens that night to align with none of those things. It has to be vastly different from what has already been and the routine, mechanical bullshit they live every day. In a way it's Liam's biggest acting challenge to date, to create as 'real' a situation as he possibly can.

Liam doesn't realize the full irony of this. Even if he did though, it might not change anything. He is who he is, and he's only able to face things with Jacen as he is able to.

As they get to the top of the landing, Liam takes Jacen by the hand and pulls him toward Jacen's bedroom.

"In here," he says, certain that he can't go through with it in *his* bed, needing that little bit of separation at least with his own, private existence.

Jacen doesn't argue, going along with Liam into the darkened room. Liam's eyes flicker back and forth like they're scanning invisible instructions, written in mid-air.

"Liam?"

Liam ignores him, too lost in thought. "Lights. We need light," he decides, and goes to click on the lamp on the nightstand.

Jacen watches him pace back to the bed and away again, closing the drapes, shutting the door.

"Maybe we should just relax, ease into it," Jacen suggests, seeing clearly how focused Liam suddenly is. Liam is pulling away; he's wrapping himself in all of his ideas of how things should be in order to get the most out of the experience. He's over-thinking it.

"Lee, stop. Just c'mere. Look at me," Jacen urges as Liam strips off his sweatshirt, folding it over and setting it on a chair. Every second that passes sees Liam transform more and more into his self-appointed role and it aggravates Jacen to no end.

"Hey. This isn't a job. It doesn't have to be perfect. Liam. *Liam!*"

Eyes trained on the ground at Jacen's feet, Liam finally stirs. Looking up, he meets his friend's gaze. Jacen is instantly shocked at what's looking back at him — seething, uncaged, animalistic lust.

"Liam?"

The tight t-shirt clinging to Liam's chest, twisted up a little around his waist, gets peeled away. Jacen's eyes flick down to the metal bars piercing Liam's nipples and he kind of hates himself for it, for being so easy. But all the same, his mouth starts to water. His dick perks up.

Heart beating faster now, throat threatening to constrict and deny his next inhale of much-needed oxygen, Jacen tries, "Ma-maybe we should, you know...."

Liam grabs the bottom of Jacen's shirt, pulling it up and off of him.

"...talk about this a little m-more...."

Jacen's fly gets yanked open. The snap pops. The zipper parts.

"...first."

Liam sinks to his knees after pushing Jacen roughly backward, causing him to fall back over the edge of the bed, his feet still planted on the floor and the rest of him sprawled on the mattress. A second after that, his pants are off. He's not wearing underwear. Liam guides Jacen's thighs apart.

"*Fuck.*"

The last coherent thought Jacen has is dull curiosity regarding where Liam is going to produce the condoms from, if he always carries some in his pockets, or what. But Liam's hands caress up the insides of Jacen's thighs, over the dark, fine hair covering them, closing up on a place Jacen is very much not used to having Liam's hands.

The first syllable of Liam's name stutters from Jacen's lips.

Simultaneously, Liam's right hand circles the base of Jacen's dick, guiding it upright while his left hand flattens, rolling over Jacen's balls. It draws a startled, choked sound from Jacen and then one of the hands pivots at the wrist to rub underneath, back over his hole. Half-hard already, blood rushes in a torrent to fill Jacen's flesh when Liam squeezes up it once, dragging a thumb over the silky crown. Liam's fingertips play at his rim, making Jacen want to close up his thighs because *what the fuck?*

It happens in slow motion, Jacen swears to it later. Liam's head dips. Jacen stares helplessly down the length of his body. Liam's mouth falls open, his tongue pushing forward to lick a wide, wet stripe up Jacen's dick, from the root all the way up over the pulsing vein running along the underside to the divot in the head. It wraps there and Liam's lips close around the tip, sealing tight as he *sucks*.

Jacen bucks up reflexively into Liam's mouth, and Liam lets him. He quickly adjusts his angle and relaxes his throat as Jacen fills it, lodging deeply. The velvety, wet glove of heat wraps him, constricting, rippling as Liam swallows. Jacen pushes up helplessly into it, trying to get deeper, hips spasming. Slowly, very slowly, Liam eases back, increasing the suction he's giving Jacen and moaning at the thick taste of him, at the feel of Jacen filling his mouth, cradled bare on his tongue.

Jacen's hands find Liam's face, framing it. Using the contact, Jacen fights for sanity and guides Liam up and off. Jacen's dick falls wet and flushed dark from between his friend's pink, shining lips.

"What the FUCK was that?! What's wrong with you?! It's not safe! Condom, Lee! Christ!"

"Oops," Liam says with a wicked gleam in his eye, kitten-licking Jacen's penis.

"'Oops?!' I could give you something!"

"Uh-huh," Liam grunts, licking repeatedly over the bulbous head, wriggling the tip of his tongue at the slit. Liam's eyes close in delirious pleasure as Jacen makes a strangled moan. He feeds Jacen back between his lips, making a tight seal, taking a slow, wet pull.

Jacen's argument stutters from his lips, his teeth clacking together, his sense shattering. Palming the back of Liam's head with one hand, Jacen's hips chase up into the sinfully perfect, damning sensation. It's the first, real, passionate, consenting, condom-less blowjob he's ever had the pleasure to receive, and the feel of the delicate tissues of Liam's throat, the soft inside of his cheeks, the wickedly talented muscle of his tongue, the silken kiss of his full lips, it's too much to process.

"It's a lot better without the rubber, huh?" Liam chuckles. He licks Jacen's bare flesh in long, unhurried strokes, in defiance of all logic and mental arguments regarding safe sex practices with another prostitute. All that matters is Jacen's silken heat and flavor, connecting to him on that base level, and to hell with the repercussions. "Mm, you taste fucking *amazing*."

Coming right apart on the bed, Jacen gulps down air, glancing down his body as Liam kisses his way up it; over his belly, up his ribcage to his left nipple, licking it and continuing on, up the side of Jacen's neck. Liam's arms are hooked under Jacen's legs, folding them back, pulling him open.

"I have to feel you, Jace. Get inside you. Can I? Is it okay?" Liam rasps, his already husky voice roughened even more than usual. Hope and desire shine in his eyes. Jacen is so unused to seeing Liam in such a state that he doesn't even consider saying no.

No sooner is he nodding in answer, then Liam is pushing two saliva-coated fingers into him, scissoring them apart to work Jacen loose. His breath catching, Jacen lets his eyes close, tiny frown lines forming on his brow. Liam tries to kiss them away. Jacen cups the side of Liam's face, so very confused, just needing something actual to hold on to. He brings Liam in for a soft kiss, gasping into his mouth as Liam makes quick work of the prep. Just the fact that Liam doesn't draw it out, that he frantically coaxes Jacen loose, fumbles in a back pocket for a condom, breathing just as roughly as Jacen is, if not more, speaks to the reality of Liam's passion. It makes Jacen's head spin, the determination and focus on Liam's face when he frees himself, rolls the condom on and breaches Jacen with little ceremony.

Jacen moans brokenly at the sudden feeling of fullness as Liam drapes himself over Jacen's long body, breathing in jagged gasps against the side of Jacen's neck, barely inside him, nudging gently deeper.

Liam's hands are everywhere, touching. Hands on Jacen's chest, hands sliding down his sides, hands palming his bottom, fingernails scratching lightly down Jacen's legs, pushing one of them back at a sharper angle in order to plunge farther into his body. Considering the desperation with which Liam entered him, the easy, languorous pace of his lovemaking, once he's nestled completely in Jacen, is surprising. Taking his time, savoring the miraculous connection between them, now that they're finally so intimately joined, Liam moves slowly and never stops touching, touching everywhere.

Jacen watches through his lowered, dark eyelashes, with so much to say, so much to ask, but speechless. The ability to find his voice is stolen by how incredibly vulnerable he suddenly feels. For all of the fucking in his life, it may be the very first time Jacen has ever been made love to. It's not about the sex at all, but it's also all about the sex. It's Liam inside him, Liam touching him, Liam moaning his name, being so careful, trying to hold back some of his urgency.

The anguish grows in Liam's face as his rhythm quickens. Growling through his teeth, Liam is gasping, lip quivering, clutching to Jacen, pulling him in with his hands even as he pushes his cock in deeper, burrowing further, taking and taking and taking. Taking it all.

Nuzzling the side of Jacen's neck. Liam stops abruptly, trembling a little, straining. The moment draws out and Jacen can't figure out why until Liam resumes movement, pushing frantically into him, snapping his hips in shallow pushes, skin slapping against skin. Liam cries out softly, his parted lips dragging over Jacen's neck, rocking into him as he comes down.

Sniffling, Liam pulls back slightly, enough so that Jacen can see the wreck of Liam's face, his bloodshot, damp eyes, damp cheeks, lips and chin. Running the back of a hand under his nose, Liam sniffs again as Jacen wipes away some dampness that looks a lot like tears from under Liam's eyes with the pads of his thumbs.

Jacen still doesn't know what to say. But he knows something else—a truth, a very important truth, one that helps him find some peace with it all. He knows without an ounce of uncertainty that he loves this man, with all of his heart.

Liam collects himself. A flimsy curtain descends behind his green eyes, dulling some of the raw ache there. He pulls out, strips off the condom, shimmies out of his pants and promptly climbs on top of Jacen, straddling his hips.

"Oh, fuck," Jacen moans.

"C'mon. Get me open," Liam croaks, settling into place, taking his weight on his knees, braced on the bed at Jacen's sides.

"Um," Jacen blurts dumbly. *He's not even ready. He's always ready. He always gets himself lubed up and stretched open before. But this is different, isn't it? It's not a job. Of course he's not ready.* "Lube?"

Liam takes Jacen's right hand, bringing it to his come-soaked cock, folding Jacen's hand up around it, squeezing up the length and groaning at the friction to his over-sensitive flesh. The hand comes away wet.

"Lube," Liam grunts.

Almost afraid to ask, Jacen says, "C-condom?"

"Just touch me," Liam begs.

Already hard enough to be dizzy from it, Jacen feels an added rush of blood surging to his balls at Liam's gorgeously wanton pleading. Pushing his hand under Liam, Jacen rubs once over the tight knot of his hole, moaning shamelessly at finally having permission to do such a thing. He slowly but steadily inserts his middle finger to the hilt, watching Liam's mouth fall open in a soundless gasp.

"*Liam.*" Jacen palms the side of Liam's face, just loving him, loving him completely.

Liam rears up, pulling himself off of Jacen's finger until only the tip remains inside. A second finger slips quickly inside before Liam pushes back down.

Liam cries out softly, beginning to ride Jacen's hand, bouncing lightly on it as Jacen strokes gently over Liam's inner walls, feeling the perfect, supple softness of him. Clearly Jacen isn't being efficient enough for Liam, so he starts circling his hips, taking Jacen in to the last knuckle. Holding the arm touching his face with one hand, using it to steady himself, Liam also grasps the one between his legs that extends under his body. Following it up to the wrist, then circling the hand with his own, Liam moves Jacen's fingers for him, feeling out where their bodies meet, jabbing Jacen's fingers into himself harder with each push.

It feels right in a way Liam had almost forgotten was possible, to have Jacen inside him, violating him, impaling him, filling his empty places. It makes him greedy, selfish. He works himself onto the fingers even as he touches them and himself. Jacen's thumb drags across Liam's cheek to his lips, tracing them as they part softly. Turning into the touch, Liam's tongue slips out, teasing over the tip of the thumb. Jacen pushes into the wet heat of Liam's mouth, moaning as Liam suckles around the digit, playing it with his tongue.

Liam wants to get off just like that, on Jacen's fingers stuffing him full, rubbing so gently in and out, and sucking on Jacen's thick, long thumb. But it's because he knows Jacen needs to get off too, because he wants to be clenched up around Jacen's thick, gorgeous cock and wring every last drop of pleasure out of it for him, that Liam pulls off. He climbs off the bed.

"Condoms?"

"Nightstand. In the drawer."

A few fevered seconds later, after some cursing and digging in the junk cluttering the small drawer, Liam is back on Jacen's lap, fitting the condom onto him, rolling it over his reddened shaft.

This is happening. This is actually happening, Jacen thinks deliriously, even as his ass throbs with a dull ache for missing Liam filling it up.

"C'mon... c'mon...." Liam sounds so impatient that Jacen cracks a smile, his eyes rolling up as Liam lowers himself onto Jacen and doesn't even give them both a second to adjust or savor the novelty of it. As soon as he has Jacen fed halfway inside, Liam starts rocking down onto him, taking even more of him, moaning like it's the best thing in the world. And then he's just riding Jacen, bouncing on his cock, clenched up so tightly that it makes Jacen's toes curl. Head thrown back, his back bowing, Jacen chokes out a rough cry, hands clamped to Liam's bare thighs.

Slow down. He has to slow down.

Jacen bucks up into Liam, meeting every downward push with an upward thrust, their bodies slamming together, Liam hugged around him so exquisitely that Jacen knows it won't last long at all.

Growling and grunting, cursing and sweating, all Jacen knows is the *slap* of Liam's bare ass against his pelvis, the hot, tight, wet, soft hugging him.

He comes with a whimper, pulling Liam down onto him, holding him there. Liam rotates his hips, coaxing him through it, hands splayed on Jacen's chest, tweaking his nipples. The room tilts and bends.

Things get hazy and unfocused. One minute Liam is lying on Jacen's chest, catching his breath, pressing tender kisses to his sweaty skin, arms curled around him, bodies interlocked. The next, the heat enveloping Jacen is gone. So is the condom. Liam's fingers stroke him up and down, playing through the mess of his spend, smearing it over his over-sensitive shaft, collecting it and then dragging it over Jacen's stomach and chest. A thumb coats one dark, erect nipple, then the other in the milky fluid of Jacen's come. As it slowly dries it makes the skin feel tight and cool.

"Lee. Lee, what're you—"

Climbing back onto the bed, Liam kneels, leaning over him, and guides Jacen's legs up to wind around behind his back. Hovering over him, Liam fingers Jacen's rim, rubbing around it in small circles. They kiss and it begins soft and sweet, but in moments Liam is tongue-fucking Jacen hungrily. Not even aware of when or how Liam gets another condom on himself, all Jacen knows is the stretch and pressure of Liam entering him a second time. The wide, rounded head squeezes through his outer ring. Jacen's fingers card through the soft, velvety texture of Liam's short hair as full lips pepper kisses over his cheek.

"You shouldn't give this away," Liam hisses at him. "I won't let you. I won't let you give this to just anyone. Not anymore."

"Yeah? Gonna make me yours," Jacen asks, slurring a little in his daze.

"Yeah. I am, actually. Mine. This is mine, now. No one else gets to have it. No one."

Distantly, Jacen wonders if it's true, if Liam means it or if he's just saying it because he thinks it's what Jacen wants to hear. But does Jacen even want that? To belong to someone? He's never considered it. It's never been something he has craved before. He's been happy experiencing a variety of partners, being free. The suggestion gets into his head, though. He imagines it as Liam makes love to him for a second time, splitting Jacen in half with his cock even as his fingers continue to move in wicked ways over Jacen's skin, whispering over it and leaving trails of the sticky film of bodily fluid, like Liam has to mark him in every dirty way to make it come true, to obscure the remembered touch of hundreds of other men and women. He has to own him and fill him and claim every inch of him, inside and out. Liam's. Jacen is Liam's.

A shiver races down Jacen's spine. His cock struggles to get hard again. Liam feels it twitch against his belly, so he fists it, squeezing it in steady, rhythmic pulses. Jacen rocks, into Liam's hand, against Liam's cock.

"C'mon, baby. That's it. You want it?"

"Yeah..."

"Lemme feel you. Lemme feel how much you want it. Does it feel good?"

"*Liam....*"

"You feel incredible. You're so perfect. Too—" Liam gasps. "Perfect. Knew... knew you would be. Knew you'd be perfect."

Liam adjusts his angle so that he's dragging over Jacen's sweet spot on every thrust. Crying out, Jacen pulses. Liam rubs through the pre-come and keeps at it, milking him dry, turning him inside out. It goes on and on longer than Jacen dreams it can, marveling at Liam's stamina. Every nerve, every fiber of Jacen's being lights up, sizzling. He comes with a shudder, coating Liam's hand, his stomach, Liam's chest. The squelching of Liam's hand squeezing through the mess is loud in the quiet room. In a moment of pure obscenity, Liam brings his index finger to his lips, licking Jacen's come with a heady moan. Boneless, spent, full and then empty, Jacen feels Liam pull out. The soft, slight sound of the rubber coming off tickles at Jacen's ears. One of Liam's hands pulls apart Jacen's cheeks. The cool air of the room teases over Jacen's winking hole and then he feels the splash, hears the moan as Liam comes, too, marking him in yet another way.

Liam unloads every drop while aiming right for Jacen's opening, shivering all the way to his bones at the sight of his come dripping down Jacen's ass crack, pearlescent over his flushed pink wrinkled knot.

Awareness slips through Jacen's fingers, leaving his grasp.

Jacen wakes an uncertain amount of time later, in his bed, covered in a sheet. Sticky everywhere, sore and used and wrung out, but in the best of ways, a sliver of shame still manages to wriggle down into the pit of his gut. Because he's alone.

There's no one else there.

His heart hardens in his chest, turning to stone, ready to

shatter.

Without any hope of getting an answer, he calls, "Liam?"

The water runs in the adjoining bathroom. Someone spits into the sink.

"Yeah," Liam mumbles. Jacen turns his head and he sees him, peeking through the doorway with a toothbrush in his mouth.

Everything in Jacen loosens. His relief is so palpable, he can't bear to look at Liam anymore or he might die from the acuteness of his foolish, love-struck hope.

Jacen's small, swallowed-back sob perks Liam's attention.

"Hey. You all right?"

Jacen nods. He wipes at his eyes, his face, drawing his legs up. "I thought you left."

Liam walks over to the bed, toothbrush still in hand.

He's dressed, Jacen realizes.

Liam has showered and dressed in the cotton, drawstring pants that he sleeps in. Lying there completely soiled and debauched, Jacen is the counterpoint to Liam's immaculateness. It leaves Jacen feeling cold.

"I'm right here."

For how long? Jacen wonders.

"I think we need to talk," Jacen says with less conviction than he intends.

With a mouthful of toothpaste, Liam digests this and nods. Holding up a finger, he retreats to the bathroom to rinse his mouth, pausing to gaze at his reflection in an attempt to find himself there, not really recognizing much of what he sees. The urge to flee is there, as it always is, but it is surprisingly easy enough to conquer. The depth of his devotion to Jacen is what stays him.

Scooping water into his mouth, he swishes it around, spitting it out. Liam sets down the toothbrush. He wipes off his face and goes to meet whatever might be in store for him. It's his own choices that have put them there. There is no hiding from this. Not anymore.

Chapter 11
Closeted Skeletons

After a brief hesitation, Liam moves to lie down beside Jacen on the bed, settling on top of the covers and facing him. There is so much as yet left unsaid between them that cannot be ignored or pushed aside any longer that it thickens the air around them, suffocating them, threatening to drown them. The tension makes Liam in particular want to instinctively bolt from the room or maybe even the whole house just out of an instinctive need to fill his lungs with currently sparse oxygen. It feels as unnatural for him to stay there as it would for a fish to continue to flop around on jagged rocks while beside plentiful, soothing waters.

The bed springs shift as Liam tries to get comfortable, pulling a pillow under his head. There are so many questions behind Jacen's eyes, so much fragility and fear. Liam knows he is the one that put those things there. He also knows that just as the two of them are closer than they've ever been, they are also, conversely, just as distant from each other. Miles and miles seem to separate them, though in reality it's barely inches.

Everything is off-kilter. Neither of them knows where to start.

"So."

"So?"

"You're a top," Jacen says, starting with the basics. "I didn't expect that."

"Well, not *all* the time."

"No, I mean *you*. When you're not doing things out of necessity for other people, if it's just about what you want, you're... a very expressive top. Who loves to kiss, and appreciates the more *tactile* aspects of sex. I'm just trying to figure it all out. Figure *you* out. For my own sake."

Without confirming or denying any of that, Liam says, "Do you want to get a shower before we do this?"

"Do you *want me* to get a shower before we do this?"

"No. Not really. I like you just like this."

"Deliberately smeared with both of our bodily fluids? Sweaty? Fucked, by you, into exhaustion?"

"Yeah. All of the above," Liam smiles.

"That's," Jacen says slowly, "interesting."

"Why?"

"Because I thought this was going to be about me being with *you* in order to, like, break the ice. Or something. Before our job with Claudia. And instead *I'm* on my back with my legs in the air, alternately with my cock down your throat or with your dick up my ass."

"Your dick was up my ass, too. For the record."

"Yeah, because you put it there," Jacen points out.

"I did," Liam agrees.

"I guess I just didn't—" Jacen tries, then stops mid-sentence. A moment later he starts again, "Um, think this was going to be about *me*."

"Of course it's about you. There's only the two of us, Jace. You're kind of a crucial element."

"That's not what I'm talking about."

"Then what are you talking about? Are you asking me to clarify that when it comes to having sex with you, my preference is to be the giver? I suppose it is. When I think about having the chance to be with you, what I immediately want is to get inside you. But I love having you fuck me, too. Clearly."

Jacen tries to analyze Liam's face when he says all of this, like if he can just correctly interpret the quirk of his lips or the meaning behind his eyes, Jacen will be able to tell if it's all bullshit or not. It leaves him still feeling confused and unsure. One thing is clear, though. "But you like to be in control."

Not refuting this, Liam asks, "Is that a problem?"

At first Jacen has no answer. Silence descends between them.

Liam's hand snakes over, intertwining with Jacen's as Jacen's fear grows noticeably larger in the heaving of his chest, the tension in his body.

"I guess it shouldn't surprise me. You are a control freak. Maybe it's more about realizing that I make you want that from me."

Jacen falls quiet again. The sadness painted on his face worries Liam.

"What's wrong?"

Brushing a lock of dark hair out of Jacen's face, Liam sighs as Jacen's eyes close and his frown deepens.

"What do you want, Lee?" Jacen asks somewhat desperately. "What is this? All of those things you said. Did you mean them? Were they just part of your character? Were they real? I mean — "

Taken aback, Liam stiffens. "I'm not *in character*, Jacen."

"Aren't you?"

"No!"

Jacen nods pensively. "Okay. You said you weren't going to let me give myself to anyone else. What was that?"

Liam's eyes glaze over as he disengages.

"Liam, *talk to me*," Jacen pleads. "I just... gave you *so much* of me and you can't just brush it off like it was nothing!"

Something hard and brittle breaks in Liam. It snaps cleanly in two, allowing secret things to slip out through the cracks.

"I followed you," he blurts, not meeting Jacen's gaze. "This morning. I followed you to Patrick's. I wanted — no, I *needed* to make sure you'd be okay, and go in there to castrate that mother-fucker myself if he hurt you. So, I saw. I saw everything. Or mostly everything."

Jacen withdraws his hand. Liam grabs it, brings it back. "You had *no right*."

"I couldn't let you go to him by yourself, okay?! No fucking way!"

"Duke was there. And I can defend myself if I need to. I was safe," Jacen argues quietly.

"Bullshit! There is no safety with guys like Patrick," Liam rages. "You can't go back to him. I forbid it."

"What do you expect me to do, Liam? This isn't my call!"

"It *is* your call! It's *your* life. It's your *body*. That's all that matters!"

"So, you're demanding that I try to break my very much binding contract with The Company? Hide myself from them for god knows how long so they don't force me to work it off? Live like a fugitive? And you're what to me that you get to make those demands? Hmm? What are you, Liam? My concerned best friend? My roommate?"

Suddenly, for Liam, there is no air left in the room. There is none at all. Only Jacen has the air, so Liam moves closer to him and touches his lips to Jacen's in a timid kiss. Breathing out a sigh, filling Liam with much-needed oxygen, Jacen kisses him back, whispering words like damnation, "I'm in love with you. Liam. Liam, I'm in love with you. That's why it's hard for me to be okay with all of this. I don't understand."

Liam doesn't respond with words, he just kisses Jacen quiet and holds on to him tighter.

Of all of the ways that Liam has classified and categorized his life, Jacen has been the one thing that he could never fit easily under any sort of label. Jacen just is. He's the biggest, most constant part of Liam's life. Without Jacen, everything is hollow and ugly. Without Jacen, there is no reason to do anything, to try or strive or hope. There used to be. There used to be many reasons—to be successful, to find excitement and pleasure in his job, in his roles, to get rich, to be adored. None of those reasons fit anymore. Nothing is what it should be. Everything is in chaos.

"Ask me something," Liam begs, on the verge of tears by the sound of it.

"Do you care about me?"

"Yes," Liam gasps urgently.

"Do you love me?"

"*Yes.*" A tear slides down Liam's cheek, dampening Jacen's skin.

"What do you want from me?"

"Don't sell yourself anymore. Ever. Come. Come away with me. We'll leave. We'll just take our stuff or, hell, just get in the car and drive. We'll clean out our accounts and just go. They won't look for us forever. And we can outsmart them. I know we can."

"Go where?"

"Doesn't matter. Anywhere. Anywhere but here. We lay low so that they can't track us down. It's more cost effective for them to replace us anyway than to waste resources searching. We'll put all of this shit behind us and start fresh."

"But why," Jacen hisses. "*Why*, Liam? Why risk it?"

Angry, determined, Liam growls, "Because I won't let this kill you too! I won't. *I won't let it!* I won't let it have you. It's already —" Liam is shaking in Jacen's arms, raging at something. Jacen doesn't know what. Sucking in a rough breath, Liam continues, "Everyone I care about! *Everyone that matters.* They just... *leave.* They get stolen away from me before I can stop it or change it and I won't let it happen to you too! *I won't!*"

"Baby, what are you talking about?"

Liam turns in Jacen's arms, pushing back until Jacen is spooned up flush against him. Forcing himself to take a deep breath, he draws Jacen's arms around him like a living, breathing blanket.

"I don't know how to talk about this," Liam warns. "It's not something I've ever had to put into words."

"Try for me."

And he does, he really does, but it just won't come.

"Ask me something."

"Who died?"

"My parents. And —"

"And?"

Liam shakes his head, putting his hands to his face and growling roughly into them. Pulling them away he rasps, "Timothy."

His voice breaks on the name, barely whispered, soft as silk.

Liam flushes hot and shudders as he fights not to cry or splinter apart into fragments, even as the tears start to stream.

"Who is Timothy?"

"I loved him, *so much.* I loved him with all I had. And I still — I'm still in love with him. I'll always be in love with him. What I had with him was the truest thing in my whole life. He was my first love, my dream. He was everything. He was the world to me."

Sensing that Liam has no more to give, that he needs to first be ready to talk more about this than he has, Jacen waits. He falls quiet and holds Liam, giving him time, letting him decide. They lie there for almost an hour, in the dark, in silence.

And then, slowly, Liam begins to explain.

"My name was Avery Williams. I grew up in foster care. My mom and dad died before I was old enough to remember them. There was no one else, so I went into the system. So many different placements, different families and temporary foster parents. And I tried. I tried *so hard* to be everything they wanted me to be — the perfect son, helpful, obedient, hard-working, honest, loyal, just a good kid. I tried my best in school, got decent grades and listened and did everything I was asked to do. All I wanted, more than anything, was to be adopted; for someone to care enough to want to keep me. But no one did. *No one* adopted me. No matter what I did or who I became for them. It was never enough. They always wound up giving me back. My life was like a dance, home to home, bed to bed, never staying in one place long. And it was all empty, shallow. Right when I began to love my foster brothers and sisters, they'd separate us. One of us would leave and I'd never see or hear from them again. Do you have any idea what that does to someone?"

Jacen presses a tender kiss to the back of Liam's ear, hugging him.

"I aged out. Eighteen-years-old. Minimum wage job. Homeless. I found some of my old foster siblings living together in this beat-up old house. I moved in there with them. We all tried to hold down jobs. We all contributed to paying the bills. It was nice. It was the closest to happy I ever was in my whole childhood. Timothy was there. He was the oldest of us, at nineteen. He used to be my foster brother, just for a few months when I was eleven. We all looked up to him so much. There wasn't anything that scared him. Nothing at all. He was so brave. It made us feel safe, protected. All he wanted was to be a family. And then, well, we fell in love. He was everything to me, he took care of me, and I worshipped him completely. I gave him everything I had."

"But...."

"But things in the house started to go — the furnace, the refrigerator, the roof. The landlord was non-existent. He took off, abandoned the place. It was up to us, and it was decomposing around us. It was our *home*, you know? And we didn't have the money to fix it or leave. The bills were so expensive. Thousands of dollars. We didn't have that kind of cash, not even pooling all of our paychecks."

Jacen sighs by Liam's ear, knowing what comes next before it's spoken.

"Timothy started coming home with money. Hundreds at a time. It added up fast. We fixed the roof. We got the furnace working. We bought a new fridge."

"He was turning tricks."

"Yeah. I couldn't even be mad at him for it, because he was doing it to take care of us, our family. He didn't want to. He never would have started if we hadn't needed the money so badly."

For a long time Liam doesn't say anything. It gives Jacen plenty of time to wonder what manner of death Timothy suffered in his efforts to provide for the people he loved so dearly.

The words sound hollow when Liam speaks them—hopeless, resigned. "He was twenty when he got full-blown AIDS. It progressed really fast. He couldn't work anymore and he needed medication to stay alive. He was in and out of the hospital all the time. The bills were just... astronomical. I had no choice. I never chose this, you understand? I *never* wanted this. I had to do it. It was easy, too. It was just like growing up. All I had to do was try to be whatever the other person wanted, to read them and adjust accordingly. It was easier, actually. A few minutes, an hour tops, I was out of there with cash in hand. And I was able to keep him alive another year. We had a little bit longer together. He was mad at me, though, for most of it. He hated that I was doing it. But it kept the meds coming. It kept the hospital from ignoring us and letting us sit in the lobby for hours, waiting for a bed when he needed care badly. It kept him with me. It was worth it.

"Then he was dead and nothing else mattered. Whoring was all I had left to define me. There was no reason to stop."

There is nothing to be said. Jacen can only hold Liam and infuse every pore of his body with love, letting him feel connected to someone and no longer alone with the darkness in his past.

Sniffling, Liam turns his head slightly and asks with a shy kind of smile, "You want to see him?"

Without waiting for a reply, Liam scoots out of bed and walks from the room, reappearing quickly with his wallet in his hands. He opens it and holds it out for Jacen.

The worn-edged, slightly crumpled picture in the little plastic sleeve shows a sandy-haired, brown-eyed boy with a carefree grin.

"That was a year before he died," Liam says softly. "I love that picture of him. He looks so happy. All I ever wanted was to see him smile like that."

"God, he's just a *baby*." When Jacen looks up and sees the fond pride and unabashed love shining clear as crystal in Liam's eyes, Jacen feels the pure sincerity of it. This is Liam, he sees. *This* is Liam at last. The masks and personas have fallen away.

Liam climbs back into bed, facing Jacen this time, taking the wallet back and holding it between them, some of his smile lingering at the corners of his lips.

Using that lingering connection to what's now just a ghost, a memory, Jacen poses the question, "What would Timothy want you to do?"

"To quit," Liam answers instantly, certain. "To leave with you and make a new, better life somewhere else. That's what he'd tell me. He would want me to be happy. You know, for a long time I was really angry at him for leaving me. Doing this, selling myself, my love, was like payback for him leaving me all alone. But I don't want to hurt him anymore. I want him to be proud of me for once."

Reaching out, Jacen takes hold of Liam's hand, and whispers, "I'm proud of you, Lee."

With a sad smile, and a small laugh thick with emotion, Liam nods and stares at their hands, intertwined.

Chapter 12
Helpless Child, Gruesome Deeds

When the wallet gets set aside, Liam's attention turns to Jacen, plain straightforward expectancy shining out at him. "Tell me. Tell me how you got here. Please."

"It's a long story."

"I've got time. And I think it's kind of important to know why the man who's become the most important thing in my life became a hooker."

"I get that," Jacen allows. "But I really don't want to talk about it."

"Jacen, *please*. You can tell me anything. There's nothing to be ashamed of."

"Yeah, well, not all of us are as perfect as you."

Liam rolls his eyes. "You know I'm not leaving or letting you shower or sleep until you talk to me. I can be quite annoying when I have to be."

"Christ," Jacen groans.

"Just start talking. Start at the beginning and go from there."

"You really want to hear this?"

"Yes. Now go. Start. Do it."

"Fine," he grumbles. "Okay. The beginning: I grew up in a big family but a poor one. Really poor, like, embarrassingly so. On a dairy farm in the Midwest. But my grades were good and I was the oldest in the family. My parents put all their hopes on me and dreamed of me going off to college, making something of myself. Becoming something important. Getting out of there. I wanted to study law, maybe become a politician someday. I'd have power and responsibility. I could make an impact. People would look up to me. I wouldn't just be useless trash anymore.

"They saved every dime, every penny. I worked any odd job I could find from as soon as I was able to swing a hammer or push a mower or work a register. It all went into the college fund. I applied for grants too, and I did get a couple. I tried my hand at sports, thinking maybe I could get a scholarship, but that didn't happen. Wasn't really my thing, I guess. But it was enough, anyway, the rest of it. It was enough, even though the banks kept denying our loan or aid applications.

"I got accepted to the local university. It was far enough away that I couldn't commute from home, so I had to live in town. I got a crappy apartment that was about the size of a closet and lived there. It was awesome. It was my own place. My parents, they're super conservative, super Catholic and really old fashioned. Being at college and getting away from all of that... it was a whole new world opening up for me. For once I wasn't living under their thumb. I could make my own choices and be whoever I wanted to be. I was on my own, one hundred percent. I was free. No one was there to judge me. All I had to do was work as hard as I could and follow my dreams. My whole future was laid out in front of me and anything was possible. I wasn't doomed to live on a farm and milk cows my whole life. I could be someone. With a college degree, any college degree, I could get a job good enough to take me anywhere I wanted to go in the world."

Jacen pauses there, like he wants to live in that moment longer, savoring the remembered possibility of old hopes. His tone of voice is vastly different when he starts speaking again. The hope is gone, replaced by bitter resentment.

"The... well, the beginning of my sophomore year, I'd just finished busting my ass with three different jobs over the summer, working as an intern in a law office, bussing tables, and working as a janitor at my school. I never slept and I was fucking exhausted all the time but it was worth it. I was making it work. I went home to see my family for Thanksgiving break, to share my worldly tales with all of my brothers and sisters." Jacen stops, laughing at himself with more malice than Liam can bear.

"My brother, Dennis, seventeen-years-old, had just got himself a car," Jacen sneers. "It was an old Ford pickup. He paid for it himself, just like I had done, working hard, saving up. I was so proud of him. He wanted to show it off, you know? Take it for a spin. So we went for a drive, just the two of us, cruising around."

Concern darkens Liam's eyes. "What happened?"

"We got sideswiped by a drunk going eighty in a twenty-five mile-per-hour zone. The truck rolled down an embankment and the other guy drove off before the cops came. When I woke up, I had six different broken bones, two in my left arm, and the rest in my legs and feet where they'd been crushed by the car. It took me almost a full year of rehab before I was able to walk again."

"Oh my god," Liam groans. "And Dennis? I'm afraid to ask...."

"Brain damage," Jacen replies, staring straight ahead. "He had broken bones, too, but it didn't even seem to matter, because he was gone. We'd never get him back the way he used to be. He'd never get better. My baby brother, whom I loved with all my heart, was *gone*. And you want to know what the worst part is? I hated him for it. I hated him for taking me out in that piece of shit truck like a show-off fool. All of that work, all of that *money* I had saved up... it went to pay the medical bills. My whole future, my dreams. Pfft. *Gone*. Gone just like him. But you know, just because life sucks doesn't mean you get to stop living it, so I pushed myself to get back on my feet just to get away from him and my parents. I was *so angry*, Lee. In one moment, everything good in my life was stolen from me."

With a grimace that masks profound sadness, Jacen hesitates for a moment, remembering a life he used to have. When he begins to speak again, it's with determination, but Liam can still feel Jacen's grief, under the surface. "But I did it. I did my PT and eventually I got better. I moved out and didn't keep in touch. I found some of my friends from school and got my old place back. I had enough time to work without school to worry about, so rent was no problem. I'd work 24/7 if I had to. The anger never dulled, though. So I acted out. I had this opportunity fall into my lap. Some rich guys from one of the frats were offering cash to anyone who'd be willing to suck them off whenever the mood struck. It was more money than I'd make in a week, at all of my jobs combined, just for some BJs. After that, I got addicted to it. It was like a drug, all of that money, and how easy it was to get. I started to place ads in the personals, you know? Escort service things. Really vague. I got a couple of older, bored housewives calling me for sex, and that was awesome. It became my career. That's how I got into it. It's not as dramatic as your story, but it is what it is. I'm not angry anymore. I like my life, especially now that you're in it."

Liam studies Jacen's face like it's a book, like Jacen tends to do to him, his eyes sharpening as if, should he stare hard enough, he might be able to crack the code of Jacen's words to find what's hidden underneath.

"I'm sorry, but I don't buy it."

Dumbstruck, Jacen blinks, "Excuse me?"

"I don't buy it. I don't accept that you started this because you were so fucking greedy that the easy money was just too tempting. That's not who you are," Liam accuses.

Hurt, Jacen pulls away. Liam pulls him back. "Maybe you're wrong. Maybe you don't know me at all."

"You said you were raised in a religious home! Conservative! How do you go from being an innocent farm boy to sucking guys off for a few hundred bucks? You're not a shallow person, Jacen! Even the hard work, the accident, losing your dream, it wouldn't be enough. It shouldn't be enough to cause this," Liam argues.

"You're wrong. It was plenty."

"No. I refuse to accept that. There's something you aren't telling me, and I can't figure out if it's to protect me or to protect yourself. Either way, it's scaring the shit out of me and you have to tell me what it is."

Jacen's face hardens. He sets his jaw and grits his teeth, blinking his eyes clear. It works for a little while, but Liam's resolve is stronger than Jacen's.

"You can trust me," Liam says softly.

"That *was* the truth," Jacen struggles to say. The words stick in his throat.

"No. Not all of it."

"Why? Because it's so easy to see how *damaged* I am? How

fucked up? Is it just so apparent that I'm easy to fuck over? That's an awesome thing to say to someone you care about. Maybe you just want me to be something I'm not. Did that ever occur to you?"

"Who did this to you?"

Jacen's eyes dart away.

"Someone in your family?"

Releasing a sharp exhale, Jacen tenses, closing off, pushing Liam away mentally.

"No. Then who?"

"There's nothing wrong with me," Jacen insists, sounding like he wants to believe it and can't quite manage it.

"Jacen, *please* tell me what happened. Tell me who. It's okay. I promise it's okay."

"Can't you see I don't want to talk about this?!"

"So there is something. You aren't denying it. Someone hurt you. Was it a relative? Was it a teacher? Was it your priest? Come on! Jacen, give me *something*! Talk to me! Just say a name. Say it! Spit it out. Say the name. Just the name."

Jacen whispers something.

"What...?"

There's a long pause. Jacen's face is a mask. He takes a deep breath and then stops fighting, stops hiding, stops caring.

"Mr. Andrews," Jacen says a little more clearly. "Brian Andrews."

Liam gets very still, his heart pounding. His eyes widen. "Who is Brian Andrews?"

"He was our neighbor."

Liam gazes over at Jacen with enough naked affection that it penetrates the invisible outer shell he's built up around himself over the years. The real, vivid concern for his well-being, for the naïve, long-lost little boy he used to be, enables Jacen to speak the truth aloud for the very first time.

"He owned the land next to my family's property and he told me he was going to buy us out and kick us off of it if I told anyone. He could have easily done it. My brothers and I were friends and schoolmates with his kids. My parents thought I went over there to play and when I came home with money, they thought I'd been doing *chores*."

"How long?"

"Forever."

"Jacen, *how long*?"

"You don't want to know."

"*Jacen*," Liam begs, shaken, sitting up, his face going pale and slightly green.

"You don't want to know, Liam. Trust me. And it never stopped. It only stopped when I wasn't living there. He even found me when I was in a fucking wheelchair after the accident."

"Younger than fifteen?" Nothing. No reaction. "Younger than ten?"

Jacen looks at him coldly. "It wasn't only about sex and being attracted to little boys; he told me I was his *favorite*. It was an *obsession*. He got off on terrorizing me when I was an eighteen-year-old in that wheelchair as much as he did molesting me as a little boy. I was more than an opportunity, I was a *project*."

Liam presses the back of his hand to his mouth and closes his eyes as helplessness, nausea and rage at the cruelty in the world paralyses him.

Now that Jacen has started to let out some of the pent-up bitterness, it unleashes a flood of admissions, bottled up for much too long. "And when the fear of losing our home and livelihood wasn't effective enough, he'd threaten to go after my brothers. He threatened to go after *Dennis*. I knew he would have done it too, to fuck with my head, but he didn't need to. All he had to do was make me understand that he could. Or he'd just make it hurt a lot. He was good at that, hurting me in creative ways. When I left for good once I could walk again, I took some of the tapes he'd made of us over the years and sent them to the local police department. I sent some to the local news station, too. I had no choice! I couldn't let that be my life a single second longer, but I couldn't escape without showing the world the monster he was. I had to *show them*. That's one of the reasons why I'm never going back. I changed my name, moved far away, and put it all behind me. I'm not that person anymore. As far as my family knows, I'm dead. I plan to keep it that way. After seeing what he'd done to their child, right under their noses, for all of those years? I'd rather be dead to them."

Jacen sits up too, pulling the covers with him in a sad attempt at modesty. "So that's why Spencer's not a big deal to me, okay? I've had worse, and at least with him it's not personal. He doesn't care about me; it's all selfish and physical. That's why Patrick's not so scary either. I'm bigger than him. I can defend myself if I have to. And I didn't want your pity, Liam, or have to face this shit again. It was done. It was buried.

"I'd like you to leave," Jacen says quietly.

Closing his eyes, Jacen takes a shaky breath. There is no sign of Liam getting off the bed. No footsteps receding out into the hall. On the contrary, the bed shifts, as Liam comes closer.

"*Please* leave," Jacen prays.

Liam swings a leg over Jacen's lap, settling down on it, winding his legs behind Jacen's back, pulling Jacen's arms open and wrapping him in a close, intimate embrace.

"I'm never leaving you," Liam promises. "This wasn't your fault. None of it."

"I'm disgusting."

"You're beautiful."

"You can't fix me."

"I want to try to heal you."

"You don't really love me."

"I do. And I'll prove it."

Jacen sighs. Liam is warm breath and a solid weight, anchoring him, soothing him.

"I'm running away again, aren't I?"

"Yes. One last time. It'll be okay. We'll do it together."

Jacen wants to believe it. He wants that with all of his heart. But his faith in others, in the world, and God died long ago in the hands of an evil, very sick man. There is no other choice though, than to give in to Liam. Jacen has said so himself, and very recently, that he can't do this anymore. His life is one that he hates and it does not fit who he is any longer. There is nothing in it for him other than Liam, so where Liam goes, Jacen is helpless but to follow.

Chapter 13
Running in Circles

As tired as Jacen is, he will not be getting any sleep that night. The day had started out just like any other, with him submitting to Patrick, his client, and his changeable whims; but it led, somehow, to Jacen making and professing love to Liam. With crickets chirping outside the window, standing in the upstairs office of their house with Liam seated at the desk as he pours over numbers and contracts, Jacen nurses his cup of espresso and tries to stay focused.

"This is insane," he murmurs. The entirety of what they need to accomplish in the next eighteen hours is mind boggling.

"We can always leave after my job," Liam tells him.

"No."

"It's just the cowboy. He's not going to get weird with me, and I might even be able to convince him to receive this time instead of me. It'd buy us another... nine hours... before your appointment with Bruce, to get out of town."

"No."

"Jacen, we need to be reasonable," Liam sighs. "I'm supposed to be there at noon. That gives us roughly six hours of daylight to get everything done and get far enough away to elude these bastards."

"If you get to make rules about who I have sex with, then I want the same privilege," Jacen argues quietly. "I don't want him touching you. Even if he is nice."

Reactions flit over Liam's face. He knows that Jacen's rationale is logical, that Liam shouldn't expect to dish it out without getting some right back. And there's no way in hell that he's backing down on his stance on Jacen taking any more jobs. It's just that no one, not even Timothy, ever got to tell Liam what to do with his own body when it came to this, the way he has always made his living.

"This shouldn't be too much to ask, Lee," Jacen tells him gently.

It's a matter of principle, maintaining control of his own life, more than wanting to fuck other people. Though there is a small voice at the back of Liam's mind reminding him how much he had been hoping for and looking forward to another job with Tucker. If Liam was to date one of his clients, excluding Jacen of course, Tucker would be the one. Liam liked him a lot.

But he *loves* Jacen.

"We'll give it a shot," Liam relents. "Okay? And try to get out of here by noon. But if it doesn't happen, then...." Liam leaves it hanging there, but the anxiousness in Jacen's face moves him to add, "I'd be doing it for us. Hell, I've been doing this for a decade, since I was nineteen. One more time won't kill me."

"One time is all it takes," Jacen counters, thinking of Timothy, but not able to actually throw his tragic fate directly in Liam's face. "If we're saying we're done with this, I want to be done. Both of us. For good."

Trying to steer the conversation in another direction, Liam says, "I don't want to argue with you. Let's go over this again. I moved all of my money to one of my private accounts that isn't connected to The Company, and set everything in motion to close the others tomorrow, the next business day. I set up a new account for you in your legal name, with new account numbers. It's all there. It won't all transfer until the morning, when the banks open. And we need to pack. I don't know about you but I don't have that much I need to take. Do we have boxes?"

"Yeah. There should be enough. There's a bunch stashed in the attic from when I moved in. I do kind of have a lot to pack, all the kitchen stuff, the cookware. I'm taking that with me."

"We can buy new kitchen stuff," Liam tells him.

"I know. But it's mine. I don't have a lot that's mine. If I have to drop everything and go, I'm at least taking what I can."

"Fine. Okay. What else. How about transportation?"

"We can't take either of our trucks," Jacen says. "Even if we got new plates somehow, we don't know if they're tracking them in other ways. They told us they had security measures in place considering we went on jobs in our own vehicles. It's fully possible they planted something on them and it'd take too long to check them thoroughly and make sure they're totally clean. We have to leave them."

Liam sighs, knowing he's right.

"When the dealerships open I'll go buy a new truck. Cash. We'll load the bed with our stuff and take that," Jacen says. "And where are we going?"

"One of the guys I used to live with, another foster brother; I, um, used to be in email contact with him, but that was years ago. I can put out a message to him, see if he gets back to me. Last I heard he was up near San Luis Obispo. That's where I'd go, and it's still close enough to Yasha that, theoretically, you could meet up for visits if you wanted to. I know it's important to you to stay in contact with him. But I'd rather have some sort of connection and not just go out there blind."

"So, we go north to San Luis Obispo. Get a room somewhere for a few days while we decide what to do, where to settle down?"

"Yeah," Liam nods.

"This is insane."

"Yeah," Liam agrees. "You got a better plan?"

"Nope," Jacen admits with widened eyes dancing with caffeine-generated energy. "What's your friend's name?"

"Dice."

"*Dice*?"

"Yeah. Well, his real name's Clay Martinez, but his deal used to be that he'd hustle people with table games. So... Dice."

"We're ditching our whole lives and putting our faith in someone named Dice that you haven't even spoken to in years?"

"He's my brother. I trust him completely. And you're putting your faith in *Yasha*, so...."

"Touché."

"It's gonna be fine, Jace. You'll see." The words seem convincing enough, but the dark, sunken look to Liam's eyes, the strain in his face, his posture, the fear... it portends differently. "We should start packing our stuff and clean house. Time's running out."

Jacen nods, hands cupped around the warm ceramic mug, his body throbbing from being with Liam, reminding him keenly how very much things have changed already.

It takes them all night to scour the house, gathering every scrap or shred of important or personal information, every possession, every token, every single thing that they can't bear to leave. Jacen's apron from Liam, his spices, pots and pans, knives and cookbooks, it all gets packed away, along with their magnets and the collection of post-it notes from Jacen that Liam has saved in a little stack with a purple paperclip holding them together — previously tucked away in a drawer by the sink, but now safely stowed in one of their boxes. The big things, like furniture, linens, towels, electronics, lamps, are all deemed replaceable and stay.

They both stuff their suitcases with clothes but most of their abundant wardrobes do not come with them. Their more outlandish costumes and footwear, used solely for pleasing their clients, are not wanted or needed. Most of what Liam decides to pack is a collection of clothing, toiletries and mementos. The biggest items he packs are his leather jacket and the handmade quilt given to him one Christmas when he was five by a grandmotherly lady he was in the care of at the time, and who passed away shortly after.

The dawn creeps up on them. Jacen throws together a bizarre yet elaborate breakfast from some of the more decadent ingredients in their fridge, just to use it all up. Then he leaves to buy a new truck.

Liam wanders through the house that is owned by The Company, to whom they pay rent. He gathers everything that they've packed near the side door, to be loaded in the new truck once Jacen gets back. He tries to let himself believe that this is truly the last morning he will ever be in that place, or be whom he currently is. Overnight, he will shed his skin and be reborn as something he cannot yet fathom. For all of his determination to get himself and Jacen away from there, and to safety, it scares Liam most of all to anticipate what life will be like when he does not have his familiar routine and duties to hide behind.

Out of his whole life, there was only a small portion of it, a gathering of mere months, in which he was nothing but himself, Liam, living only for what he wanted. He's not sure he knows how to be that person any longer. How will he be able to make Jacen happy, to be a whole person and take care of him, when Liam doesn't even know who he is when he looks in the mirror? And even if he figures it out, how can he dare give his heart away to someone to be broken for the second time? Is there even enough of his heart left to give? Is all he is an act? When it's all stripped away, what remains?

It's too late, the ghost of Timothy whispers to him. *You know that. Don't lie to yourself. You couldn't leave him now any more than you could leave me when you found out why I was getting so sick, so fast. You were scared then, too. It didn't change anything.*

"What if I'm not enough? He deserves better than me," Liam voices into the empty air.

All he wants is you.

"You don't know that. You're not even real; you're a voice in my head."

A few hours later, and a few miles away, Jacen is being handed the keys to a slightly used blue Chevy pickup. On the way back to the house with it, he calls Yasha.

"Hey," he says tiredly when Yasha picks up. "I'm leaving town. Today. Now. Liam and I are going, together."

After a pause, Yasha says quietly and with audible confusion, "Okay. This is sudden."

"It has to be. Neither of us wants the other to have to do this anymore, and we both have jobs booked today, so we're getting out before anyone knows we're going."

"This is a mutual desire to change careers, or...?"

"He said last night that he wanted to sleep together before we had to do it for the job, and he convinced me to trust him enough to go through with it. And it was intense. Turns out there were some feelings there on his part. More than I expected. He got really protective of me. But look, it's kind of a long story. He oversaw me with one of my rougher clients and it spooked him. And," Jacen takes a

116

deep breath and admits, "we talked. About our pasts. How we got into the business."

"You told him?" There is noticeable shock in Yasha's voice.

"Yeah. So now he thinks he has to save me from my life."

"You disagree?"

Jacen considers this. "No. I don't I just see it more like finally having a reason to move on."

"And Liam doesn't?"

"I don't know."

"But you want to do this, right? You're doing this because it's time and because you're ready? Not just because Liam is telling you to do it and convincing you that things will be worse if you don't do what he says?"

"I am," Jacen says, not knowing if it's a lie or not, but fully aware that it might seem like he is allowing himself to be manipulated again. There's a prolonged moment in which Jacen can sense Yasha's unease but he has no idea how to counter it.

"Where are you going? Can you tell me?"

"I'll call you when we get there. It'll be from another number. But I'd like to see you in a few days, if you can manage it. They don't know our history — that we're... good friends — so they shouldn't think to watch you, but you'd have to be careful just in case. It'll help me not freak out so much if I know you're still a part of my life."

Yasha doesn't have a response at first. Jacen listens to him breathing, holding the phone closely to his ear. "Be careful," Yasha urges somewhat desperately. "Please. I'll help in whatever way I can. Just let me know what I can do."

"Thanks," Jacen sighs. "I mean it. Thank you."

"Call as soon as you can."

"I will."

There's a surreal moment for Jacen when he pulls into the driveway and sees Liam waiting on the front stoop, his thumbs hooked in the belt loops of his form-hugging jeans Dressed in cowboy boots and an earthy-hued button down, he looks completely ready for his date with Tucker, instead of prepared to abscond with Jacen. It's like their talk never happened, that Jacen daydreamed the whole thing out of a pitifully desperate delusion designed to comfort him in his turmoil over the past few bad jobs.

That's why they don't talk about it. Jacen swallows his hurt pride and wordlessly loads the boxes, full of their possessions, into the new truck with Liam, packing them in tightly and then covering it all with a tarp, using bungee cords to secure it in place.

It's quarter after eleven in the morning when Jacen arrives with the new truck, and eleven thirty five when they have everything ready to go at last. There hasn't been a call or email from Dice, and because they are cutting it so close to Liam's scheduled job, it is silently agreed between them to do what seems necessary, if not desired.

Liam gets into his old truck. Jacen gets behind the wheel of the new truck.

Jacen marvels that at that very moment, as they drive together across town to a hotel they have both frequented hundreds of times, professions of love warming their hearts and the dull, not unwelcome ache left in their bodies from their lovemaking the previous night, Liam has completely prepared himself, bodily and mentally, to fuck another man. And it seems just as impossible that Jacen is driving with him to the place, and will sit there, in the truck bought with ten thousand dollars cash from his private accounts, transferred by Liam not hours ago to give them a fresh start together, while the man he loves has sex with someone else.

It's not supposed to go like this, he tells himself. *It's supposed to be better than this.*

They park at the hotel at five of noon. Liam gets out of his truck and locks it. He stands there beside it for a second, debating something, his face unreadable to Jacen until Liam turns and makes right for him. The driver's side window is rolled down, a breeze blowing Jacen's dark hair back as Liam steps up to him. Faced forward, his hands clenched around the steering wheel, Jacen hides his hurt as best he can, but he can't meet Liam's eyes.

Liam exhales sharply and takes Jacen's face in his hands, turning it gently toward him. Kissing him softly, Liam hisses. "I'll be right back. I'm sorry. I love you."

It's the first time he's ever said it outright, and that he said it there, like this, is a poisoned arrow through Jacen's heart.

Jacen doesn't say a word, just closes his eyes and lets himself be kissed, because that's his job—to comply and be moved, be touched, be conquered. Liam's lips briefly touch Jacen's forehead and then he's going. He's gone.

Chapter 14
Fly, Fly Away

The message on Liam's phone tells him to go to room 402. He takes the elevator up to the fourth floor and follows the signs to the correct door.

He stands there, at door 402, until his watch tells him that it's five past, unable to knock. All he can see, clouding out everything else, is Jacen's anguished, resigned betrayal, written in the sad quirk of his lips, the furrows in his brow. Behind that, darkly, he sees Timothy's feelings of betrayal, the desperation in him every time Liam left to walk the streets, alone, with the bills piling up and no other perceived choice.

Knuckles rap upon the hotel door and though they are Liam's, they feel disconnected from his arm. His feet anchor themselves to the hallway floor, prohibiting his retreat, but then the door opens and it's too late.

"Tucker," Liam says, lips curling in a smile that doesn't reach his eyes — the only part of him still drowning in the guilt and horror of it all.

"William, hey. It's good to see you," Tucker grins. That same sweet awkwardness that initially captivated Liam is still there, like all of the wicked temptations from his past beckoning to him as Tucker fidgets in the opened doorway, but though Tucker was the one stumbling over his doubt and lack of self-confidence the first time they met, it is now Liam that begs without speaking for salvation. "Come in."

"Yeah," Liam says, glancing down the hall to the exit as his feet carry him inside. It all begins to unfold in his head as Tucker closes the door behind him. They will undress. Tucker's lips will drag over Liam's skin, touching him, using him in defiance of the man currently seated just outside the building—Jacen is Liam's future where Timothy was the past, part of Liam's previous life as a boy called Avery and here he is, somewhere in the middle, doing the unthinkable.

How could you? Don't you love me? Why would you do this to me? To us?

The ghostly echo of a voice sounds like Timothy, accusing him still, ten years later, but Liam's mind is filled with Jacen. It's happening again, he realizes—turning like a circle. Gathering his character around him like a shroud, burying Liam like he buried Avery so long ago, he tries to be neither of them, only a nameless cowboy, looking for a fuck. It used to feel good and incredibly freeing to deny Avery and be an Other, a creation of his imagination. The baggage would fall away. The heartbreak, the sadness, it melted under the heat of strangers' desire for his body, the proof that there were still people alive and aroused and vital in the world; men who, in that moment, wanted only that temporary facet of Avery Williams' soul. It would grant him release from any and all troubles clouding his heart, and make life, for those few, precious minutes, seem bearable.

The nameless cowboy steps up to Tucker, hooking a finger behind the man's belt and drawing him near.

"What's wrong?" Tucker asks softly.

"Nothing's wrong." Liam's palm rubs over Tucker's chest, feeling his heartbeat thumping. He tries to push the rest away, to focus only on that connection, but the hope, of all things, is what damns him. When it was Timothy Avery was denying, he was overcoming death and suffering. Now, as Liam, he's trying to deny Jacen, who is the promise of a future, and freedom, and he can't manage it. He can't kill hope when it's barely bloomed.

A gentle hand touches Liam's face, which is painted with sorrow. Closing his eyes against the kindness, Liam flounders. Then Tucker does the one thing that Liam doesn't know how to fight against or work with, and wraps him in a hug, holding on and trying to soothe. There is no other choice, Liam grabs on, hugs back and exhales heavily.

"I'm sorry," he says, not thinking, just reacting without a filter or knowing what rules to play by. All is chaos. "I met someone. He's outside, right now and as soon as I leave this hotel we're going to go start a new life and god, why the hell am I telling you this? What's wrong with me?" He pulls back sharply, searching Tucker's face, really seeing him for the first time since the door opened, and the unfamiliar, soft concern in his eyes. Liam looks down at him, the long hair fallen around Tucker's shoulders, the crisp lines of his tailored shirt. It's the mental image of Tucker ironing his clothes in preparation for William's arrival that breaks through some of the fog. "What do you want?" he blurts, desperation making him shameless. "Anything, anything you want, just name it. I'll do *any-thing* if you'll forget what I just said. Please?"

Tucker is looking at him strangely. That eager, nervous happiness lifts away, and some of what his female groupies must see colors his expression instead. With regret and a sadness of his own, Tucker nods slightly. "I like you, you know. Been thinkin' about you, more than I should. It would've been fun."

His hand drops away from where it was resting against the side of Liam's face. Tucker takes a backward step. "I'll wait three hours or so before calling in that you were a no-show. That should give you some time to play with."

"What?" Liam blurts stupidly.

"Go on. Be in love. It looks good on you."

Liam is unable to believe it, even as Tucker folds his arms, closing off, and waits for him to understand and leave.

"We could still..." Liam tries to offer.

"No. We couldn't. I wouldn't feel right about it. It's okay. Really. Go on, now."

Liam stares at Tucker, but for a long moment his feet won't move. It's only when he quickly closes the gap between them and places a soft, tender kiss to Tucker's lips, before hissing an urgent, "Thank you," against them that the spell breaks. Tucker kisses him back after a pause, and it feels like goodbye.

Twenty minutes after he disappeared into the hotel lobby, Liam emerges from it, running.

He runs to Jacen's truck, *their* truck, with everything that matters nestled safely in it.

Breathless and fevered, Liam rasps as he yanks open the passenger side door, "I couldn't. I couldn't do it."

Jacen sighs heavily, his lips forming the words to a whispered prayer of thanks.

"Gimme your phone. Quick. We've gotta get the hell out of here. Now."

Liam takes both phones, puts them on the pavement just behind the front driver's side wheel of the truck. Standing back, Liam watches as Jacen leans out the window slightly to see as he backs the truck over them, crushing them. The brittle snapping and crunch of the plastic is immensely satisfying.

With a bright, happy smile, Liam jumps into his seat and they take off, laughing.

Flying down the road as fast as they legally can, at least until they're past the city limits and on more open, less patrolled roads, they hold on and keep hoping, praying that they make it, that they can just go.

An hour later, they are still driving, the road receding behind them, just as new ones keep opening up before them. It's like a miracle.

"We did it."

"Not yet. Don't jinx it."

Jacen smiles and bites anxiously at his thumbnail.

"We really can do this, can't we? We're doing it."

"Yeah," Liam agrees.

"I'm glad. I'm so glad, Lee. And thank you, for not going through with it. I know it makes it scarier for you to not have that cushion of time."

"I know," Liam murmurs. "I don't know what I was thinking, to do that to you. Can we just forget about it?"

"Yeah," Jacen nods.

A few minutes later, something in the glove compartment starts to ring.

Liam's eyes go wide as sudden panic surges through him.

"Oh! I forgot." Jacen pulls over and fumbles out two new

phones, finding the one that's ringing. It's the green one — Liam's. He hands it over. "It's for you."

Dumbstruck, Liam says, "Who would be calling me on a phone I've never seen before?"

"When I bought them this morning, I sent the number to your friend, er, brother. Dice. Just in case."

Liam blinks. "You are awesome."

"Yeah, I'm pretty awesome," Jacen grins as Liam answers on the fifth ring and puts it on speakerphone.

Hesitantly, he asks, "Dice?"

"Pigeon?" the husky voice on the other end of the line counters. Jacen gives Liam an amused, curious glance but Liam doesn't catch it.

"Oh my god, no one's called me that in *years*, dude," Liam grins.

"Yeah, right back at'cha," he laughs richly. "I usually just go by Clay now. Or Officer Martinez for the civilians."

"You're a cop! No way," Liam says, shocked. "That's ironic."

Clay laughs again, "Yeah, yeah. I'm a long way from the stupid kid I used to be, that's for sure. How are you, man? What is it you go by now, if it's not Pidge."

Liam groans through a laugh. "Liam," he says.

"Nice. Back to the classics, I see."

"Look, Clay. Man, that's weird. I don't want to impose or anything. I know you've got your own shit going on, but I'm kind of having a situation. And I need some help."

"That's my speciality, helping. What can I do for you?"

"Well," Liam says slowly, looking like he's having trouble stating the facts. "I never really ventured far from my original career path. Until today. I just quit. I'm driving right now, up to San Luis Obispo. Looking to start fresh, get on the straight and narrow, but I don't exactly have family or anyone to go to. I've got the means, I just was looking for a friendly face I guess, as I get set up in a new town, find somewhere to live, a job, all of that."

"Pidge, you've got family," Clay tsks. "What's up? You got people looking for you or somethin'?"

"Something like that. And all I want is a chance to get away from all of that for good. And be safe. It's not just about me, either. There's someone I'm involved with. Someone I care about. He's with me right now. His name is Jacen," Liam adds after a quick glance to check if it's okay to divulge that much. "We left together."

"Better late than never, I guess. It breaks my heart thinkin' you never broke free of that shit. I'm a little disappointed in you, kid. But if there's anything I can do to get you situated, I'll do it. When are you gonna be in the area?"

"I don't know. Maybe in an hour?"

"Cool. Cool. Um, let's see...."

"Is there a motel or something you could recommend?"

"There is. A nice place close to the precinct. Clean, respectable. And close to where I am. I'll send you the address, okay?"

"That'd be fantastic. Thank you."

"I think I can get away for some late lunch if you're interested. Talk face-to-face. We can discuss if you'll be needing any protection."

"Yeah. I think Jacen and I would both like that. We appreciate the help."

"Hey, it's what I do. And anything for a brother. Gimme a call when you get closer, or if anything comes up. I'll text you the directions to a diner down the road from me."

"Thanks, Dice," Liam says urgently. "Really. Thank you."

"No problem, little bro. See ya soon."

Liam hangs up and lets his head fall back against the headrest, a small but honest smile lightening his mood and expression.

"Um," Jacen says, not sure how to continue.

Liam glances sideways at him then straightens in his seat. "We gave each other nicknames, okay? You don't pick your own, you're given it. I had no say."

"But... why?"

Liam rolls his eyes, flushing pink with embarrassment. "They said I was this harmless looking little scrap of a kid. Big eyes, quiet, street-smart, non-threatening. And I'd swoop in, take what I needed, usually without much warning or conversation about it, and then fly away with the spoils."

Jacen smiles. It starts small but quickly grows huge, shifting into happy laughter, dimpling his cheeks and breaking a lot of the tension that has been lingering all day long.

"*Try* to be less entertained," Liam pleads. "Please. I beg of you."

"But it's so adorable, I can't even.... Were you always adorable? You were, weren't you?"

"Jacen..." Liam warns.

"And, hey, pigeons are very smart. Great sense of direction. They used to deliver the mail and everything."

"Can we not? Please?"

"But you're sexy as hell when you blush, and your eyes get all sparkly."

Liam turns sideways and stares seriously at Jacen until he gives it up. Softening, Jacen says, "So we've got a cop on our side? Can't hurt, can it? Maybe someone's watching out for us up there," Jacen suggests, glancing heavenward.

Growing shyer and more pensive, Liam stares down at his lap and considers this. After a moment, Jacen reaches out and takes his hand, holding on to it. Then, when Liam doesn't pull away, he laces their fingers together.

For a long, long time, Liam is perfectly content, sitting there, staring at their entwined hands, enjoying the warmth radiating from Jacen's palm, even though it feels strange, and new.

Jacen picks at his fries, trying to reconnect to the conversation and order his thoughts into a more sensible form. The continued surreal nature of it all is making it a struggle just to get from one moment to the next. The only thing he has to anchor him is Liam's determination, the presence of him at Jacen's side, and the first item on the shifting to-do list floating in his mind.

Find a place to stay. That's what's important. That's as far as he can think.

He had a brief phone call with Yasha, in which his friend's doubt of Jacen's ability to pull this all off was too stark to bear for longer than a minute or so. Promising to drive up to see him soon and to check in with them via phone regularly, Yasha has left Jacen to find his footing and get something to eat.

Now, sitting at the table with Liam and the dark-skinned, hugely tall, broad, physically intimidating Dice, aka Officer Martinez, aka Clay, Jacen lets Liam do the talking. More animated than Jacen has seen him in a long time, Liam can't seem to stop smiling as he gets caught up with his old acquaintance. Clay tells them how he was taken under the wing of an officer involved with a youth outreach program, and was inspired to begin a career in law enforcement, especially when he saw friend after friend, brother after brother, get their futures taken away from them due to bad decisions and bad luck. Clay wanted to make his own luck, and do his part to keep kids off the streets. Liam listens avidly, and Jacen tries to. Then Liam tells an abbreviated tale of the different places he has lived, the brothers and sisters he used to keep in touch with, asking Clay if he's aware of whatever happened to this person or that.

As much as Jacen enjoys seeing Liam reconnect with Clay, though, they have their own pressing matters to attend to.

The motel is in sight of the diner. It seems sufficient to their needs, from what Jacen can tell. But then what?

"You two need a cover. New identities," says Clay. "If you want to distance yourself from who you have been, and keep people from finding you, you need new names, new back stories, and new jobs. I can help you navigate the paperwork and skirt the legal side of it all. But the most important thing to start with are the names. Don't check in to the motel under your old ones. Don't leave a trail anyone can follow. It's so easy to search for people these days. You need to be off the grid. Don't make it easy for them."

"Okay," Liam nods. "We can do that. We'll talk about it, figure out what to do."

"Good. I'll send you the info on the forms and applications you'll need. And I'm guessing you don't want to be in the motel longer than you have to. Get yourself a local paper, check the real estate listings. There's a lot available in the area. I'll vouch for you, whatever you decide."

With a fond farewell, a firm handshake and reassuring smile for Jacen and a hug for Liam, Clay excuses himself as his break comes to an end, promising he'll be in touch.

Reading the weary, lost look on Jacen's face, Liam gives him a confident grin.

"Eat up. We've got boxes to move. You'll need the energy boost," he says.

"Yeah. But, um, like Clay said, we can't check in with our names. What do we do? Any ideas?"

Liam takes a bite of his rapidly diminishing burger, and thinks it over. "Yeah. I do, actually. People within The Company are aware of a small fraction of our pasts, right? Speaking for myself, they know one or two of the names I used to use. It has to be something new. Something they can't connect us with."

Jacen grunts, "Yeah, okay. Makes sense."

"They knew of some of my aliases. But they didn't know the circumstances, or my friends," Liam says, thinking aloud. "And it just goes back a couple of years. Beyond that there's no way to track me. I moved around so much. Fifteen different cities in ten years, and a different name in each one."

"So, what? We just pick something random? Open a phone book, close our eyes and point?"

Liam's gaze drifts up from his plate to Jacen's face.

"I know that look. What? What are you thinking?" Jacen wonders suspiciously.

Fierce color blooms high on Liam's cheeks. He masks a bashful smile behind a hand.

"What?" Jacen presses. "Tell me."

"It's totally out of left field, but that's a good thing, right?"

"Well, I don't know until you tell me."

"They're looking for two friends travelling together. There's not much we can do about that, unless...."

Jacen stares blankly at Liam, with no idea where he's going with this.

"Yes?" he prods.

"What if we take the same name? Like a couple, a married couple. 'Cause, with Prop 8 overturned, it would be technically feasible and all. We might even be able to keep our first names, and just take new last names. It'd be a good back story. And we know enough about each other to pull it off."

"That is the *lamest* marriage proposal I have ever heard," Jacen tells him, shaking his head with disappointment. Liam blushes harder and elbows Jacen in his side.

"God, I shouldn't have even said it," Liam moans.

"You totally want to marry me! That's—" *ridiculous*, Jacen intends to say. But the word doesn't manage to come out. Because in his heart, he thinks it's a great idea. Surprised into a giddy smile, Jacen licks his lips and tries to overcome his own sudden bout of shyness.

"Okay! It's a stupid idea. I'm sorry."

"It's not stupid," Jacen admonishes. "I think it's a great idea."

"No, you don't."

"No, I do. I swear. Let's do it. Yes, I will marry you, Lee. So, what's our name going to be? Anything is fine with me, except maybe Lipchitz. Or Gaylord. That's a hard one to pull off."

"Um. Well," Liam starts, stealing one of Jacen's fries and breaking it up nervously into tiny pieces, popping one in his mouth. "I was thinking, as good luck or something, and since it's something important to me, and if we're doing this, I don't want it to be meaningless. I want it to be for a reason. I was thinking, maybe, Timothy?"

"Oh my god, Liam," Jacen sighs.

"It's a bad idea, isn't it? I knew it. I—" Liam starts, but is silenced when Jacen catches his mouth and kisses him tenderly.

"I'd be honored," Jacen whispers over Liam's lips, caressing Liam's cheek.

"It doesn't, you know, have to be *real*. It can just be our way to stay safe. I think he'd like that."

Jacen doesn't say it immediately. At first, the swelling hope in the words make them too big, too poignant to voice.

"Maybe it should be. Real. I mean, we might need the marriage certificate to prove our identities, right?"

He can see Liam's chest rising and falling with quickened breath, the anxious questioning in his eyes, the hesitancy, the oh-so-fragile flowering of unfamiliar optimism.

"What do you say?" Jacen asks softly, sitting in a greasy diner, under flickering fluorescent lights on the east side of San Luis Obispo, California. "Wanna get married?"

Liam laughs, his green eyes sparkling even more than before, and kisses Jacen firmly in answer.

"This is insane," Liam interjects between presses of their lips. He catches an older woman at the next table smirking at them from over Jacen's shoulder.

"Not any more insane than the rest of today."

"No, actually, it kind of is."

And that is how, with the help of someone working both within and just to the side of the law, William Taye, originally born Avery Williams, changed his name to Liam Timothy and, in just a few days' time, legally wed in a civil union service, Jacen Pruski; though for the sake of the records he went by his legal name, Travis Saxon (Pruski being his mother's maiden name and Jacen one of two middle names, the other being Michael). Travis Jacen Saxon became Travis Jacen Timothy, husband of Liam Timothy.

With their possessions in boxes, stacked along one wall, living out of suitcases in a well-used motel room located two blocks from the police station in San Luis Obispo, the two friends find themselves suddenly spouses, with new identities. The enormity of the change, though technical more so than actual, lifts some of the load from their shoulders. A handful of days pass in a blur, and they come out on the other side as new people. It's a quiet dash of time, with the shock and stress stilling their tongues. They share the only bed in their room, but the nights are chaste. The most they touch is to hold hands when they need the comfort of the connection, to hug before bed, and the kiss they share when they are pronounced wed.

But that evening, when they return to their room, closing themselves away from the world, with plans brewing in their heads, and old dreams finding new life, Liam and Jacen can feel it in the air between them, that expectations, desires, are there. They are no longer friends, nor co-workers, nor roommates. They are so much more than that. Yes, it has happened in a way both stranger and quicker than it should have, but it has happened nonetheless.

Sitting side-by-side in the dark, on a worn, old couch in the

Seabreeze Motel, the blue, neon-tinged light filtering in from the city streets just past the window, Liam's hand slips inside Jacen's.

"Guess you're stuck with me now, old man," Jacen sighs.

"Hey, right back at'cha. At least I married someone that can cook."

"At least I married someone as crazy as me. And whose ass looks *fantastic* in a pair of jeans."

"Wow, you're so shallow sometimes," Liam laments with a smirk.

"Yeah. Well. You're my trophy husband. Get used to it."

Liam nudges Jacen's side.

It's not real, though, Jacen tells himself sadly. *It's just another game. New characters to play.*

The shimmering silver rings on their fingers feel real enough. But what feels more real is the absence of deception or distance in Liam's eyes when Jacen holds his gaze, searching it, trying to read it.

"What are you thinking about?" Jacen asks.

"I'm just glad. I feel like I can breathe. It's really going to be okay. It seems possible now. I mean, I know it just seems like none of this really happened, like it's all a bizarre vacation or some weird, long assignment we were sent on. But we don't owe anyone anything anymore, no one but ourselves, and each other. No one else gets to tell us what to do, or what to be, or who to be with. We can be whatever we want to be."

"And what do you want to be?"

"Safe. I want to be safe and wherever you are."

"What else?"

"Hmm. I'm still figuring that out. Right now what I want is to celebrate. We should celebrate this. We did it. We really did it, Jace."

"Yeah, we did," Jacen smiles.

Chapter 15
First Times

Liam emerges from the bathroom in pair of loose-fitting flannel pajama pants, immediately putting Jacen more at ease just because he didn't try to come up with a special outfit in an attempt to characterize their marriage celebration. Going directly to the bed, Liam flops down on the empty side, right beside where Jacen is leaned back against the headboard, fiddling with his new ring.

"I still can't believe you're pierced," Jacen mutters, eyeing Liam's bare chest.

"Why?"

Jacen shrugs, glancing between the shining, shimmering symbol of his new union with Liam and the equally brilliant jewelry embedded in his companion's dark, semi-erect nipples.

"You don't seem like the type," he says finally.

"What's 'the type'?"

"I don't know."

"They feel good. They make sex feel even better. That was kind of a bonus for me," Liam says dryly. "Why, you don't like 'em?"

"Doesn't matter if I like 'em," Jacen murmurs, staring at his hands, not really thinking about what he's saying, too bogged down in everything buzzing around in his head.

"Um. Yeah. It kind of does matter," Liam argues, sitting up and spinning around to sit cross-legged, facing Jacen.

Jacen's eyes flutter closed. "I didn't," he sighs, stops and tries again. "That's not what I meant. I like them. They're just really distracting. They keep making me lose my train of thought and it's kind of aggravating."

Repressing a smile, Liam clarifies, "My nipple studs make you lose your train of thought."

"Only when you go flashing them around," Jacen says, shaking his hands slightly and wiggling the fingers in the air. Because his tone is perfectly serious, Liam snorts with laughter.

"I'm deeply sorry about that. Should I get a shirt? Take them out? Or maybe just remove my pants so you can enjoy the complete set."

"Don't even get me started on the penis one. That one's *totally* unfair. I can't even look in the general direction of your crotch without thinking about it."

"Do you look at my crotch often?" Liam asks with a smirk. It doesn't get much of a reaction from Jacen, he only sinks deeper into his funk, frowning. His fingers twist together, his wrists resting on his drawn-up knees. "Hey, what's wrong?"

Jacen's lips purse as he shakes his head, dismissing the worry in Liam's voice. "It's nothing. Yasha's going to drive up and visit us tomorrow. He doesn't know about this," Jacen says, raising his left hand and wiggling the ring finger.

Understanding unfolds. Liam hums thoughtfully. "So, can we talk about this? Yasha? You? Can you tell me a little of what happened there? As far as your past goes? I mean, does he know about it?"

"The molestation? Yeah. He knows. He's the only other person I've told. Or, well, not *outright*. He kind of guessed from the way I was reacting to certain things and I didn't deny it."

"You initially told me you slept together because it was your first time."

With an icy smile, Jacen replies, "Yeah. No, that wasn't my first time. It was just the first time it was consensual."

Liam reaches out and takes Jacen's restless left hand, stilling it, holding on to it.

"I had issues," Jacen continues, sounding like the words are coming out faster than he wants them to. "Clearly. Yasha... helped. His background with counseling was a bonus. And he was a trusted friend. He showed me how good it could be, that it wasn't always scary. I can never repay him for everything he did for me. He cared, you know?"

"I was always kind of jealous of Yasha for being so close to you. But I get it now. I'm glad he was able to help."

"Me too," Jacen nods, softening when Liam gives his hand a gentle squeeze. With a sideways glance, and after a thoughtful pause, Jacen ventures, "What was your first time like? Who was it with?"

Exhaling around a smile that doesn't reach his eyes, Liam says, "That was a long time ago."

"Tell me about it. Was it with Timothy?"

Liam's grin widens, but stays cold. "Nah. Sex really wasn't a big deal to me any more by the time I was with Tim."

"But you were eighteen," Jacen frowns. "How old were you when you lost your virginity?"

"Hmm, let's see. It was when I lived on the ranch in Minnesota, so... eleven? Twelve? Maybe. I can't remember. There were three of us. All boys. Foster brothers. They had us staying in this big room over the garage, and during the day we'd be responsible for chores. That's why they'd wanted to foster older boys — to work. And as you can probably imagine, they didn't really go out of their way to be affectionate parental figures. We were pretty much the help. I was the youngest, and the smallest — didn't get a good growth spurt until I was older — so it was harder for me. My brothers were sixteen and seventeen. God, I can't even remember their names," Liam says quietly, to himself, with emotionless amazement.

He'd been lying in the double bed under the room's one window, which was opened to let in some of the cooling night-time breeze. That summer was a hot one, and their room was nearly always stifling. The only thing they would sleep in was their underwear, with a thin sheet covering them. There were two beds in the room. Avery and the sixteen-year-old shared one, and the seventeen-year-old took the other.

"I was starved for attention. When my brothers were nice to me, that was like the best part of my day," Liam explains. "When the younger of the two started to touch me one night — just running his hand lightly over my body, a caress — it was nice. It started slow. Gentle."

The hand moved over the sheet covering the both of them, restless.

When it ventured farther, bit by bit, slowly, down between Avery's legs, at first he tried to draw up his knees. Laying on his back, he felt the playful squeeze of his penis, and heard the whispered, "This okay?" He was swayed more by curiosity than anything sexual to let his much physically larger sibling do what he wanted. The squeeze shifted into kneading and stroking. From the other bed, a low, post-pubescent voice said, "Take the sheet off. Lemme see."

Liam makes the mistake of glancing up at Jacen's face. His expression is one of growing rage, as if he wants to reach back through time and defend the child in that bed. Jacen sits up straighter. Dropping his gaze to his hands, Liam presses on. "I didn't know what was happening. I was too young to get it, but it felt good when he touched me. And hardly anyone ever did, even to hug me. So I let him. They threw the sheet back, slid off my briefs, positioned me so that they could both see everything." Sensing Jacen's movement, Liam looks up at him. He's shading his eyes with both hands, jaw clenched, breathing like a freight train. "Should I stop? If this is upsetting you...."

"Finish," Jacen breathes, his baritone voice more vibration than sound.

"Okay," Liam says doubtfully. "It was just manual stimulation for a while. I closed my eyes and went with it. I could feel my face was, like, beet-fuckin'-red, but their attention was just locked on me. I wasn't used to that kind of scrutiny. Kind of made me feel powerful. Special.

"My older brother tossed a bottle of lube and a rubber onto our bed. The one jacking me stopped and looked over at him, deciding, I guess. I think they were saying stuff like, 'Go on, he's into it,' and arguing about if I was too young, but it didn't last long and I didn't catch most of it. The one touching me, I remember he had such dark eyes, like almost black. Dark hair, sun-browned skin.... He got between my legs, hooked 'em over his shoulders and leaned down over me."

Cold and wet, the first finger entered him in a slow push, and it was such a strange, foreign sensation that a scared, startled little noise erupted from Avery. "Feels weird, huh?" Avery nodded, grunted in agreement, the sound of it wavering. He tried to see what was happening between his

135

legs, but couldn't quite. The finger pumped in and out, smearing lube, coaxing the muscle. The boy on the other bed moved to get a better view, told his brother to add another finger. Avery's face felt so incredibly hot, the blood made the skin tight. Sweat broke out freely over his lithe, pale body, glowing in moonlight that fell in pools through the window above. "You like that?" he was asked, as a lube-coated palm squeezed up his shaft. Wriggling, he grunted again, frowning. The blood roared loudly in his ears, the heat of the body pressing down on him stifling, the probing of the fingers moving inside his body — it started to overwhelm him. A scared whimper left him as it started to become far too much, too fast.

"Come on. He's ready."

"M-maybe. Uh," Avery tried, voice trembling.

"Relax, okay? I'll take good care of ya."

The finger withdraws and the friction is startling. His brother picks up the condom.

"Um," Avery blurts, trying to sit up and see what's going on, unable to. "What — Are...are you going to put it in me?"

"My dick? Yeah," his brother told him with a nod as he rolled the rubber on, watching Avery stare at the thickened flesh cradled in his hand. "Don't worry. You'll like it."

"He was small, which was good for me, I guess. It didn't hurt as much as it would have otherwise. He had me take these deep breaths, and every time I exhaled, he'd thrust. Once he was in me, it felt... real. Like, it'd happened. It was done. No going back. I was scared, and I was probably making a lot of noise, but he was gentle with me. I calmed down once I started to get used to feeling full of him. He was really worked up. Sweating, trembling, flushed, moaning. I thought it was funny. After he finished, he brought me off too and I think I fell asleep. I don't really remember."

"They took advantage of you," Jacen accuses, sounding incensed, bordering on furious.

Calmly holding his gaze, Liam shrugs. "I don't know, it didn't feel like that at the time. I looked up to them. They appreciated me, took care of me. I felt kind of proud to be able to make them so happy. And it felt nice. I liked it."

"Was that the only time you slept with a brother?"

Liam chuckles. "What do you think? Once I'd started, why stop?

I mean, I'd only fuck the ones that were interested."

"Jesus Christ, Lee." Jacen's disapproval oozes from the words. Shaking his head slightly, he seems tired, very tired. He rubs his eyes and turns his face slightly away. After a moment, he turns back and asks, "Was it always guys?"

"No, some of my foster sisters would come on to me. Hey, I was cute, I guess. And we'd screw around, for the hell of it, but," Liam scrunches his nose, "wasn't my thing. I wasn't really into it. How about you? Did you ever try messing around with a guy when it wasn't for money?"

Jacen shakes his head.

"Did you ever want to?"

"No. Not really," Jacen admits. "It was always girls. When it was just for fun, it was girls."

"Huh." Feeling the possessive fire burning hot and strong enough to scorch flesh behind the intensely piercing look Jacen is giving him, Liam clears his throat and resolves to shift the conversational gears away from the murkiness of their pasts. "Okay. I have another question. Needs to be asked."

"Lay it on me."

"Are we going to be monogamous?"

At first, Jacen looks somewhat offended that Liam would need to ask such a thing, when most of their attention for the past few days has been on getting married. Slowly though, anger brewed out of possessive, protective anger of Liam, hearing the nature of his first sexual encounter, drains away. Reality, stark and actual seeps back into Jacen's awareness. Aqua eyes opened wide, he starts to more completely understand the question, what it means, what it implies.

"This is usually something that's covered *before* people get married, I know. But we need to agree on this."

"Wow. I've," Jacen starts and sputters. "I've never been monogamous with anyone in my whole life. How sad is that? Have you?"

"Yeah," Liam nods. "For a few months with Timothy. Until he started... you know. That was the only time."

"Do you want to be?"

"Yes," Liam says after taking time to consider this. "I admit I wasn't sure at first. It's gonna be weird to not, you know.... Given what our lives have been like recently. But yes. I'd like that. I'm ready to be done with the person that I was. I want to try to listen to what *I* want for a change, and all I want is this. Right here. With you. It's your call, though. After thinking about it the past few days, I don't feel like I can tell you what you should do when it comes to sex. Not to that extent. But I need to know if there're going to be others. I feel like I deserve that much."

Liam waits for it, for Jacen to admit that he wants to have the freedom to have sex with women too, especially after hearing him admit that in his adolescence, he wasn't even attracted to guys. Bracing for it, he prepares for the hurt he knows he'll feel.

But, with an expression so forlorn that it breaks Liam's heart, Jacen mutters, "Yes. I want to be monogamous."

"Yeah? Well, good. Okay." The agreement hangs in the air between them, shocking. A shy smile threatens to curl up the corners of Liam's lips so he fights to swallow it back, trying not to look as happy as he feels. "We should get tested. Again," he clarifies, since they have been going to get tested regularly, every other week or so, anyway, up until their hasty escape from L.A. "Tomorrow."

"I agree."

"Good."

With that, Liam lays down, bringing one of the soft pillows under his head, curling up with it. Jacen absent-mindedly caresses the line of Liam's jaw, freshly shaven, the side of his throat, thinking about everything that's been said, letting it sink in, trying to accept it, trying to let go of the rest of his anger and the blind urge to defend someone that doesn't exist anymore. Time slips by.

After a while, when simple nearness to a half-naked Liam starts to make him hard, Jacen says, "Hey. I thought we said were going to celebrate."

"Hmm." Liam glances at their suitcases with their clothes, the door. Tugging the pillow even closer, his lips twist up on one side. "What'd you have in mind?"

"Well," he scans the room, their meager possessions stacked in piles. "There's a few bottles of wine in that box. We could order pizza?"

Liam chuckles. "I like your style."
"I hope so. You're kinda shit outta luck otherwise."

Chapter 16
Hooker's Honeymoon

"Gotta admit," Jacen says a moment later while digging out the phonebook in the nightstand, flipping to P for pizza. "This is not how I pictured my wedding night."

"You pictured your wedding night? Really?"

Jacen shrugs, biting a thumb as he judges pizzerias based on the meager content of their advertisements. "Sometimes."

"I'm sorry to disappoint," Liam murmurs, slipping a hand under the pillow to warm it.

"You're not a disappointment, Lee," Jacen says with gentle conviction. "The most important part of how I pictured it came true. I'm here with my best friend in the world, aren't I?"

Trying not to look as pleased with the compliment as he feels, Liam asks, "So are we gonna consummate this marriage or not?"

For a second, Jacen keeps reading through menus and envisioning various topping combinations, the fantasy of having his own pizza oven someday even flitting around at the back of his mind. What Liam said doesn't register. Then it does. "Oh, you mean with me?"

Liam snorts. "Do you see anyone else? I ain't talking to myself. I mean, I guess I could always go out there and walk around for a while until I find someone who's interested."

Tossing the phonebook aside, Jacen pounces onto a prone Liam, getting astride his legs, rolling him gently to his back. Palming the thick swell of his left pectoral muscle, Jacen slips his other hand around the side of Liam's neck, stroking along the edge of his jaw. Jacen grins down at Liam.

"Wow. That was sudden," Liam blinks. "You're like a puma."

Jacen laughs. "You look nervous," he observes.

Cheeks coloring, squirming slightly, Liam presses up into Jacen's hand unconsciously, reflexively, as it rubs firmly over his chest. Of their own accord, his hips roll forward in a slow drag against Jacen's hard body. Tilting his head to one side to expose his neck more, just out of habit, Liam stops acting out of automatic instinct and realizes that he *is* nervous.

"Um."

Jacen is heavy on his legs, unmovable, huge. There is obvious hunger in his watchful eyes, so light and bright, framed in the dark, almost black waves of his tousled tresses. It's something like what Liam saw in Claudia's chambers that night not so long ago. In a flash, Liam can see it all happening, Jacen making him powerless, devouring him, just like he did on that remembered evening, but in Liam's vision it goes farther. He sees Jacen licking him open, his wicked, twisting fingers everywhere, inside and out, taking Liam apart and then fucking his brains out, holding Liam down and pounding his ass until it's throbbing and Liam is begging, simply *begging* for release, for more, for anything and everything.

Beet red, heart racing, starting to sweat, more than a little claustrophobic, Liam closes his eyes and takes a deep, shuddering, cleansing breath that does nothing to calm his anxiety.

"How about we eat first and try this again another way," Jacen suggests, feeling Liam's tension and seeing glimpses of the biting fear he's trying to hide.

"Yes, please," Liam manages, the plea coming out more strained that he expects it to.

Jacen pulls away, backs off, measuring Liam with a steady look.

"J-Jacen...?"

Smooth as velvet he replies, "Yeah?"

Hesitating, he reaches for Jacen's face, cupping it in a hand, drawing him back in. Their lips hover a hair's breadth apart as they breathe over each other, Liam's soft, nervous gasps audible and utterly intoxicating. Jacen can feel Liam's heart racing under his palm, skipping away.

"Hey. It's fine," Jacen whispers.

Liam makes a soft sound back in his throat, his brow furrowing with regret and self-recrimination. "I'm sorry. It's just — "

"Really. I understand."

"Do you? 'Cause I don't."

"Yeah," Jacen says tenderly.

Sighing, Liam brings him in for a light but lingering kiss. When it's finished, and Jacen leaves him there to go and order the pizza (without bothering to ask Liam what he wants, knowing that Liam always orders the same kind of pizza every time anyway), Liam observes him silently, drawing one knee up to conceal some of his hard-on.

With the pizza ordered, Jacen fishes out the wine, using the plastic cups that came with the room to serve it. Offering Liam a glass, they touch rims and Jacen says, "To the future and our happiness."

"I like that," Liam grins, sipping from his cup, rolling the full, rich taste of the wine back over his tongue.

After nodding to the remote and getting an approving grunt from Liam, Jacen turns on the television and begins to surf through the channels, shifting up to cuddle next to Liam on the bed as they drink their wine.

"Man, I can't wait until we have our own place. Let's drive around a little tomorrow and check some out."

"Okay. Sure."

They find some cheesy game shows and zone out watching them for a while until Liam admits, "This is the longest I've gone without having sex since I was a teenager. It's so bizarre. And sad. It's only been about a week and it feels like forever."

"Do you miss it?"

"Hmm. Yes and no. More yes than no. Mostly because when I think about who it is I'd be having sex with if I *was* having it, now, it makes me miss it."

Jacen hums, rolling to face Liam, nuzzling against his hair, breathing him in. Resting a hand on Liam's side, Jacen rubs down over his waist, around to the small of his back, down over the curve of his ass, palming it.

"Pizza," Liam blurts. "Pizza's coming any minute."

Moaning in complaint, Jacen goes still but doesn't move his hand from its claim, wrapping the side of Liam's ass.

"Fucking pizza," Jacen grimaces.

And Liam is right. Not two minutes later, there's a knock at the door.

They quickly realize how hungry they are and enjoy every bite of their food, though Jacen does eat his share at a faster clip than he usually would.

It's an hour later before they've cleaned up and Liam is ready to go through with it.

Sitting on the edge of the bed, Jacen watches as Liam moves around the room, turning off lights, ensuring drapes are closed, turning off phones and making more than a couple of trips to the bathroom. Once satisfied that everything is in order, he finds some lube and goes to the bed with it. Jacen takes off his shirt, drawing Liam's gaze instantly to his bulging muscles and bare chest.

Stepping up between his legs, Liam fingers through Jacen's hair. He coaxes Jacen backward, up farther onto the bed, guiding him back until he's resting against the pillows that had been propped against the headboard, to lean against while they ate. Jacen gets settled, and shivers slightly when Liam's fingertips skim down the length of his body to the waistband of his pants.

"I'm gonna take these off, okay?"

"Yeah."

Once again, Jacen has no idea what Liam has in mind, only that he doesn't seem so overwhelmed or anxious any more, now that he doesn't have Jacen bearing down on him. The pants slip off, leaving him naked. Liam guides Jacen's thighs open, presses his legs apart and settles on the bed between them, sitting on his heels. Jacen bends his knees, letting his legs fall open wide, even though it makes him uncomfortable to be so very exposed to Liam. One of Liam's hands rubs up Jacen's washboard abs, over his sternum, all the way up to his neck and back down again while the other carefully cradles his heavy, rapidly swelling cock — not moving to stroke it, just holding him.

Jacen shivers, getting harder. Closing his eyes, he rocks gently into the hand as his nipples pebble and his cock jumps. Liam rolls the pad of his thumb over the silken head.

"I just want to touch you for a little while. Is that all right?"

Not trusting his voice, Jacen nods and tries to get comfortable and relax, but it's difficult. He's jittery and tense with anticipation. Liam still feels more like a friend than a lover; the mental shift in roles hasn't entirely kicked in for Jacen. Every thought, every sensation is focused on Liam's hand wrapped around his erection, playing with it, fondling it.

"I never really, you know, get to enjoy someone I like. There's always gotta be a goal. Get off. Finish. Leave. But," Liam says, lightly tracing with a fingertip the thick, pulsing vein twisting around under the skin of Jacen's shaft. "There aren't any rules with you. It's nice. I'm just starting to realize, actually, how much more interesting sex can be now. We can just," with an opened palm, he brushes feather-light, up and down against the underside of Jacen's straining flesh, moving with it as it twitches and swells. "...play."

Jacen groans, fighting to be still and not just greedily hump Liam's hand like he wants to, like his body is telling him to.

"I can just play with you like this for hours, any time I want to," he says thoughtfully.

"I'm, *uh*," Jacen grunts. "Pretty sure that might kill me."

"I think you underestimate your stamina," Liam smiles. "Do you know how gorgeous your body is? I'm just," he twists a hand around Jacen, tugging on him, guiding him to a different angle, making his hips tilt up off the bed, "kind of in constant awe of how hot you are. And this? I love you like this; letting me touch you even though you're kind of afraid to completely relax. Smooth, silky and rock hard at the same time. Your body is *obscenely* fuckable."

"Mm." Jacen undulates and then forces himself to loosen up again. "Liam."

With a tight squeeze up Jacen's length, Liam brings a low, rolling moan from Jacen's lips. Pumping him in a slow, steady rhythm, Liam draws it out as long as he dares. There isn't much more that Jacen is willing to sit back and take.

"Especially since now you're all mine. Knowing that I don't have to share you, with *anyone*? It's intoxicating. And the best thing to happen to me in a long, long time."

Once released, Jacen lets out a sigh. Liam slips out of his pants and straddles Jacen's lap. He takes Jacen's right hand, squirts lubricant onto the fingers, spreading it around and in between them. It's very welcome permission and brings a wide, happy smile to Jacen's face.

Wishing he could see Liam better, that there was more light, Jacen debates lunging for the nearest lamp and grunts, "Yeah?"

"Yeah."

"But I thought you'd want to, with me."

"Oh I do. I mean, if you'd rather...."

Cupping the back of Liam's head to keep him close, his lips right there, warm, full and soft, and a small but noticeable amount of trepidation in his eyes, Jacen drinks him in as his other hand cups under Liam's ass, the fingertips slipping up between his cheeks. A shiver races through Liam's body. Jacen feels it and senses Liam's nervous energy. It's taking a lot for Liam to give Jacen this much, and freely. It's as much as he can give right now, and Jacen feels honored to receive it, and him.

Liam's lips drag back over the scruff covering Jacen's jawline, the rough texture tickling. His small, sharp inhales are soft but audible.

Jacen slips the tip of one finger in up to the first knuckle after tracing around Liam's tightly clenched opening. He parts easily enough with gentle pressure. The hot, soft grip of him around Jacen's finger brings out Jacen's animalistic need. Everything in Jacen tells him to push and get farther inside Liam, to pull him open and thrust inside and move, right there. Holding back with marked effort, he feels Liam shiver again as the finger slides slowly deeper. Liam's fingers claw at Jacen, gripping on to him to remain steady as Jacen enters him.

Gradually, gently, Liam begins to rock, rearing up, and when Jacen just chases after him, moaning quietly as Liam pushes down onto the invading digit.

Kissing the side of Liam's neck, back by his ear, Jacen groans, "God, you're so tight."

Clenching up at the words, Liam seals his lips to hold in a louder, swallowed moan. The grips he has on Jacen's back and shoulder are almost painful in their intensity but Jacen bears it with no problem or complaint. Liam battles his way through his own fears, letting it happen, letting Jacen take what he wants without the buffer of a character or charade to hide behind. Bad things have always happened to him when he's let a loved one in too deeply: hearts get broken, lives are ruined, and happiness is obliterated. Liam tries to trust while hoping it doesn't destroy him in the process. It helps that he's technically on top, and could get away if he needs to. That small detail is the only thing staying him. After committing to Jacen so completely, to their shared future together after so brief a 'courtship', if you could even call it that, Liam needs to preserve something for himself, just for now, but for fear of what, he doesn't even know.

"If you aren't ready for this, I understand," Jacen tells him. The sadness exuding from Liam is palpable. "You wanna be in charge? I'm okay with that if it makes it easier."

"I'm sorry," Liam hisses.

"Hey. You don't ever have to be sorry with me. Just be honest. Okay?"

"Okay."

"Tell me what to do, boss."

He can feel Liam smile against his cheek. "Add another one."

"Yes, sir."

Liam chuckles but it breaks apart with the burn of the stretch. He surges up, pulling almost all the way off and away, and this time Jacen lets him.

"Wanna stop?"

"No," Liam says, shaking his head, sinking back down, and taking Jacen in. Staring at Jacen's earlobe, his shaggy brown hair tucked behind it, Liam anchors himself to reality. "It's okay. I'm okay," he repeats to himself.

Gripping his jaw with strong, gentle pressure, Jacen guides Liam's head back a few inches, just enough to see him as Liam moves in a shallow rocking, dipping rhythm, riding his two fingers. Not a word is said, but Jacen asks clearly enough with his eyes.

Liam replies, somewhat breathlessly, "This'd be so much easier if you didn't give a shit about me."

"You don't have to be anything but you. You don't have to be perfect, or a fantasy. You're allowed to fuck up, or be scared. There aren't any rules here, Lee."

"Just kiss me," Liam asks.

Nodding, Jacen leans in as Liam does. They meet in the middle. Eyes closed, tasting each other, lips and tongues sliding together, their closeness helps dull the edges of things. In a sense they stop being separate beings, Liam and Jacen, and meld into something else, some other creature with two parts, symbiotic.

Liam's movements gain in strength and depth. Scissoring his fingers apart, stroking and twisting, Jacen worships Liam's body with each touch, each kiss. Rolling his hips back, Liam thrusts forward, right against Jacen's straining cock. Their flesh rubs, dragging together. Gasping, clutching at each other, it happens again. Liam thrusts up against Jacen, savoring the way it makes Jacen try to buck and pulse. Reaching down between their bodies, Liam wraps them both in a hand and tugs.

Jacen grunts. When Liam does it a third time, a fourth, Jacen tries and fails to rut up against Liam's silky, steely shaft with Liam's weight holding him down. It continues a little longer, but quickly Jacen is trembling, breathing hard, ready to come.

Liam decides for them, wanting to feel Jacen buried deeply when he climaxes, so he lets him go. Intending to ask Jacen to pull out, the plan changes when Liam gets up on his knees. Jacen strokes in and out of his clenched heat, the lube making it slick and easy. Remembering his old secret fantasy from before any of this happened, before *Claudia* happened, of having Jacen's fingers stretching him out instead of what Liam is used to doing the job—a cold, hard toy—Liam starts to really get off on it. It's empowering that it's Liam provoking Jacen's soft moans, and in that moment there is nothing better than the bending, changing push and tug of the long, thick fingers penetrating him, coaxing his sphincter loose so that Jacen can stuff it full of his fattened cock and fuck Liam's ass to orgasm.

Liam's cries grow slightly louder, sharpening. He exhales shakily against Jacen's sweat-dampened skin.

"Feels good?"

The answer Jacen gets is a whimper. Liam is perfectly still, unmoving, kneeling astride Jacen's lap, letting Jacen fingerfuck him without any help or guidance. Snapping his wrist, Jacen thrusts deep, up to the hilt, then slowly rubs his way out over the velvety soft tissue of Liam's rectum, tugging out completely through his rim only to rub around it, teasing him for a long second before pushing back inside, sighing as he reclaims the place he most wants to be.

"Liam...."

Unthinking, just reacting, Liam grabs his aching cock, jacking himself off. Breath labored, shuddering with desperate need as Jacen caresses over Liam's body, simply touching him, not for any selfish reason other than to give Liam pleasure and because he cares. He cares about *Liam*, not his body, not what Liam can do to him or what Liam can take from him. It's more than that. It's everything that counts. It's everything Liam has, until that moment, not realized he has been missing.

Exhaling sharply at the sweet sounds of Liam's rapidly approaching climax, Jacen kisses him searchingly, tasting Liam's desire, his frantic lust.

With Jacen's fingers playing in his ass, Liam comes with a small cry, painting Jacen's chest with his spend.

Before Liam has even begun to come down, Jacen frees his hand, palms a rubber and gets it on without missing a step after years of practice at it. Grabbing hold of Liam by the hips, Jacen adjusts his angle with a tilt of his pelvis, lining up. He draws Liam down onto him, shifting his hands around to pull Liam's cheeks apart. Once they're aligned, Liam whimpers again into Jacen's mouth. Liam's hand slips over to Jacen's throat, wrapping a come-smeared palm around it to feel Jacen's Adam's apple move as he moans.

A hard grunt is startled out of Liam as Jacen breaches him. After a full week of no sex, his body has begun to recover from some of the abuse it had endured from overuse, tightening back up, so it aches and burns as Jacen stretches Liam wide. Hugged around him, Liam breathes through it, focusing on Jacen, who sounds like he's trying not to blow his load right there, before he's even fully seated. Taking some pride in Jacen's devastated panting and tensed, controlled but sharp thrusts, Liam lets him in, closing his eyes and humming at the possessive pleasure of owning Jacen so intimately for only the second time.

His whole body strung tight, from his arms, his back, his abs, his thighs, even down to his curled toes, Jacen bites back his orgasm, losing his mind from the exquisite snugness of Liam gripping him. Finally, Liam's body weight pulls him down flush to Jacen's pelvis. Observing Jacen's inner battle with a small but pleased grin, Liam only gives him a moment to fight it out with himself before he begins to roll his hips, working himself on Jacen's cock.

"Oh fuck! Li-Liam! I, I can't," Jacen grunts, growling.

Liam's smile widens. His hands rub up Jacen's chest, kneading his pecs, tweaking his erect nipples. After only a few tight figure eights, he pulls up and presses down, beginning to slap down against Jacen's skin, bouncing on his lap.

"God, you *suck*," Jacen complains. "Lee, I'm gonna — I'm gonna come. You have to slow down."

Liam chuckles. "Don't you dare come. I forbid it."

Jacen growls with frustration, tensed up from head to toe, ready to shoot. Gritting his teeth, he lets Liam torment him a few seconds longer before his raw need wins out. Wrapping Liam with an arm wound around his back, the hand clasping to the nape of Liam's neck, Jacen guides him forward, crushing their bodies flush together, chest-to-chest, and plants his feet on the bed.

Jacen begins to snap his hips, fucking Liam roughly, pounding up into him and taking him deeply.

A wrenching moan is surprised from Liam, as he plants a hand on the headboard behind Jacen's head to steady himself, each digging rut of Jacen's huge cock driving the air from his lungs. Blood surges, as Liam struggles to attain a second erection. Sticking out his ass to meet each push, Liam lets Jacen use him, and gets off on it.

Hands palming Liam's bottom, Jacen holds him open and keeps him right where he wants him. With only a few more quick slaps of skin on skin, he's coming with a sharp, thunderous shout, panting and sweating.

"Oh my god. Oh my *god*," he groans, tingling from head to toe, not wanting to let Liam go.

The room steadies once more. Their breathing evens out. Jacen can feel Liam's dick nudging him, the hard line of it. But Liam is quiet, almost too quiet. A small, secret voice in the recesses of Jacen's mind suggests that Liam is probably waiting for his chance to take off, to sneak away to the bathroom, maybe purely from habit, and an instinct of self-preservation.

But Jacen doesn't want to let him go. Closing Liam up in a gentle, complete embrace, pressing kisses in a line to his neck, Jacen makes it last as long as he can.

"Want me to suck you?" he asks quietly.

Liam's chest falls as he exhales in a rush. "No, I'm good."

"You sure?"

"Yeah."

A few minutes later finds Liam locked away in the motel room's bathroom. The sound of the water running in the shower is loud, drowning out what Jacen suspects might be the soft gasps brought on by Liam's second release as he masturbates in the shower.

Once Liam has finished cleaning up, they switch places. When Jacen—freshly showered—returns to the bed, Liam is dressed in pajama pants once more. The sheet is drawn up over him, tangled around him. Climbing into bed beside him, Jacen whispers, "You good?"

Liam rolls toward him. He's smiling. The sight of it lets Jacen breathe easier. Palming his cheek, Jacen smiles back at him. "Yeah. I'm good," Liam sighs.

Loving Liam so much in that moment that he's unable to speak the words, Jacen is grateful when Liam shifts closer, slipping a hand around Jacen's waist. They fall asleep like that, safe in each other's arms.

Chapter 17
Carnal Knowledge

"Do we tell him about this?" Liam asks, holding up his left hand, the ring finger adorned with a gleaming silver band. "Last chance to say no."

"It's Yasha. We can trust him," Jacen says. He scans the diner's menu with a baffled expression. "You know there's seriously every entrée known to man on here. How am I supposed to pick something?"

They have decided to meet Yasha clear across town and far away from their motel, just in case. In case of what, exactly, they don't even permit themselves to speculate. They just know that it makes them feel better about showing their faces to someone who knows who they really are and how to find them. Jacen and Liam have both been friendly with almost all of the employees of The Company, though some more than others. They are also acquainted with some people who have worked their ten-years, like Yasha, and gotten away free and clear. But without specific knowledge of the closeness between Jacen and Yasha, and the assumption that The Company can't be tailing everyone all the time, they are consenting to take the risk of meeting Yasha, though they have asked him to double back a few times to ensure he is not followed on the drive.

"If you say so, but this is our lives, Jace. This isn't a game."

"I never said it was a game." Jacen sets the menu down and glances at the other customers around them. No one is paying the pair of men sitting in a booth by the window any attention, so Jacen continues. "He knows everything about me. He's the only friend we have to depend on, apart from someone you just got in touch with after how many years?"

"About ten," Liam admits.

"Yes, we need to disappear, but it doesn't mean we can't trust anybody."

"Actually, that is what it means. If Yasha knows our names, where we live, our new backstory, he has the ability to fuck everything up, and I don't want to take that chance. I won't do it. It's one thing to meet up with him, and stay in contact over the phone, but I don't want him to have any more leverage on us than he already does."

Jacen sighs and takes a sip of water. "Okay. Compromise," he suggests. "We don't tell him our new name, and we don't tell him where we're staying. No facts. Nothing to help anyone track us."

"But you want to tell him we got hitched?"

There's a pause. Glancing away, off into the parking lot, Jacen says, "Yeah. I mean, it's kind of a big deal to me."

Liam suspects Jacen is thinking about his family and all of the ways they can't share in his life or his victories and be there to catch him when he falls. And Liam agrees that it isn't fair. It isn't fair at all. It feels cruel to deny Jacen this small request, so Liam relents.

"Okay. You can tell him. But that's it. That's as far as it goes."

"Thanks," Jacen beams.

"Yeah yeah."

They don't have long to wait before a familiar motorcycle pulls into the parking lot, swinging around to a spot on the side of the building. There are two people riding it.

"You didn't say he was bringing anyone," Liam frowns.

"It's just Valery. She and Yasha are like a package deal, believe me. Nothing that involves Yasha doesn't involve her, too, at some level. She's very trustworthy."

His patience sorely tried, Liam is momentarily distracted by this. "Wait. Does that mean that when you and Yasha—"

"Later. Okay?" Jacen says, cutting off the question right there and thereby pretty much answering it anyway.

Scowling, Liam picks at the edge of his menu as the couple on the bike climb off, stowing their helmets.

"Wow. That's kind of flattering," Jacen smirks, slouching back in his seat with a dark but proud glimmer in his eyes.

"Excuse me?"

"Nothing."

"No. I want to know what exactly that's supposed to mean," Liam argues. "I didn't say anything. I'm letting it go."

"No, you're not. It bothers you. I can actually tell that it bothers you."

"And what is it that's supposed to be bothering me?"

Jacen swallows his grin, forces his expression to return to a more serious one. Leaning forward, with one eye on the entryway, watching as Yasha and Valery get closer to it, Jacen says, barely above a whisper, "That they both know me in ways you don't yet. Carnally or otherwise. You're jealous."

"Oh, I know you pretty well," Liam scoffs, doing an even poorer job hiding his true thoughts on the matter.

"I agree," Jacen allows. "Is this part of why you didn't want to tell them?"

Liam rolls his eyes and drums his fingertips against the table. Yasha and Valery are nearly within earshot so he doesn't bother answering. Instead he gives Jacen a sly grin, satisfied that the conversation is being thoroughly interrupted and vowing to take out some of his churning, surging possessiveness later by fucking Jacen until he can't even stand.

"Hey! Look who it is," Liam smiles charmingly. Sliding from his seat, he stands politely as Yasha and Valery arrive at their table.

"Liam, good to see you," Yasha nods, shaking Liam's hand.

"Likewise," Liam returns, accepting a one-armed hug from Valery and a light kiss on the cheek. "Valery, if I'm not mistaken?"

"You got it," she smiles, pushing her dark curly hair behind one ear. "But call me Val. Nice to meet you at last. Though I wish it were under better circumstances."

"Oh, I think the circumstances are pretty damn acceptable," Jacen says, getting halfway to his feet as Yasha leans in to kiss Jacen hello, as they always do. One brief smooch later, Liam is frowning again and Valery is leaning in for her own piece of Jacen's lips.

"Shall I move, or..." Liam starts, indicating the seating arrangement.

"This is fine," Yasha says, sliding in beside Jacen as Valery sits beside Liam. "So. Should we order first or get right to the hysterical outrage and astonishment?"

"Order first, I think," Jacen grumbles at a sharp look from Yasha.

"Fine." Following a short visit from their waitress during which Jacen settles on the meatloaf after a non-verbal scolding from Liam when he nearly goes for the fettuccine instead, the scolding coming from Liam's knowledge of Jacen's lactose intolerance, they all sip at their glasses of water and wait for someone to start.

"Okay, I'll go," Yasha says, clearing his throat. "What the fuck were you thinking?"

"That we didn't want to be prostitutes anymore and we want to have respectable lives," Jacen hisses under his breath. "I don't think that's too difficult to understand. We quit, just like you did. We just want to start over."

"This isn't the best way to do it, and you know it. I didn't quit, I worked off my time. There's a big difference. You just sneak away? Breach of contract, The Company on your asses...."

"We had no choice," Liam says sternly. "We wanted out without being screwed any more, figuratively and literally, than we already were. No strings, no time frames, no explanations." Pointing at Jacen, Liam hisses, "He had *nine years* left. You expect me to let them have free rein to do whatever the hell they want to him for nine years?"

"But you called me. That's a string. This is an explanation."

"Jacen wanted to include you to some extent. Your friendship is an important thing for him to maintain, and I won't deny him that if it means that much."

"Why are you together? Wouldn't it be safer to be apart?"

"We left in order to be together," Jacen says quietly. "Or at least that's my take on it."

"It was my idea," Liam says. "I didn't want Jacen anywhere near those lowlifes. I convinced him it was time to go."

"And what does Jacen get out of all of this? Homelessness? Joblessness? A lack of direction in his life?"

"He gets a family who loves him and the freedom to do whatever he wants, without anyone to answer to."

"'Cept for you," Jacen smiles, warming at Liam's defense of him.

"Wait," Valery interjects. "What does that mean? What family?"

Jacen lifts his hands above the table, resting them there in front of him, his wedding ring shining under the fluorescents.

"Whoa," Yasha gapes. "You got married?! Who did you marry?"

They all turn and simultaneously look at Liam, who clears his throat and unfolds his own hands, displaying his own, matching ring.

For what seems like too long a time, no one says anything. Then Yasha, his face a storm of outrage, shouts, "*Horseshit!*"

"Shh!" Valery scolds him, grabbing his hand to pull him back into his seat when he tries to stand and come around to grab Liam by the throat. "Stop it. Don't make a scene!"

"You don't care about him!" Yasha growls, lowering his voice with effort. "You *married* him?! Mister Two-Face-Fucking-Taye? The guy who played you for his own amusement just the other day, leaving you miserable and showing up on our doorstep just to help you figure out what you could have possibly done to insult his Highness who flat-out ditched you? Fuck and run. That's who you are, Liam. Why the *fuck* would you two get married?! Even as a cover, it's insulting."

"Insulting?!" Liam nearly shouts, his voice sharpening with the cutting edge of defensiveness.

"Yes! He deserves better!" Yasha rages, pointing to Jacen.

"It's not a cover! I mean, okay, yeah it is to some extent but that's not why we did it. If it was just for the name we would have done it without bothering to see a judge and dealing with all the legal hassle of that. We did it because it was what we wanted and I do care about him! I care about him a hell of a lot more than you do!"

"Oh yeah? Prove it," Yasha dares.

"Would you cut it out, please?" Valery hisses to her husband. "You aren't helping and you know it."

"I *will* prove it. Just give me a chance. Ask Jacen what he thinks.

Ask him if he's happy, if he's glad we did it. Don't take my word for it."

"I'm sure he is happy, but he's also delusional if he really believes you care about him. You're a professional con artist and you're playing him for a fool," Yasha spits. "You're taking advantage of the fact that he has a big heart and an innate need to be cared about in order to make yourself feel better."

"Get up," Jacen barks at Yasha. "Get out of the fucking booth."

Confused, Yasha obeys, sliding out of the seat, letting Jacen push past him.

"Jacen," Liam calls apprehensively. "Jacen?!"

He tries to get up, but he's blocked by Valery.

"Jacen!"

Jacen is at the door opening out onto the parking lot by the time Yasha snaps out of it, though he manages it before Liam is able to free himself from his seat to pursue his new husband.

"Fuck. I'll get him," Yasha groans, the fight draining from him in a flash.

As soon as Yasha is darting after Jacen, Valery groans into her palms. Hanging her head, she says urgently, "Liam, I'm so sorry for that. He's just got this soft spot for Jacen and I swear that despite what he said it's not a personal attack against you. Ever since Jacen signed that contract, even after Yasha tried as hard as he could to talk him out of it.... Jacen only found out about The Company because of Yasha's past, and he's always felt solely responsible for that, and him. He's just worried sick about Jacen's safety and he's freaked out. "

"I know," Liam sighs, battling down his temper and panic. It helps that he can still see Jacen, standing right outside, now with Yasha in his face, talking passionately to him, alternately gesturing with his hands and holding Jacen's shoulders like he's afraid Jacen will take off again.

"He loves him. He's been in love with him ever since... well. But, anyway, you really did it, huh? Jacen's your husband," she marvels.

"Yeah. He is. He's—" Liam takes a deep breath, holds it and lets it back out, "—everything to me. Making him happy. Keeping him safe. Hearing him laugh. That's all I care about. He's the only thing in my life that matters. Took me long enough to figure that out. Anyway, I mean, yeah, maybe we went about it the wrong way, but it was with good intentions."

"I can see that," she says gently. "He makes you want to be a better man."

Liam nods, laughing with self-consciousness, morosely. It quickly threatens to turn into a sob. He covers his mouth with the back of a hand, waiting for it to pass. Valery rubs his back and tsks Yasha again.

"Jacen was so excited to tell him about this," Liam admits quietly. "What we did, getting married. I told him it was a bad idea, but he wouldn't listen. He was just so happy to share good news, and...." He can't get any more out, pained by the thought of Jacen's innocent, dashed hope.

Valery sighs. "Dammit Yasha."

Outside the diner, located at the tail end of sunny San Luis Obispo, California, Jacen folds his arms over his broad chest and tries diligently to ignore the man he trusts most in the world.

"Just come back inside and sit down," Yasha pleads. "I promise that large pointy stick that was previously lodged up my ass has been removed. Clearly I'm the jerk here, and I'm sorry. Jacen? Hey. Come on. Jacen?"

"So I'm a sucker? An easily manipulated idiot who doesn't have the balls to stand up for himself? That's what you think of me? Now I know, I guess."

"That's not what I think of you. You can be..." Yasha debates what the right word is and settles on, "sensitive. That's not necessarily a bad thing but I meant what I said about you having a big heart. You care too much, sometimes, even when you're trying not to, and more than is healthy. Look, it doesn't matter if I think this is a bad idea. If you're content and out of harm's way, that's good enough for me. Is he taking care of you?"

Jacen sets his jaw, staying silent.

"Does he love you as much as you love him?"

Jacen is able to mask his rising emotion only a few seconds longer before dampness pricks at his eyes. They redden and his tears threaten to spill over. He holds them in. "He's my husband now. He bound himself to me. I don't have to explain anything to you. I only told you because I *foolishly* thought you'd be happy for me, but clearly I was very wrong about that. I regret calling you. We should have just made a clean break and left everything behind."

"I'm glad you didn't leave us behind," Yasha says tenderly, marveling at how far Jacen has come from the damaged, jaded kid he used to be. That he cares enough to want to hold on to their friendship even after he's fled speaks volumes. Once upon a time, Jacen was able to walk away from his entire family, dissolving all ties to them, but for some reason, he wants to retain his friendship with Yasha. He doesn't want to lose everything again. And that's remarkable progress.

"I love you, Jacen. Do you know what it would have done to me, to find you'd gone missing and just vanished? To never see or hear from you again? You don't, do you?" Closing a hand over Jacen's forearm, Yasha tells him, "I really am sorry for hurting you. I didn't think before I spoke, and I should have. I, um, reacted emotionally rather than with consideration or forethought and that wasn't fair to you, or to Liam. Please don't shut me out, TJ. Your friendship means too much to me to lose it like this."

The use of the old nickname, one from Jacen's childhood, hits him sharply. Squeezing his eyes closed, he doesn't pull away when Yasha hugs him. After a moment, Jacen hugs him back.

By the time they get back to the table, their food is being laid out by the waitress. Jacen follows behind Yasha, whose gaze is locked on Liam rather than his wife's disapproving glare.

"Liam, I'm sorry for the things I said," Yasha professes. "Both you and Jacen deserve better than that from someone who's supposed to be a supportive friend. Congratulations on your union. I wish you both a long lifetime filled with happiness together. It's just a shame you don't have more people to celebrate with."

"You don't have to pretend you approve," Jacen mutters, sitting down. Liam reaches across the table, taking Jacen's hand, brushing the back of it with the pad of his thumb and holding his gaze with a look of loving concern.

"What *I* think is irrelevant. If this is what you want, if this is the life you want, then I support it one hundred percent." Yasha unfolds his napkin and asks, "Are you two at all curious about what's happening in L.A.? The chaos you caused?"

"We caused chaos?"

"I touched base with Ryan and David," Yasha explains. "Just out of general curiosity as to why William hasn't returned my calls regarding some information I needed for someone I've been treating. They have no idea what happened to you two. No leads, from what anyone can tell. The talk is, the higher ups were furious but now that they can't find you, they are refocusing on keeping the clients happy and bulking up staff as quickly as possible. They've decided it's a waste of resources to continue searching for you."

Liam and Jacen share a queasy look. "Great. So some poor, naïve kids get to take our places."

"There's always a poor kid or five waiting in the wings. You can't save everyone," Yasha tells him. "Luckily The Company treats its employees fairly well for the business they're in. Considering."

"Yeah," Liam groans morosely.

"What are you two going to do next? Travel?" Valery asks.

"Find somewhere to live," Jacen says. "Get a real job."

"Make a home," she smiles fondly. "With a shitty job and some shitty kids."

"Exactly," Jacen smiles back. "My dream come true." At Liam's questioning cock-eyed glance, Jacen tells him, "I'll explain later. It's... a thing."

"If you say so," he says with confusion.

"You really do seem content, Jace," she says. "I think it's incredible. And I think Liam is incredible if this is the direction things are going for you. Is there anything at all that we can do to help?"

"Keep an eye out and an ear to the ground. Most of all, don't let on that you know where we are. And stay in touch."

"No problem," she nods with a grin.

Chapter 18

Seeing From the Other Side

After an afternoon spent driving around aimlessly, scouting out available houses, townhouses, condos and even apartment buildings, leaving nothing off the table and sure they'll know where they're meant to live when they see it, Jacen and Liam have a wonderfully mundane evening at the motel. Jacen makes do cooking a supper of gourmet burgers and fresh salad in their room, using a tiny plug-in grill and a plethora of veggies from a farmer's market nearby. Liam can't stop smiling the entire time, watching Jacen crouch on the sidewalk outside their door, hunching over the ridiculously small grill and poking at the burgers with a plastic fork. Liam helps with preparing the produce, but once he starts chopping things that needn't be chopped, Jacen steers him back to their collection of newspapers, placing a highlighter in his hand and patting his head.

The food is delicious. Liam sees Jacen's cooking skills as miraculous or magical, and tells him that he should consider using them to find a job. The suggestion surprises Jacen with how very intrigued he is by it. He falls silent, thinking it through, trying to figure out how it could work, given he has no formal training or experience.

Once everything is cleaned up and stowed away, the pair finds themselves sitting side-by-side on the couch, their fingers tangled loosely together on the cushion between them. In front of them, the TV is on but muted.

"I wish it had gone differently today," Liam says. "I wish he'd just been happy for you."

"I know. Me too."

"But I get it. I mean, who am I? Some whore you moved in with a few months ago, who's been oblivious to exactly how amazing you are until very, very recently, and after I abscond you away, I talk you into getting hitched in a shotgun wedding that's completely ludicrous."

Jacen processes this, pauses, opens his mouth to speak, shuts it, and then a wide smile blooms on his face. "We're married."

"Jesus," Liam sighs, but laughs. "That's all you took from that, huh?"

"There was more? I mean, I did hear something about me being amazing. Tell me more about that."

Liam swats Jacen's leg.

"It's good that he's protective of you like that—Yasha. Makes me like him more. And Valery. She's great."

"Yeah," Jacen smiles fondly.

Neither of them speaks for a long while. The wind whistles and blows outside as a storm rolls in. It's entrancing and soothing in a profound way. Rain patters against the windows, then teems. Tap-tap-tapping one minute, beating against the roof and walls the next.

"Tell me about him?" Jacen asks hesitantly, only looking over at Liam after he gets the question out. "Timothy? What was he like?"

"He was... huh. I... wow. I guess I'm just realizing that I never had to classify him before. The only people that knew of him, knew him personally, so I never had to, like, introduce him to anyone. And I've never, you know, spoken of him since."

"You don't have to. I'm just interested. He means so much to you, so you should be able to talk about him. He lights you up. It's kind of beautiful."

Liam looks over at Jacen, holding his gaze, searching his face and Jacen has a moment of pure undiluted happiness that he has this, this closeness with Liam. "Show me the wallet again."

Liam debates it a second, then relents and slips it out, handing it over. Jacen opens it to the tattered photo of Liam's first, true love.

"He always had these wild ideas, you know," Liam starts. "'Liam, I've got this great idea,' he'd say, almost falling over himself he was so excited to tell me about it and get started on whatever it was."

"He called you Liam?"

"Yeah, sometimes. Usually when it was all of us together. When it was just him and me, alone, he called me by my first name."

"Avery?"

"Yeah. That's why I changed it. I'm not that guy anymore. Avery is dead. Just like Tim."

The absence of emotion in those cruel words hurts Jacen. He takes a moment to mourn those lost young boys, taking on the whole world all by themselves and suffering for it. For what might be the first time, his childhood doesn't seem so bad. At least he had parents, shelter, food.

Liam's hand slips over Jacen's long leg, brushing absent-mindedly over the fabric encasing it. "He was a good kid," he says softly. "Tried as hard as he could to do what his heart told him to do, without apology. He just..." Liam sighs thickly. "He didn't think stuff out like he should have and made some really bad calls. But what do you expect? He was a teenager with no guidance, no parents or guardians whoopin' his ass to get him to toe the line. He thought he was invincible. And he wasn't. So he wasted away right before my eyes until he was a shell of himself, hollow, empty and grey. And then one day he closed his eyes and just never opened 'em again. You know, I never had any fanciful notions of what the world is like. I had a hard-ass upbringing. But I never really got it until then. The truth is that sometimes nightmares come true and there's no way out. You have no choice but to survive and keep getting out of bed in the morning."

"Lee, I'm so damn sorry," Jacen says urgently.

"No, it's okay. It is. Because I can finally say that I did what he's been whispering in my ear to do for *years*. I stopped wallowing like a coward and now I have a chance to really act on that vibrant spirit that drove him. Maybe there's a reason for all of it. Maybe I can do something good for the people trapped in this world before I leave it. And I feel so guilty for being as happy as I am. For years I tried to figure out why it had to be him, and not me. But I'll never know why, and maybe that's all right. I'm really happy, Jace. And that's all you."

Jacen places the wallet back in Liam's hand and kisses his cheek. "You love me."

"I do love you," Liam agrees solemnly. "Can I ask you something? Since we're in a pensive sort of mood anyway."

"Sure. Go for it."

"Do you always hate it? Receiving? And I feel like shit for not asking you sooner, but I'm asking now. Please be honest with me," Liam asks.

"Not anymore," Jacen says with almost peaceful calmness. "I learned to like it. It can feel so good to trust someone that much and give that much pleasure to the other person. Makes me feel kind of powerful. It's all in how you look at it."

"Yasha taught you that."

Jacen pauses, staring out at a point in mid-air. "Yeah," he says slowly. "But it's totally different with you. You're the first person I've been with that makes me feel so completely safe and cared for. With you, I can tell that you want me like that because it's *me*, and it's not just about the sex. I like that. Even with Yasha, there was still a sense of duty behind it."

Quiet falls for a long moment and then Liam turns suddenly, catching Jacen's mouth in a slow, searching kiss.

When they break, Liam seems anguished. "After all you went through, you have this strength inside of you that I just don't. It's incredible. I wish I was strong like you. I wish I could stop being afraid. I don't even know what I'm afraid of anymore."

"Hey," Jacen urges. "You'll be ready when you're ready. I understand why you're tired of giving away pieces of yourself to others. If you need time to heal some more before you're comfortable letting go, then that's okay. It's okay to need to be in control of something."

"I just don't know why I can't just...." Liam exhales sharply, frustrated. "Just relax and let you — "

"*I* do. I know why. You were forced to be okay with it the first time you submitted to me. That leaves scars. I know all about shit like that. And I have no expectations of you getting over that really fast. I have news for you, Lee, I'm not going anywhere. If it takes ten years I'll still be right beside you, waiting for you, and cherishing every second I have with you and every kiss you give me and every time you make love to me."

"You want me like that, though, don't you?" Liam asks like he already knows the answer.

"It's just how I am," Jacen admits. "I've always enjoyed dominating and being the giver. There's less baggage for me that way, and it's just a preference, just like you've got a similar preference. Doesn't mean we can't enjoy other things, too."

Liam glances away, hiding his expression from Jacen.

"What? What'd I say?"

"That's not my preference," he says in barely a whisper. It's mumbled and low, embarrassed.

"Oh. God, I should have realized. That's why it's hard for you," Jacen realizes, looking more closely at Liam. "You're a bottom."

"I—" Liam starts. His mouth works soundlessly for a few moments, then closes again.

Jacen sits up straighter, staring at Liam with growing heat behind his eyes, remembering their few passionate moments together, looking at them in a whole new way. Feeling the weight and sharpness of Jacen's gaze upon him, Liam tries to will himself invisible. "I have a mental block, okay? When I think about you, the way you were that night with Claudia, how you looked at me, like every filthy thing you wanted to do to me was about to happen simply because you wanted it to, and you *knew* you could seduce me into it, and maybe also knew I'd have to let you because it was my job to let you.... You have no idea how much I want to be okay with that, but then I just can't seem to pretend to be anything but myself, no matter how hard I try and—"

Liam is pressed back lengthwise on the couch, his head pillowed by the armrest as Jacen surges down on top of him, trapping him as he catches Liam's mouth in a dirty, hungry kiss. Liam swallows a groan and feels his heart leap into his chest when Jacen roughly pulls Liam's outer leg up around Jacen's lower back, hooking it there, opening him up. Then Jacen rubs in a greedy push up the underside of Liam's leg, up his thigh all the way to his ass, palming it as they kiss.

At first Liam is okay. Jacen tongue-fucks his mouth and squeezes his ass. Then Jacen begins to grind against him, thrusting against the junction of Liam's legs. Easing the leg wrapping around his back higher, Jacen rocks against Liam's bottom. His fingers hook inside the waistband of Liam's pants. They're chest-to-chest and Jacen can feel Liam's heart jumping, beating too wildly, the quickened gasping of Liam's breath, more panic than anything.

Instantly, Jacen tries to put on the brakes. He stops thrusting and stills his movements. Putting a buffer of space between them after guiding Liam's leg back down, Jacen kisses in a line down Liam's throat to his collarbone. Intending to break away, he's instead lured in by the clean taste and heat of Liam's skin, and sucks hard at his pulse point. Liam surges up into the contact, grabbing a handful of Jacen's hair and moaning loudly as Jacen nips and sucks and marks him, leaving a dark bruise.

"Let-let me up," Liam growls. "Jace. Let me up."

His pupils blown black, Jacen can't even pretend to hide how hard up he is, how crazy with lust. Enough of his brain is still working to inform him that he's being a jackass for trying to take from Liam exactly what he's just confessed he wasn't ready for, so he hangs his head and hides his face in his hands, elbows planted on his knees as Liam gets up off the couch.

Once I'm more composed, Jacen tells himself, *I'll apologize profusely.*

He doesn't get the chance. Liam shoves Jacen back against the cushions, grabs his knees and yanks them forward, making Jacen sag even farther into the back of the seat. Roughly yanking Jacen's pants open, tugging them down to mid-thigh, Liam settles on his knees between Jacen's feet, holding his gaze with a steady, dangerous look. Fitting Jacen's massive hard-on in the junction of his thumb and forefinger, Liam extends his tongue and licks in a wide stripe over the head, rolling the taste of him back into his mouth, moaning at the salty, thick flavor. Jacen palms the back of Liam's head and, wasting no time, Liam wraps his lips around Jacen and feeds him slowly back over his tongue, taking a few inches, hollowing his cheeks and pulling back off. Then he does it again, feeding him a little deeper, pressing with his tongue along the underside and sucking as hard as he's able as he pulls off a second time with a slurp.

"Li-Liam," Jacen pants, wrecked already. "Fuck your mouth."

With a wicked grin, Liam plants his hands on Jacen's thighs, holding on to him as he begins to suck him off. Head bobbing in Jacen's lap, Jacen's flushed length slips wet, pumping in and out from between Liam's sinful lips, stretched wide with his mouthful. Liam takes Jacen deeply enough to get his hips bucking up off the couch. Jacen's free hand flies to Liam's head, to better hold on to it, guiding his pace, and scratching desperately over his scalp as Jacen's need coils like a snake ready to strike.

Before he erupts, Jacen drags Liam up off of the floor, his fist twisted in Liam's shirtfront. With a growl, Jacen licks back into Liam's mouth, sucking the taste of himself from Liam's lips. But Liam doesn't ease up, letting Jacen have his mouth as he manually brings Jacen off, hungrily drinking down Jacen's explosive, breathless cry.

"It's—" Jacen gasps, trying to recover " —official. I'm the luckiest bastard in the world. Hands down. Goddammit."

Liam chuckles, "You're welcome." Leaning close to Jacen's ear, Liam clears his throat and asks in a gruff voice, "Can I?"

"Baby, you can do whatever the fuck you want to do."

"Good. 'Cause all I want's to be balls deep in you right the fuck now."

"Is it always going to be this much fun to work through our issues?" Jacen asks deliriously, his voice breaking as Liam yanks Jacen's pants the rest of the way off and manhandles him around so that he's kneeling on the cushions, holding the back of the couch.

Spitting thickly onto his fingers, wriggling them up into Jacen, getting harder at the low grunt Jacen makes in response, Liam scissors his fingers apart and leers, "Nah, once we get the test results back and know for sure that we're clean and I can finally do you bareback, it's gonna be *so much fuckin' better*."

Pulling his fingers free, Liam fits his condom-sheathed member to Jacen's opening, letting gentle pressure stretch him open the rest of the way. Jacen shudders and shivers, his head falling as he pushes back against Liam, swallowing him up.

"And once I get over my shit," Liam promises, "you can hold

me down, tie me up, stuff me full of that gorgeous cock and fuck me 'til I scream any goddamned time you want to."

Jacen moans sharply and starts to fuck himself back onto Liam. "Because no one else gets to have that from you but me."

"That's right," Liam grins. "And *no one*," he growls, snapping his hips, plunging in up to the hilt, driving the breath from Jacen's lungs, "gets to have *you*," he draws back and does it again, holding Jacen's hips to keep him still, "like *this*," one more time. "But *me*."

"Yours," Jacen gasps.

"Damn fuckin' right. Anyone else tries to touch you, I break their goddamned hand."

The possessive, protective, wildness in Liam's words gets Jacen off fast. He comes at the same time that Liam does, and hopes the dull ache from the force of Liam's movements lasts all night long, to serve as a reminder of the promises made.

Chapter 19
Asking for It

The speed with which Liam and Jacen found themselves dislodged from their previous existence was dizzying. Realities shifted overnight. Up became down. Night became day. Nothing was certain. Given this fact, and their subsequently frazzled mental states, Liam in particular is lured into a conviction that things will begin to slow down and stabilize again seeing as how they've attained a modicum of safety. Sure, the motel isn't ideal, but it works for their basic needs and there is no reason to rush any more major decisions. This is why Liam is utterly unprepared for it when Jacen comes back from an emergency panini run with not just a bag full of hot, fantastic-smelling food, but a job to boot.

After tossing the bag down onto the motel room's small table, Jacen spills the news in a torrent of words. "It was incredible, Lee. I saw the help wanted sign posted but didn't really think much of it until I got talking with the woman that was serving me. Her dad owns the place and they had a really bad experience with their last chef. He had this massive ego, I guess, came right out of culinary school and they're looking for someone who they'll get along with better. They said they don't mind someone learning on the job if they're a good fit and I don't know. One minute I was placing my order and the next I'm sitting in the back office answering questions about my cooking style and availability and they hired me. I start tomorrow afternoon. Joe Barbara, he's the owner, he wants to see how I do with the current menu. The crowd won't be too crazy since it's a Tuesday, so I can ease into it, but can you believe it? I don't have training, or, you know, experience, but they were willing to look past that and this is huge. This is like a dream come true! I want to take you down there. I mean, we should eat first, of course, but I want you to see it. You never know, our luck could hold out and we might see some place on the market in the area and it could be our new home."

"Whoa. Slow down. Take a breath, sit down. You look like you just ran all the way back here." Liam pulls out a chair for Jacen and glances over the Barbara's Bistro logomark on the paper bag.

"I could have!" Jacen gushes, his skin flushed hot and glistening with a light sheen of sweat. "I feel so energized, like I could run clear across the state if I wanted to."

"This is just really sudden. Are you sure this is the right fit?"

"Yes, it's the right fit! It's a perfect fit. Why? You don't think so?" The light begins to die in Jacen's eyes, crushing his overjoyed, enlivened spirit, so Liam holds his tongue, pushes past his concerns and smiles.

"I think it's awesome. I don't think I've ever seen you this excited about something before. I guess I was just surprised."

"Me too! It was just... *bam!*"

"And you don't think it's taking on too much? I mean you said it yourself; you don't have formal training in this type of thing. We've both been pretty stressed from the move and all. I just don't want to see you jumping into this only to be disappointed."

"Lee, I swear I can handle this. All I was praying for was a chance, just a chance to show someone that I can do it. I'll work my butt off. I'll listen and take direction and use every trick I know."

Hands flattened on the tabletop as if he's bracing himself against the blistering speed of Jacen's decision-making, Liam looks over at Jacen, who is bursting with joy and renewed faith in the universe. "You're going to be amazing, Jace, I know it. I believe in you."

Jacen's cheeks dimple deeply as he grins, surging toward Liam, sweeping him off his feet in a bear hug and groaning loudly against him.

He sets Liam down and flops into a chair, doling out the food and patting Liam's seat to get him to settle into it. "The pay isn't extravagant. It's nothing like we're used to pulling in, but there's a health plan and retirement benefits and dental and it's totally legit."

Jacen's eyes sparkle at the idea. "And we've got enough saved to last us a lifetime as long as we're not stupid about it, so the salary's just gravy anyway. I've got a job. A real job. I can provide for us, and once we find a home we're set. God, I want to tell everybody but I can't so I feel like I'm just going to explode with happiness."

Liam lets Jacen ramble on, exploring every idea that passes through his mind aloud as the reality of what he's accomplished settles in. Liam eats while Jacen talks, and the food is good. Jacen finishes his own sandwich in huge bites which he tries to talk around, causing Liam to fear the obvious choking hazard. It would be spectacularly ironic, after all, for Jacen to die by the sandwich that sparked his good fortune just as all his dreams seem to be coming true.

It's two in the afternoon when they head out, bellies full and Jacen itching to show Liam his new place of employment. It's a ten minute drive. They park in a small lot set back off of the road, which they cross as they walk in the direction of the bistro. The neighborhood is quaint but bustling, with shops as far as the eye can see; a coffee bar, a bank, a community center and any number of businesses lining the road. People filter in and out of the buildings, drinks or shopping bags clutched in hand. Still about half a block from their destination, Liam tries to soak it all in, scanning the street. He pauses, reading the signs labeling the stores as Jacen goes on ahead, impatient.

Liam is getting ready to hurry and catch up again when a group of attractive, well-dressed women emerge from the coffee place on the corner and pass very close to Jacen on the sidewalk. One of them is a petite, platinum blonde and, judging purely by the superficial, Liam decides there's no chance she wasn't a snooty cheerleader type in high school. She smiles seductively up at Jacen and purrs, "Hi."

"Hey," Jacen smiles back at her, years of instinct coming into play as his natural charm and adorably dimpled grin radiate warmth and friendliness. Pushing his long, dark hair back with a hand, his attention lingers with her a moment longer.

"I'm Logan," she says, extending a hand to him.

"He's taken," Liam interjects, finally catching up to Jacen's side, hands balled up into fists, hidden in the front pockets of his jeans.

There's an awkward couple of seconds when Jacen seems to struggle to figure out what's going on, what he's doing, what Liam is doing, and so on.

"Maybe you should let him decide that," Logan says before turning her back to Liam, facing Jacen once more.

"I have actually. He's not interested. Back off."

"Seems interested enough to me," she retorts, planting her hands on her dainty hips.

Liam fumes, jaw clenched, eyes blazing.

Logan scoffs, "What's your problem, anyway?"

Jacen looks on, dumbstruck, as Liam spits, "My problem is with you trying to hit on my husband."

Now it's Logan's turn to be dumbstruck as Jacen finally finds his tongue. "Liam. Be cool. It's okay," Jacen says calmly, taking his arm. "Come on."

He guides Liam away from the growing crowd of onlookers, and down a fairly deserted side street. Liam yanks his arm free and steps into an alcove, hissing under his breath, "'Be cool'? What the fuck was that?"

"What? I just said hello."

"That wasn't just hello. You smiled at her like you were flirting with her. I know the difference between hello and *hello*."

"You're being crazy," Jacen says quietly, blocking the stares of a few nearby people with his broad back. "It's polite to say hi to someone who acknowledges you. What do you want me to do, ignore people?"

"You're trying to teach me etiquette now? Some bimbo just tried to pick you up on the street and you want to turn it into a lesson in manners?"

"Liam," Jacen says, stepping closer to him, lowering his voice even more. "No one's picking me up. There's nothing to worry about. We're here, together, to check out the area because the restaurant that just hired me is nearby. I'm glad you're so quick to defend my honor, but really, I've got this."

Liam tells himself that Jacen wouldn't have engaged Logan any farther than a brief exchange. He wouldn't have tried to pick her up like he was out here working the street, but seeing with his own eyes how fast Jacen slipped into that suave, disarmingly charming role he plays so well—flirtatious and sensual—causes Liam to drown in a surge of jealousy and fearful possessiveness that he can control no more than he can control the way that, even now, people are looking at them, watching their heated exchange. And then he remembers everything Jacen has told him about how he got his job offer, that he fell into conversation with a waitress at the bistro and she was all too happy to tell him about the open position. That makes it worse.

Biting his tongue, digging his fists deeper into his pockets, Liam attempts to master his reaction and remain silent rather than say something he might later regret.

"Should we just go back to the room?" Jacen remains aggravatingly passive and composed, not a feather ruffled, a counterpoint to Liam's formless inner uproar.

This is supposed to be about him, Liam reminds himself with effort. *We're supposed to be here so that he can include me in this victory and I'm shitting all over it, just like Yasha did with the marriage announcement.*

After taking a deep breath in, holding it, and then letting it back out, Liam reins in his temper.

"No, I'm fine. Show me where you work. I want to see it."

"If you're not up for it, then..." Jacen starts.

The apology won't come, no matter how hard Liam tries to formulate it. He's not sorry for speaking up when he did. Part of the problem is lingering stubbornness and maybe even remnants of anger initially brought on by having to witness Jacen and Patrick together.

"I'm fine," Liam repeats a little more forcefully.

Liam isn't sure why Jacen does it, all he knows is that one moment he's standing there, slouching, glowering, jaw clenched, trying to see everything at once—Jacen, the people beyond Jacen who are milling about, the cars driving past, even the patrons inside the stores and restaurants, just on the very unlikely off-chance that a spy from The Company is there, somewhere. The next moment, Jacen's big, warm hand is wrapping lightly around the side of his throat as he leans in to kiss Liam pointedly. It's firm and possessive, determined, and Liam bends to it instantly, letting himself be thoroughly kissed.

When Jacen straightens, his fingers slip downward to find Liam's wrist, tugging his hand free of his pocket and claiming that too.

The fight drains from Liam. Lips tingling, hyperaware of Jacen's hulking presence by his side, their hands joined, Liam feels shaken and fumbles, "Look, I really...."

"We'll discuss it later. For now just walk with me."

For what might be the first time since Timothy died, Liam doesn't feel in control at all. Jacen has all of the control, but it's somehow okay. It doesn't make him nervous at all.

Jacen leads them through the crowd, keeping Liam close, not making eye contact with anyone if he can help it. He's able to feel the heat baking off of Liam, now quiet and chastened. But Liam's initial surge of energy was brought on because he was tense and irate, completely out of control of his reaction to something as innocent as a hello with a stranger, when Jacen knows for a fact that Liam has weathered much worse with less trouble. It's empowering and enlightening for Jacen to see how much his behavior affects his new partner, hard proof of the shifting dynamic between them. And somehow Jacen knew that all he had to do to balance things back out was to give Liam back some of his cherished coping mechanisms.

By leaving words behind, just kissing him instead, Jacen had managed to underline, for anyone looking on, exactly what the nature of their relationship was, should anyone continue to doubt it or should Logan still be near enough to see, for Liam's sake more than anything. Jacen had also taken the disagreement back to a more intimate, physical level, showing Liam what his role is to play. And Jacen felt the precise moment when Liam chose to obey and submitted completely. It was a flickering change behind his eyes, a shift in his posture, a softening of the intensity that had thus far been vibrating from him.

They reach their destination, Barbara's Bistro. Not intending to go inside, they remain out front, taking it in—the dark, heavy, ornately carved decorations on the exterior, even more of the same rich wood continuing inside in the beams in the ceiling, the molding, and the floor. The restaurant is filled with neat little round tables covered with crisp white linens which are flanked by high-backed, decadently upholstered chairs which add to the ambiance. Tasteful candles on the tables and similar, larger sconces on the walls light the space with soft, flickering warmth.

"There's a wine tasting bar on the side," Jacen explains, pointing it out. "And they specialize right now in slow-cooked meats. It smells *amazing* in there, Lee. It's like heaven. Joe told me he used to love to travel all over the world, but especially to Paris, so when he settled down with his daughter, Lily, he decided to open this place to remind him of where he'd loved to eat when he was abroad."

"I love it. It's gorgeous." Liam weaves his fingers more closely between Jacen's. "You really are a lucky bastard, aren't you?"

Jacen grins down at him, nudging him with an arm.

"Damn. I'm gonna need to join a gym or something, because if you're gonna be cooking all the time, or bringing home all of this incredible food, I've gotta find a new way to burn the calories."

"Maybe I'd like a little more meat on your bones," Jacen whispers conspiratorially to him, right by his left ear. "More to grab on to when I'm having my way with you."

Liam squints up at him. "Or you just don't wanna chance the sweaty, juiced-up, muscle-heads at the gym flirting with me while you're off at work."

"Mm," Jacen hums thoughtfully. "They can look. But they can't touch." He briefly takes hold of Liam's chin, his gaze sliding in a long measuring glance down Liam's body. It makes Liam shiver, butterflies knocking around in his stomach. He feels himself growing inexplicably shyer by the second.

When Jacen just keeps looking hungrily at Liam like *he's* a piece of slow-cooked meat, one he's more than ready to sink his teeth into or roll around in his mouth for a while, Liam clears his throat and points out, "Okay. We *were* discussing your new, fabulous job. I know you just wanted to take a look, but should we go in, or...."

"Nah. Let's just walk around a little more."

"Mm. So you, um, you didn't want to get out of here? Head back to the room?" Liam murmurs, rubbing a hand back through his short hair.

A slow, purely wicked grin spreads over Jacen's face, making his eyes spark bright and hot.

"Why would we want to go back to the room?"

"Well," Liam mumbles, his gaze skittering around the side-walk, still watching out, looking at everything but the way Jacen is eye-fucking him. "You know, on the off chance that you wanted to, I mean... come on. We're both in a period of adjustment right now. And, for my part, at least, I'm used to a certain level of... activity. Like daily. Sometimes hourly. And it feels strange to not, uh, have that anymore. So I think we should try to maybe kick the frequency up a little bit more than we have been. Just for the sake of a smooth-er transition."

Jacen swallows a dark chuckle, his smile only growing, with eyes only for Liam in his sweetly awkward horniness, just drinking it up like nectar.

"Stop smiling at me like that," Liam scolds. "I'm serious."

"I can tell," Jacen agrees. "Come on." He tugs on Liam's hand, but in the opposite direction from where the truck is parked.

"You're going the wrong way. We're back here," Liam says, thumbing over his shoulder.

"Oh, I know. We're not leaving yet."

"Why not?"

Chuckling again, Jacen guides Liam farther down the block. A shadowy alleyway gets gradually closer and Liam blurts, "You're not really—I mean, I guess it's faster, and convenient, but...."

Jacen pauses, following Liam's gaze to the dark, narrow pas-sage between the buildings. "Lee," Jacen says with clear amuse-ment. "I'm not fucking you in the alley."

"Why not?"

Deep, rolling laughter erupts from Jacen, surprising him. "Oh, wow. This is going to be more fun than I thought."

"What?"

Jacen glances back at Liam from over his shoulder, his blue eyes flashing with promise as hot and brilliant as sunlight striking calm waters. Tossing his hair back with a flip of his head, he pulls Liam on, walking past the alleyway.

"Jacen?"

"*Liam,*" Jacen teases, mimicking him in a low, sing-songy

voice.

"Come on! What good's a trophy husband if you don't use him for dirty sex a few times a day?"

Jacen has no reply other than another one of those heady, piercing looks.

"Jacen!"

"*Liam*," Jacen teases again.

"I don't want to look at real estate possibilities right now, I want to get fucked," Liam growls quietly.

"Oh, I've noticed," Jacen assures him. "We have received the message, loud and clear. But I think you're too much fun when you're desperate for it to actually give it to you just yet."

Liam's eyes narrow.

Jacen blinks calmly down at him.

"Well, maybe I'll just be less fun, then."

"You can try," Jacen smirks. "Now get your sweet ass moving. I see some 'For Sale' signs up ahead."

"Maybe if we were talking about renting, but as it is, it's too damn much," Liam argues. He tosses his emptied take-out container onto a table and sinks down onto the couch. His skin feels too tight and he's itchy, fidgeting restlessly. His knees bounce. His right hand scratches over the back of the left, and most of all he can't look at Jacen. The calm determination Jacen is exuding is even more panic-inducing, because it looks very much like Jacen has already made up his mind about this, and is just seeking ways to convince Liam to go along with it.

"I told you, it's not too much. We have over a million dollars between us, and that's without the stocks. Doing this is a smart investment. We'll be making our money back every month with the rent we charge and that's not even counting the real estate value itself."

"Jacen, we can't buy a whole building."

"Sure we can. And hey, it solves the problem of you finding a job outside the house. It's even safer this way. You can tend to the building and the grounds as the landlord. I'll be hunkered down in the kitchen at the bistro. Not a whole lot of face time with the public, less chance of being recognized, less chance of getting hurt. I think it's perfect. And the realtor said there are already tenants in four of the six units. With us in the fifth that leaves only one open to rent. What about it don't you like, specifically?"

"The hallways are yellow."

"We can paint them. Anything else?"

"What if I don't want to be a landlord? I don't know how to fix crap," Liam says, throwing his arms out widely.

"You can learn. You're a pretty quick study. And I have faith in you," Jacen smiles. "One of the most important things to people is their home. You know what I'm talking about. This is your chance to be there for other people and keep them safe, too. It doesn't have to be your job if you don't want it. We can share the responsibility if you'd rather find some other sort of work."

"I'm not like you, Jace. I don't have any secret talents, besides giving good head. I'm fairly useless. The last thing I want right now is to have a whole other group of people counting on me to take care of them. I kind of feel like I have a full plate as it is, with keeping us alive and off the streets. Can we just take this a little bit slower? I think it's awesome that you found a job so fast, but I'm not in a huge rush to commit to something this big."

"Hey," Jacen says tenderly, but still with that hard, unmovable glint in his aqua eyes. He takes a seat on the coffee table in front of Liam, staring eye-to-eye with him. "It's not only your job to handle things with us. We're sharing this. If you need me to take over sometimes, then I will do that, no questions asked. You can count on me, Lee, and you can lean on me. I won't break. Can you please just trust that I have a good feeling about this? I want to do this. I'll handle everything with settlement and the legal shit. I already sent Clay the address to see if he thinks it's a good plan or not, since he knows the neighborhoods better than anyone."

"But why does it have to be so soon?"

"I guess I just like knowing where I belong. I feel like I belong there."

"What if they find us? What if they track us to San Luis Obispo and we've committed to a mortgage on a six-unit apartment building. Then what? We skip town again and have the banks on our asses too?"

"We can always manage the building from off-site. We hire a landlord and rent out the sixth apartment. We do it remotely. We don't skip out on anybody, but we can go off-radar if we have to. It's actually easier to do it with something like this than if we were just buying a place for ourselves. Then if we had to leave, we *would* be in trouble with the banks. And renting somewhere is just throwing hard-earned money down the toilet. Financially, this is a better long-term solution. We make our money back. It's our second income *and* our home."

"This is insane," Liam says adamantly.

"Hey, I think that's my line," Jacen smirks. He takes Liam's hands, folding them inside his own. "Do you really hate it? Honestly?"

Liam bows his head. Jacen palms his cheek and caresses his skin, rough with blond stubble.

With a small shake of his head, Liam murmurs, "No, I don't hate it."

"Trust me," Jacen coaxes.

Eyes downcast, but warming slightly at Jacen's touch, Liam agrees with a muted, "Okay."

Eagerly, Jacen asks, "Yeah?"

Liam nods.

Giddy excitement floods Jacen's system. Grabbing Liam, he kisses him quick. Liam lets him, feeling like he's falling.

"It's going to be great," Jacen declares, absolutely certain of himself, catching Liam's bottom lip in another fervent kiss. "You'll see."

Tentatively, Liam glances up. He's drowning in anxiety, feeling self-conscious and powerless and unsure. But when he looks at Jacen, who's been through hell itself and not only lived through it, but came out the strong, self-assured man now kissing him passionately with nothing but loyalty and devotion, Liam whispers, "I love you."

Jacen grins widely, "Yeah, but I love you more."

Chapter 20
Performance for Jacen

Without regular jobs to perform and Johns to service, time continues to slip by astonishingly quickly for Liam. One day they're settling into their motel room after getting the hell out of L.A., the next they're packing again in preparation for the move to the apartment building they've just purchased. And with Jacen away nearly every day at his new job at the bistro, there is even less activity to punctuate Liam's time. So when Jacen and Liam do manage to be at the motel together, and aren't organizing boxes or sifting through paperwork or returning calls to their realtor or Clay, Liam feels added pressure to perform and keep Jacen interested and happy by having sex. The problem is that Liam doesn't want to have sex.

More and more, since finding out about Jacen's past, Liam feels guilty for wanting Jacen to be the one to receive, so he begins to try to convince himself that he doesn't want Jacen that way, or at least that it's off-limits. But in addition to that, with all of the upheaval, the stress of their changing lives, Liam is as far away from being mentally able to submit to Jacen sexually as ever.

Two chaste weeks pass. Then, on a Friday evening at around one in the morning, Liam's guilt gets the better of him. Without saying a word, he knocks on the bathroom door when Jacen is getting ready to take a shower after a long shift.

"Yeah, come in," is the reply.

Liam opens the door and stares at Jacen's chest, stripped bare of his discarded, dirty shirt. Jacen is unfastening his watchband, his pants unbuttoned and hanging from his narrow hips.

Tiredly but cheerfully as ever, Jacen asks, "What's up?"

Responding with only a tight shake of his head, Liam walks up to him, laying an opened hand on the center of Jacen's chest. He feels warm and vital and Liam sinks into the natural musky scent of Jacen's skin, letting it block out everything else clamoring for attention in his mind. The one thing Liam doesn't want just then is talk, so as soon as Jacen seems to be getting ready to press him again for an explanation, Liam caresses down Jacen's body, over his chest, the taut planes and firm ripples of his stomach, his fingers hooking inside the waistband of Jacen's boxer briefs. Sinking to his knees, Liam keeps his eyes focused only on smooth skin and the dark, soft curls of hair dusting Jacen's groin. Liam eases his husband's pants down a little farther and pulls his member free. Stroking it with gentle squeezes, Liam begins to lick and kiss inside the hollow of the cradle of Jacen's hips, up the inner crease of his thigh, just under his navel, making his way gradually closer to the center of his interest.

"Liam," Jacen sighs. "Hey, let me get cleaned up first. I probably smell like grilled meat. We can move this to the bed, take our time."

Liam doesn't want that at all. He fears it actually, so he moves more decisively, guiding Jacen's cock up to his lips, sucking lightly at the tip.

Jacen groans, "Lee, not that I don't appreciate it, because I really do...."

Opening his mouth more widely, feeding Jacen's thickening, pulsing flesh back over the wet muscle of his tongue, Liam closes his lips loosely around Jacen's shaft. Sucking on it, he pulls back off, almost all the way before diving in again, taking Jacen all the way back until he's lodging in Liam's throat. Humming, tasting Jacen, Liam keeps one hand on Jacen's hip. Jacen's hands fly to the sides of Liam's head, holding on to him as he moans. Easing back on Jacen's cock far enough to breathe through his nose, Liam sets a steady, increasing pace, giving Jacen the power to guide him. Both of Liam's hands fall to his sides only to clasp behind his back, his wrists resting against the curve of his ass as he lets Jacen use his mouth.

"Jesus," Jacen groans, getting achingly hard fast after too long without any release. Gazing down the length of his body, hips rocking forward and back of their own accord, moving out of pure need, pumping in shallow thrusts, he watches his flushed, stiffening cock slide wet between Liam's stretched lips, listens to him suck and slurp and swallow. Hooking his hands around Liam's ears, feeling his jaw work, Jacen exhales sharply and bites at his bottom lip, completely undone by the innate submissiveness emoting from Liam. It's there in the downward cast of Liam's half-lidded eyes, the easy fold of his hands behind his back, the way he bends and takes and yields so readily. But as complicit and demure as Liam seems, Jacen knows what this is, that it's a play, a ploy to distract and subdue. As submissive as Liam seems, he's the one that has all of the power here, and that's just as he intends it to be. As much as Jacen wants to call Liam on it and not play right into his hands, Jacen is at the mercy of his libido and helplessly fucks Liam's mouth until he orgasms with a swallowed moan, watching avidly as Liam's throat works, swallowing his load of come without a sound of protest, working him through each quiver and pulse.

Letting Jacen fall wet and softening from his lips, Liam momentarily nuzzles his lover's skin and says in a hoarse voice, "Missed you."

Jacen frowns heavily, clutching Liam to him. "C'mere. Let me see you. Let me kiss you."

"Mmm," Liam grunts, resistant. "Gonna hit the hay. Kind of tired. I just wanted to, before."

Without allowing Jacen a chance to argue the point, Liam gets to his feet, wiping self-consciously at his lips with his fingertips and slipping from the bathroom with a brief, seemingly shy flicker of a smile.

Jacen takes his sorely needed shower and re-enters the bedroom to find Liam is indeed in bed, his eyes closed and the lights off. Climbing under the covers, Jacen shifts close to him. Reclined on his back, Liam lays with his hands wound up over his head, resting on top of his pillow and against the headboard. He looks comfortable and Jacen might have believed he was asleep if there hadn't been so many nights during which to study Liam in his most unguarded moments in order to learn the differences between when he's faking contentment and actually feeling it.

Reaching for Liam, Jacen closes his large right hand over both of Liam's wrists. Jacen inhales the scent of Liam's skin and pushes the bed sheets impatiently away. The only thing barring his way is Liam's sleep pants, so Jacen grabs at the ties and tugs the knot free, pushing the garment down with a questing hand.

This all happens quickly. Liam's eyes open once Jacen has his arms pinned down. He looks with resignation at Jacen as Jacen pulls a small object from a pocket, sucking on it briefly.

"Jacen," Liam whines, pleading, drawing his legs up to disguise his growing hard-on, now exposed with his pants pulled down so far.

Jacen only stares at him in his fierce, determined way, like Liam's struggle only adds to his amusement. He brings the saliva-dampened butt plug down, reaching under Liam's bent legs. Anticipating the touch of the toy, Liam gasps and wriggles when instead he feels Jacen stick his ring finger up his hole, working it in and out. Twisting on it, Liam's mouth falls open just as his eyes shut.

"Is this okay?" Jacen says soothingly, sounding like he's going through with it anyway, no matter what Liam says, since he knows enough now to read between the lines of Liam's lies and feigned protests. Stroking his silky soft, hot inner walls, Jacen hums as Liam flutters and clenches around his finger. Quickly plucking the digit out, he replaces it with the plug, pushing firmly enough to pop it through his sphincter, rubbing with his fingertips around Liam's rim as it closes back up around it, the toy nestled snugly inside.

"Jacen," Liam whimpers. He looks to be on the verge of tears, fighting an internal battle with himself, writhing between where he's held tightly by Jacen's hand gripped around his crossed arms and where Jacen is rotating and playing with the toy he's just stuck up Liam's ass.

"Yeah, baby?" Jacen hushes.

The toy feels like a promise of more, that Jacen is getting him ready for what Jacen has had every right to take for weeks, but hasn't.

The protests won't come. Liam wonders if it's because he's simply too used to letting people have at him in whatever way they want to, as long as it makes them happy, or if it's because he doesn't want to say no to Jacen. Either way, Jacen presses firmly at the base of the plug, making sure it's in place and then shifts the hand above Liam's legs which fall immediately to the bed, straightening out until Jacen wraps Liam's erection in a tight fist and squeezes around it, pulling gently. Then Liam's legs curl up again, parting, as he throws his head back and lets out a broken cry.

"Look at me," Jacen says forcefully but with affection.

"I can't," Liam admits.

Jacen shifts, drawing up, propping himself on his right elbow and looks down at Liam. Liam's green eyes open wide, looking shiny wet and bloodshot. His lips, so recently and obscenely stuffed full of Jacen's cock, now pout in a sweetly vulnerable expression.

"You really are a puzzle," Jacen hums, his gaze roaming down Liam's body, strung tight, his hips canting up into Jacen's unyielding grip around his dick.

Jacen's hand, momentarily steady, suddenly begins pumping Liam at double speed and it causes Liam to moan loud and long, pulling at his trapped arms. His spine curves as he arches up off the bed. The breath huffs out of him in a rush only to suck back in. He holds it as long as he can bear it then does it again, whimpering sharply on the inhale.

Jacen bends closer, dragging his lips in soft trails of kisses up the side of Liam's neck, back to Liam's ear as his hand works him at frenzied speed. When Liam whimpers his name again, Jacen comes up to meet his eyes, staring down into their questioning hugeness with steady assurance. Trying to wriggle his hips away, Liam gets Jacen to cease his manipulations but instead of pumping him, he simply fondles, fingering lightly, exploring the slick head of his dick, around the ridge, the divot on the underside, plays with his slit.

Part of Jacen knows that if he asks, Liam will find the voice to say no, so he doesn't. He just takes. Leaning down, he catches Liam's pout in a kiss, licking over his plump lips and into his mouth, tongue-fucking it deeply, forcing Liam's jaws wide. As Liam moans into Jacen's mouth, he bucks and pulses pre-come. Jacen closes his hand up around the crown of Liam's cock, and squeezes it in pulses as he maps Liam's mouth with his tongue. Held fast to the bed, trapped and vulnerable, Liam's only fight is to suck down air through his nose and to be still as Jacen coaxes him closer to orgasm. When he's like steel sheathed in silk in Jacen's palm, Jacen breaks the kiss to get a better look at Liam who tries to catch Jacen's mouth but is unable to reclaim his lips. Corkscrewing his fist down and back up Liam's length, then doing it again, Jacen sees Liam's mouth work as his climax surges up his balls and splashes in long, wet streaks over his belly.

"Good. That's it. Come for me, Lee. Let me hear you."

Liam gasps and mewls, shuddering, eyes closing over.

A few more pumps and he's milked dry, shivering with the aftershocks. Jacen releases him only to manhandle him over onto his belly, fitting a pillow under his hips to tilt them.

"Jay... Jacen... *Jacen,*" Liam keens as Jacen settles on the backs of Liam's legs and fits his fingers around the base of the toy, rotating it as he withdraws it slowly, tilting it at an angle to pry Liam open wider before he's free of it.

Tearing open a packet of lube with his teeth, Jacen spits the piece of wrapper out and inserts two fingers into Liam, spreading them apart and squirting the lube in between. Liam shivers as the fluid slithers up inside him then grunts when Jacen smears it further.

"Your choice, Lee. Grab the headboard or tell me to fuck off. I won't take it personally."

Liam grabs the headboard and bows his back, sticking his ass up in invitation. Jacen settles between Liam's legs, steadies his cock at the root and finds his angle. He enters Liam with a growl, pulling Liam's hips back as, simultaneously, Jacen strengthens his thrust, moving slowly but deliberately. The head breaches Liam's outer ring and slides more easily as Jacen presses farther, pulling back now and then before resuming.

"Take it," Jacen grunts.

The possessive fierceness in it makes Liam purr. He pushes back into Jacen's thrust to meet him, even as he gasps through the burn of the stretch.

"God," Jacen hisses, thrumming with the need to rut and move. "Feel so soft. Feel incredible."

They'd gotten the results of the STD panel days ago and they were both clean, thankfully, but had yet to take advantage of not needing rubbers anymore. Unlike Jacen, Liam had not always used condoms with clients, one of the perks to purchasing Liam's very expensive services as he was one of the more higher-end offerings at The Company. If the client requested it, they could partake in condom-less blowjobs, though no bareback anal sex was permitted no matter how clean your lab work showed you to be. So even with their former lovers, neither man had ever gone bareback before. Liam and Timothy used condoms every time, even with their first Johns. They knew that much. Just as they knew that condoms weren't a foolproof guarantee, as Timothy so tragically found out.

Now none of that matters. All they know is the intimate feel of each other, without boundaries. Jacen quickly gets high off of it, the tight, heated hug of Liam's sphincter around his dick, the delicate tissues so very hot, velvety soft, giving when pushed, and fluttering in ripples around him as Liam battles his nervousness.

"Liam," Jacen moans. "I love you so much."

"Don't," Liam begs, needing Jacen to move and fuck him and not make this more of an emotional trial than it is.

"I do. I love you. That's what this is Me loving you," he argues, hunching down closer to Liam, running an opened hand up Liam's back, feeling him arch into the touch, still clenching in gentle pulses around the violation of Jacen inside him. "And I love that you're letting me."

Jacen settles even closer, flush to Liam's back. Liam turns his head into Jacen's touch when Jacen nuzzles at his neck. His breath hitching, Liam tries to hide the fact that he's crying. Jacen rocks in and out of him, riding him tenderly. With one hand sliding up and down along Liam's side, just needing to touch and savor him, Jacen feels the cool tickle of Liam's tears against his cheek and moves to kiss them away, tasting their saltiness and hushing Liam when he whines softly back in his throat.

"Am I hurting you?"

"No," Liam gasps, shaking his head, rolling his hips counter to Jacen's movements, knowing just how to get the most out of it for him.

"Good. How does it feel?"

Liam exhales sharply, turning his face away.

"Hmm?"

Jacen's restless hand shifts, wedging under Liam's belly, finding his cock. It drags shallowly against the bed with each rocking nudge Jacen makes at his body.

"You're hard," Jacen observes. "You want this sweet or rough?"

"I want your come leaking out of my ass," Liam grunts.

Moaning out a sigh, Jacen's lips crash into him, sucking a dirty kiss to Liam's mouth.

For all his bravado, Jacen's lovemaking remains tender if also intense. The sensations are too new and exquisite for him to last long, but he takes comfort in knowing Liam is his to have whenever he needs him now.

As Jacen is moving shallowly in his own spend, he marvels at the slick, wet slide and the way it sounds, the soft squelching, the way it would be so easy to keep going, to grind against Liam until he was hard enough again for round two. But there's something he wants more.

"Come on," he urges, pulling Liam up off the bed, getting him on his hands and knees then just his knees as they both straighten to a kneeling position.

Liam moans loudly as Jacen changes their pose without pulling out, shifting inside him.

"That's it. On your knees." Jacen steadies him, holding him up. He caresses up through the soft curls of golden hair under Liam's arms as Liam brings his bent arms back and over his head, his back arched beautifully, connected at one end to Jacen's pelvis and the other to Jacen's lips pressing kisses to anywhere he can reach, nip and bite. Jacen's hands move back down, over Liam's belly, twisting to fit between it and Liam's curved, bobbing member, dragging in wet lines over the back of Jacen's hand. "Touch yourself. I wanna watch you jerk off," Jacen whispers near Liam's ear.

Liam shivers and undulates, reacting to Jacen's touches and words alike.

His training kicks in as he obeys, ignoring what he wants, just giving in to his partner's command. Curling one hand around his shaft without really thinking about it, he starts to tug lightly, making sure he tilts his head so that Jacen has a good view.

"You feel so wet, Lee. Every time I move I can feel my come dripping down the inside of you. Feels so fucking dirty. You know what it makes me wanna do?"

"What?" Liam croaks, snapping his wrist, tugging faster even as part of his psyche detaches, floating away somewhere else, somewhere safer.

"Makes me wanna bury my face between your thighs, spread your cheeks and lick you open. I wanna bury my tongue in your come-soaked hole and taste myself dripping out of you. Then I'd get my lips on your dirty little hole and suck on it. I'd suck my come out of you."

"Mother*fuck*," Liam groans, all thought shorting out, focused only on Jacen.

"Never done that before, have you, babydoll? I bet you'd like it. I bet you'd beg and whimper real sweet and then ask me to do it some more. You want that? My tongue licking the come out of your cherry hole?"

"Jacen," Liam moans, close to the edge, getting desperate, the soft smacking of his hand at his dick making Jacen's cock twitch where it's buried balls-deep in Liam's body.

"Say please," Jacen teases.

"Please," Liam gasps.

"Tell me you want it."

"I want it," Liam moans. "I want you to eat me out... feel your tongue in me... feel you moan when you taste it... God, fuck. So fucking dirty, Jace..."

"Just for you. Don't want anyone else. No one. No one but you. Gonna let me be dirty with you, baby?"

"Yeah," Liam whines, gritting his teeth.

"Stop. Stop touching it," Jacen orders.

Very reluctantly, Liam's hand falls away. A long moment later, it's replaced by Jacen's. He touches Liam, feather-light, barely grazing over his reddened, throbbing cock, playing with the head, palming the shaft, blood vessels pulsing thickly as he strains, trying to rock into the touch and get off. Then he fondles lower, over Liam's full, drawn-up balls, tugging gently on them.

"Jacen, *please*," Liam begs shamelessly.

"Just enjoy it," Jacen coaxes. "You're so close. Everything's so sensitive...."

Liam keens, his cock jumps, pulsing pre-come. Jacen drags a fingertip through it, painting Liam's cock in the wet streaks.

"You like the feel of my thick cock stuffed up your ass? I hope so, 'cause I'm 'bout to fuck it again," Jacen warns darkly.

"Shit," Liam hisses, and that's it. He comes like a gunshot, blowing his load all over his belly and Jacen's hand, splatters reaching as far as his chin.

"Beautiful," Jacen purrs.

And still it goes on. Jacen has Liam grab the headboard again and fucks him roughly for a second time, pounding Liam's ass until it's throbbing. Once he spills, hot and messy, filling Liam with another load of come, Jacen manhandles him over onto his back, pressing Liam's bent legs back toward his shoulders and holding him in the pose as he settles down below Liam on the bed. With long, curling licks, Jacen tastes every inch of Liam's skin and his come-smeared groin, mapping it, not missing a spot. Liam is half-hard again when Jacen's busy tongue finally finds Liam's opening, breaching it with a slow push, moaning into Liam's body as it hugs around the wet muscle of Jacen's tongue obscenely and Jacen licks as deeply inside as he can reach. The suction of Jacen's lips, pressed so tightly around the well-used, slightly swollen opening as he draws the come out of him, makes Liam crazy. But the thought of it, his glimpses of what's happening—Jacen eating his own spend from Liam's ass, gets Liam screaming with pleasure. He writhes and twists, trying to hold in his cries and failing. His flesh stirs, trying to somehow get hard again, wanting to get hard again, then Jacen begins playing with Liam's balls and cock while he licks and sucks and tongue-fucks and the world tilts, blacking out at the edges.

But as much as he gets off on it, the cold, tight knot in Liam's chest remains and tears continue to fall from the corners of his eyes. He's able to push through the panic, the hurt, and bear it. And when Jacen is through with him, and tiredness—emotional and physical—draws Liam down into the blackness, he doesn't fight against it. He gives in and lets it consume him. There is no regret, no anger at Jacen, only rage at himself and his own failings.

"Can you forgive me?" Jacen asks him quietly. "I know you wanted me to wait until you said you were ready, but it felt like it was time."

"Yeah," Liam mutters drowsily, nodding and closing his eyes. "'S okay."

"I love you," Jacen whispers to him, brushing Liam's sweat-streaked hair back from his forehead.

"Love you too," Liam murmurs in reply, falling into sleep.

For a long while, Jacen watches him sleeping, wondering what the morning will bring, if Liam will truly have forgiven him or if there will be fresh layers of hurt there now to heal, and carefully placed trust abused.

Chapter 21
Nothing Left to Take

The alarm goes off at nine the next morning. Grumbling, Jacen rolls over and swats at it, silencing the shrill beeping. Exhaling deeply into the bedding, Jacen groans, "What's with the fuckin' alarm, Lee? Yash isn't gonna be here 'til nine with the truck. Plenty of time. I... Lee? Lee? Wha—?"

The fog clears from Jacen's senses and he realizes he's talking to himself. Liam isn't there.

"Goddammit, Liam," he groans. Seeing the cell phone on the nightstand, he lunges for it and discovers the note left underneath. He's still reading it as he dials and puts the phone to his ear.

"Mornin'!"

"Where're you?" Jacen complains, slurring slightly and rubbing at his eyes.

"Picking up breakfast."

"Why didn't you tell me you were leaving? You could've woke me up instead of sneaking out."

"I didn't sneak out; you were tired so I let you sleep a little longer. But Yasha and Valery will be there any minute so you'd better at least put some pants on. And a shower wouldn't be out of line either, considering."

"Considering where my mouth and my dick were just a few hours ago, you mean?"

Liam smiles politely at the teenage red-headed girl behind the counter at the donut shop and hands over a twenty dollar bill. After taking the change from her, he stuffs it in his pocket and grabs the bag with the food, tucking it under an arm and then hefting up the coffee cup carrier.

He knows his silence will only speak of his bashfulness, but it can't be helped, and it's only partly because of where he is. The longer he says nothing, the more clearly he can sense Jacen's wicked grin at the other end of the line. He can practically feel Jacen's tongue dragging in warm, wet lines up his ass crack, wriggling into him as that evil, teasing glimmer lights his eyes and those big hands hold tightly to his thighs to keep him still and open.

A grandmotherly woman holds the door for him as he heads out to the parking lot, doing a quick scan of the occupants out of habit, looking for anyone suspicious.

"You're awfully quiet." Jacen observes with a smile in his voice.

"I'm trying to get to the truck and not drop scalding hot coffee all over myself *and* hold the bag *and* not drop the phone all at the same time," Liam complains.

"That's all? You're not even thinking about how hard I pounded you and how good it felt when I sucked on your balls?"

"Jesus. Stop," Liam hisses into the phone. "Gimme a few minutes and I'll be home. Go get ready. And for Christ's sake, hide the butt plug and the lube so I don't literally die of embarrassment when Yasha gets there. See you in a few."

He hangs up and gets the food settled on the floor of the cab. Pushing his sunglasses up the bridge of his nose he tries not look at himself in the rearview mirror as he reverses out of the spot.

Jacen doesn't call back but it's only a three minute drive back to the motel. Yasha's motorcycle and the rental truck are parked in the lot when Liam gets there. Cursing under his breath, Liam does his best to mask his expression and goes to join the others.

They had given up on the plan of keeping their location a secret from Yasha and Valery. It didn't really feel like doing so would accomplish much in the way of keeping them safe. It felt only childish and foolish when they so very much desired the aid of the pair of friends, especially given their hurried second move.

The motel room's door is slightly ajar. The sound of voices lilts out onto the balcony as Liam gets to the room and pushes his way inside.

Yasha is eyeing the small mountain of boxes and Valery is looking at a road map of the area. They both glance up when Liam enters. Hiding as much of his expression as he's able to behind dark sunglasses, Liam tries also to shrink into his leather jacket, setting the bag and coffee on the table nearby.

"Hey," Liam smiles. "Thanks for helping with the move. How've you guys been?"

"Fine. Just fine," Valery grins, coming over to give him a one-armed hug.

Yasha seems to zero in on the way Liam is avoiding eye contact and his hunched posture. For a second Liam wrongly suspects that the wariness and hints of sadness he detects in Yasha are caused by this and not something else.

"Good," Liam nods, extending a hand to Yasha before he can try to hug Liam too.

Shaking with him, Yasha anticipates Liam's question before he can ask and says, "Jacen's in the bathroom."

"Oh," Liam grunts lamely. To have something to do, he unpacks the food bag. "There're bagels and donuts for everyone. And coffee, obviously. Clay's going to meet us over there a little later. So, how's L.A.? Any news?"

"Same as it always is," Yasha answers a little too quickly. "Thanks for the coffee. After that drive, I could use it."

"Is everything okay?" Liam asks, concerned.

"Yeah," Yasha assures him. "It's just been one of those weeks, you know?"

Looking to Valery for visual confirmation of this, at the very least, Liam gets a warm smile from her and relaxes slightly.

The bathroom door opens and Liam instantly stiffens.

"Hey! You're back," Jacen beams. He makes his way over, wearing nothing but a pair of old, grungy jeans. He presses up close to Liam's back and catches his mouth in a fervent but soft kiss over Liam's shoulder. Liam responds and kisses back but can't meet Yasha or Valery's gaze once Jacen breaks away. Eyes downcast, Liam takes a donut and a coffee cup, partaking of some refreshment before it's time to begin the manual labor.

"So, how's married life treating you?" Yasha quips.

"Awesome," Jacen says happily.

Liam, somehow, manages to blush *more* and takes a big bite of donut. Jacen reaches over and takes the sunglasses from off of Liam's face and when their eyes meet, Liam smiles despite himself, his face lighting up.

"You two seem different," Valery observes.

Jacen squints, "Different?"

"Different good," she assures him. "Guess you made the right call, huh?"

"Yeah," Jacen nods in agreement, sipping from one of the unclaimed coffee cups and pressing a quick kiss to Liam's temple before going in search of a shirt. "I think we can get this done in one go. That furniture we bought is stacked in boxes on that wall. We should load that first and then stack the rest in after."

"Okay," Yasha nods thoughtfully, still distracted. "We'll get started on those while you guys have some breakfast. We grabbed some on the way up."

"You don't have to," Jacen says. "It'll just be another minute."

"No problem. That's what we're here for, right?"

Valery and Yasha lift a long, flat box from either end. Slowly they make their way out of the motel room and down toward the stairs to the parking lot. Wiggling into a t-shirt, Jacen tugs it loosely down and circles Liam in his arms from behind.

"Mm. You okay?"

"Yeah," Liam hums, sighing.

"I was worried when you took off like that. Even if it was for a valid reason. If I'm ever out of line or...."

"Jace, really. We're cool," Liam says softly, pulling away, turning around to face him.

Jacen gazes down at him, wondering if it's true, trying to judge from subtle cues whether it's Liam trying to make him feel better and put off a "talk" or if it's genuine.

"I know what you're doing," Liam tells him.

"And what's that?" Jacen asks, playing coy.

They lock eyes and Liam palms the back of Jacen's head, bringing him in. Their lips touch, brushing together. Liam's mouth parts slightly. He closes his full lips around Jacen's, sucking a gentle kiss to them. Moaning, Jacen presses in, seeking more contact. Liam's tongue slips into his mouth, tasting like coffee.

They don't hear Yasha and Valery re-enter until they chuckle, speaking quietly and deciding what to take next.

Liam breaks the kiss and Jacen straightens. Running a hand back through his tousled hair, Jacen goes to help with the boxes.

"Please, don't stop on our account," Yasha says. "In fact I'm offended by the lack of groping and dry-humping going on here."

Jacen throws him a look and Valery puts a hand on Jacen's arm. "Eat," she instructs. And after a moment's pause in which Yasha opens his mouth to add something to that directive, Valery clarifies, "Eat *breakfast*."

"Buzz kill," Yasha tsks.

The morning passes without incident. They crank up the radio and quickly get the trucks loaded with all of their belongings. After checking over the room one last time, Liam checks them out of the motel and pays the bill with cash. Then the four of them all drive over to the recently purchased apartment building.

Yasha drives the rental truck. Valery drives the motorcycle, and Jacen and Liam take their truck.

On the drive, Liam asks hesitantly, "Um, they don't seem weird to you today, do they? Yasha and Val?"

"What do you mean?"

"I don't know. Quiet, or thoughtful, or like they're hiding something?"

Jacen considers this.

"Maybe I'm just being paranoid," Liam says, thinking, *or maybe it's because I feel like they know what we did last night just by looking at us and I don't like it.*

"Mm," Jacen grunts. "I guess Yasha did seem a little reserved. We're almost there; we can just ask them what's going on."

"Yeah," Liam hums.

Clay is there waiting when their caravan pulls up. Clasping hands with Liam and drawing him in for a sound clap on the back,

Clay laughs brightly and says, "How's it goin', man? The place is lookin' nice, I've gotta say. And perfect weather for a move."

The sun shines down on them, a cool breeze ruffling their hair. Yasha and Valery head over to join the other three standing around on the sidewalk. Liam handles the introductions.

"Yasha, Val, this is Dice... er, Officer Clay Martinez. Sorry, force of habit," Liam apologizes.

"Nice to meet you both. Liam and Jacen have told me how cool you've been, supporting them and all."

"You know, you two don't look like brothers," Yasha says dryly, observing Clay's huge, stocky build and mocha skin tone in contrast to Liam's lean frame and paler countenance.

"Brothers from another mother," Clay chuckles, shaking Yasha's hand, then Valery's.

"It's definitely a load off our minds, knowing they have you looking out for them," Valery tells Clay sincerely.

Clay slaps a hand down onto Jacen's shoulder in greeting, eyeing the trucks. "We ready to get started? It's gonna be a haul getting everything up three flights of steps. Guess we should open the place up, make sure it's all ready to go and that there aren't any surprises."

"Yeah, but before we get to that," Jacen starts, pausing to collect his thoughts. He turns to Yasha and Valery. "Is there anything going on that you guys haven't told us? Because it just seems...."

Yasha sighs, giving Valery a sidelong glance.

"Tell them," she urges. "Go on."

"Okay. It's probably nothing," he says up front. "But Ryan didn't check in with his roommate after his job on Thursday night, and he hasn't been home since. There was—" He stops, looking around at the tense, focused expressions on everyone's faces. "There was a rumor that he was going to try to take off, like you guys did, to get out of his contract. I heard it through a friend of Ryan's, and just the fact that it got back to me doesn't speak well for Ryan's conscientiousness for his own well-being."

"You think they got to him, don't you?" Jacen says severely, his expression clouded and dark. Circling Liam's shoulders with an arm, Jacen holds on to him like it will keep him safer. "The

Company?"

"To be plain, yes," Yasha nods. "I do. I think they'd want to make an example of him to scare the rest of their employees into toeing the line."

"*Fuck*," Jacen curses, pain etched in his face.

"What can we do?" Liam asks quietly, sounding fearful but determined.

"There's nothing you can do," Yasha says. "You need to be concerned about your own well-being. You need to keep yourselves safe at this point. Whatever happened to Ryan, which could be nothing, is out of your hands. His roommate and friends are talking about filing a missing person's report but it could get Ryan in even more trouble with prostitution charges and the like."

"But it does mean The Company is angry, for whatever reason Ryan disappeared," Valery inputs. "If it *was* them behind it then that's even more reason for you and Liam to keep a low profile and stay hidden. We still haven't heard a peep about you from anyone in L.A. Yasha and I do think they gave you up for lost, but it's important to be careful."

Liam turns to Clay and meets his gaze. "They're right," Clay says sadly. "There's nothing you can do for him without overly endangering yourselves. I'd encourage his friends to file the report and even have Ryan talk with the police if he turns up. Maybe they could cut him a deal for information on The Company."

Grunting, seething with frustration, Liam rakes his fingers back through his hair. Jacen grips his shoulder and urges, "Come on. No use dwelling on it right now. Let's get the place unlocked."

Letting Jacen take his hand, lacing their fingers together, Liam follows him to the building's entrance, keys in hand.

Though he may try to convince himself otherwise, Liam knows right away after hearing about Ryan what he wants to do about the situation. So he does everything in his power to bury his churning thoughts, at least when Jacen is around to possibly notice. Liam knows that if he's going to do what he knows needs to be done,

Jacen can't know or suspect.

The apartment is on the top floor, so the whole gang is kept busy taking boxes and belongings up to it. It's easy for Liam to avoid always being within sight of Jacen. He bides his time, looking for the right opening, knowing Jacen wouldn't approve of what he's planning, but intent on going through with it anyway. Liam knows that some of the reason behind why he wants to do something that will make Jacen angry is that part of him wants payback for the helplessness and emotional uproar Liam has been experiencing. For weeks he's been forced to endure huge changes and take part in things that Jacen has helped coax Liam to be okay with. Sure, maybe Liam should have tried to stand up for himself more along the way, and maybe being okay with scaring Jacen is a very wrong path to take, but Liam doesn't see a lot of options.

Toward the middle of the day, when Jacen is having a coffee break and talking to Valery in the new apartment, Liam heads downstairs to the trucks. Clay is down there, checking through the remaining couple of things in the back of the moving truck.

Liam waves to him and holds up his phone, "Making a quick call, okay?" He thumbs back at the alley along the right side of the building; it's secluded but still rather brightly lit and deserted.

"Sure, Pidge," Clay calls back.

Liam checks over his shoulder, glancing all around and even up at the windows along the various stories of their building. No one is watching from what he can tell. He jogs through the alley, out the other side and in the direction of the convenience store across the street. Five minutes later he has a prepaid, disposable cell phone in hand. Once he's back in the alley, he dials a number from memory and presses the cheap phone to his ear, praying silently to himself while it rings.

Not actually expecting it to be picked up, as much as he wants it to be, Liam is shocked when Ryan answers his phone.

His groggy, rough sounding voice says, "Yeah. Who is this?"

"Ry, it's Will. Are you okay?"

"Will?! Holy shit! What happened to you, man?"

"What happened to *me*? What happened to *you*? Everyone's freaking out, thinking you've been offed and tossed in a river somewhere."

"Oh, yeah. I've heard. Nah, nothing so dramatic. One of my clients got a little carried away. I ended up in the ER and, Christ, Della was losing her *shit*, you should've seen it; it was kinda priceless, man. Completely worth the stitches and rectal exam, just to see her freaking out to that extent. I thought her head was gonna pop right off. She was so freaked over having to lose another client and scaring all the employees once they found out how bad I got hurt, thinking of all the money they'd lose."

"She kept it quiet, didn't she, what happened to you? She didn't want anyone to know."

"Bing! Right on the nose. You're a smart cookie, Willy baby. It was sweet. Private medical treatment in this suite downtown, and I'm on some *exquisite* meds right now, got everything I could possibly need, right at my fingertips. It's fantastic."

"So they didn't threaten you. You're okay?"

"Of course I'm okay! Della's so desperate to keep me shiny, she'd do *anything*, man, and I do mean anything. Got her wrapped around my little finger."

"What about your injuries? You'll heal? What happened?"

"Oh, someone got a little too friendly with the knifeplay, but nothing either of us haven't dealt with before. It's been handled, like I said. No worries. But enough about me, what the fuck happened to you and Jacen? The higher ups, they figured you two long gone. Weren't sure if Patrick did something nasty or what. They were going through your whole client list, investigating everyone. They tried to track you down, had absolutely no fucking clue what happened. Are you and Jacen okay?"

"I can't talk about it. Let's just say I've made some changes and I'm far enough away that no one needs to worry about me anymore, but I'm happy. I really am. But listen, Ry. I've gotta go. You take care of yourself, ya hear?"

"You too. If you see Jacen, tell him I said howdy."

"Not too likely, but roger that," Liam says before hanging up.

Breathing out a profound sigh of relief, a wide smile curling his lips, Liam sags back against the brick wall of the building. He begins to try to decide the best way to smash the phone and which dumpster to toss the remains in.

"What the hell is going on? Who did you just call?"

Liam turns with a start, cursing, "Fuck! You scared me!"

Jacen stands wide-eyed and breathless just a few feet away. "Clay said you took off down here to call somebody, but who in the hell would you have to call, Lee?"

His face burning with embarrassment at being caught, Liam tries to decide what to say. Jacen stares at him, takes a few steps closer and backs Liam up to the wall.

"Come on! Talk to me! You look guilty as hell and I don't like it. You're scaring me."

"I took a chance. I had to. For us. I had to know, and I'm the only one he'd talk to."

"What are you talking about?" Jacen demands. "Who?"

"Ryan," Liam admits. "I called Ryan."

"Are you *out of your fucking mind*?!" Jacen exclaims, throwing his arms wide, his mouth hanging open.

"Maybe. But it was worth it. I think I called at the perfect time. It was a miracle he answered at all, they probably have him guarded and well-secluded. Probably was the drugs that made him forget he's not supposed to talk to anyone right now."

"Liam Timothy, you explain to me what the fuck you're talking about, right now," Jacen rasps, his voice ragged from shouting and from fear. He looms large over Liam, a massive hulk of a man.

Shrinking in on himself at the way Jacen is trying to physically intimidate him into answering and at the unexpected use of his full, married name, Liam sinks into the guilt. It chews up his guts with sharp, needle-like teeth, making him wince. "Baby, I'm sorry...."

"Tell me," Jacen growls, his eyes blazing, his breath quickening, like he's getting ready for a fight, or maybe, rather, trying not to lose himself to the panic. "Now."

"I called him on a prepaid phone, not my phone. I'm not that stupid." Liam holds it up for him to see. "We've been getting all of our information third- or fourth-hand through Yasha, and not that I don't trust Yasha, I just needed to know, right from the source, what's going on in L.A. Ryan has been a friend for years. I *know* him. Just like I know how quickly rumors start circulating in our former circle of acquaintances. So I took a chance and called him. I didn't stay on the line long enough for the call to be traced, and I'm not even paranoid enough to believe they're equipped to do such a thing if they wanted to... but anyway, I found out the truth. The actual truth, Jacen. They didn't bump off Ryan out of some malicious desire to make an example of him and scare everyone. They were discreetly getting him medical attention after a bad job and trying to pamper his ass to make nice and keep him happy. They don't want to lose any more employees or clients. That's all that's going on. And Ryan said they have given up on us."

"What about when they hear that Ryan talked to you on the goddamned phone? Huh?"

"He was way too high for it to even be believable, even if he did say something. And so what if he does tell them? They know we're gone. They've moved on. They don't want to come after us when they've got plenty of other shit to handle. We're done, don't you see? They're done with us. It's okay. It's really going to be okay."

Jacen battles with himself, processing Liam's words, his own storming emotions. His face twists, as he fights with holding back everything that threatens to bubble up—anger, betrayal, confusion, fear, relief.

"You should've talked to me first. We should've talked about this, as a couple, before you did anything so stupid."

"We should've talked about a lot of things," Liam says coldly, feeling very small and alone.

"What's that supposed to mean?"

At first, the words won't come. Then, they do. Meekly, Liam says, his voice soft and low and rattled, "Y-you should've listened to me when I asked you to slow down. With everything. A-all...." He sighs shakily, gesturing around at their surroundings. "All of this. It's too much. It's too much for me, and you should've waited until you had my permission. You didn't wait. You just *took*. Just like *they* do. Just like they've always done. You took from me the only thing I had left to keep me sane. You knew I wasn't ready and *you took it anyway*."

With a hand clapped tightly over his mouth, muffling a moan of pure horror, Jacen shatters into a million pieces.

Liam pushes past him, away down the alley, away from the building and Jacen.

Before he disappears out of sight, Jacen finds his voice and cries with devastation, "Liam! Liam, please! I'm sorry! *Liam, I'm sorry!*"

But it's too late. Liam is gone.

Chapter 22

The Peace Beyond the Pain

The whiskey burns its way down Liam's throat and loosens up some of the tension knotting nearly every muscle in his body. The drunker he gets, the more relaxed and steady he feels. Everything around him, the ghosts of Jacen and everyone else in his "new life", the ghosts of his old life too, it all recedes more and more, chased by the strength of the amber liquid in his glass.

He hunches over the edge of the bar, his booted feet hooked on the rungs of his barstool. Swirling his whiskey, savoring the heat and dark, crowded atmosphere of the pub, Liam feels like he could stay right where he is for hours. Which is handy because he hasn't got anywhere else to go.

The wedding ring on the third finger of his left hand glints in the low light, reminding him coolly of his responsibilities. He tucks that finger in, to hide the gleam, and then runs the pad of his thumb over the band's slick metal. Through the din of conversation and the clinking of glasses and the shuffling of boots, a raspy, southern drawl sings mournfully through the speakers playing a local radio station. Recognizing Tucker's voice instantly, skin pebbling with a chilly crawl of goosebumps, Liam feels pulled strongly in two opposing directions. He falls easily right back into the persona of the cowboy that he had with the man—the whore that seduced the singer, before the singer set him free—but he's also far beyond that. He's now someone that he doesn't even recognize or know how to be. Tucker's voice is Liam's past—sinful, indulgent, and gone. With a large swallow of whiskey, Liam burns the memories away.

The place is fairly crowded, and he feels inconspicuous. Someone walks up to the bar from farther back in the darker recesses of the room and calls to the bartender for a lager. He takes the stool to Liam's left. With a subtle glance, Liam measures the man—an inch or two past his own height, an impressive build and tan, weathered skin hinting that he's a laborer of some type.

"How's it goin'?" he says in a gruff murmur to Liam.

"Not bad. You?"

"Can't complain."

It happens quickly, and discreetly. With nothing more than a sweeping, lingering look down the length of Liam's body, the dark-eyed newcomer communicates his interest, letting Liam notice, leaving it up to him to acknowledge it or not.

Liam responds instinctively, ducking his head to sip from his glass, smiling faintly with just a slight curl of the corner of his lips.

The man clears his throat and draws something from the breast pocket of his flannel shirt. With a sly shift of his fingers, his hand curled and resting on the bar top, a fold of bills is revealed. The two of them lock eyes and the exit is indicated with a nod of the stranger's head.

God, it would be so easy, Liam realizes. *He's cute. It'd be nothing to me to turn my head and go through with it. Money in my pocket, maybe enough to buy a bus ticket out of here. It could all go away. Just keep moving, keep running, keep changing. He'd forget me eventually. He'd be safer without me. Happier too.*

As if in a daze, Liam stands, gulping down the last swallow of his whiskey, gritting his teeth against the burn. With hunger in his eyes, the dark-haired man at Liam's left finds his feet and starts toward the door. The over-loud music thumps through Liam's skin, seeps into his brain like a heavy cloud, covering over and muting all rationality. A moment later they're outside, around the building. A thick hand wraps Liam's waist. Another wraps the side of his neck. He's pushed back against unyielding brick.

"I don't kiss," he warns as strange lips lean in.

The questing rub of someone else's fingers over his body, something Liam has experienced so often for so long that he's become easily numb to it, surprises him in the way it sends a dull, queasy tickle writhing deeper and deeper into his stomach. Shame floods his system. Bile rises in his throat which quickly closes up around a horrified groan.

"Look. I'm sorry," Liam protests, finally. "I thought I could. I. I can't. I can't do this. Sorry."

He pushes the guy off of him and sprints away, getting swallowed up in the dense shadows of night before he's able to be tracked and followed.

Seated behind the wheel of his squad car, Clay rolls up beside Liam, who is hunched over and sitting on a bench by the side of a downtown park. It's fully dark out. The only illumination is an orange glow from a nearby streetlamp. Leaning out of the window in his t-shirt and jeans rather than his uniform, Clay says, "There you are. Your boy's crawling the goddamn *walls*, you know, looking for you."

"I'm not hiding," Liam sighs, well past exhaustion. He hunches forward even more and holds his face in his hands. "I'm not even really mad at him. I just said things that I shouldn't... and now...."

"Lemme take you home, Pidge. Wouldn't be able to live with myself if I allowed your husband any more worry 'bout your well-being. What d'you say?"

Liam's anxiousness grows, spreading over his face. He doesn't move a muscle.

"I have to call him," Clay warns.

"I know," Liam nods wearily.

Clay dials and says only a second later, "Found him."

Liam can hear the shrillness of Jacen's voice through the phone from many feet away and it just makes him feel worse.

"Nah, I'll bring him to you. Jay... Jacen. Jacen! Hey, I know. But he's fine. We'll be there in five. Won't let him out of my sight. Scout's honor."

Liam stares blankly down the mostly abandoned, tree-lined street, with a few stars coming out in the clear, cloudless sky. He's unable to meet Clay's gaze after he hangs up.

"Come on. Get in the car."

"But the things I said to him," Liam aches. "When he was only trying to protect me and do what he thought was best for us, for me...."

"If you're worried about whether he's going to forgive you, no need to worry. He was so convinced he'd lost you for good, you're pretty much golden right now."

The shame is too great, though. Liam remains frozen to the spot, unable to imagine facing Jacen when he sounded like he knew, positively *knew* that Liam was lying dead in a gutter somewhere — caught at last by the boogeyman or possibly done in by his own hand.

As Liam bites at his fingers, marveling at his own ability to so deeply disappoint people he loves, Clay plays his last card, saying simply, "Avery, get in the goddamned car before you break that poor kid's heart for good."

Expelling a held breath sharply, half-laughing, half-sobbing, Liam bites down on his tongue hard enough to draw blood and gets to his feet.

Yasha twists Jacen's arms up behind his back, pinning them there and keeping his death grip on the thick ropes of muscle running through them as Valery leans all of her meager weight against Jacen's chest, her hands splayed across it.

"Jacen," she says soothingly, "Sit the fuck down."

"Let me go! *Let me go!*" he rages, fighting against them.

"They're on their way here! You need to wait. Two minutes. *Two minutes* and they'll be here."

"Get *OFF OF ME!*"

"No. We're not letting you run out there and hurt or kill yourself for no good reason. You're not in your right mind."

Suddenly, Jacen stops his fierce wrestling against them and goes perfectly still. "Okay. Okay, I'm cool. I swear. I'll sit down. Maybe you can get me a drink? There's bourbon in that box in the corner."

"Yeah?" Valery asks.

"Yeah," Jacen pants, catching his breath.

Slowly, she eases off of him and stands up straight, her gaze darting to Yasha's face every now and then. Just as slowly, Yasha releases Jacen's arms. They fall to Jacen's sides and he flexes them, his chest rising and falling heavily.

"Easy," Yasha coos. "Easy...."

For a full ten seconds, Valery and Yasha actually believe that Jacen has really, finally become rational once more. Yasha is the one to detect otherwise and shouts to his wife, "Grab him!"

Growling like a crazed animal, seething and spitting, Jacen tries to get past her before she can, but Valery's right hand shoots out, grabbing hold of Jacen by his weakest, most vulnerable spot, knowing there's no other way to subdue him given the difference in their sizes.

Jacen cries out with exquisite pain, his voice rising a number of octaves as Valery's fist closes up like a vise around Jacen's testicles.

"Sit the fuck down. *Now*," she commands viciously.

Jacen's mouth works around a silent, choking scream as he crumples to the floor. He nods, defeated.

"Good boy," she sighs.

The crazed, off-kilter, maybe-the-fastest-way-to-the-sidewalk-is-a-leap-from-the-window look on Jacen's face starts to fade at last. Yasha takes a deep steadying breath, bracing his hands on his thighs. Valery goes to look for the bourbon. She finds it and some plastic cups, pouring the booze into three and handing them out. Jacen downs his in one gulp and refuses to meet their eyes.

"It's gonna be okay, sweetie," she assures him. "I know you don't believe that one bit, but it will. Clay knows him better than anyone."

Jacen takes it like a slap, wincing, but it's evident that scenarios are still playing out in Jacen's mind—Liam running off again, getting away from Clay and disappearing into the night, this time for good. A drive-by hit as the phone call from earlier is traced to San Luis Obispo and Liam is spotted on the side of the road, taken out by one well-aimed gunshot to the center of the head. Liam deciding that maybe all he's good for after all is a fuck, letting the one wrong guy get too close and taking a knife to the belly, bleeding out on the pavement or in the back of someone's van.

He twitches forward with a scared whimper, teeth gritted and ready to spring toward the door, to get to his feet again, but Yasha circles his neck from behind, hugging his chest, pulling him back flat on his ass once more, his back flush to the large box behind him, on which Yasha now sits.

"He—he could... he could be...."

"Shh."

"He could... I-I have... I have to...."

"No. You don't. Not this time, TJ."

Every muscle in Jacen's body tenses and he battles against the waking nightmares, seething through his teeth, fighting not to drown in terror.

Valery straddles his legs and sits down on them. Settling onto Jacen's lap, she closes the circle, embracing him from the front as Yasha holds on to him from behind. She presses a tender kiss to Jacen's temple.

"Not all the nightmares come true," she whispers to him. "He's going to be fine."

But what if he's not? every fiber of Jacen's being cries out.

Yasha and Valery look at one another, each thinking the same thing—that Jacen is holding on too tightly to this. That Liam is the only thing keeping him anchored to the world, and if that tenuous hold snaps, Jacen will truly be gone, lost to them forever, taken by madness. The demons chewing at the tattered edges of his soul will win.

Jacen shudders, trembling violently as they wait, like that, for Liam to return, as if Jacen knows on a base level that there is no returning for Liam, that Jacen has been forsaken for his sins, doomed to an eternity of hell, alone, without a single ray of hope left.

For the first time, Jacen thinks to himself that it would have been easier if they'd been quickly tracked and found by The Company. At least then he would have had something tangible to fight against, something concrete to lay hands on and do battle with. There would not be this creeping dread, this niggling certainty that the man he loved more than life itself was destined to endure horrors beyond Jacen's imagining, in penance for the simple crime of finding some happiness at last, after a lifetime of subjugation.

Jacen swallows back a small, hurt, hopeless sound and Valery caresses him, soothingly.

"He's going to be fine."

"You're not this much of a bastard," Clay accuses.

They're parked in front of Liam and Jacen's building, just a few feet from the stairs that lead up to where Jacen is waiting. They've been sitting there for long minutes, in stalemate.

"You don't know me anymore. I'm not that stupid kid I used to be. I know what the world is like. There is no happily ever after. That's just a sad joke idiots hold on to so they don't go and eat a bullet. The only thing waiting out there is more pain. And this time I'm the one causing it. I'm not ready for this. I can't do this."

"You're right, you are causing it. Jacen is up there, waiting for you, going out of his mind, and you're just *sitting here*!" Clay shouts.

Liam doesn't blink or flinch. He just stares straight ahead, blankly, out toward the road unwinding before them.

"Is this really who you are now? You're the kind of guy that just gives up? Throws in the towel and lets the people who matter to him suffer needlessly? The kind of guy that would have let Tim suffer and die alone because it was too hard for *you* to bear?"

Liam sneers, laughing maliciously, his gaze piercing like daggers. "Fuck you. Really. Fuck you."

Clay snaps. He gets quickly out of the squad car and walks around to the passenger side. He pulls the door open and says, "Get out of the car."

Liam doesn't react.

"Let me rephrase. Get out of the car or I'll make you get out of the car."

Laughing again, Liam's expression is cold as he gazes up at his brother and says with a grin, "Whatever way you wanna play it, baby. I like it rough."

Clay hauls him out by the front of his shirt, dragging him to his feet and slamming him back against the side of the vehicle.

Chuckling, sucking in oxygen after the wind is forced from his lungs from the impact, Liam says, "You know, an hour or so ago I let some guy pick me up in a bar, let him take me into the alley...."

It's perfectly clear to Clay that Liam is being completely truthful, despite the strong smell of whiskey on his breath, and the searing anger of Clay's reaction overtakes him before he can catch himself. He punches Liam in the mouth, connecting sharply and drawing blood.

Wincing, Liam touches the tip of his tongue to his bleeding lip. He spits out a thick wad of red-tinged saliva. Liam meets Clay's blazing eyes head-on, not backing down an inch.

"It was kind of like old times, back when Tim was home, in agony, struggling just to breathe, withered and rotting in our bed, and I was out sucking dick for a few bucks a pop, pretending Tim didn't even exist, pretending I was someone else, *anyone* else but the stupid fuck that cared about him."

A measure of peace comes over Liam's face just before the second punch connects, willing it, inviting it. After he's knocked momentarily unconscious, he struggles to think of something else to say, anything else that'll keep Clay pounding on him, beating him to a pulp. Because the pain feels good. It feels earned, a perfect echo of the internal torment flaying Liam's soul.

When the world swims back into actuality, Liam slurs, with a bloody, swollen lip, "Come on, you pussy. That the best you can do? Hit me again. Hit me! HIT ME!"

Liam draws back his arm, preparing to let it go, to release a punch, blindly, as his eye starts to swell just like his lip.

"HIT ME!"

He swings. Clay catches his fist and denies him the satisfaction.

"COME ON! COME ON, HIT ME!"

Clay lets go of Liam's fist and catches him instead, wrapping him in strong arms as Liam rails against him, whimpering and starting to sob, his voice cracking.

"What's wrong with you?! You know I need this! You know I deserve this!"

"No. You don't," Clay laments, not letting go, just holding Liam to him. "You didn't deserve any of it."

Liam's legs give out and he releases a long-stifled, gut-deep, wailing cry of pure pain and loss, one that he's been holding in for years, for decades.

"Come on, Pidge. I'm sorry for losing my temper like that. You sure know how to play a guy, don't you? Come on. Time to make it right. Life is short. We've gotta hold on to the good stuff while we still can."

"What if I can't? What if I don't know how? What if there isn't enough of me left under all the bullshit to give to him? He deserves better than someone like me."

"Hey. Timothy is dead," Clay says seriously. "He's been dead for a long damn time, but *you're* still alive. You can do anything you want to, as long as you stop trying to hurt yourself. It's not your fault he got sick and it's not your fault he's gone. Now how about you start being the sort of man he'd want you to be, instead of the kind of douchebag that hides from his problems?"

Liam's fingers claw at Clay as he loses himself in the embrace for one more precious moment.

"Oh god. I hate this. I'm... scared," he admits.

Clay gives him a supportive smile as Liam regains his feet and backs off a step, his mouth bloody and right eye preparing to sport a healthy, dark bruise. "He's gonna be real happy to see you. I think I'm the one should be scared once he sees your face."

Liam laughs. It's a bright, honest sound that lifts years of weight from his shoulders. Drawing himself up, gathering his resolve, he nods. "Okay. Let's go up."

Chapter 23

With Opened Arms and a Willing Heart

They take the stairs, slowly. Each step is a battle, and the closer Liam gets to the third floor, the more he wants to give up, be a coward and run the other way. It becomes nearly unbearable. Somehow he makes it. They stand awkwardly at the closed door for a prolonged moment, as Liam is unable to bring himself to knock. Rolling his eyes, Clay warns, "You owe me for the ass whoopin' your boy's about to give me."

Liam nods gravely, going paler by the second which only makes his injuries stand out more starkly. "If you want to take off, I can handle this. Probably."

"Yeah. Right. I bet it's real easy to handle confronting a closed door."

Clay knocks soundly, and his fist is barely able to draw back away from the door when it swings open, revealing Valery Savaria wearing a hugely relieved expression of pure joy. "Oh thank *Christ*," she swears.

They get a partial glimpse of Jacen struggling to his feet and Yasha behind him before Jacen barrels toward them. Valery gets hastily out of his way before Jacen throws the door open wide. He scans Liam's face, registering the state of it but unable to stop himself long enough to react to it before he's scooping him up in his arms, lifting him off the ground and moaning desperately into the side of his neck.

"Maybe we should go," Valery starts to say, looking to her husband. "Let you two talk...."

Liam returns the embrace, though he holds on to Jacen somewhat more gingerly. At first the apology is too big to voice. It lodges in his throat, threatening to stick there and choke him to death. When Jacen seems unable to relax his grip or put him down, Liam gives in, surrendering. His voice is hushed and shame-filled as he hisses, "I never meant to hurt you."

Valery waffles, wanting to give privacy, and Jacen shows no sign of letting go of Liam. Yasha speaks up with a much-needed authority as Clay awaits the backlash of Jacen's anger for hitting Liam. "TJ, put him down. He's bleeding and we need to make sure he's okay before you suffocate him."

The words spur Jacen to action. He sets Liam down but doesn't let go, merely pulling back enough to be able to see him. Liam's eyes are downcast, the right one nearly swollen shut, beginning to color with an ugly bruise. His lip is split and bleeding, the flesh there swelling up as well.

"I'm fine," Liam mutters. "It's not a big deal. Really. It's not important."

"Not important," Jacen echoes robotically. "I thought you were dead. I thought I'd never see you again! I—I thought—"

Liam catches echoes of Jacen's nightmares, reflected in his tortured gaze. He hushes softly, "I'm okay, baby."

"It's all my fault. You left because of me. Because of what I did. To you. But you came back. You came back to me. I thought I'd lost you. Lee... Lee I was so scared." His voice breaks apart, cracking, "I was so scared."

Liam nuzzles against Jacen's neck and holds on to him more tightly. "It's okay."

"I'm so sorry, Lee. Please, I'll do better. I'll be better for you. I'll do anything. Anything, just please don't leave me. Please. I need you. I love you so much and I'm nothing without you. Without you nothing matters."

"I love you too. I promise not to leave again. I won't leave you. Okay?"

"What happened? You're hurt. Who hurt you? What...?"

Liam tries to dismiss it with a shrugging shake of his head, but

Jacen catches his chin, tilts it up so that he can examine Liam's injured eye, his mouth.

"Are you hurt anywhere else?"

"No. Jace, can we not get into it right now? Please? I swear I'm fine. It's really not a big deal, and it's kind of my fault anyway."

"No, I want to know what happened to you," Jacen frowns. "Do you need to go to the hospital? Do we need to file a police report? Why didn't you say he was hurt? You said he was fine!" Jacen accuses, shouting at Clay who is still standing behind Liam in the hall.

"That's because he *was* fine," Clay argues, riling at Jacen's anger. "Look, I—"

"We got in a fight," Liam interrupts before Clay can say anything else. "Me and Clay, downstairs. But we're cool now. It was an old argument. It was my fault."

"*You hit him*?!" Jacen releases Liam, turning to Clay, his fists balling up tightly at his sides, his arms and shoulders tensing, the muscles flexing in preparation.

"Jacen," Liam says, catching hold of him, pushing him back.

"You fucking *hit him*?! You're supposed to protect him! What kind of a brother are you? What kind of a *cop* are you, to hit someone when they're clearly already in pain?! I'll fucking... I'll fucking kill you, you piece of shit...."

Liam speaks up, "Yasha, help me! Jacen, stop! It's not his fault! It's *my fault*!"

"And you have him making *excuses* for you, too?!" Murder shines red and ready in Jacen's eyes. Clay says not a word, unwilling to throw Liam's angry confessions, his professed behavior that night with a stranger, in Jacen's face in defense of his own actions.

Yasha helps Liam pull Jacen back into the apartment. Some of the other tenants are peeking out from their own doorways now, looking up the stairwell to see what the fuss is about.

"Jacen, please," Liam sobs, broken, with almost no more fight left in him. "I wanted him to. I was egging him on. I was doing everything I could to get him to hit me; it's not his fault. He's my *family*. Don't hurt him. Please. *Please,* just let it go," he begs. "Please."

"I apologize for hurting Liam," Clay says calmly. "We've got a heavy past, and I should have known better. He's my little brother and I love him, and you two obviously have a lot of talking you need to do, so I'm going to go and give you your space."

"Get the fuck out of here," Jacen spits. "I don't want to fucking see your face again and if you lay your goddamn hands on my husband again you'll fucking regret it. I guarantee it."

Liam moans. Valery reads the utter lack of strength left in him, the nearness to collapse put off by sheer force of will alone, and winds an arm around him, bringing him to the kitchen to sit. Once she has him seated in one of the few available chairs, she grabs a handful of ice cubes from the freezer, wraps them in paper towels and presses the compress gingerly to his injuries. "Steady," she says softly to him. "Just breathe. That's it. Don't worry about them, okay? We're gonna take care of you now."

Yasha plants a hand on Jacen's chest, pushing him back. "Clay, it was nice to meet you. I promise that Jacen is just acting this way because he's had a very rough day. My apologies on his behalf."

"No problem. I'm just glad I was able to find Avery. Take care of him."

Clay reinforces the words with a heavy stare and turns to leave, descending rapidly back down the three flights of steps. Yasha gets Jacen back inside and shuts the door, standing between him and it.

"Jacen!" Valery calls from the kitchen, leaning over Liam. "Get your head out of your ass!"

The sharp edge to her voice more than anything is what snaps Jacen out of his rage-filled haze. He turns to see Liam shivering faintly with a fearful pallor, his eyes closed and seemingly ready to fall over. The chair and Valery are the only things keeping him upright.

"You need to get the mattress out and ready so we can lay him down and let him rest," she instructs. "Yash, get Liam a glass of water."

"I'm fine. I just need a sec," Liam protests. "Just got kind of dizzy but I'm fine."

"So you keep telling us," Valery frowns, watching Jacen hurry to the bedroom to drag their mattress set into place. Yasha returns with a cup of water from the tap and sets it in front of Liam, who doesn't even register the cup's presence. There's a disturbing emptiness behind his barely-opened eyes. It's a look both Valery and Yasha have seen before in their combined experience with counseling—that of a person who's pushed themselves past their limit of tolerance for survival's sake alone, and who's run out of both the fuel to sustain their course and the ability to maintain a functional state of being. As they watch Liam, and catch each other's reactions, communicating wordlessly about the things they've observed throughout the day and night, they see him gradually come undone. It's quite subtle and could almost be mistaken for calmness, but as the tension in Liam's face slowly disappears, smoothing out fine lines around his eyes and mouth, the sense of poorly-masked emptiness only grows. He's not calming down at all, he's giving up and mentally breaking apart, letting the stark desperation of his condition wrest loose his hold on things.

I don't like this, Valery tells Yasha with a glance.

Neither do I, he agrees.

The nightmare lasts an eternity. It goes on and on for hours, folding in on itself at times, doubling back, replaying on a loop where the soundtrack is nothing but screaming—bloody, raw, soul-shredding.

Liam has always loved his characters, his creations—the people he becomes for the pleasure of others. They are his haven, the roles that he plays to keep sane, the hard shell of his exoskeleton in which he hides, safe from harm. He clings to them like he clings to nothing else in the whole of his life. No one can take them away. And they are his outlet, his way to bleed out the creeping urges, the simmering curiosities, and the untapped reserves of his consciousness. They are all him, but they are also none of them him.

In the nightmare, he is his creations, each of them in turn.

He's a punk. He's a gentleman. He's a twink.

He's Leah, in a cornflower blue silk slip of a dress that skims over his thighs like a cool breath. The soft auburn curls of his cascading wig tickle his shoulders, his middle back, and the sides of his neck. His open-toed shoes bite at his feet, but it's a good kind of pain. He doesn't mind it. The flowery perfume he's sprayed on fills his senses, anchoring him to the persona. He's more at home in her than he's been in any building he's routinely slept in as far back as he can remember.

In his mind, he knows the room number. It keeps changing, though. Sometimes it's twelve, sometimes it's twenty-one, sometimes it's one hundred and twelve, and sometimes it's all of them at the same time. Standing in front of the door, he sees all of the numbers at once and each of them alone.

I've been here, he thinks. *This is the place.*

He knocks, slightly alters his pose, composes his expression, shifts his stance, and pushes out his hip, his fake breasts.

When he hears the footsteps approaching from the other side of the door, that's when the dream splinters.

He's confident and ready.

He's panicked and sweating; a voice inside his head yells at him to *RUN! RUN NOW! RUN!*

He's sobbing and stumbling.

The door opens.

There's a heavyset bald man standing there.

There's no one standing there.

Dice is standing there.

It shifts back to being the bald man but Liam knows that if he looks too closely at him, his face will melt off and drip down to the carpet and Liam will see who it really is, and if he sees that, he'll lose his mind. His sanity will break clean off like a rotten limb bearing a too-heavy weight.

Liam says his lines and follows his client inside. Being Leah is easy, because he *is* Leah. They are the same. She is at least as real as anyone else Liam has claimed to be.

He's standing in a darkened hotel room and the sense of impending doom twists his gut up in sickening knots. Madness claws at the edges of his brain. The person before him flickers like an old-fashioned movie, in and out, bright and dim, this and that. They change and morph. He doesn't dare look directly at them because the constant changing makes him want to gouge out his eyes rather than endure the sight. They shrink, grow, get fat, thin, they have a beard, they're clean-shaven. They're every race and color. But the worst part, the very worst part, is that it doesn't matter what they look like, Liam still knows. He knows who it is, underneath. It's the same person it's always been. It's always the same person. Every time he knocks at a door, waiting for an answer, he's calling on the same person, over and over and over and over again. But it's never who he needs it to be.

But in the dream, it is. The dream is the truth. The dream is his completion. The dream is his damnation.

The apology swells in his throat, growing in substance and size until it's too big to pass his lips. He sobs, trying to force it out. He cries, and the tears make his mascara run in black smears down his cheeks.

I'm sorry, he cries. *I'm sorry. I'm sorry. Please. Please forgive me. Please. I'm sorry.*

The man's hands tear at his dress, ripping the delicate shoulder strap, splitting the seam. The sound of it is stark in his ears, over-loud, offensive. The dress falls away and he's standing there in his bra, stuffed with falsies, his stockings and panties.

Look at you! Why?! Why would you do this to me?! You're disgusting! You're a LIAR! STOP LYING! Pervert! You're a disgrace! You make me sick! Take it off! Take it off and stop LYING!

The bra is torn off next, the elastic snaps back, biting at his skin, but the tears burn even more. They rake down his throat, searing his lungs. He tries to collapse to the floor, to cover himself, but it's no use. He's not as strong as he should be. He's weak. Weak and pathetic.

Fingers grab and tear at his stockings, his shoes, his panties. They are all brutally torn from him. It's Leah being murdered, spit and shit upon while he's helpless to save her.

Please, he begs, pleads. *I'm sorry!*

You fucking LIAR! You're a joke! You're pathetic! Take this shit off! All of it! NOW!

He's naked and still he's being clawed at, short-clipped nails drag over his skin, trying to pull that off too. He falls to his knees, holding himself, rocking, sucking in rough breaths through his wrenching cries, the world awash, smeared, horrific.

You're nothing! You're nothing but a filthy LIAR and you make me sick! You're nothing! NOTHING!

I'M SORRY, Liam screams until his voice is in shreds, as his body falls away in strips of crimson ribbon made of skin and muscle, revealing the abyss where his soul used to be, the emptiness that's been inside him for long, long years. Maybe forever. *Timothy, please, I love you! I just didn't know what else to do! This is all I have! This is who I am now! PLEASE! I'M SORRY!*

Timothy stands there over him, his normally sweet face contorted with rage, his voice so sharp and so jagged that if Liam had ears left they'd be bleeding, *Everything we had, you ruined! You shit on it and now you mean NOTHING to me! WHY DID I EVER LOVE YOU?! You make me SICK! You WHORE! You stupid, filthy, fucking WHORE! I hate you! I HATE YOU!*

The pain wins. Liam's will gives out. He welcomes death as it ends him, as the darkness swallows him up, leaving nothing left but the lies he's told.

The dream folds in on itself again, as it has done over and over, all night long.

He's standing in the hall, outside the room of his next client. He's a cowboy, with authentic leather boots handcrafted in Dallas, Texas, and slim-fitting, perfectly worn clothes that hug his body like a second skin. The woody scent of his cologne, the grip of his thick leather belt around his hips, the cool touch of his silver lucky horseshoe necklace resting on his chest all serve to remind him of all of the times he's worn this identity, and how well it fits him. Smiling, happy, contented, Liam steps up to the door as the numbers change but stay the same.

But it doesn't last long. The dread creeps into him, burrowing under his skin, making it crawl, because a part of him knows what's coming, what's waiting for him on the other side of the door. It's the same thing that's always waiting there.

And that's why he knocks. That's why he acts, inviting without a shred of doubt the worst thing he could ever imagine. He beckons to it with opened arms and a willing heart, ready to die, ready for Timothy to tear him down and end him, again and again and again, all the while shouting his disgust, his disdain. Because Liam deserves this. This is what he's earned. This is all he gets to have. He savors it. He dives in, turns inside out and outside in, begging his forgiveness, knowing he'll never get it. Not ever.

He's nothing but a stupid fucking whore anyway.

Liam whimpers softly. It's a pure, heartbroken sound.

He stirs, rising up and up through the thick fog of his sleep. Gasping, the tears burn his eyes and the burning radiates out, awakening all of the throbbing pain laced through his face. He wonders if it all became real, if he'll find his face in ribbons, like it was in the nightmare.

More of the heavy weight of the dream clears away and all that it reveals is more pain. He makes a small, hurt sound, halfway to a sob and brings a hand up to touch his face. When his fingertips connect with the flesh, he hisses. The hand reflexively draws away and more tenderly, he traces the swollen tissue. He's confused, so very confused.

Where am I? What happened to me? Did I fall asleep on a job? Do I need to call Della and see the doc? God, I hope I don't need stitches. That'll put me out of commission for weeks. No one wants to fuck Frankenstein.

Gotta find my phone. Gotta figure out if the John's still here. If he's the one that did this to my face, I've gotta beat a hasty retreat, get the fuck back to my car.

He tries to open his eyes. They won't go. His left eye cracks open. Bright light scorches his retinas and he grunts, blinking his vision clear of tears. But his right eye won't budge. The lid is anchored shut. It sends a small cold slithering terror wriggling down to his stomach.

He begins to yawn. When his lips part, the tissue pulls, threatening to reopen a recently healed wound. Wincing and grimacing, he fights against the vestiges of sleep as every new discovery unsettles him more than the last.

Turning his head to scan the room, his heart thumping wildly in his chest, he freezes as he sees....

"Val." The name on his tongue is ragged and thin.

Some realization flickers, but it's as ephemeral as a mayfly.

Valery's expression twists with obvious concern as Liam's face perfectly displays how very lost he is, how scared.

"You have a black eye and a fat lip," she provides softly. "Hi."

She's lying on his right side, the side he can't see out of, so he turns toward her, rolling onto his right side. With a quick scan, he finds her wearing an oversized tee shirt and not much else. The shirt is familiar. He stares at it, knowing she might mistakenly think he's staring at her breasts, trying to puzzle it out.

Jacen's. It's Jacen's shirt. That's why it looks so big on her.

"It was our husbands' idea."

"Jacen?"

Her tone is so motherly, soothing in a way Liam has very rarely experienced, even as a child, that it in turn pushes his emotions closer to the surface.

"He's sleeping on an air mattress in the next room with Yasha." She shifts so that her head is propped on her hand rather than just the pillow. Dark, soft curls spill over the white linen. "You know, I've never really seen him this sick over something. He's really afraid of hurting you, but he won't say why."

Liam sees the now-thawed ice pack beside the mattress on the floor, the pill bottles, a bowl, a cup with a straw. It all comes back to him — the fight, the long hours he spent wandering San Luis Obispo, the bar he wound up in, the guy who picked him up there, the face-off with Clay, the chaos when he found the balls to show his face to Jacen again. Glancing at the door with his good eye, he tries to picture Jacen out there, on an air mattress that would barely be big enough to hold him let alone him *and* Yasha. The curtainless room and the sunlight it's flooded with lead him to assume it's late enough that he's the only one still trying to wake up. But why wouldn't Jacen be in here? Why would he ask Valery to take his place as Liam's nursemaid?

Then Liam recalls the things he said to Jacen when he was caught in the alley with the phone after calling Ryan, and truly understands how much pain Jacen must be in, too.

Valery watches Liam's misery, his silence. He curls up beside her on the mattress, the sheet gathered up almost to his chin, with no sign of wanting to get up or rejoin the world. He and Jacen had seemed so happy to her before, the gulf that's opened between them is baffling. It doesn't make sense.

"Can I ask you something?" she tries hesitantly. "It's totally none of my business so feel free to tell me to fuck off."

Liam looks right at her, his one eye opened and aware, much more so than it was the night before when all was empty and broken. He waits for her to continue, mere inches separating them as they lie on their sides, facing each other.

"Liam, he's your husband. Why would it hurt you to sleep next to him? What happened? You two seemed so great, I just...." She shrugs. Liam tentatively licks at his sore lip, moistening it so that he can speak without further injuring himself. The vivid, dark coloring of his black eye is painful to look at, so she can only guess at what it must actually feel like for Liam. But she can tell that Liam's face is the least of his concerns right now.

"Our fight," he starts. Then he stops there. The flash of pure vulnerability in his expression says more than words ever could.

"Go on," she coaxes gently, "I can tell you want to. I'm a pretty good listener, if you want to talk about it."

He looks at her, and she seems so fragile, delicate. She's a wife, and has been for a while. She's been through years of marriage, and there's an awe inspiring amount of strength and intelligence contained inside her small frame. *Maybe she'll understand,* he hopes. *Maybe out of anyone, she would.*

"I wasn't ready," he tells her, and the amount of urgency and betrayal he fills those three little hesitant words with explain it all, before he goes any further. "I wasn't ready to let him have sex with me and he did it anyway. How ironic, you know? I'm a whore. An old whore. And it's my job to put out for him."

It feels like a fist squeezing her heart, trying to crush it. Her chest aches and she reaches out, taking his hand, holding it. *Oh god, Liam.*

"No means no. No matter what," she says. Fight enters her voice, the same fight that's always present when there's someone before her badly used, a spirit damaged by the careless or cruel actions of another. Hearing it, how she takes his side just like that, without question, Liam's frown deepens. His lips turn down at the edges and he squeezes her hand, trying to hold it together. "Jacen knows that. Better than anyone. There is *no* excuse."

"But I didn't exactly say it. I didn't *say*... but...."

"He should have known. Right? He should have realized."

Yeah, he should have, Liam thinks. *He should have realized. And stopped.* But then he thinks back, to when he first took Jacen, the force that he used, the coercion. *I have no right to be upset about this. I was owed this.*

And still, the betrayal of it, after everything that Liam gave Jacen, the faith, the trust, after everything was stripped away, all of his control, his control mechanisms. All that Liam had left was the trust he placed in the man he loved. He remembers how it felt when Jacen fucked him without permission, using his body, fucking with his mind too, as he professed his love while making crude use of the vessel of Liam's body.

Liam fights not to cry, but as his lips try to draw back with his grimace, the flesh tears, drawing fresh blood. His hand goes to his face, hiding behind it, he squeezes his good eye shut and holds his breath, holds it in as the hopelessness of it all settles on him again.

Valery sighs with her anguish at witnessing Liam's torment. She grabs a tissue and sets it in his hand, then draws his hand from his face and grips it tightly.

Pushing on, pushing him past the horror of it all and into action, she says steadily, with steel behind the words, along with an unspoken promise not to abandon him until this is figured out, "Do you feel safe being alone with him? Be honest with me."

"Yeah, I do. It just..." he takes a deep breath and slowly lets it back out, confessing in a small voice, "It hurt."

"I know," she tells him, proud of him for being able to admit to that. Closing up their joined hands with her other, she kisses his knuckles and waits.

"Thanks. For staying with me. If I'd woken up with him it might have freaked me out. But don't tell him that, okay?"

"Okay." Taking a cool cloth from the bowl on the floor by her side, she presses it gingerly to his bruised eye, dabs at his bleeding lip. "What happened here? Why'd Clay want to hit you?"

"Long story. I provoked him."

"That's no excuse."

"Yeah, it is," he disagrees.

"So, what? You deserved it? Just like you deserved Jacen forcing himself on you? Come on, Liam. Tell me it's not the same. I dare you. Let's see how good a liar you really are."

The sting from that catches Liam by surprise. It hits far too close to home, too close to the truth, and he chokes on fresh sobs. She winds an arm around him, hugging him tenderly. He holds on to her and cries into her soft curls.

"I just..." he hisses, not able to let go of her, murmuring against the warmth of her skin. "I couldn't leave. But I couldn't come back, either. I couldn't be who I was and I don't know how to be the person I'm supposed to be now."

"You need to learn how to speak up for what you want. That's my advice to you in a nutshell. Say it with me, even if it seems stupid. Come on. *No.*"

"...No," Liam repeats. The word feels foreign on his tongue, a new weapon that he's never had the use of before.

Valery smiles.

Chapter 24
Pride, Proving and Taking Time

"Do you want me and Yasha to take off so that you two can talk?"

Liam stands by the room's closed door, one hand flat on the wood, thinking over Valery's offer. Then he admits, "I don't know. Before yesterday I would have said yes."

Valery walks up to him, gripping his shoulder supportively. "You can't hide in here all day. You need to eat, get some fresh ice on that eye."

"Yeah," he sighs. "You know, I really don't want to talk about it at all, but I guess I have to. I'm afraid to see him. There's just so much shit between us right now." He shakes his head with annoyance, as if to clear it. "Fuck it."

Liam opens the door. Dressed in a short-sleeved shirt and sweatpants, he shuffles out of the bedroom, glancing around as he goes, looking out for Yasha or Jacen. Valery stays with him, a step behind. It doesn't take long to find the others. Jacen is seated cross-legged at the end of the hallway, blocking the way with furniture parts strewn all around — wood, screws, screwdrivers, and a lot of other things Liam can't identify on first glance. Yasha is standing over Jacen, sipping coffee and pretending to supervise. They're both wearing the same clothes as they were the day before.

Jacen senses Liam there before he hears or sees him, like a bloodhound, his head snapping up as his attention is piqued. He jumps to his feet and pauses, frozen, momentarily incapable of movement, stunned by the battered state of his lover.

Yasha's impassive expression shifts, instead becoming quickly one of alarm at something subtle he sees in Valery's eyes and the quirk of her mouth. "Shit," he hisses, as much from the angriness of Liam's wounds as from the tension in the air.

Looking from Liam's angry black eye to his split, swollen lip, to Valery, Jacen feels how she exudes a surprising and fiercely protective air as she lightly touches Liam's arm. He twitches forward, wanting with all of his being to hug Liam, but he doesn't dare. Not yet.

Gathering his courage, his pride, Liam can't find the words, at first.

"I'm so sorry, Lee," Jacen urges softly.

Yasha glances from his wife to his best friend to Liam, trying to put it together, trying to figure out why Valery is just barely managing to not strike out bodily at Jacen.

"I know there's nothing I can say to defend myself. All I can do is hope that you are able to forgive me but you have to believe that — "

Liam holds up a hand, silencing him. "I shouldn't have called Ryan without talking to you first. That was wrong. And I shouldn't have run away like I did. It was cruel of me to make you worry like that. And I should've said no, instead of just hoping you would stop. I'm not used to having the option of standing up for myself in bed, so I can't bring myself to see what happened as your fault. But I didn't deserve that. I know that now."

Valery gives his arm a firmer squeeze, bursting with pride in him. Yasha's mouth falls open. He stares at Jacen, astonished. Jacen hangs his head, covering his face with a hand, turning red and blinking away shameful tears.

Yasha's lip curls in distaste, but before he gets a word out, his wife says sharply to him, "Don't. He feels bad enough, can't you see that?"

Jacen wipes a hand over his face and looks at Liam. "This isn't your fault. You trusted me, and I knew how to play you so you'd go along with it. I'm the bad guy here."

"Stop," Liam says, tiredly. "You wanna know why Clay hit me? Why he did this to me?"

Jacen looks up at him sharply.

"He was being so nice to me, trying to bring me home to you

because he cares about us. But I didn't deserve his kindness, and I couldn't face you after how I'd acted, how I'd endangered you and the things I'd said to you. I wanted to leave, to just run away and let you go for good, but I couldn't. I couldn't go. I tried, though. I went to a bar. Had too much to drink, let a guy pick me up."

Jacen's face crumples. Every ounce of strength leaves him.

"I followed him out to the alley. He started touching me. I tried to focus on the wad of bills he'd flashed, to get me through, but it made me nauseous. I felt disgusting. I'd rather die than let anyone else but you touch me like that again, to give you up for *that*." Liam lets it hang there, before he continues. "But I let Clay think I went through with it, so that he'd want to hit me. And he did. And the pain felt really good. So I told him being with that guy made me remember back when I'd been out fucking men for cash while Timothy was home, suffering, and how I'd pretend to be someone else, someone better, how I'd pretend Tim didn't even exist, just for a couple of minutes, to get through it, and how that made me happy. That's why he hit me, okay? I begged him to keep going. But he wouldn't. He *wouldn't*. Clay's a good friend. You should know that."

He takes a step away from Valery, toward Jacen; then another. "You could never be as cruel to me as I am to myself. But I'm sick and tired of hating who I am. And yeah, I'm scared. I'm really scared that I can never be the man you think you fell in love with. All I want is to make you proud of me, and to find a way to be proud of myself. I'm deeply sorry, Jacen."

Liam hangs his head, having confessed and given everything he has to give, waiting for Jacen to tell him to get out, to rail on him the way Clay did, maybe, or to rip him to shreds the way that Timothy did in the nightmare, calling him a good-for-nothing dirty whore. He waits for it, expecting it.

So when Jacen instead wraps Liam in an oh-so-careful hug, breathing in the scent of his skin and hair, infusing the embrace with pure, powerful love, Liam moans and returns the gesture, hugging his husband back. "Let me prove that I deserve you," Liam whispers against Jacen's blanketing warmth.

Jacen holds on to him like he's never going to let go. Liam feels

Jacen's tears trickling down his neck, collecting in the hollow of his collarbone.

"Please, just give me the chance," Liam asks.

The desperation and despondency in Liam's words destroy Jacen and his ability to respond coherently. He wants to find a way to convince Liam that he deserves every good thing the world has to offer, to let Liam see himself the way that Jacen sees him, as a beautiful, magnificent man, whom Jacen is humbled and honored to know and love. But he can't. He has to let Liam get to that place on his own, somehow. He has to love him through it, with patience and devotion.

"Love you," Jacen whispers. "I'll always love you. Whatever you need, okay?"

"Thank you," Liam sighs.

Valery wipes her eyes dry and Yasha goes to her, kissing her cheek with understanding and appreciation.

A sense of normalcy begins to return. Valery and Yasha take their leave. Liam gives Valery a grateful hug at the door. She gives him a soft peck on the lips and whispers words of encouragement, asking him to call her whenever he wants to talk. Still quite unable to get past the realization of what Jacen did to Liam, it speaks volumes that Yasha says farewell to Jacen with a firm handshake and nothing more. Jacen endures Yasha's coldness, welcoming the punishment that it is, knowing he can affect it no more than he can affect Liam's turmoil.

Once they are left alone with each other, Liam goes to the kitchen for breakfast, waving Jacen off when he offers to make something for him. Jacen returns to the half-built cabinet in pieces on the floor, using the distraction to keep his mind busy. Wondering why Jacen decided to build it in the particular spot he selected, right at the end of the hall rather than in the more open space of the living room, Liam realizes that Jacen must have wanted to be as close to his husband as possible, to overhear any calls or trouble, or maybe just drawn there, unwilling to be even a few more feet apart than they had to be.

Liam takes his food into the bedroom, eating while he begins sorting the mess of boxes there.

It's the beginning of a long period of quiet between the two men. They each work at their own tasks, establishing their new home one possession at a time. All that day they work in separate rooms. Jacen cooks lunch, leaving Liam's share ready for him when he wants it. He gives Liam his space, and Liam indulges in the procured privacy.

Darkness quickly descends on them as the sun sets. Pizza is ordered for dinner. Lamps are lit and placed strategically around the rooms so that they can keep working, keep unpacking. Bedtime approaches, and Jacen doesn't know what to do. More than anything he wants to sleep next to Liam, to enjoy the comfort of his nearness in order to get some much-needed rest. Jacen had slept barely an hour or two the previous night and tiredness creeps deeply into his bones. But he makes up the air mattress again with fresh sheets and a blanket. Liam works late into the night, unpacking their clothes and putting them either into the closet or in neat piles until they can buy some bedroom furniture.

Peeking his head into the bedroom, Jacen says, "'Night, Lee. You should head to bed soon, too. Get some rest."

"Yeah. I will," Liam agrees, nodding, folding a shirt over in his hands. "'Night."

Liam watches him walk into the second bedroom where the air mattress is laid out, as a cold fist tightens around his heart in his chest, wanting to call Jacen back. Not a word is spoken. He selfishly lets Jacen go.

The next day, Jacen leaves the house at ten in the morning to be at work for the lunch rush. He gets showered and dressed, and, with dark circles under his eyes, says goodbye to Liam from across the room.

Liam thrives in the distance Jacen provides him with. He stops being afraid that Jacen will ask something of him he's not ready to give. He stops worrying about much of anything besides getting their lives in order, starting with the few hundred square feet that is now their home. That much Liam can handle. He turns on some music and smiles as the list of chores to be done unfolds in his mind.

The next day Liam goes out to buy more furniture and, when he finds some that he likes after a few hours' search, arranges to have it delivered. That he does this on his own, without Jacen's input, is a triumph for him. It feels like he's finally able to contribute to their lives, instead of standing helpless as Jacen does all of the work for them both. Each day, when Jacen comes home after work, their space feels a little more "theirs" for all of Liam's work, and a little more real. It makes him happy deep down in his heart to see Liam taking on the task of unpacking, without any prompting. The kitchen cabinets fill up, as do the closets. New artwork is hung on the walls, selected by Liam, a mix of both of their tastes. But most of all it's the small things, like the old magnets that Liam displays proudly on the fridge, that bring the warmth back to Jacen's heart. Each time he goes to the kitchen, he gently touches the ones that mean the most, like the one from the Vancouver Aquarium that, for him, symbolizes the period of time when they were first becoming friends.

Liam continues to draw in on himself, not speaking much, quietly building a normal life for the first time in his nearly thirty years. He devotes the whole of his battered soul to it, determined to do a good job. Every day he unpacks a few more boxes, determined to go through each one and find a place for everything, including all of Jacen's cooking paraphernalia. When he runs out of space, he just hangs a rack from the ceiling from which to hook Jacen's large pots and pans, and buys another armoire for storage.

As Liam organizes his personal things, he finds the few pieces of his old "costumes", the items he couldn't bring himself to leave behind in Los Angeles. Without much thinking about it, he starts to wear them, incorporating them into his daily wardrobe. A week after they've moved in, he wears the thick leather belt with the huge silver buckle. Three days after that he slips on his combat boots and a pair of cargos when he goes out food shopping. The day after that, he puts on some pale pink lip gloss, keeping the tube in his pocket to reapply throughout the day. He develops, subconsciously at first, an overpowering need to claim his personas for himself, absorbing them and reincorporating the facets of his own self that they grew out of into who he is now. It's not until the day when he wears the lip gloss that he realizes why. He's doing it, he discovers in a flash of insight, staring at himself in the bathroom mirror, in defiance of the nightmare he had in which Timothy tore him down repeatedly, trying to corrupt and besmirch the way Liam identified himself since he was nineteen-years-old.

Restlessness and the pleasant, sunny weather inspire Liam to begin taking daily walks that last for miles. He always starts from their building but explores every possible direction, heading out in a wide radius, venturing into the city that has become theirs. Two weeks from the day they moved in, Liam interrupts his walk, detouring into a drug store on his route. He grabs a basket to shop with and loads it up, buying mascara, eyeliner, nail polish, a waxing kit, and a few shades of lipstick. He buys them only because it feels right to do so, and for no other conscious reason. Purchases in hand, he continues on his walk, going two more miles out before doubling back.

When he gets home he hides the things he bought in one of the drawers of his new bureau, concealing them under a carefully folded stack of long-sleeved shirts. That night, when Jacen gets home, exhausted and irritable, Liam watches him from the hallway, leaning against the wall, picking at his nails as Jacen digs his wallet and keys from his pocket and kicks off his shoes. Stacked in the far corner of the living room are the sheets, blanket and pillow that Jacen uses every night when he sleeps on the couch, as he's done every night since they had it delivered, favoring it over the air mattress. Liam stares at the linens, then sees Jacen stretch his arms, trying to work a knot out of his back. The dark circles under his eyes are still there, and a profound sullenness has pervaded Jacen's being for weeks, ever since the fight. Thinking of this and his new purchases, which feel like a secret but powerful accomplishment, buoying his spirit, Liam clears his throat to get Jacen's attention and says to him, "Hey. How was work?"

Noticing him for the first time, Jacen turns. "You're still up? Thought you'd be in bed. It's almost one a.m."

Liam shrugs. "I got a call from Mrs. O'Donnell in 1B. Her kitchen sink's been leaking. I was online doing some 'plumbing for dummies' research. You know they actually have a book for that? I might pick it up if I can't figure out what to do on my own. Anyway, I told her I'd head down there first thing tomorrow morning to take a look. She seemed really grateful."

Jacen goes to the sink for a glass of water, shooting Liam an amused half-smile, squinting a little at him in disbelief. "Yeah? I mean if you don't want to I can always make time or call someone in."

"Nah. I want to," Liam argues. He smiles, then ducks his head bashfully. He traps his bottom lip between his teeth and glances surreptitiously to the master bedroom. "Are you gonna come to bed soon?"

Jacen stops moving. He slowly puts down his glass of water and stares at Liam, not comprehending. Liam meets his stare, backing up the question with a level, steady look, not backing down, daring Jacen to make him repeat the inquiry. "I was gonna take a shower first," Jacen says after a pause.

"Okay. Don't be too long." Liam turns, walking back to the bedroom with his hands in his pockets.

Jacen watches him go, then smiles hugely, chuckling to himself, flushing with joy.

He speeds through the shower, but doing a thorough job. While drying off he realizes his pajamas are back in the living room where he'd left them that morning. Tucking a towel around his waist he goes in search of them. The pile of linens and his pajamas aren't there though. Jacen walks back to the bedroom. Liam is there, one lamp casting a soft golden glow over the new dark wood of the bedroom set Liam picked out for them, the king sized bed, the matching bureaus, the high-backed chair near the window. Thus far Jacen has only ever been in the bedroom to get his clothes and get out as fast as he can, to not intrude on Liam's space more than he needs to. Liam has the bed turned back and passes Jacen his pajamas.

"Thanks," Jacen says.

Liam goes to his side of the bed and climbs in, averting his eyes as Jacen gets dressed. He lies down on his side, facing Jacen, curled up around the pillow tucked under his head. Once dressed, Jacen joins him under the covers.

Sighing with the pleasure of pure, luxurious comfort, Jacen smiles and murmurs, "'Night, Lee."

"Goodnight," Liam smiles back. His gaze darts down to Jacen's mouth and he begins to move closer, bridging the gap between them. Acting desperately on the implied permission, Jacen meets him in the middle, kissing Liam tenderly, a mere press of lips on lips. Cupping a hand around the side of Liam's jaw, Jacen draws it out a few more precious moments. He's all dimples and happiness when they break apart. That night brings Jacen the best sleep he's had in all his life.

Early the next morning, Jacen feels the mattress shift when Liam gets out of bed. A short while later, after falling back asleep, he stirs as a soft kiss is applied to his temple. Liam whispers to him, "I'm going down to 1B. Call if you need me."

"Mm," Jacen hums without even opening his eyes, "'Kay."

A few seconds later, he's asleep again.

By the time he has to leave for work again, Liam is still gone, so Jacen calls him.

"Hey, how's it going down there?"

"Oh, not bad. I had to replace the one line. Just got back from picking up supplies. Should be done in a little bit."

"Cool. Very impressive," Jacen grins into the phone. "I'm headin' out now but I shouldn't be home as late tonight."

"Oh. Shit. I didn't realize how late it was. I didn't even get to see you today."

"Eh, I'll see you later. I don't expect to be as sleepy tonight. The bed was great."

There's lightness to his gruff voice that Jacen adores when Liam replies, "It's a date, then. Have a good day at work, baby."

Chapter 25
Getting As Good As You Give

Shortly before eleven, Jacen gets home from work, anticipating his "date" with Liam. The progress they had made the night before buoyed his spirits all day, and he's still chipper when he returns. He hurries over to Liam for a quick kiss before hitting the shower. Standing at the kitchen sink, Liam is hand-washing some new crystal wine goblets. He smiles over his shoulder in welcome as Jacen circles him from behind in a brief hug, pecking a kiss to Liam's neck.

"Hey, handsome," Jacen grins. "Missed you."

"Me too," Liam allows shyly.

"These new?" Jacen asks, indicating the glasses.

"Yep. I picked up some wine for tonight and remembered we didn't have the right glasses."

"They're really great. I like 'em."

"Good."

Liam shuts off the water and dries his hands, taking his time. Then he turns to face Jacen. With a sort of proud defiance, he gazes up at his husband, locking eyes with him.

Jacen notices right away. But more than that, he *understands*. It's because of this understanding that he reaches up, brushing the pad of his thumb over the delicate skin near the corner of Liam's eye.

"What's this?"

Over the past number of days, stretching into weeks, Jacen had not always been around when Liam had dressed in the pieces of his old costumes. Liam tended to stay in pajamas until nearly lunchtime, and Jacen typically returned from his shift at the bistro late at night, when Liam was back in pajamas again. But he did notice the combat boots in their bedroom, and saw Liam wearing his cargos. He also saw the lip gloss on the bathroom counter. And this evening, Liam is wearing one of the black button-down shirts he would pair with an expensive suit when going to see higher end clients with a taste for someone refined. Liam is also wearing eyeliner, a carefully applied, thin, black line of it, ringing his big, beautiful green eyes. The effect is powerful, bringing out perfectly just how vivid and gorgeous Liam's eyes really are, but when Jacen notices the faint pink tint to his lips, the remnant of lipstick applied hours ago, Jacen feels it as a low throbbing heat between his legs that swells and grows.

Liam doesn't flinch or glance away. He stares back into Jacen's eyes as heat starts to burn there, too, and says, "I bought a few things. I like wearing it."

There's a definite moment then, in which Liam waits for Jacen to laugh or criticize. He half-dares him to, expecting the fates to find new ways to mock and destroy him. Jacen sees this expectation in Liam's face, reading it as clearly as if Liam had scrawled a declaration of self-consciousness in black letters across his face with the same stick of eyeliner. Acknowledging this discovery, Jacen moves right past it, driven by his own reaction, one much more powerful than Liam's bashfulness.

Jacen's lips curl in the beginnings of a smile, and Liam's heart stops. His eyes grow fractionally wider. And then his heart starts beating again, but beating rapidly, thumping heavily in his chest. Because Jacen's smile is not one of amusement, it's pure undiluted *hunger*.

Things happen quickly after that. Jacen moves in, wrapping his right hand around the gentle swell of Liam's left pectoral muscle, rolling his thumb over the piercing embedded in his nipple. It punctuates the course of Jacen's focus. Bowing his head slightly, Jacen parts his lips and touches them to Liam's stained lips, gently at first, then more firmly as their kiss deepens. Jacen growls low in his throat, savoring the taste of the lip gloss, the soft sound Liam makes at the stimulation to his nipple, the kiss itself. Liam opens for him, readily, and Jacen enters him, determined, needy, and possessive. Their tongues twist together. Jacen maps Liam's mouth, rediscovering it, taking from it all of the pleasure Jacen could want.

A semblance of self-control reclaims Jacen. He ends the kiss reluctantly, pulling back. His pupils are blown wide and black with lust. His interest nudges Liam's hip.

"It looks good," Jacen says hoarsely, wrecked and fighting back hard against the rising tide of his passion. "I'm gonna take a shower."

Liam nods, his lips pursed in amusement, his dark-lined eyes twinkling. He stands there by the sink as Jacen goes into the bathroom. The water starts to run, pounding against the tile. Liam slowly makes his way over to the bathroom door, listening, savoring the tingle and throb in his lips from Jacen's hunger. Then he hears it, Jacen's swallowed grunts, the wet slap of skin on skin as he masturbates. Smiling wickedly with satisfaction, Liam strains his ears to catch every single thing.

In the shower, Jacen tugs fast and hard at his cock, thinking of Liam, his eyes ringed black, his lips painted pink, wondering if he was wearing it all day, even to go fix the plumbing. It's the thought of Liam on his back, under the sink, sweaty, cursing, in an old t-shirt and make-up that gets Jacen off as much as the heat of their kiss.

After the shower, spent and calmed, Jacen gets dressed. Liam is back in the kitchen, opening the wine, pouring it into two of the freshly-washed glasses. He's chosen a white, Sauvignon Blanc, and the sweet aroma tickles Jacen's nose, makes him smile. They sit in their new living room furniture, with Jacen in the armchair, Liam on the couch. Jacen chooses the chair so that he can enjoy a better view of Liam than he would get if they were side-by-side. Liam kicks his feet up on the ottoman, sighing and taking a sip.

"So, honey, how was work?"

Jacen's smirk widens, at both the lightness of Liam's mood and the endearment. "Isn't it funny? We used to say that as a joke, but now...."

Liam rolls the wine around on his tongue, drawing out the flavor, his eyes closing over with satisfaction. Puckering around the rich taste, he swallows and glances up at Jacen. There's so much there in his expression, Jacen is almost stunned. So many of Liam's defenses are down, down and gone, that truth shines out golden and miraculous from the depths. Liam used to be defined by his defenses. Every retort, every word or gesture was laden with some persona or another. Jacen had to seek out the actuality of him, digging down deep before he even scratched the surface. Now it's all laid bare, and Jacen feels blessed.

"It wasn't a joke to me," Liam says, unsmiling. "It was the only way I knew to feel close to you."

And there, right there, as Liam locks eyes with him, Jacen sees that Liam heard. He had heard everything that he did in the shower. More than that, he's letting Jacen know that he heard, that he wanted to hear, that he understands the heat he stirs even now in Jacen. Liam digests the knowledge of what he does to Jacen, drinking it down like nectar or the wine currently slipping over his lower lip as he lifts his glass once more. It warms Liam from the inside out, giving him back some of the power he's lost. His ability to seduce Jacen with such little effort on his own part, merely by revealing a side of himself that he has been leery of showing thus far, a few beguiling words, an interest in Jacen's life apart from Liam; Liam holds on to it, gripping the understanding like a precious jewel.

With a slight tilt of his head and a raise of his eyebrow, Liam indicates that Jacen never answered his initial question and that he's waiting for a response.

Jacen licks his lips and takes a deep drink of his wine. "Tough. It was tough. Always is. They have really high standards, so all I can do is bust my ass to do things the right way the first time and wait for the thumbs up or down. Standing by the ovens all day, working frantically and just constantly, turning out dish after dish, filling the orders as quickly as I can so that the customers get fed in a timely manner. I love it, don't get me wrong. It makes me feel really alive, and happy. Wanting to please them, to get even the smallest praise from Joe, it's kind of what it's all about for me."

"It suits you, the hard work. Plus, it's kind of hot."

Bowing his head at the compliment, Jacen looks up again and lifts his glass a few inches in a small toast. "Thanks."

"You're welcome."

"How about you?" Jacen debates asking and then says, "Are you lonely yet?"

Liam breathes out a small laugh. "I do miss all of the constant attention sometimes. Keeps the ego inflated, you know? But mostly I'm good. Maybe I'm just finally growing up. It's been great to meet the tenants and I'm gonna dive into fixing up the empty apartment tomorrow. Valery might even come up later in the day to help me paint."

"Well, if you ever want some more attention," Jacen offers, his voice sounding rough in a way that holds Liam's attention, his gaze sliding down Jacen's body. "I'm kind of your biggest fan."

Smiling despite himself, just for a moment, Liam basks in the heat of Jacen's stare before pulling away again, erecting a sort of invisible barrier to keep him at bay. Jacen feels it there between them, and aches. Sadness paints over Liam's face, and Jacen wants to scream, to rage at the depression that's taken hold of his lover, like that could banish it.

"I mean it, Lee. Are you happy? Can you be happy here?"

It's urgent, and plain. The straightforwardness of the question hurts because it serves to remind Liam of all of the times he tried to make Timothy see things that should have been apparent, like the dangers of prostitution and, later, why turning tricks had become a necessary evil in order to pay the medical bills. When he was Avery, Liam would speak plainly too. But rational thinking never did anything for him then and, ever since, he has learned not to scrutinize his circumstances and decisions too closely. He has adopted Timothy's compulsive nature, and some of the cynicism which came in force once his health deteriorated. It feels like Jacen is asking Liam to reclaim some of Avery's long-lost naivete and positive outlook. The last thing Liam wants is to do that and open himself up to the sort of torment that came with Timothy's slow, torturous death. If he lets himself be happy and carefree with Jacen, it could all happen again — especially with The Company breathing down their necks. He could lose Jacen like he lost Timothy.

It makes Liam angry, that Jacen is trying to take him back to such a dangerous emotional place. And, at the same time, Liam resents the fact that he can't simply be happy with Jacen. Nothing is simple anymore.

"Good wine, good company, no sleazy strangers to fuck or

suck? What's not to like?" Liam indicates his empty glass, standing with it. "You want some more, too?"

Jacen just stares at him, doing everything he can not to erupt with the sheer, maddening frustration of it all. His strain and hurt meets only a wall of non-expression from Liam. After a moment, Liam stops waiting for a reply and goes to get the wine bottle. When he returns with it, and his own refilled glass, Jacen is still waiting, strangling on all of the things he wants to shout at Liam but doesn't dare.

With a bitter semblance of a grin, Liam tries to push Jacen away like Timothy used to push Avery away; Avery, who only wanted to love and be loved. Opening his arms wide, Liam says, "This is what you signed up for. What did you expect when you married a broken old whore? Sunshine and rainbows?"

The words cut deep. Wanting to throw the wine glass that Liam had bought and so carefully washed by hand, his fist tightening on it so much than he waits to feel the crystal splinter and shatter inside his grip, Jacen instead sets it down on a side table and gets to his feet. He turns like he's going to go, but then stops, his face working with the battle within him, poorly concealed. It feels like he's bleeding, like Liam has somehow reached inside Jacen and ripped out something vital. He shoots a look full of accusation and injury at his husband.

But Jacen knows what this is, it's Liam building up that wall, moving back rather than forward, and Jacen won't stand for it, no matter what kind of pain Liam is in. He closes the gap between them, a matter of two or three feet. Jacen grabs the wine glass and the bottle from Liam, setting them carefully down too, beside his own glass. Then he faces Liam, fuming, determined.

"What are you so goddamned afraid of? Huh? Is it me? Are you afraid of me, Lee? Or is it you that you're afraid of? I'm in this for the long haul, no matter what, because I love you. I love *you*. And I'll be here, waiting for you to be comfortable enough to be *you*, and not all of the people you feel like you should be instead. You want to pretend to be an asshole? You want to pretend to be a victim of your own decisions? Well you can go right ahead, but I know that's not you. It's a fucking act and when you figure out what I already know about you, then we'll talk, okay? In the meantime, you need to find a way to respect the fact that I will always care about you, no matter what shit you want to throw at me on the way."

The rise and fall of Liam's chest, increasing at the same rate as the color in his cheeks, is what Jacen fixates on. He examines every facet of Liam's reaction, the wicked gleam in his narrowed eyes only growing as he sees him taken aback, shocked silent. Jacen holds his ground, bearing down on Liam emotionally and physically, towering over him, stronger in every sense of the word.

Something breaks. The wall forms a crack, letting vulnerability spill out, gushing faster and faster. A tremble works its way through Liam's form and he sets his jaw with stubbornness. *How dare you*, his beautiful eyes blaze.

"God, I hate you sometimes," Liam growls even as he moves, surging in and Jacen swoops and claims his prey. He grabs hold of Liam in two places — the base of his skull and his waist, fingers clawing, letting some of that bottled-up hunger rush out of his every pore. Liam kisses him but Jacen forces his mouth open wider, makes him bend and submit to it. It's furious and passionate.

Liam moans thickly as Jacen's tongue enters and takes him. Liam feels it all the way to his toes and he lets Jacen wrap him up, enveloping him completely, their bodies flush from thigh to chest. Jacen's interest swells but Liam's is almost painful in its intensity. Fighting not to rut and fuck himself against Jacen's hot, hard body, Liam shudders and swallows, tasting wine, tasting Jacen.

For a heady second, Jacen pulls back, biting at Liam's lip as he does, tugging at the plump flesh and tilting his head to the other side only to claim Liam's mouth once more. It's so good, Liam gets dizzy. No one has ever wanted Liam with such purity and intensity. No one. And Liam has never wanted to give himself over as completely as he does with Jacen, to drop all his defenses, to open up more utterly than he ever has and be the void that Jacen fills, with his lust and love. Liam's body throbs with that want. He moans again, more desperately, as Jacen scratches and bites at him, trying to consume him, using Liam's mouth with the talented muscle of his twisting, darting tongue until Liam's jaw aches and his pulse thrums just under the skin, every inch of him tingling and on edge.

With a snarl and a flash of darkly animalistic, feline eyes, Jacen abruptly ends the kiss, taking a backward step to put distance between them as Liam almost follows after him, chasing after more contact, more of the kiss.

"You're not ready," Jacen rasps. Closing his eyes against the strong tide of his want, Jacen forces it down, drawing up some control over himself, somehow. "I don't want to do this if I can't have you, and I refuse to hurt you any more. When you're ready, let me know."

He walks away quickly, around the chair, grabbing the wine bottle and upending it, taking a long couple of swigs, then breathing out sharply and putting the vessel on a kitchen counter. "I'm gonna cool off and go to bed. It's been a long day."

Helpless, wanting, *needing*, Liam exhales a shaky breath and wills the world to stop its spinning. He falls down to the couch, collapsing back into it with a groan of, "Jesus...."

Chapter 26
Regarding Jacen's Wife

A quiet moment finds Jacen as he stands in the kitchen of the bistro. Meat is in the broiler and soup is on the stove, simmering lightly. For a few minutes, there is nothing more to be done. Standing there, with one hand braced on the countertop, he stares at his fingers. It used to be very important to him to maintain nicely manicured fingernails, to be spotless and free of mark or visible injury. Now his hand is riddled with small, insignificant cuts. His nails are broken in places, the edges uneven. The skin is slightly raw from scrubbing it clean over and over again. The contrast between then and now is right in front of his face, concrete. He loves the way his hands are hard-worked and bear the proof of his labors.

Joe and Lily walk into the kitchen and at first Jacen doesn't realize he has company. Misreading the reason why he's looking so intently at his hand, Joe says to Jacen, "Why don't you ever talk about her? I don't mean to pry. It's your business, after all."

"Hmm?" Jacen turns, snapping out of his daydream.

"Your wife. You said you were married, but there's never a peep about her. We don't even know her name."

Lily smiles mischievously at Jacen from behind her father. Jacen sighs and squints at her in playful accusation, knowing this was probably her idea. Her curiosity has prompted many leading queries over the month and a half he has been employed at Barbara's, but so far Jacen had managed to keep his private business private. Jacen could imagine her talking with Joe in idle conversation, putting the idea intentionally in Joe's head, knowing he'd be more likely than her to get an answer out of Jacen.

He hasn't been keeping his marriage a secret out of embarrassment or shame. It's mainly been an effort to keep a low profile, and to mask Liam's identity for as long as possible, for the safety of both of them.

Jacen takes a deep breath and looks down at his silver wedding band, turning it around his finger. His sullen air prompts further comment from Joe, "Hey, if it's a sore subject, forget I asked. I know how that goes too."

"I don't have a wife," Jacen says with clear resignation.

Their expressions change abruptly. Lily's eyes go wide and Joe seems to immediately regret he brought it up.

"I always thought I would, you know, someday. But I wasn't really good at committing to the women I, um, dated. That all changed when I met Liam. He's my best friend. I didn't plan on falling in love with him, and I didn't even know that I had for a while. Then it just hit me. I was in love with him. We've only been married for a couple of months. Newlyweds, I guess."

Jacen sees Lily positively melt. He's actually surprised he doesn't get a full-out "aww" from her.

"Yer gay?" Joe blinks, his face screwing up a little around his confusion.

"No," Jacen scoffs.

"You're married to another man."

"Yeah," Jacen allows. "I'm just not a big fan of labels."

Joe rolls his eyes and shakes his head. "You kids give me a damn headache with your P.C. bullcrap. So when do we get to meet Liam?"

"What?" Jacen blurts.

"Your old man," Joe clarifies helpfully.

Jacen smiles at that, his dimples popping as he chuckles. "I don't know. Hadn't thought about it. I guess I could have him come in."

"What's he do?"

"Right now he's managing our building. Supervisor. Landlord. That kind of thing. And helping get us settled in after all the moving around."

"Hmm," Joe hums, nodding.

Lily pipes up at last, "Is he as cute as you?"

"Cuter," Jacen grins.

They close early that day. Joe and Lily have a funeral to attend for a friend's father and they give Jacen the rest of the day off. A number of things knock around in his head on the drive home, which he takes slow and easy. He wonders about all the hinting comments Liam has been making recently, just in passing, about maybe getting another piercing. Each time Jacen presses him on it, Liam clams up and won't say any more than that, not even giving Jacen an idea where the new piercing might be located. All Jacen has been able to offer is support and assurance that whatever Liam wants to do with his own body, he can do. And it's not like it's a huge secret how hot Jacen's thinks the three piercings Liam already has are.

That prompts Jacen's thoughts to roll over and catch on to the fact that he hasn't bottomed during sex with Liam for at least a month, maybe two. And the way things are going, he might not ever again. Liam has backed off completely, giving no sign that he needs that from Jacen anymore. In a way it's a relief. It's been a long time since Jacen wasn't required to be okay with submitting to anal sex. He considers a life in which that isn't a part of and after thinking it through, realizes for the first time, maybe even for the first time in the whole of his life, that he doesn't want that. He likes receiving from Liam.

Part of the dull ache that he's been living with recently is due to the fact that he hasn't gotten that from Liam in longer than he would like. So far, Jacen had attributed his unshakable gloom to the utter lack of sex in his marriage. It's been four weeks since the day of the move and the big fight. Jacen is starting to go insane from the lack of release. At first it was nice to have a break. Now it just feels wrong. It claws at him from within, the need, itching under his skin, scratching at his thoughts all night and day. He's become a serial masturbator out of sheer desperation and every time he indulges, he gets the nagging suspicion that Liam knows he's doing it, that Liam might even be listening in, and it just makes it worse. But Jacen's determination holds out. He will not entice or ask sex of Liam if he's not ready. He just won't. Not after coming so close to raping the man he loves more than his own life. Jacen would rather be celibate.

Fantasies begin to rise in Jacen's mind, of submitting to Liam, suspecting that Liam might actually be okay with something like that if properly persuaded that Jacen was the instigator and not doing it for any reason that wasn't selfish. These fantasies gloss over everything else, his lingering thoughts about work and the next day's menu, his low mood and constant fears about The Company, his wonderings about Liam's state of mind.

Jacen pulls up to their building, parking on the street out front. He shifts the truck into park and considers losing himself in the fantasy a little longer, maybe even jerking off in the cab before going inside. Hell, the truck's got tinted windows and he's done more with less privacy.

As he moves to cup himself, he notices the person by the corner of the apartment building's brick walls. He freezes but even as his consciousness first refuses to acknowledge who it is, there is no fear or panic, just shock.

He breathes out a throaty groan and shuts his eyes against the vision, willing it away because he can't handle it. It's not fair. Not after everything. There's only so much a person should be expected to handle before they just have a mental breakdown and give up the fight.

Reopening his eyes with a profound dread crawling up his gut, Jacen gets them half-lifted and gazes heavily out the window.

"Sweet fuck," he moans. "So unfair."

He can't look away.

"He's trying to kill me. He's actually trying to kill me."

Standing by the cluster of mailboxes for each of the building's six apartments is a man with golden blond hair, grown shaggy and long on top. It curls sweetly over his forehead. His eyes are masked by dark, wrap-around sunglasses. His skin is sun-baked a warm golden brown, the tan gleaming on his bare arms and shoulders. His body is lean and toned from diet and regular, daily exercise, the contours of muscle stark and sharp in the bright afternoon sun. Each shadow and hollow seems etched by a chisel, but the flesh glistens with a light sheen of sweat, highlighting his body perfectly, as if it's a statue placed on the lawn for all that pass by to admire.

That's all bad enough, causing heat to flare and rise, flushing Jacen's skin pink, causing his blood to pump faster, pulsing hotly. But what Liam is wearing is worst of all.

A sinfully tight, black tank top is stretched over his chest so that his nipple studs stand out clearly beneath the thin cotton fabric. Around his hips, slung low, is a black kilt. It catches the breeze, lifting on currents of air. His feet are clad in knee-high combat boots with thick black leather straps wrapping his lower legs from bottom to top.

Jacen whimpers and squeezes his cock through his jeans, kneading it to relieve pressure as his balls throb painfully. Imagining Liam is naked under the kilt, his pierced dick rubbing against the coarse fabric of the kilt every time he moves. Jacen is aroused so fast that it hurts. There's a vivid half-second flash of a fantasy that lights Jacen's taxed brain, of pushing Liam up against the rough bricks of the wall, flipping up the back of the kilt, getting it out of the way and mindlessly fucking into and rutting inside of his tight heat.

A hard shudder rips through Jacen's massive frame and his vision narrows, centered wholly on Liam, sweating and flexing in the sunshine as he swings a hammer and embeds a nail in the wood bracing the metal mailboxes. Liam bends over, crouching. He plucks another nail from the box of them at his feet, sticking one between his rosy lips, holding another between his fingers and lining it up before using the hammer to tap it in place. His shoulders and back muscles flex and he shifts his hips, the kilt swaying.

"Fuck me running." Jacen covers his eyes with a hand, blocking out the vision. He fills his lungs with deep inhales through his nose, blowing the air back out through his mouth, kneading his aching balls and willing his erection to wilt enough to allow him to stand and walk from the car to the front door.

Somehow he manages it. By the time he's stepping out of the truck, his gaze fixed to the sidewalk, Liam is finishing his task and gathering his supplies. Jacen locks the vehicle and focuses on getting past Liam, into the building. He thinks of his menu for the next day, listing off entrees and appetizers one by one, methodically. Maybe Liam won't see him. Maybe Jacen can get inside and upstairs unnoticed, and can barricade himself in the bathroom for a good, hard jerk before his testicles fill to bursting.

He's almost at the door. One more step and he can grab the handle.

"Hey! You're home early," a rough, raspy voice calls happily.

"Fuuuck," Jacen moans miserably. He wishes he had his sunglasses on too, but he'd left them at home that day. They're upstairs on the counter in the kitchen next to the coffee pot.

He's utterly unable to mask his thoughts as he turns to Liam. There's raging, wild lust in his liquid-blue eyes, along with a sense of barely controlled composure. First his eyes catch on the nipple piercings; then his gaze skitters down to where he imagines Liam's cock hangs, dangling in the breeze.

Easy access....

Jacen can't even pretend to be able to formulate words into anything sensible. He just stares at Liam, eye-fucking him.

Liam's full lips twist into a wicked grin. He reaches up and slides the dark glasses from his face. Licking his lips wet, he tries to catch Jacen's eye and fails. So he clears his throat and says, "Hey."

That does it. Jacen's eyes dart upwards long enough to catch on Liam's face. When he sees what Liam wants him to, something in Jacen breaks and shifts darkly. His thick, huge hand comes up to wrap the side of Liam's sweet face, and Liam knows as surely as he stands there that he needs to get them inside, now.

"Come on," Liam urges, pulling Jacen toward the door, glancing around to see if they're observed.

They take the stairs with Liam climbing them in front of Jacen, his ass shifting with every step and he feels Jacen's eyes on him like a caress, moving over his skin as tangibly as if he was groping his bottom as they walk.

Liam fumbles his keys out, unlocking the door with Jacen right at his back, breathing hot and heavy over the back of Liam's neck, causing his skin to pebble. Then they're inside and Liam turns the lock behind them. It's all Jacen can do not to *grab* and *take* and *plunder* so Liam maintains control for both of their sakes. Holding Jacen's gaze, Liam's eyes are wide and assured and calm. The new dermal piercing on the top of his cheekbone just about an inch below the outer corner of his right eye catches the fading daylight filtered in through the windows. Sparkling like a diamond chip, the tiny adornment is like a tear freshly slipped from Liam's big, shining eyes, making him seem vulnerable, fragile, and exquisitely beautiful.

Jacen's resolve is slipping through his fingers, and desperation radiates from him. Wordlessly pleading with Liam, Jacen knows he cannot ask so he warns Liam to get away, and quickly.

"Bedroom. Come on," Liam whispers, nodding toward the hall. "It's okay."

"Lee," Jacen warns.

"It's okay," Liam repeats.

A fresh shudder races through Jacen's body, his desire threatening to overwhelm his system, overtaking logic. Because he can see in Liam's eyes as clearly as Liam sees Jacen's wild need that he's not ready yet. He's still not ready, after all this time.

"Baby, I can't," Jacen almost sobs.

Liam sighs, he moves right up against Jacen's front, putting their bodies flush together, feeling the heat baking from Jacen's skin, the hardness jutting between his legs. He teases the tip of his tongue over the swell of Jacen's bottom lip then sucks a light kiss there.

"I won't hurt you again," Jacen hisses.

"I know," Liam replies gently. "Just trust me, okay?"

Jacen goes, letting Liam pull him along, and it feels like damnation.

Chapter 27
Heavenly Devil

They're in the bedroom and Jacen stands by the foot of the bed. Squeezing his eyes shut against the temptation of Liam's body, Jacen feels his lover's hand slip away.

Liam peels off his shirt, letting it fall to the floor. "I want you to watch. I want to see how much you want me."

Jacen stares at the discarded shirt, refusing to look at Liam himself even as he hovers there in the periphery of his vision. "Leave the kilt on. And the boots," he says roughly.

Liam sits on the edge of the bed and then slides up toward the pillows, laying back on them, letting them prop him up. He plants his feet on the bed widely, letting his knees fall open.

He's naked under the kilt. Jacen moans thickly.

Reaching down between his legs, Liam slides the kilt up and begins to fondle himself. The black leather of the boots is stark next to the paler skin of Liam's groin. His cock hangs dark and heavy between his legs, the skin there recently waxed clean of all hair and Jacen can't *not* look. He's helpless.

"Let me see how hard you are," Liam instructs. His fingers trace the line of his dick, root to tip, around the head, along the edge of the silver metal of his piercing. The flesh stirs, twitching, thickening. Wrapping his shaft in a hand, Liam tugs. Again. His free hand slides over his chest, rubbing hard, clawing at the taut muscle and leaving faint pink lines in his nails' wake. His fingers find the piercing in his left nipple, pulling at it.

Jacen's eyes flutter momentarily closed as he swallows another moan. Clawing at his pants, he gets them quickly opened, undoing the belt, tugging down the zipper, pushing the denim down enough to free his member. He cradles the heavy weight of it in his hand, not daring to stroke, not yet. He wants to savor this, to make it last.

It starts slowly. Liam strokes his cock, getting it really hard, flushed red. He squirts some lube in his palm, slicking the fluid over himself. His fingers play at his nipple, stimulating it easily. Then his fingernails scratch downward, over his abs. He reaches down over the bunched fabric of the kilt, between his spread legs. His right wrist snaps, working his cock at a steady pace while, with his left hand, he rolls his balls, tugging gently on them. His hips come slightly off the bed but he doesn't play it up too much, knowing that Jacen would be able to tell if he was faking. Instead, Liam gets lost in the freedom of it, the unbearable lust in his lover's eyes, only for him. Pumping his cock until pre-come oozes from the slit, Liam hums and purrs, pushing his hips up into his hand at a steady pace. Then his left hand quests lower and the pad of his middle finger traces the clenched knot of his hole.

A ragged breath leaves Jacen. He closes his eyes to gather himself and props his left foot on the base of the bed. Liam stares at Jacen's hand kneading his cock, jacking it as slowly as he can stand. But, as Liam's finger circles around and around his opening, his legs falling even more widely opened, his hips tilting up to give Jacen a better view, Jacen's need grows. Looking away, Liam lets his head fall back on the pillows and he relaxes into it, the feel of his hand sliding on his lubed cock, and inserts his middle finger steadily, until it's fully seated in his anus.

Jacen grunts thickly and he tugs harder, breathing shakily. Liam opens his lips and lets a soft moan slip free as he tugs the finger back out, savoring the friction. He hasn't touched himself or been touched in so long, the muscles have closed back up and regained a tightness he hasn't enjoyed since he first became sexually active. The finger pumps slowly in and out. He fucks himself with it, knowing how it must look, the pink ring hugged up around the digit, taking each push, puckering obscenely with each withdraw. He jacks himself faster, enjoying it, getting off on it. He needs more so he adds another finger, pushing his index finger in alongside the one already there. It's almost enough. He plucks the fingers out and rubs over his hole, stimulating the engorging flesh as blood rushes there, making everything that much more sensitive. Lightly he taps the opening and Jacen grunts harder, hissing a curse under his breath.

Liam senses movement but he keeps his eyes closed over, playing with himself, not letting his concentration get broken, trusting Jacen. Feather-light, a finger traces the edge of his cleft chin and Liam knows what Jacen is giving him. Parting his lips, letting them soften, he waits to be kissed. The dark shadow of Jacen's form looms over him and his heat radiates into Liam's skin. Sighing softly, Liam feels Jacen's lips skim over his. Liam's tongue pushes forward, finding Jacen's lips and the tip of his tongue. It remains light and they explore each other, lips brushing over lips, tongues barely touching, breathing into each other as Liam brings himself closer to orgasm. He knows without looking to confirm it that Jacen is still watching him, that Jacen is still manipulating himself closer and closer to release. He feels it in every breath, in every tender touch of Jacen's lips — the passion and devotion, the way Liam has taken Jacen apart. It's one of the most amazing experiences of Liam's life, because it's the complete opposite of what he's used to — being kissed so lovingly, so gently while no one touches his body in any other way, but instead lets him do the touching. Liam gets off all on his own, brought there by Jacen's love and the knowledge that Jacen watches with desperate, avid passion.

Fully expecting Jacen to come first, Liam is surprised by his own orgasm. It blooms like a flower, unfolding between his spread legs. Fingering himself quickly, tugging rapidly, he comes in a few thick pulses of semen that he struggles to catch in his hand, rather than soil himself. He uses the viscous fluid to further slick his cock. It slides so wet and hot in his hand and Liam moans thunderously into Jacen's mouth, bucking into his hand, stuffing his fingers as far up his hole as he can reach, just to feel full like he loves to be. The inner muscles clench and grip his fingers with the beat of his heart as he comes and comes down.

Trembling, his heart racing, Liam tries to catch his breath. Jacen nuzzles his cheek and oh-so-gently kisses beside the new piercing, seeing the skin there to be inflamed and tender as it heals.

Liam reopens his eyes at last, and sees Jacen is hugely erect, desperate and wanting. He's held off for some reason, some purpose that Liam can't interpret or begin to guess at.

"Grab me that towel?" Liam asks quietly, bringing his knees back together, growing slightly self-conscious.

Jacen does as asked, reaching for one of the towels stacked on the nearby chair and passing it to Liam, watching as Liam wipes his hands and genitals clean.

Then Liam waits, knowing Jacen needs to be the one to ask and clarify his purpose.

It takes longer than Liam expects. Jacen straightens. He'd been bent over the side of the bed, grasping the headboard for stability as he leaned over Liam for their languorous kiss. Laid out on the bed, Liam feels exceedingly vulnerable, so he gets up onto his knees instead, facing Jacen. The kilt falls back into place, concealing Liam's nakedness.

"Tell me," Liam urges, coaxing Jacen to confess.

Jacen rolls his eyes wearily at himself. His face grows pinker as a blush not born of desire heats the skin.

"I want you to fuck me," he murmurs, the words only audible due to the stillness of the apartment. "I waited until you came to tell you because... I don't know."

"Yeah, you do," Liam says, not falling for the lie. If he thought Jacen's blush of embarrassment couldn't get darker, he was wrong. "If you need me to do this, you have to say it. You have to convince me I'm not hurting you either. Two-way street."

Jacen hesitates.

Liam continues, "Baby, this isn't gonna work if we can't trust each other enough to talk about this."

"Goddamn it," Jacen curses softly. He raises his gaze to lock with Liam's. "Okay. I want to get off while you finger me. I really like that. Um...."

"What?" Liam presses, seeing a new confession sitting there on the tip of Jacen's tongue, but quickly bitten back.

"...Yasha..." Jacen finally confesses.

"Oh." Liam says, trying not to imagine it. "It's how he got you off."

"It became more about focusing on me feeling pleasure, without fear or pain. That makes sense, right?"

"Yeah," Liam sighs, attempting to stifle any gathering resentment. "It does."

"But I want more than that from you," Jacen continues. "I miss feeling you in me, Lee. I need you like this. No condoms, no barriers, just you. I want to feel you enjoy it. And I don't want you to be gentle. I don't want you to make love to me. I want you to *fuck* me."

"C'mere," Liam breathes, pulling Jacen in. They kiss and Liam takes it deeper than before, putting urgency and heart-stopping affection into the contact. He kisses Jacen breathless as he works to get Jacen's jeans down over his hips. "If you wanna fuck, you're gonna have to give me a few minutes to, uh, recover."

"Yeah, I know," Jacen admits impatiently. "Fingers...."

"Right. So, how do you want this?"

Jacen thinks it over, but it's difficult to decide even that, his brain's circuits are so fried. "I wanna see you."

"Okay," Liam nods, turning them around so that Jacen is the one on the bed. He guides Jacen back down onto the mattress and pulls his jeans and boxers off. Jacen plants his feet on the edge of the bed, tilting his hips up in invitation. Stepping right up between Jacen's spread legs, Liam slicks plenty of lube on his hand. He penetrates Jacen with two fingers. Stroking his inner walls, working his hand in and out, Liam lets him ease into it. Scissoring his fingers apart, he coaxes the muscle loose. Jacen's blush doesn't fade—his face a deep red—and soon he gives in to the demands of his body. His hand falls between his legs as Liam corkscrews the digits, bending and twisting them up into Jacen repeatedly.

"I know why you're really tight," Liam says. "It's been a damn long time, hasn't it? I wanna get four fingers in here but I'm not sure they'll fit. But see, what I don't understand is why you're so tense."

Jacen exhales sharply, then holds the breath.

"You gettin' shy on me, baby?"

"Maybe," Jacen grunts, trying not to watch as Liam watches him jerk off. "Maybe it's just the fucking kilt and piercing."

Liam chuckles. As he slips in a third finger, and Jacen's mouth works around an unvoiced cry, he says with dark amusement, "You like 'em that much, huh? Good to know."

His wrist pivots and he intentionally triggers Jacen's prostate. Jacen's mouth works again, but this time the cry is voiced. It's hoarse and jagged; like Liam pulls it from him no matter how hard Jacen tries to claw it back down. "Mmm, you liked that too? What's it gonna take for you to come so I can fuck this? How about four? Can you take four?"

"Lee-Liam... *fuck!*" Jacen bucks, fucking his own hand, moving reflexively as Liam massages his prostate gland. "God... DAMN it."

Liam inserts finger number four and Jacen growls through gritted teeth. The tapered wedge of Liam's hand opens him wider than he's been in a long time. *Jesus Christ, it feels good*, he moans inwardly. Then the moan breaks free, loud and strong, as Jacen finally finds release, coming in a milky flood over his fingers.

Without letting up, thrusting his hand into Jacen over and over again, twisting it to get deeper on each push, Liam leans down and licks over Jacen's fingers, cleaning away his come as he continues to pulse and clench around Liam's hand. Opening wider, he suckles the reddened head of Jacen's cock, held tightly in Jacen's fist and that's it. Jacen is done. He'd give Liam anything—absolutely anything he wanted—in that moment. Liam *owns* him.

Letting go of his spent flesh, Jacen grabs his thighs and holds his legs, pressed back toward his chest. He blows out a breath and then again, trying to steady himself and calm down. But Liam withdraws his hand only to press back inside, more firmly than ever and gets most of it, all the way up to the base of his thumb, into Jacen.

Jacen growls, blowing out his sharp inhale even as his dick struggles, futilely, to stiffen again.

"I'm just a thumb away from fisting you," Liam tells him, his typically bright eyes dark with lust. The twinkling sparkle from the dermal piercing is like a mockery, daring Jacen to think Liam so innocent and vulnerable now.

"I'd do it," Liam whispers. "I want to. But it's more important to me that you really feel my cock when I'm pounding it into you."

Just like that, the hand tugs out, leaving him too open, gaping, empty.

"Flip over. Ass-up, sweetheart."

And Jacen wants it — badly — so he flips over as gracefully as he can, keeping his knees planted widely to make plenty of room for Liam to get nice and close. He keeps his ass up high as instructed but locks his arms, bracing them against the bed with a double-handful of bedding for what he knows is coming. Flipping his hair back from his face, Jacen turns, looking back over his shoulder just in time to see Liam flipping up the front of the kilt. He squeezes up his shaft twice, then fits it to Jacen's hole. With a hard thrust, he's nestled deep and Jacen croaks a wrenching moan, pushing back into Liam's pelvis, inviting more.

"Come on, fuck me. Hard," Jacen rasps.

Liam's upper lip curls in a hungry sneer, animalistic and primal. He draws his hips back and Jacen feels the friction keenly. The first thrust is just the beginning as Liam sets a brutal pace, his pelvis slapping loudly against Jacen's nicely presented ass. His cheeks get quickly pink. Jacen moans low and long and works himself onto Liam, pressing back against every thrust, pulling forward on the withdrawal. His movements are greedy, wanton.

"Harder. Fuckin' harder," Jacen grunts. He dares another look and sears what he sees into his brain, the image of Liam, dressed as he is, wild as he is, fucking him with all his strength until Jacen knows he's going to feel the bruises the next day. The air is driven from Jacen's lungs on every impact, knocked from him with the force of Liam's cock, and it is *so* good.

Liam holds him by the hips and gives up on bothering to pull out so far on each thrust; he stays buried to the root in Jacen's heat and beats the cradle of his pelvis against Jacen's ass over and over. Liam's breath begins leaving him in ragged tears as he empties himself into Jacen, climaxing hard enough for his vision to momentarily white out.

They both collapse down onto the bed, exhausted. And, as Liam doesn't have the energy or interest to pull out, they stay intimately joined. Jacen moans loudly into the mattress below him, letting out all his remaining pent-up cares, going limp and boneless. The weight of Liam on top of him and between his legs is welcome and comforting. He has only enough left in him to reach back and find Liam's hand, weaving their fingers together as he loses himself in sleep.

An uncertain amount of time later, Jacen wakes, having forgotten what he's been up to, and, to his astonishment, finds Liam still with him — or rather, within him.

"Jesus, you're still up my ass?"

Liam laughs and presses a kiss to Jacen's back. "I ain't done with it yet."

"Clearly. How long have you been hard?"

"Long enough," Liam says gruffly as he begins to rock in a smooth, rolling motion, working himself in Jacen's snug orifice.

Jacen groans. He lifts his hips, bowing his back to accept Liam deeper. This time it's sweeter, more lovemaking than fucking, though still urgent and passionate enough that Jacen grows restless. He dutifully lets Liam use him, trying not to rut against the bed to get off himself. But when Liam catches on, he shifts the position so that Jacen is on his side, his leg drawn up and open so that Liam can bring Jacen off as he moves inside him.

Afterward, Liam lays there with him, pressing soft, warm kisses to his skin, until Jacen stirs, rolling from his side to his back. It causes Liam to pull free of him. For a few long, comfortably quiet minutes they just lay there together. Then Jacen reaches down and touches himself, feeling the tenderness of his rim. When he pushes a finger inside, he's amazed at how wet he is. He can feel Liam's sticky fluids there, dripping down from deep inside, leaking out and running down the inside of his leg and up through his cheeks.

"God, I'm a mess. It's so strange," he says with wonder. "But nice. I like feeling like I'm yours."

"Oh, you're mine all right. No gettin' out of it now," Liam smirks, clearly enjoying Jacen's depravity very much.

"Good." Jacen stares at Liam's mouth, twisted up with happiness. "I'm gonna get cleaned up. Then I'll cook you whatever you're in the mood for."

"Deal. I'm a lucky bitch."

Jacen bites his lip, smiling. Then he clambers off the bed, heading toward the bathroom.

The steam and strong spray from the showerhead revives Jacen. Refreshed, he returns to the bedroom for clean clothes. Once he is dressed he goes in search of Liam.

Jacen smiles broadly as he discovers him just down the hall, in the kitchen. He's leaning bent over the counter, reading the newspaper, sipping from a bottle of water and still dressed as he was — in the kilt, boots and black tank. Shaking his head, Jacen walks past Liam toward the fridge. On the way, he quickly lifts the back of the kilt and directs a firm smack to Liam's bare behind.

With a yelp and a squinty-eyed glance over his shoulder, Liam gives his husband a smirk.

Jacen fetches his own bottle of water and stands on the opposite side of the counter, facing Liam.

"So," Jacen starts. "Since I'm clearly very offended by your choice of outfit today, I have to ask, why the hell are you wearing this? What happened to the guy who was perpetually in sweats and a baseball cap nearly the whole time I've known him?"

Liam breathes out a laugh, his smile changes. Glancing down at the counter, he sets down his bottle and says, "Well, that's what you expected me to wear, right? So that's what I wore. It's all part of the game. And I guess..." he pauses, running his tongue over the ridges of his teeth. "I guess it helped me pretend that when I took off the costumes, I could leave the rest of it behind. Like I wasn't really the same person that fucked for money. But I've been thinking about it a lot lately — what makes me happy. And I've decided to dress in whatever makes me happy."

Jacen thinks about that — Liam dressing like one of the guys just to make Jacen more comfortable, just like Liam used to act like Jacen's "friend" because he didn't know how to really be his friend. It makes him sad, but it helps that Liam is finally seeing through his self-deceptions. "And the piercing?"

"Hell, I've wanted it for years," he says, holding Jacen's gaze with big, green eyes, the metal embedded in his cheek glinting brilliantly in the sunlight. "But I couldn't screw with this, could I?" He draws a circle in the air, around his face. "It might scare off business."

The sense of pervading sadness grows, threatening to weigh fledgling happiness down again, so Jacen lifts his bottle, in a toast. "To my husband, the gorgeous, sexy, kinky bitch that he is. I wouldn't have you any other way, babydoll. The blue balls might just kill me, but what a way to go."

Liam breaks into bright, free laughter and hops up, arms braced on the countertop, leaning over it to kiss Jacen squarely on the lips. Trying not to fixate on the way it makes Liam's ass push out perfectly, Jacen groans and accepts the kiss. "So unfair," he laments again. "Can I at least put a bag over your head and wrap you in a blanket until my balls and my ass stop throbbing?"

"Oh, now where's the fun in that?" Eyes alight, he touches his bottle to Jacen's and takes a drink.

Chapter 28
The Beauty Within

Liam stands back and surveys his work now that the paint has mostly dried. He scans the walls, looking for any spot he missed or that will need another coat. The scrutiny is intense, but with the abundance of quiet in the vacant apartment across from his own, he can hear the approaching footsteps from a long way off, and audibly tracks them as they weave their way up the flights of steps right to the door and then through the door to him. It's only because he refuses to let the old paranoia continue to win out that he doesn't run to the windows to check for a black Lincoln parked out front or plot an escape route down the fire escape. He simply stands where he is, waiting.

His self-manicured fingers scratch at a stray bit of beige splattered on his forearm, where it would have gotten in his arm hair if he had any. Every time he waxes, which he does regularly and by himself now, he waxes more territory than the last. A few nights ago he had waxed most of his torso and all of his arms.

The newcomer walks up to him, and he smiles before even turning to see her, her familiar scent and the barest glimpse of her long hair an instant comfort.

"Hey, babe."

"God, it's good to see you," he sighs, turning to give Valery a hug.

She notes the new piercing, which they have already spoken of over the phone. Amused at Liam's tight purple tank top that has the word 'flirt' scrawled across it in big glittery script, coupled with his grungy cargos, she says, "So you let just anyone wander in here these days?"

"Pretty much," he answers, not mentioning that by the speed and volume of her steps alone he could rule out any threat. She didn't sound like one of The Company's goons or match the dainty *click-clack* of Della's cherished stilettos. "Thanks for coming."

"My pleasure. You look good. The jewelry's hot. What did Jacen say?"

He laughs, gathering his painting supplies into a neat pile near the sink. "It was less a verbal reaction than a physical one."

"Wow, that good, huh?" Liam raises an eyebrow and shrugs, aligning stacked paint cans and straightening brushes laid out to dry on paper towels. Taking another step closer, she presses him with, "How are things with you two? You don't usually like to talk about it on the phone, so...."

"I don't like to talk about it at all," he clarifies quietly.

"Yeah, believe me, I've noticed. But if you had some sort of *physical* celebration of your new accoutrement, then that means...."

He sighs, rolling his eyes up to the ceiling.

"Hey, if you really don't want to talk about it, we can just discuss nail polish brands again. Which are you wearing anyway? It looks really good on you. It hasn't even chipped with all the manual work you've done today. How many coats did you put on?"

Liam turns to face her, looking down at her, dark glasses perched on her nose, her hair fallen back over her shoulders. From the seriousness in his expression she hopes she's finally pushed him past his barriers, until he says, "You don't tell Yasha we talk about nail polish and all, do you?"

She breaks into a chuckle, shaking her head. "Do you tell Jacen?" she counters.

"I don't know. Not really." She makes a face at him and he huffs, "What? Yasha fucked my husband! A lot, I'm told. I kind of have this psychological need to be a bigger man around him."

"Sweetheart, he's fucked a lot of people's husbands. You aren't so special."

"You know what I mean. He's like... like my...."

"He's not your competition."

"Not anymore, obviously. But how do I know Jacen isn't, like, comparing and contrasting us in his head. And they still talk all the time. If Yasha thinks I'm turning into a big sissy and he tells Jacen he made a huge mistake being with me...."

"Liam. You're being irrational again. What do you care what Yasha thinks about you? And for the record, he loves that we talk about nail polish and he would try to buy that shirt from you if he saw it. I could take a picture with my cell of it right now and send it to him and in seconds he'd be calling to harass you with price offers. What is this really about? Talk to me. That's why you like to hang out in person like this, right? So come on, I'm here. Spill. Give me details."

With a sigh, he palms his keys from the counter and says, "Fine. Let's go over to my place. I need to get cleaned up anyway. We're meeting Clay at the diner in an hour."

"We are?"

"Yeah. It'll make sense once I explain."

"Okay."

They cross the hall after locking up the vacant apartment, unlock Liam's door and head right back to the bedroom once the bolt's been slid into place. Valery flops down on the bed, sitting crosslegged as Liam goes to the sink in the adjoining bathroom to wet a washcloth. He brings it back to the bed, sits and uses it to clean off paint splatters as they talk.

"The place looks great by the way. Every time I come here it looks homier."

"Guess it just needed a sissy's touch to make it a home, huh?" he teases. She nudges him.

"Don't be so mean to yourself."

"Yeah, that's what they keep tellin' me," he mutters. "Um. So. What do you want to know?"

"No, uh-uh. That's not how this works. What do you want to tell me? What's on your mind?"

Liam shrugs.

"Okay then, let's start back where we were before. You and Jacen were intimate recently? Was that the first time since...?" She lets it hang there, but sees he needs to hear it so she chooses to finish by saying, "Since the fight?"

"You mean, since I failed to say 'No' to him? Yeah. But it wasn't—" He takes a breath and tries again, scratching nervously at his neck. "I topped him. I haven't let him touch me that much, and we haven't, you know, switched. I'm still working up to letting him have that much power over me again."

"But it was something. And it went well?"

"Yeah. Yeah, it was fantastic. Better than fantastic. It was the only time though. In how long?"

"It's not a contest," she tells him. "That's a huge accomplishment, you know. It's awesome that you guys have gotten that far. Are you happy? Getting along okay?"

"Yeah. To both," he smiles at her. "It's been better than ever, really. A lot more, um, honest?"

"So, what's the problem?"

Liam seems to focus more on the washcloth and his cleaning, tuning out the question. Valery takes the rag from him and his hands finally become still.

"What if there was a part of myself that I still haven't shown anyone, not even Jacen." He remembers the nightmare, in a gut-wrenching, cutting flash that's there and gone. It's powerful enough to make him wince. "What if I have to make peace with that before things can finally be okay?"

He killed her. Timothy killed her. Ripping and tearing. Or did he? Maybe it was me. Maybe I killed her.

Nonsensically, tears spring to his eyes and he sniffs, hunching forward over himself.

Valery takes his hand, holding it. She gives it a squeeze. "If it's a part of *you*," she says. "Then he will love that part as much as the rest."

"How do you know? How do you know it'll be okay? What if it's not, and it ruins everything?"

"It's okay," she whispers conspiratorially, like it's a given, a fact. He just hopes she's right.

The drive to the diner is a short one. Jacen has the truck as he's off at work for the day, so Valery takes Liam on her motorcycle. There isn't much time or ability for conversation, but when they get to the diner, Liam springs a random question on his companion.

They park the bike and tug off their helmets. Liam hangs his on the back and says offhandedly, "Do you ever get jealous of Yasha being with other people?"

Valery blinks at him. "Where'd this come from?"

He shrugs. "I don't know. I've always wondered. You guys are so committed to each other, and I really admire that. But I can't work out how you're okay with him doing that. I mean, hell, I *still* think about when I saw Jacen and Patrick together. It's like this horror that's burned in my head and won't go away. So maybe it's just my own hang ups."

She stares at him, thinking this over, trying to figure out what exactly Liam is asking and why. Then she says, slowly, "It's all about give and take. Balance. Trust. I trust him. And his clients might get to touch him, but they don't *have* him, you know? Plus, Yasha isn't the only one that gets to be with other people."

Liam's eyes pop. Valery laughs brightly.

"Pshh," he scoffs. "I knew that. I mean, I *actually* knew that, in, um, never mind."

Valery keeps giggling. "You don't hold it against me that I've had sex with Jacen but you hold it against Yasha? Double standard, man."

"Yeah, well...."

"It should be more of an issue with me being with people, shouldn't it? I don't even have the excuse of it bringing in income."

"Hmm, I hadn't exactly thought of it that way."

"It's not the lifestyle for everyone. But it works for us." She smiles up at him and adjusts her glasses. He smiles back and pulls her in for a hug, nearly swallowing her up with his arms given their size difference.

"Yeah, I love you too. Come on, ya big softie," she says.

Clay is waiting for them inside at a booth, hunched over a cup of coffee and scanning the menu. He grins when he sees Liam and Valery, standing to welcome them.

"Hey. You're a sight for sore eyes," Clay beams, drawing Liam into a bear hug. "How are ya, kid? You look good."

"I am good."

Clay puts more space between them, holding Liam's face in his hands to look the new piercing over. He clucks his tongue against the roof of his mouth and shakes his head. "As if you needed more of a shine to that pretty-boy face."

Liam laughs. Clay shakes hands with Valery and ushers them into the booth.

"So, I guess you're wondering why I called you all here today," Liam says formally.

"I am actually. But for Christ's sake, Pidge, lemme finish my coffee first. You've got that heavy look and I need some fuel before we get into any shit."

"No shit, I promise."

Liam and Valery look over the menus. Clay catches Valery's eye while Liam bites at the pad of his thumb and frowns at the listing of omelets. Valery shrugs at Clay's questioning glance, with no more clue than he has of what this is about.

"Does the husband still wanna kick my ass?"

"Hmm. I don't know, actually," Liam admits. "We haven't talked a whole lot about that night, period. I think Jacen's afraid of scaring me off or upsetting me if he brings it up and *I* haven't brought it up."

"Why not?"

He shrugs and says shortly. "Trying to look forward, not backward."

"Mm. I hear that."

They order their food and more coffee.

"You can't see the bruises anymore. I'm glad," Clay says with an apologetic tone.

Liam glances up at him from across the table and holds his stare.

"I'm real damn sorry about that," Clay tells him softly.

"Stop it," Liam grunts.

"No, I mean it."

"I know."

"So, you're good?"

"I'm good," Liam agrees.

"What does that mean?"

"It means no more running away. No more confusing the past with the present. It means being a fucking man and dealing with my issues."

Clay nods approvingly.

Their coffee comes. Valery watches Liam repeatedly run the tip of his thumb over the smooth gloss covering his polished fingernail, getting lost in thought.

He starts to talk quietly, without focusing on anything, like he's channeling something from deep down, buried far underneath layers and layers. "Val, you've got your whole history of counseling and helping people, right? You've been doing that for a while."

"Yeah," she nods.

"And Clay, you've been active in the community around here. That's the reason you became a cop, isn't it? To give back and make a positive impact rather than a negative one?"

"What's this about, man?"

"I want to give back too. I want to help someone. At least one person. If I can do even that much, I feel like all of this will be worth it. Everything I've done for so long has just been selfish and... dark. I want to be able to look in the mirror and be proud of who I see. And I like that now when I do look in the mirror, I see Jacen's spouse, but I want more. It's not enough. I need your help, both of you. I can't do this without either of you. Will you help me? Please?"

Clay smiles first. Valery catches it and adds her own. A silent agreement is made. They're both invested as of that moment, without even hearing Liam's idea. Turning to him, they ask, "What do you have in mind?"

Chapter 29

In With the New

The next day, sitting in the truck, parked in the lot across from Barbara's Bistro, Liam taps his foot and stares at the clock, watching time tick by whether he likes it or not. He has a few minutes left to kill before going across the street, filled with shadows and dark figures, to meet Jacen's co-workers and employer for the first time. He had dropped Jacen off at work earlier, knowing that this was the plan, for him to come back that night and pick Jacen up. Joe has been asking to meet Liam and Jacen had finally caved, agreeing to have Liam come by for the formal, long-awaited introductions.

But after months of solitude, with only Yasha, Valery and Clay for regular company, other than Jacen, Liam's nerves automatically crank up at the prospect of broadening his little circle. He might have been even more panicked than he is, though, if not for the little meeting the day before with Valery and Clay at the diner. It had boosted Liam's spirits and given him confidence unlike any he'd ever experienced before. Anything seems possible, if only he would want it badly enough. And now, Liam is finally becoming able to zero in on what that is, to a precise degree.

His plans spin out in his mind, unwinding like glistening ribbons of hope stretching out in all directions, turning everything that might otherwise be dark and ominous, golden and enlightening. There is so much he wants to accomplish, and it feels not only feasible, with Valery and Clay's help, but destined to be.

Smiling to himself, Liam basks in his newfound confidence and joy. It radiates out from him, changing his posture, his appearance, his energy. The goals he has set for himself are big, and they threaten to outshine everything else in his universe. But they don't. There are still other things there, hovering in orbit. Some are also good things. Some aren't.

One of them, one difficult to classify, is Leah. The nightmare that Liam suffered the day of the move, after running away from Jacen and their life and then offering himself up as Clay's punching bag, has not faded or receded. It's as stark and haunting as it was when he first woke with Valery by his side. He's become much more able to analyze it, what caused it, what it means, but there are still aspects that have implications for his future, coloring his decisions and influencing his mindset. Leah is a big piece of the unsolved puzzle that is Liam's psyche. The specter of Timothy tore down most of Liam's personalities, without bias, with the one exception of Leah. The hate and judgment that was there when Leah died at Timothy's hands disturbs Liam on a base level.

It's like one of the foundations of who Liam is has been knocked askew and until he's able to shore the critical pillar, everything that defines his soul is in danger of tumbling down. Even now, sitting behind the wheel of the truck, with pedestrians milling about feet away, the world carrying on as if nothing is wrong, Liam can feel the cracks. The temptation to worry at them, to pick at the edges is nearly overpowering. He could do it. He could fixate his attention on the weak spots and that damaged support would buckle. If he imagined with all his strength the idea of Jacen facing Leah as Timothy did, and having the same reaction — pure disgust — that would do it. It would break him beyond the ability to recover. Horribly, the idea of that has its appeal. The abyss beyond it feels welcoming and blissfully absolute. No more worry, no more fear or pain.

Leah is everything vulnerable in Liam. It's not an issue of male versus female, or of choosing one or the other. Not really. The appeal of being her, a woman, is that it lets Liam be everything he's afraid to be otherwise — utterly submissive, spectacularly delicate. She has a sort of power over Liam that nothing else in creation does. Even the thought of her, of being her, just for a little while, sends gut-deep shivers racing through his body, pebbling his skin, stirring his cock. He wants to let Leah live again. He needs it for his own survival. If he could restore her, bring her back from the un-life that has trapped her since the nightmare, he would be whole again. The parts of his personality that she brings out could meld with the rest. Leah would cease to be distinct, vulnerable to attack. Liam could own his full self, and, just like that, he would be free.

Hot and cold, aroused and focused, a portrait in contradictions, Liam gets out of the truck. He locks the doors and pushes the keys into his pockets. Straightening his tie, running a hand back over his slicked-back hair, tugging at the hem of his suit jacket, he lets all his cares fall away and prepares to step forward into whatever the future holds.

The night is particularly cool. He can feel the bite of the air even through layers of clothes, enough that he is troubled with a dull sort of concern for the women he passes, dressed in micro-minis and sleeveless blouses made of sheer silk. But that only stirs more thoughts of Leah so he pushes the distractions away.

The bistro is empty, but the lights are on. When he tries the door, it's locked, so he knocks gently on the glass and smiles at the young woman who jogs over to let him in.

"Liam?"

"Yep. You must be Lily."

He extends a hand. She's adorable with a chestnut brown pixie cut and warm eyes. Everything about her sings of youthful exuberance and positivity. Liam likes her instantly.

Lily blushes and bites self-consciously at her lower lip. It seems foreign to her spirit, the sudden shyness. "Yeah, it's so nice to finally meet you." She takes his hand, letting him fold her much-smaller fingers up in his palm as they shake. "You're not quite what I pictured."

His smile grows as he chuckles, letting her hand go after a pause. His voice deepening subtly he asks with a conspiratorial edge, "And how, exactly, did you picture me?"

Lily giggles and she nervously pushes back a lock of hair. "Um...."

All of the particulars of Liam's appearance catch her attention — the diamond-like piercing on his cheekbone, his eyes outlined with a smoky charcoal grey pencil, his full lips, the broad span of his shoulders in his tailored, dark grey suit, the line of his matching grey silk tie running down the center of his body. He sees her looking at him while simultaneously trying not to look at him, at least noticeably.

"J-Jacen is back this way. I can, uh, show you." Flustered, she flashes him a huge grin that tries to wordlessly apologize for her skittish behavior. As she turns away, toward their destination, he sees her roll her eyes at herself and cringe. He tries to mask his amusement at her discomfort, knowing it for what it is—the very thing he's learned to stir in people since he was a teenager: desire, lust, attraction.

And even under current circumstances, it makes him proud to have succeeded in luring her in.

Maybe he dressed up because he wanted to impress them. More likely it was a blatant attempt to boost his own ego by playing the part of someone who has no problem being confident. But it's different than it used to be. He doesn't feel like he's being a character. He simply feels like he's willing himself to express the part of his own self that is confident and assured. And that distinction is a huge success already.

They pass the bar, behind which is, at the far end, an older man with a neat brown and grey beard and knowing eyes, as warm as those of his daughter. He's hunched over, studying receipts.

"Dad, this is Liam," Lily tells him with an endearing little curtsy. "Jacen's Liam."

"The old man," Joe says with interest, setting the slips of paper aside. "Well, I'll be. Jacen! Company for you!"

The choice of wording jolts Liam faintly, but then it passes when, a moment later, Jacen emerges through the door leading back to the kitchen, wiping his hands on a towel. "Oh. Hey, you're here! So, introductions. Lily, Joe, this is Liam," Jacen says, gesturing to each of them, but Liam is momentarily distracted by the particular look in Jacen's eyes. "Everyone else took off as soon as we closed."

"But we're the only ones that count anyway," Joe winks. He extends a hand and shakes with Liam. "Nice to meet you, Liam. I don't know. With Jacen being such an enormous pretty boy I expected you to be the yin to his yang, but look at'cha. Another enormous pretty boy."

Liam laughs. "Well, thank you, I guess. This is a nice place you've got here. I'm sorry it's taken me this long to stop by, but I have to thank you personally for giving Jacen the opportunity that you did."

Joe waves a hand to dismiss this. "Nonsense. We're lucky to have him. Never had an employee work so damn hard before," he says with a pointed look at his daughter. "Yes, that includes you, princess."

"Dad," Lily groans.

"I know from what little Jacen has told me," Joe adds with a more serious tone. "That you two don't have much of a support system, and that you're trying to put some rough times behind you. I don't know any of the specifics, now, but I wanted to tell both of you to your faces that if there's anything we can do to put your minds at ease or lend a helping hand, we'd be more than happy to do so."

The offer affects Liam noticeably. He has trouble finding his voice at first before replying, "Thank you, Joe; that means a lot."

"Jacen's a good guy, and if you're anything like him, which I think you are, then that's really the least I can do. Now how about a tour?"

"That sounds great," Liam smiles.

Jacen follows along behind the small group as Joe and Lily take Liam through the bistro, showing him the space, the bar, the kitchen and the office in back. He lets them run the show, distracted as he is by Liam's appearance. The perfectly pressed suit with its crisp lines, the grey on grey palette, his perfectly, painstakingly polished dress shoes and the elegance of the combined effect offset by smoky eye make-up and the obvious facial piercing, his slicked-back blond hair, it all works just as Liam intends it to. He looks like himself. He's debonair, refined, sensual, and most of all, beautiful. It makes Jacen smile happily to see Lily fall for him so fast, taken in by Liam's natural charm. And the lack of judgment from Joe, the way he welcomed Liam in with opened arms—it's like a dream come true. It makes Jacen feel that he really does belong here, with them.

And he's never loved Liam more than he does in that moment. Jacen's never been prouder of him.

They catch each other's eye now and then, communicating what they each feel without anything as cumbersome as words. Jacen's pride and his desire is countered by Liam's ease, patience and wicked knowing. Liam feels Jacen looking at him, undressing him with his eyes, and Liam invites it eagerly, lips soft and smiling, squaring his shoulders, and sending Jacen sultry, heated glances.

As they wind their way behind the imposing, finely crafted bar, Liam is the one to spot Joe's self-defense system—a huge shotgun stowed under the bar's countertop, within reach.

"You have much need of this?" Liam asks, indicating the weapon.

"Nah, but you never know. I had to bust my butt and earn through plain and simple hard work everything I've got in this life. Well, 'til my Auntie Laura kicked it a good fifteen years ago—old money from politicin', oil and cattle ranchin'—and went and left it all to her only living relative, yours truly. She always did have a soft spot for Lily, who was only a baby then, and me a single father trying to provide for her. I wouldn't have my home or the bistro without that capital to fund it. Fiercely protecting my assets has come naturally to me ever since. My employees—and my daughter—are kind enough to indulge my eccentricities. I guess that's what happens when you give a blue-collar guy white-collar opportunities. I watch over them like they're all my kids. If that means making them use that silly little phone app to check in when they're at work, so that I can see where my delivery guys are, and see who's in the building when I'm off-site or out for the day, they humor me—your husband included. If it means being okay with that shotgun's presence, then they can either accept it or find somewhere else to work. And I tell 'em if they ask, that a few years back the store to our left was held up at gunpoint. That's when I brought this in, just in case."

"Are you good with it?"

"Hell yeah, I'm good with it. I have a cabin that I use when I go hunting. Mine is a military family on my father's side. Auntie Laura was my mother's sister. We were trained at a young age to know how to defend ourselves and handle a wide array of weaponry. I've been taking Lily to the shooting range since she was this big," Joe says, holding his hand up at about chest height.

"I gotta say, it does make me feel like Jacen is safer, knowing all of that," Liam tells him. "Maybe I'll start using that phone app to keep tabs with him. And, you know what? I might ask you for the location of that shooting range. Get some target practice in. Couldn't hurt."

He can feel Jacen's hard stare, but Liam doesn't meet it this time.

"Yeah? In that case, I'll take you to the range myself. I'd be happy to. You pick the date, just as long as it's a morning or a Monday when we're closed."

"Sounds great. Let me check my calendar and I'll let you know."

"Liam," Jacen starts, then bites his tongue.

"I think it's a good idea," Liam tells his husband, finally locking eyes with him. "Think I'll look into getting a license to carry, too. For protection."

Jacen's expression tells him clearly, *We'll talk about this later.*

Sensing Jacen's displeasure, Joe clears his throat and says, "Can I offer you both a drink on the house before you go?"

"Thanks, Joe, but it's getting late and we should head home. Next time, for sure."

"It was very nice to finally meet you both," Liam says, shaking their hands again, favoring them with a warm smile of gratitude. "I'll be in touch."

"You have my number," Joe nods.

After Jacen gathers his things from the back room, they walk out of the bistro and back to the car, not really paying much attention to their surroundings, giving cursory glances to the traffic as they cross the road.

"You want a *gun* now?!"

"I think you know there are very good reasons for us to be armed," Liam counters. "With proper training I think it'd be the perfect way for us to feel safer."

"Do you know how easy it is to have a deadly accident with a gun? For it to be taken and turned on you? I don't like it, Lee, at all. Every time I've been in a situation where there were weapons like that... it never was a good thing. For anyone."

"I don't want to argue about it," Liam sighs. "If you're that adamant about it, then we can talk about it later, before doing anything. All right? I just thought it might help."

Jacen, frowning, takes the keys from Liam, who holds them out. He walks to the driver's side of the truck and looks at Liam from across the hood, not aware that their whole exchange is being observed.

"Okay?" Liam adds, holding his hands up in surrender. "I'm officially dropping it."

Jacen remains stubborn for a moment longer, battling to remain calm despite the grisly images flashing in his head of Liam having a gun put to his head, of Liam getting shot, bleeding out and dying in his arms.

"Baby...."

"Okay," Jacen relents. "Let's go home. It's late. I'm just tired."

Liam nods and they both open their doors, settling into the seats. Gunning the engine, Jacen uses the mirrors to reverse out of the spot, checking to make sure there isn't anyone walking behind the vehicle as he clears the front end and turns to pull forward. As they coast up to the exit, a black Lincoln Towncar with its lights off slowly creeps out of its own parking spot nearby. The person in the passenger seat sets down the long-range camera in their hands and picks up a cell phone instead.

The truck joins the flow of traffic on the main road. A few cars behind them, the Lincoln follows.

Chapter 30
A Sense of Foreboding

The tension between Liam and Jacen, spurred by the argument over whether Liam should get a gun, lasts all night and into the next morning. Jacen's ever-present paranoia of finally being found by the representatives of The Company is given new life by the mention of possibly arming themselves. He has also not stopped fearing that the phone call between Liam and Ryan could, at long last, produce results. Just like the night when Liam ran away after the fight following that call, Jacen is plagued by nightmares, daymares and horrifying visions of what could come to pass if their fragile luck happens to suddenly run out. Not wanting to blame Liam for his uneasiness, Jacen closes off and tries to deal with it on his own, thereby leaving Liam out in the cold.

They hardly speak to one another after they get home that night. Jacen goes to bed soon after getting his shower, but isn't able to relax or surrender to sleep until very late. In the morning, Liam wakes early, as usual. He attempts a peace offering in the form of a valiant but not-entirely-successful attempt at vegetable omelets. Jacen wakes and eats his share, but the strained silence continues anyway.

Once Jacen is dressed and ready to leave for work, Liam waits at the door to their apartment to say goodbye. Dressed in his pajama pants and a baggy shirt, he hugs himself, his eyes opened wide with pleading. When Jacen avoids meeting his gaze, Liam bows his head and says softly to his husband once they are standing toe-to-toe, "I'm sorry for even bringing it up in the first place. I just thought it could help put your mind at ease. If I knew it would upset you this much, I never would have—"

Jacen silences him with a tight shake of his head. "Don't. It's not your fault; it's just that I've had a tendency to focus only on the worst-case scenarios lately. Every time I close my eyes, all I see is...." Sighing heavily, he squeezes his eyes shut, willing the visions away for good. It doesn't work. Liam steps up close to Jacen, who pulls him into a gentle hug, kissing the side of his head. "All I want is to stop being so afraid all the time."

"Me too," Liam admits, folding himself into Jacen's comforting warmth while he still can.

Liam watches Jacen pull away from the building in the truck; his heart aching, the unease only building in him as Jacen disappears from sight. The feeling of *wrongness* won't leave him. He can't shake it.

Troubled, twitchy, he seeks some way to soothe his frayed nerves, even if it's a temporary balm, destined to fade quickly.

There is one thing that he knows will help, something he hasn't dared to indulge in until now. His musings from the previous night, before he went in to meet Joe and Lily and the whole debacle of the gun discussion, rise to the surface once more. Liam knows it's selfish, and more than a little crazy. But he's alone with his troubled heart and if it helps him feel better, then where's the harm in it?

He goes to the bedroom and uncovers an unopened box hidden at the back of his closet under a couple of old jackets. Very carefully, he peels back the brown packing tape sealing it shut and pries apart the cardboard flaps. Lifting out the contents, he cradles them in a hand. Even just touching them, feeling their actuality, makes him feels so much better. He takes a deep, filling breath and lets it slowly back out, knowing it's right, and it's time.

He turns off his phone, unable to face conversation with anyone in the state in which he finds himself. After a solid hour and a half of preparation, Leah emerges from the bathroom, leaving Liam temporarily behind. She busies herself around the apartment, doing laundry, cleaning up, paying bills. Time slips by.

Sometime in the early afternoon, right about when the lunch rush should really be kicking into gear at the bistro, Leah turns her attention to the leftover breakfast dishes. She turns on the radio and gazes out the window over the sink, not really seeing anything, just daydreaming happily and singing quietly along with the music.

She doesn't hear the lock turn, which might have been enough warning to allow her to hide or run to another room, out of sight. It's only when the door opens that she realizes in a second she will no longer be alone in the apartment.

Terror — icy cold and unbearably strong — freezes her to the spot. Stricken with panic, her hands in soapy water, her throat closing up around the breath of air that her body demands that she draw, Leah is suddenly lightheaded and quakes with a tremor that grows and grows. Her heart hammers wildly against her ribs, quickening to a dangerous pace as she grips the counter's edge for purchase.

She doesn't even dare look to make sure it's Jacen. From the particular music made by the way he unlocks the door and sighs, kicking off his shoes, Leah knows it's him. It might even be easier if it wasn't Jacen and was some burglar instead.

Oh my god. Oh my god. Oh my god.

She can't breathe. Her lungs refuse to work, choosing death by suffocation over the current level of her mortification.

He's not supposed to be home. He's not supposed to be home for hours.

"Hey," Leah hears from the doorway, and it's like the world is moving in slow motion, every second an hour in length. Her lungs burn the longer she goes without her next inhale, and then the burning spreads to her eyes as they threaten to produce tears in quantity.

Jacen doesn't make another sound and Leah knows he's finally seen her, standing there at the sink, wearing the blue silk dress, the one from Liam's nightmare. He'd bought it weeks ago, just to have, not to use. Along with the dress, he'd also ordered a corset that she's also wearing. With care, she had applied Leah's make-up, but that's as far as it went. She doesn't have her wig, or the right shoes, or falsies. Barefoot in her dress, Leah wants to die. Her heart tears in half, offering itself in sacrifice in order to spare her further humiliation. The rush of blood in her ears drowns out every other sound—Jacen's footsteps getting closer, the radio, the honk of car horns outside.

The nightmare is coming true, her worst fears realized, a punishment for the crime of finally owning her full self, in defiance of everyone's expectations, including Liam's own, and in defiance of Timothy's imagined scorn from beyond the grave. She senses Jacen getting closer, still silent, and actually braces herself to be struck. She grips the counter, waiting for Jacen to backhand her to the side of the head for being such a stupid fucking whore.

Then, as the tears come in a flood of pure shame, she is blind as well as deaf. She doesn't hear the choked sob she makes, astonishingly loud in the stillness.

From not even a foot away, at her back, Leah hears Jacen's hushed baritone, "There was a gas leak, so we closed early for the day."

Big, strong hands, capable of breaking bones and ripping flesh, turn Leah around, manhandling her easily so that she faces her judge and jury. Stomach muscles clenched, cringing, an even more wrenching sob of disgrace emits from Leah and still she waits for Jacen to strike out at her. It's not even a question in her mind at this point; Leah knows it will be coming. There's no use fighting anymore. All is plain and bare. It's done. This realization brings a sense of peace and acceptance. At least there isn't anything else to be afraid of. Nothing could ever be worse than this moment.

An eternity passes. Leah's vision swims with her fat, salty tears. Colors dance and shift before her, and she blinks, staring at whatever is held in Jacen's hand without comprehending.

A hand touches her face.

Tenderly.

"*Leah....*" A breath. Soft as the silk skimming her bare thighs.

A moan of desolation. Leah pushes at him, trying to run, to escape. But all of her strength is gone. Liam has no strength when he is Leah. It's who she is. She's helpless and delicate. She's everything Liam doesn't dare to be.

Jacen bars her way and Leah pushes harder. It's futile and she knows it.

"Please don't cry," Jacen begs. And, nonsensically, adds, "It's okay, baby, it's okay."

It will never be okay.

Twisting her fists in Jacen's shirt, Leah gasps, sucking in much-needed oxygen, but the subsequent exhale is a wail of pain so acute and exquisite that, within it, the truth, in all its splendor, is communicated to Jacen as if he is seeing directly into Avery's soul. Quickly, Jacen wraps her in a tight embrace, holding Leah to him lest she fall, sensing the weakness in her stance.

"These are for you. They're an apology, for how I acted earlier," Jacen tries, stumbling over the words, tripping over the roadblocks of his swelling reaction to Leah's state.

He presses the roses to the side of Leah's hand. The petals tickle her skin and then she can smell them. The perfume gets through the fog of shock. It's nothing but a vapor, the most intangible thing in the world, but Leah clings to it like it's her lifeline. She stares blankly at Jacen's shoulder, an inch from her nose.

He brought me flowers. Jacen brought me flowers.

Because he loves me.

He loves me.

"Lee... Leah. Look at me. Please, look at me."

Jacen hooks a finger under Leah's chin, tilting it up slightly.

"Let me go. Just let me get changed. I can't... God, just let me die. I wanna die. *I'm so embarrassed.*"

And Jacen can hear in her voice that it's true. The extent of Leah's mortification is written plainly across her face, in her body, her trembling, frantic energy. It makes Jacen want to hold her even more tightly, to soothe the hurt with tenderness. He sets the roses down to his right hand, using it to grasp Leah's waist as his left cups the side of Leah's jaw. The touch lets him feel the cool, liquid texture of the dress... and what's underneath the dress.

Shuddering with the force of the sudden hard, blunt edge of his want, Jacen closes his eyes and tries to master himself, knowing how quickly and easily he could lose control and ruin everything.

Leah feels Jacen become still as a statue, his face deliberately masking whatever expression was about to paint across it. This only stokes the fire of Leah's panic, because Jacen has her held tightly.

There is no getting away. Not now.

"Lemme go," Leah pleads in a small voice.

Jacen's thumb drags through the hollow of Leah's cheek. The hand at her waist pushes hungrily down and around, kneading the flesh of her backside, grabbing a handful of muscle and squeezing. Then they're moving. Jacen backs her up to the door of the fridge, doing even more to prevent escape. Dipping his head, Jacen frowns heavily, his eyes closed. Darkness sweeps over him, engulfing his tenderness entirely.

His lips ghost over Leah's.

"I'm disgusting." It's barely spoken but audible enough at that distance.

"Shut up," Jacen growls. He licks at the flavored gloss on Leah's plump lips and then greedily past them, into the heat of her, tasting her, parting her without any trouble at all. Leah unfolds for him like she's the rose. Jacen's huge hand wraps the curve of her ass, hugging just underneath of it, guiding the leg up. Leah immediately obeys, hooking it around Jacen. Moaning thunderously, Jacen ruts in a greedy thrust against Leah's pelvis, drinking in the nectar that is the taste of her as his hand pushes needfully up under the skirt, dragging over the waxed-smooth skin of Leah's thigh, questing up, up, farther until he gets to the panties. With a shuddering exhale, Jacen flushes with a fresh wave of heat. It radiates from him as he fondles Leah through the sheer silk, getting achingly hard, fast. Rolling his palm over the bulge in the front, feeling the damp spot that forms in the thin material as he rubs over the crown of Leah's dick and it weeps pre-come, she obliges by lifting her leg even higher, granting further access.

Desperate, simply needing, Jacen rubs back, over the curve of Leah's left buttock, seeking the top edge of the panties so that he can pull them down and out of the way. He stops, freezing, not even breathing, as he feels something unexpected.

He breaks their deep kiss and stares at Leah, whose eyes are half-lidded. More truths are laid brazenly bare. Jacen *sees*. The carefully applied make-up. The corset. The dress. The air of vulnerability.

Jacen moans thickly and nuzzles into the warmth of Leah's neck.

A whisper like damnation at his ear, soft and supple, irresistible, Jacen hears, "I want you."

"I have your permission?"

Leah hears how far gone Jacen is. The words are just a formality, playing at civility. She feels Jacen's fingers trace, through the panties, around the base of the silicone plug nestled snugly in her ass, and she shivers, her panties getting even wetter. The hard line of Jacen's cock drags in a slow rut against her hip.

Knowing her answer is clear, but voicing it anyway, Leah lets Jacen stare back into her eyes as he presses two fingers at the base, driving it sharply deeper. Leah gasps softly, her lips parting, quivering.

"Yes."

"You are... *so beautiful*," Jacen hisses, destroyed by his lover's exquisiteness. "Anything. Anything for you. *Anything* for you."

Leah moans.

Jacen's hold on himself snaps, breaking cleanly. He crouches for a second, grabbing Leah's other leg and drawing that one up as well so that both are wound around his waist. Then he carries her like that out of the kitchen to the bedroom, kicking the door open and barreling toward the bed. He turns, sitting heavily on it.

Leah, straddling Jacen's lap, grabs at the hem of her dress, ready to twist it up and off and pull it over her head. Jacen stops her, rasping roughly, "No. Leave it on."

Impatiently now, Jacen falls back onto the bed, prying at his fly and zipper, trying to free himself. Leah helps him get his pants open and props herself up on the bed to give Jacen some room to push the clothing down and out of the way. Once he's freed, Jacen pulls Leah back up closer to where he wants her and returns to a sitting position.

"This okay?"

Leah nods even as Jacen quests after her mouth, claiming it with a groan. His busy hands slip under the skirt and pull the panties down in the back, tugging at them until he has access to the deeply inserted toy. Tongue-fucking Leah's mouth, his balls so full that he's in real pain, Jacen gets a good grip on the base of the plug and pulls. Leah gasps softly into Jacen's mouth. The sound gets swallowed. Leah rears up as Jacen slowly withdraws the object from her body, taking his time, not because he wants to but purely to spare Leah any discomfort. Then it's free and Jacen tosses it away onto the bed, greedily inserting three fingers in the plug's place, pressing them through her opening, the hot, wet ring of muscle hugging so tightly around the digits that Jacen is wracked with another shudder of lust. Panting, he gets his fingers in to the hilt; they follow up after Leah, determined, when she writhes and starts to rock up and down on them. Jacen drinks down her small mewl and thrums with need to get his cock inside her.

"Love being inside you. God, I missed this," Jacen says roughly.

Twisting his hand, spreading the fingers apart, he tests the elasticity of the cavity, judging how much prep Leah will need. Jacen is astonished at how tight Leah is, barely able to scissor his fingers apart at all without causing her to whimper when he does. But she's wet enough, lubed up from when she inserted the sex toy. He waits only a minute as Leah rocks down onto Jacen's fingers, working herself on them, and then he can't wait anymore. He plucks the digits free of her and steadies his cock by the root, aligning it with Leah's opening and when he's got it there, tells her with a small nod that he's ready.

Biting at her lower lip, nose scrunched, Leah inhales a shaky breath and presses her weight down on the jutting length of Jacen's member.

Her small cry, broken off at the edges, only drives Jacen to thrust upward as Leah rocks down. The head breaches her and the whole of his shaft is engulfed in tight, wet heat, gripped by it mercilessly. Jacen moans sharply in Leah's ear, panting and gasping, holding her by the waist, pulling her down and making her sit on his whole cock, just pushing, pushing, pushing to burrow deeper.

"Ja-Jacen," Leah moans, wriggling, too full too fast and throbbing from it.

Jacen's eyes roll loosely as Leah clenches in flutters around him, her body almost unable to take the thickly engorged cock, fighting against the burn of the stretch. Running one hand up Leah's back, over the laces of the corset, Jacen scratches over the exposed skin at

Leah's shoulders and reclaims her mouth, sucking kisses to it. He eases them into a rhythm, twitching up into Leah who begins to roll her hips, slow and shallow at first.

"Lee... Leah... Fuck you...."

Jacen's other hand finds Leah's cock, fingering over it through the twisted up, strained fabric of the flimsy underpants. It's hard and the questing touches only make her harder, quickening her pace as she works herself down onto Jacen. Gasping in rough gulps of air, Jacen breaks the kiss and moans into Leah's neck instead, urging her ever faster, twitching up as hard as he can against the swell of her ass on every down-thrust. He rides the clenched, velvety heat of her, moves in a frenzy toward a quick orgasm. Leah rides him but it's not enough. Jacen needs more. So Jacen growls and moves them. He flips them over so that Leah is on her back, staring up at Jacen who, bent over the side of the bed with Leah's legs wide before him, hooks his arms under her knees and holds her there, pinned and spread wide.

"Oh, *God,*" Leah moans. Her breath chokes off with the force of Jacen's thrust after he is realigned, driving his full length into her in one push, making her whimper. The corset prohibits deep breaths and Leah can't seem to get enough air as Jacen fucks her hard and fast, pounding her hole, making her ache with every rutting dig. It's primal and dirty and it's all Leah can do to grab hold of Jacen's shoulders and bear it. The panties are twisted up too tight around her, binding her genitals cruelly and preventing any relief. Jacen's cock feels so thick and long, splitting her in half, taking her apart, but Leah simply lets Jacen pull her thighs more widely open and claim her as deeply as he wants.

With a snarl and a grunt, Jacen twitches, shudders and comes, filling Leah with his seed, unloading deeply into the vessel of her body and then moaning loud and long through the aftershocks.

"So... fucking... *good.*"

Jacen looks utterly spent and dazed as he scans the area around them wildly. After a moment, he sees what he's looking for and grabs at it.

"What...?" Leah starts, then chokes off a breathy grunt as Jacen tugs carefully out of her. The friction is delicious and Leah thrusts into the air, needing something to rub off against. Once freed, quickly Jacen fills her up with the plug again, watching Leah's flushed-pink, tender hole stretch around and hug the plastic, helpless but to part around it. "Oh, *fuck* me."

The dark lust is back in Jacen's eyes and Leah is overcome with self-consciousness and need as Jacen fights to get the panties down and off of her, only to settle himself down between Leah's spread thighs and begin licking her cock and balls.

"Jesus *Christ*...."

Jacen hums, tasting her. Then he opens widely and takes Leah between his lips, suckling briefly on the cockhead, then guiding her shaft back, sucking on it with shallow pulls that go deeper each time. Wrapping the silk of the dress in his fists, he takes Leah back, farther and farther until he's got all of her cradled on his tongue, filling his throat. He pulls off slowly, giving Leah intense suction. The ridge of the crown catches on Jacen's lips so he dives back in. It goes on and on. Jacen sucks as slowly as Leah can stand it, holding her down in defiance of the needy thrusts she tries to make, wanting to fuck Jacen's mouth. But Jacen makes her lie there and endure it — a lazy, unhurried blowjob.

Leah's moans and grunts become more desperate and wrecked until she's keening.

Then Jacen pulls off, moaning hungrily as he licks repeatedly up Leah's cock, playing at the piercing fed through it, and then down over her drawn-up balls, over her sac. Leah curses and fists the bedding, shamelessly loving the luxury of having to submit to this and let Jacen draw out her pleasure torturously. When Jacen licks even further back, trailing the point of his tongue around the flared base of the plug, through lube and his own semen, Leah cries out in both surprise and lust, bucking futilely at the air. Luckily Jacen can't hold out for long. Soon he's swallowing Leah back down, sucking her with quick little pulls, speeding up the pace dramatically. His hand quests up Leah's chest, playing at one of her pierced nipples. Tweaking it through the dress, he twists it until Leah snaps her hips, ready to come. Jacen eases back on her, taking only the head in his mouth, squeezing repeatedly up the shaft in a twisting motion as he tugs sharply on nipple pinched between his fingers.

Leah grunts sharply then curses, "*Fuck!*"

Leah floods Jacen's mouth with come. He swallows it and wrings out more, moaning as his lover pulses and convulses beneath him, helpless — overwhelmed with pleasure.

Dizzy and dazed, Leah is only half-aware of Jacen letting her fall wet from his lips, licking her carefully clean. Then Leah is pulling Jacen up to lie with her.

"Hold me?"

Jacen, grunting an assent, sighs and wraps himself around Leah, never wanting to let go. But after only a few moments, he does just that.

"Sit up for a second," Jacen instructs. "Just a little."

"Why?"

But Jacen is focused, determined. He takes hold of the hem of the twisted silk dress and, reverently, guides it up and over Leah's head. Then Jacen folds it, taking such care that it takes Leah's breath away. The dress is set aside, on the chair by the bed, and Jacen says, "I'll take it to be dry-cleaned later. Let me help you out of this," he says, indicating the corset. "How do I...?"

"There's laces, in the back."

Jacen frowns with concentration and picks at the bow's knot, loosening the ribbons and easing up the pressure on Leah's bound ribs. He helps her get it over her head as well and smiles contentedly at his work when Leah takes a deep breath of relief and falls back down onto the bed.

"Better?"

"Much," Leah grins shyly.

"I didn't want it to get ruined. If you want to get cleaned up...."

"No. I just want you to hold me."

Jacen stares at her, with rapture and naked devotion. "I love you, Leah."

Leah smiles, then laughs, but it sounds thick with emotion and the tears threaten to return. It brings fresh concern to Jacen's face, but Leah tells him, "I love you too. You don't have *any* idea how much this meant to me. I mean it. Thank you."

"For what? Loving you? Lee, that you gave me *this*, this part of you... that's *everything*. It's an honor to be your lover. All I want is to make you happy."

Leah grabs Jacen, hugging him tightly. All of the knots that had been twisting up her heart, soul and spirit, like the unyielding ribbons binding the recently shed corset, for as long as she can remember, give way and, just like that, Leah/Liam is free—really and truly. "I am happy. You make me *so happy*."

Soaring, unencumbered by masks or facades, Liam is lighter than air. Even so, the hard ground awaits, rushing up at them from beneath. Their happiness—his and Jacen's—is not destined to last. Fate is waiting, with fangs and teeth, crouched and ready. They both sense it on some level, hidden in their hearts. It has always been a waiting game. Happiness, no matter how acute, is the fantasy, the silly dream, bought and paid for dearly. A fleeting excitement before the nightmare returns. But at least it's a good one, worthy of sacrifice. Maybe that's why they cling so tightly, while they can, before the mirage of safety fades at long last.

Chapter 31
We All Fall Down

Like most terrible days, this one comes without warning. It begins suddenly, ripping those it ensnares away from their routines and lives, taking everything until it's had its fill and is spent, its victims left in ruins, trying somehow to pick up the pieces.

After the lunch rush clears out at Barbara's Bistro, the place is mostly deserted. Lily is kept busy with one table, ringed with six businessmen lost in heavy conversation as they discuss work over their meal. With the kitchen in order, Jacen comes out front to write the evening's specials on the chalkboard behind the bar. When he's halfway finished, deciding between green beans and asparagus for the vegetable sidedish, he sees a woman come to sit at the bar out of his peripheral vision.

"We'll be with you in a moment," he says distractedly, knowing that Joe is in the back, taking a small break from bartending duties. Since he doesn't know the first thing about mixing drinks, Jacen decides to call Lily over once she's done waiting on the table on the far end of the restaurant.

"Oh, take your time, Jacen," a familiar voice—one from his nightmares—says with malicious sweetness. "I've waited this long. What's a few more seconds?"

The chalk drops, shattering on the floor, as Jacen's hands start to shake violently with merciless, stomach-churning panic. His back is to the stools, to *her*, and he almost runs, darting away into the kitchen and out the back, but he knows better. There is no more running from this, or her. Just like when he was bound to a wheelchair, his body destroyed from the car accident when he was in college, and the boogeyman came in the guise of his next door neighbor, he knew there was no getting away. There's only one option: stay and fight, or die.

"No," he breathes. It's been so long—months—that he had begun to believe they were free. And now that dream is suddenly gone and he is in Hell.

"Yes," Della says with a smile.

Liam. Oh god, Liam.

He turns on a heel.

"What the fuck do you want?" he hisses through gritted teeth.

At first she only smiles, triumphant and calm. "Right now I just kind of want to savor this. It's pretty sweet."

"Get out. Now. Get out."

He's shaking bodily now, his hands curled in fists, all of the blood drained from his face as a cold sweat breaks out over his skin. His phone is tucked into his jeans' pocket, useless. He's surrounded by other people, some that even care about him, but they are useless, too. A quick scan of the area shows him a black car parked out front, two huge bodyguards standing by its side. With guns. He can see the straps from their holsters, their jackets flipped back on one side in case they need to draw.

Fuck.

He stares at Della, continuing to make a mental map of his surroundings. Sensing Lily nearby, he momentarily fixates on her and can feel her standing there, watching him and knowing on a base level that something is wrong. He wills with all his might that she doesn't say a word, that she leaves it alone. *If anything happens to her,* he thinks, with tears springing to his eyes.

Lily's light, soft voice calls with concern, "Jacen?"

Trying to sound normal, knowing he doesn't, biting his cheek to keep the tears inside, he says with forced easiness, "I've got this one. No worries."

"You sure?"

"Yeah!"

Where is Joe? In the kitchen? In the back office? Outside? He can't remember. The shotgun is at the other end of the bar, and they'd stop him before he could get to it, anyway.

Eyes locked with Jacen, Della says quietly and slowly, "Good boy. This is a private conversation, isn't it? And we don't want anyone to get hurt. Do we?"

She lifts something from her lap and lays it on the bar, sliding it over to him.

He glances at it and away. Terror, vice-like, clamps around his heart and squeezes. Nauseous, slightly faint, the photograph on the bar's top burned into his retinas, Jacen sinks into a deep and profound hopelessness.

It's a picture of Liam checking the mail outside of their apartment building, dressed in the outfit he wore the day before.

Understanding Della's threat, Jacen grasps frantically for a lifeline.

"What do you want," he seethes, trying to keep it together a little longer, just to keep Lily from becoming too worried and getting involved in this. He could never forgive himself if she got hurt.

"You. You're an asset of The Company and we intend to make our profits from you."

"What does that mean? William..."

"Has no more value to us. He's getting a little old," she whispers conspiratorially. "A little worn and tired. His only value to us now is leverage. Because you, Jacen, you have plenty of good years left in you — about nine of them, if I'm correct. You're strong, resilient, and you would do *anything* to keep him safe. Wouldn't you?" She gives this a chance to really sink in, and reading the profoundness of Jacen's fear, says, "So what we're going to do now, is you are going to come with me and get in the car waiting right outside. Tell your little friend over there that there's been an emergency if you have to. Then, well...then you have a job to do."

"Now?"

"Right now."

Blank, shrill, clawing horror fills his senses. He can't think. He can't think of any other choice than the one presented to him. So, trying to keep his voice even, but hearing the edge in it anyway, he calls, "Lily, I have to step out for a minute, okay?"

"Yeah, okay," she replies, confused.

"That's a boy," Della praises, tracking Jacen as he moves around the bar and joins her. Hooking a hand around his arm, she guides him out through the front entrance and over to the armed guards.

"Dad! Daddy! *Daddy*!"

Lily runs back through the kitchen, not knowing what's going on, only that it doesn't feel right. It feels wrong. *Very* wrong.

"Sweetheart, what is it," Joe gasps, jogging out from the storeroom at the sound of her call, and the alarm in it. "Is everything okay?"

"No. I don't know." She tries to catch her breath, to find a way to explain. "Jacen just left. There was a woman and she showed him something and he looked... he looked really scared, Daddy. I've never seen anyone look so scared so fast."

"What do you mean, he left?"

Joe runs past her, and Lily follows. He pushes out into the restaurant, scanning the room and then the street beyond.

"Jacen left with her, just now. They got in a black Lincoln with tinted windows and took off south," she says, pointing. "But there were men. They looked scary. Dad, I think Jacen's in trouble."

Joe takes a precious second to read her face, to decipher the clues. "Government trouble?"

"No, not government. Something else. Something bad."

"Shit," Joe hisses. He darts behind the bar and grabs the shotgun, keeping it held low and out of sight. Pulling out his cell phone, he turns it on and selects the app that he asks his employees to log in their locations with, praying harder than he has in years that Jacen remembered to use it that day and has his own phone on him. On the tiny screen in his hand, pink dots pop up over a crudely drawn map of the surrounding area, with one slowly receding from the bistro. Exhaling his small relief, Joe asks, "Truck's around back?"

"Yeah," she says with wide eyes. "Daddy?"

"Keep a lid on things here. Get Frankie out from the kitchen to watch the house. Call the cops. I'm going after Jacen."

Jacen tests the give of the metal handcuffs clasped to his wrists. The edges bite into his skin painfully and he can't move much. He's sitting in the Lincoln, one of the armed guards beside him, the cold barrel of the pistol in the man's hand pressing into Jacen's ribs. Della is in the front seat, turned around sideways to watch him.

His breath is coming so fast, bordering on hyperventilating; his feeling of faintness only gets worse. Trying to calm down, knowing it'll be harder to find a way out of this and handle himself if he succumbs to fear, Jacen tells himself he's been in worse situations than this, even if part of him knows it's a lie, if only because now he has Liam to watch out for. Everything Jacen does from here on out depends on one thing—keeping Liam safe, even if it means sacrificing himself to do it.

"So if I come back to work for you, you'll leave William alone?"

"Yes," she says with the gleam of triumph in her eyes. "You play nice and nothing will happen to William."

"How do I know that's not bullshit? How do I know you don't have him in another car, telling him the same thing about me?"

She laughs. "Well, I guess you'll just have to take my word on that, won't you? Unless you want us to swing by your place, pick him up and let him watch you work."

"No," he gasps. Dark spots crowd at the edges of his vision, pushing inward, overtaking the light. "Don't. No. I'll... I'll cooperate. Just. Just leave him alone. Please."

They've only been driving for a minute or two, not nearly long enough for him to regain any sense of self-control or get his bearings. The car rolls slowly into an alley in a part of town he doesn't recognize. It pulls up bumper to bumper with another black Lincoln, already parked there, and Jacen's tenuous hold on consciousness begins to slip from him at the sudden certainty that they have Liam after all, that he's in the other car and they're each going to be pulled out in the street and executed with two shots to the head for the crime of daring to try to live their lives in peace—made an example for the other employees of The Company who might get similar ideas.

Groaning around bitter bile that rises in his throat, he tumbles into the darkness of his mind, an inky abyss free of pain, when a sharp blow to the head from the butt of the pistol awakens him with excruciating explosions lighting up his brain.

"Don't fall asleep on us just yet, darlin'," Dellas says with warning. "Not 'til your client is satisfied."

They drag him from the car. He fights them, twisting and kicking, struggling to break free, even as thick blood oozes down his temple.

The sun is stark and blinding and he can't make out who it is climbing from the back seat of the other car. He doesn't care; he just wants to get away.

The next blow from the butt of the pistol splits the skin above his eye. Grunting thickly, another stream of blood running in his right eye and making it even harder to see, he keeps fighting for survival, pulling away, the handcuffs slicing skin away from his hands.

"No! No!"

"Again," Della says tiredly from somewhere nearby.

"NO!"

A knee connects with his gut, twice, sending the air rushing out of his lungs. Doubling over around the hurt, his fight leaves him with the third blow to his head. Ears ringing too loudly to make out any words, blind and limp, his legs given out, choking and coughing in his struggle to suck down air, he is helpless to resist it when they drape him belly-down over the front of one of the Lincolns.

Distantly, through a dense white fog that he recedes back into gratefully, hoping that if he lets go completely he'll lose consciousness and not even be aware of what they do to him, there are voices having civilized conversation. He doesn't know what they say. He doesn't care. White is folded into black and he lets go. He's gone.

The strong, stinging aroma of something—some chemical—fills his nostrils and he bucks, gasping and trying to get away from it.

"What did I say? No sleeping until the client is happy."

Della, he thinks, unwilling to focus his good eye to check to make sure it is her.

Something cold and hard presses against the back of his skull. When the barrel of the gun sends tongues of fire licking out through his skin as it grinds in deeply, he sobs and cries out.

"You gonna cooperate?" It's a male voice, laced with cruel laughter.

"Yes," he manages, trying to be still, his injuries screaming.

Hands pull at his clothing, ripping it off of him. His pants are pulled down to his ankles. Bent over the car as he is, he has nowhere to escape as something, maybe fingers, maybe something worse, are forced up his rectum. Clenching around the violation, hyper-aware of the gun now resting against his gashed temple, he sobs quietly against the gleaming metal of the car's hood. Distorted reflections are all he sees.

"You remember Spencer, don't you?" Della says from a few feet away, sounding bored as his body is invaded more deeply. So helpless and humiliated, he wants to die; wishing it, praying for it, feeling flashes of memory overlapping, of being so very young, being held down and raped much like this. "When we offered him the chance to have you again, and to do whatever he wanted to you, that wouldn't cause damage *too* permanently, he was quite interested and paid *handsomely* for the opportunity."

Buzzing, white noise fills his senses, threatening to drown everything out as his weakness only grows with blood loss. It becomes difficult to make out the words. He wonders, deliriously, if there are any pedestrians nearby, as it is the middle of the afternoon after all, just going about their business as he's beaten and molested only steps away, his whole universe ripped to shreds and shit on. There is no help for him now, he knows. There is only this, and the desperate prayer that somewhere, somehow, Liam is all right.

"GET THE FUCK AWAY FROM HIM. NOW!"

He hears it, the hoarse, barking shout penetrating his daze. And at first, all it conjures is dread and the desire for the forgetfulness of oblivion, because there's not enough left in him to dare to hope. Not anymore. *Maybe*, he thinks, *if I keep fighting they'll just shoot me.* It seems the best option, because he recognizes the voice. On some level, he does.

"Don't be a fool, old man. Put the gun down and walk away. This isn't your concern."

"I called the cops already. They'll be here any second. You

morons were too fucking stupid to bother watching your asses to—"

A gunshot splits the air. Jacen screams and it turns into a low, rolling sob.

They shot him.

They shot Joe.

This is my fault.

Oh God, please.

"Any other bright ideas?"

Joe. Jacen gulps down a breath of air, straining his ears, not daring to look or move.

"Get the fuck away from him. Now. Back up. Hands over your heads. That's right. Keep 'em where I can see 'em. No sudden movements."

A pause.

Another gunshot explodes the air. Jacen jumps, cringing, wondering vaguely if he's pissed himself yet or not. He stays close to the hood and feels the invisible, clammy fingers caressing his mind, telling him how easy it would be to stop fighting entirely and get lost in the serenity of unconsciousness once more.

"Jacen," Joe's familiar, comforting voice calls nervously. "Jacen, stay with me. Jacen!"

Jacen tells himself he's just dreaming and lets go again. This time for good.

Joe grips the shotgun like his life depends on it, which, funnily enough, it kind of does. Two shells left and three targets. If they try to run for it, he would probably only be able to take down some of them, not all, and some isn't good enough.

The truck is parked slantwise at the side of the road, at his back, his phone sitting on the dashboard and now showing two little glowing dots crowded together about two miles east of the bistro. He can hear the sirens getting closer and he wants more than anything to go to Jacen, who has just collapsed, slid from the car and crumpled to the asphalt. Not knowing if he's breathing or alive, only aware of how much blood covers the boy's face, Joe prays he's okay. Jacen's pants are pulled down as, when Joe approached the group of people in the alleyway, crowded around the beaten and bound figure of his employee, he was being subjected to something Joe tries not to comprehend with too much clarity. Joe can't go check on Jacen without taking his eyes off of the three people he's got at gunpoint, and the other one he's already shot in the kneecap, now passed out cold and no longer a concern. The second shot had taken a good chunk out of the forearm of a hulking man in a suit who had dared to reach for his handgun.

The only woman in the group looks toward the sound of the approaching police, getting skittish.

"Don't even think about it," Joe warns. "You stay right where you are."

He's fairly sure she'd have run for it anyway had he not already shot two of her bodyguards.

The man to her left has his pants open and his genitals exposed. Joe's finger twitches on the trigger, wanting to blow them clean off of the bastard for what he's done to Jacen.

An eternity later, two squad cars pull up to the entrance of the alley. Men jump out and shout at him to lower his weapon.

"That boy needs help! Please! He's hurt bad," Joe begs them.

"The ambulance is on its way, sir," one of the cops tells him as he's restrained and his rifle is taken.

"Thank God. Jacen! You hang in there, kiddo! Just a few more minutes!"

"FREEZE! HANDS IN THE AIR!"

Joe turns slightly to see as the group he'd had his sights on is disarmed and wrestled to the ground, and handcuffs are locked onto them.

"*Jesus Christ,*" one of the younger policemen groans as he sees the bloodshed and Jacen's poor body. "What the hell was goin' on here?"

"Is he breathing?! Is he okay?!"

The young cop takes Jacen's pulse and nods to his partner.

"Yeah, he's going to be okay."

But, somehow, Joe doubts the truth of that.

An hour and a half slips by, lost. Joe is taken by the police to be questioned. Jacen is whisked away in an ambulance for emergency medical treatment. No one is able to call Liam to tell him what has happened. Liam is first and foremost on Jacen's mind when he *is* conscious, in fits and starts at first, slipping in and out of awareness. All he wants is to call Liam. Afraid that he's been taken too, and is maybe even worse off than Jacen himself; the clawing panic of this fear makes it very difficult for Jacen to be still and let the EMTs, nurses and doctors treat his wounds. They wind up sedating him on the drive to the hospital, and more time slips through the hourglass, unaccounted for.

At the San Luis Obispo police station, Clay is on duty. When he hears of the Feds being called in to deal with a handful of suspects picked up in connection with a brutal assault downtown, he asks what happened. He has to question more than one officer before he gets a somewhat clear picture of what has taken place, the nature of the crime and the motive behind it: a prostitution ring, hired, armed guards, a man with a record of sexual assault charges that never went to trial, and a victim. Jacen. Jacen's name is the most difficult to get as the department tightens up in preparation for the FBI who will be taking over the case as soon as they arrive. But when Clay hears that prostitution is involved, he does not stop until he knows if his friends are connected, praying that they aren't but his heart telling him otherwise.

Once he knows Jacen was the one abducted, beaten and sexually assaulted, that he is alive and being treated at a nearby hospital, Clay knows what he needs to do, for Liam's safety as much as anything.

As Jacen is being taken for a CT scan in order to determine the extent of his head trauma, and Joe is sitting in handcuffs down at the station awaiting questioning, Clay is jumping into his patrol car and speeding over to Liam and Jacen's apartment building. He doesn't know if he will find Liam there, if The Company will have sent another team to pick him up by now. Suspecting the worst, he arrives at the building, parking crookedly in front in the street. He turns off the sirens but leaves the lights flashing as he jumps out, his hand on the butt of his gun, just in case. Giving the area a visual scan before approaching the front entrance, he spares a few precious seconds. The door bursts open and he nearly draws his weapon, but he sees with a deep sigh of relief that it's Liam.

"What?! What's going on?"

Clay stares at him, registering the question but unsure how to answer at first.

"Dice, what the fuck, man? Why are you here? Why...? What's going on? What's wrong?"

He doesn't know, Clay realizes, stricken. "Get in the car. Now. I need to get you off the street."

"No! Not until you tell me what's wrong!" The blood has drained from Liam's face and a deep, subtle tremor begins to wrack his body.

Clay moves, still scanning the streets, watching for anyone suspicious or with a weapon. He grabs Liam by the arm and stays close, moving him around the car to the passenger side.

"Get off of me!"

"Avery, get in the goddamned car! You're not safe here!"

Eyes wide with terror, Liam lets Clay push him into the car. Clay slams the door and runs around to the driver's side. When he's behind the wheel again, he reaches for the gear shift but Liam grabs his arm.

"Something's happened. Jacen," he gasps, as the earth drops away from beneath him.

Clay sees it happen in his friend's eyes, the new bloom of certainty that he's lost another lover to the indiscriminate cruelty of the world. "He was taken from the bistro. His boss followed, but he got there after they'd.... We have them in custody. The people from The Company, the assailant. Two were shot."

"WHAT HAPPENED TO JACEN?!" Liam screams.

"He's alive. He's at the hospital. That's where I'm taking you. I don't know the details. But he was beaten. And the report mentions sexual assault."

Liam's hand falls away. His eyes glaze over.

Clay turns the sirens back on and shifts into drive.

Chapter 32

Losing You

Almost two hours after the attack, Liam and Clay arrive at the hospital. They run inside and demand from the woman at the front desk to know where Jacen is being treated. She gets on the phone to inquire about him and Liam rages with desperate impatience. Clay pulls him away and tries to get him under control but it's like Liam isn't even hearing him. He's detached and all that matters is finding Jacen. He tries to bolt for the elevators before hearing what floor to try, so Clay grips him tightly and keeps him there, threatening to put him in handcuffs if that's what it takes to get him to cooperate.

Finally, they find out that Jacen is most likely somewhere on the third floor, not yet admitted but being treated for his injuries.

They take the elevator up, and when they get to the third floor, Liam sprints down the hall with Clay jogging after him. He doesn't have to go far before he sees Jacen, looking worse for wear but standing by a bed and arguing with a nurse.

The profundity of Liam's relief drains him of the energy or ability to move. He stands there, remembering, finally, to breathe, his heart resuming beating at a regular pace.

"Jacen," he gasps. He shouts the name louder when Jacen doesn't hear him over his dispute with the attendant. "Jacen!"

Jacen looks for the source of the voice and then sees Liam. His eyes close with a prayer of thanks and he deflates, argument forgotten.

"Sir!" the nurse calls, annoyed beyond tolerance, "Mister Timothy, please!"

Jacen pushes past her, going to Liam. With a soft sob of gratitude he folds Liam into his arms.

"Thank God. You're okay, you're okay. You're really okay," Jacen whispers, his hands moving over Liam's body to ensure his actuality and health. "I've been trying to call but you didn't pick up and I thought.... Then they wanted to admit me but I had to make sure you were okay."

"Oh. Fuck, I left the cell in the apartment when Clay showed up." Liam pries Jacen loose, just enough to get a look at him. His forehead has been stitched closed over his right eyebrow and also up near his hairline. He looks bruised, battered and his skin tone is a horrible lifeless grey. Wearing his jeans and a hospital gown, Jacen is also barefoot. Holding Jacen's face in his hands, Liam gasps, "Baby, what did they do to you?"

Jacen avoids his gaze, glancing instead at the cops stationed nearby to keep an eye on him. They're talking to Clay and, lowering his voice, Jacen says, "Come on, I want to get out of here. They said they need to talk to me down at the station, and I was going to try to slip 'em to find you, but since you're here I guess we should get it over with so we can get the fuck out of here already. I just want to go home."

"What?" Liam blurts, confused. "No, we need to make sure you're okay first."

"Sir," the nurse interjects, approaching them with a second nurse she's retrieved to help her get Jacen to cooperate. "We need you to get in the bed and let us admit you so that we can keep an eye on that concussion."

"You have a concussion?" Liam echoes quietly.

"No. I told you, I'm refusing treatment," Jacen growls.

"What? Why? No, you have to let them treat you," Liam argues.

"No. I don't. I just want to go home."

Two men in suits emerge from the elevator bay. They approach the officers and Clay, taking something out from their suit pockets that neither Liam nor Jacen can make out.

"Feds," Liam says.

Jacen starts, looking between Liam and the newcomers. "Shit."

One of the suited men approaches. He flashes his badge and

asks, "Are you Travis Saxon, aka Travis Jacen Timothy?"

Jacen rolls his eyes wearily, looking like he's barely able to remain on his feet. "Yeah," he sighs. "That's me."

"Sir, please," the nurse urges, frowning at his pallor.

Surrendering, he lets her usher him back to bed. As she produces an ear thermometer and a blood pressure cuff to check Jacen's status, the agent consults his notepad, then turns to Liam.

"And are you Avery Williams, aka Liam Timothy?"

"Yeah," Liam murmurs, folding his arms across his chest and coloring with something akin to guilt, though he's not sure why or for what.

"Excellent. We're going to need to talk to both of you, but in the meantime I'm keeping you in protective custody."

"Why?"

"It's for your own safety, sir. The assailants, from what we know, have been tracking you both for some time and we want to make sure things are in order."

As this is the first time Liam has heard such a thing, and at the evidence of the authorities being aware not only of his and Jacen's aliases but the fact that they've been tracked by their former employer, he clams up. The slight strength he'd found at the proof of Jacen being all right evaporates, leaving him lightheaded.

Clay comes over, concerned, "Hey. Pidge, sit down. Come on. I'll get you something to drink."

He guides Liam down into a chair that a nurse brings over for him. Jacen stares at his hands, folded in his lap as an IV is prepped for him.

"I just want to know what the hell is going on," Liam says. Jacen sets his jaw and stays silent.

"Don't worry, we'll get you caught up," the agent tells him.

"Thanks," Liam murmurs, taking a cup of water and watching his husband, battered and broken, afraid for him, and of his quietness.

"What do you know about an organization known as The

Company?"

Joe sips his cup of bitter, weak coffee. He's seated in an interrogation room across from a female federal agent. He's forgotten her name as he's talked to about six different people by now.

"Nothing," he tells her. "I've never heard of 'em."

"If you haven't heard of them, what's your involvement with the incident today?"

"I already told you people, Jacen works for me. He's a chef at my restaurant. He disappeared during his shift under suspicious circumstances, so I followed him using my phone to track his location. And when I found him, he was .. was...." The memory is so potent, it forbids further scrutiny. He rips his thoughts away from the remembered sight of what he saw, because if he doesn't, he'll drive himself crazy with worry. He hasn't been told anything about Jacen's condition or if he's even alive.

"So you opened fire?"

Anger rises. They keep prodding him with the same questions over and over, like it'll change his story. He's tired of it. He wants them to finish with him so that he can get some answers of his own.

"You didn't see him!" Joe flounders for the right words, but they don't exist. "They were surrounding him. One of them pulled his pistol so I shot the bastard. I told 'em to get away from the kid, but another one pulled, so I shot 'im too!"

The agent nods. "Thank you, Mr. Barbara. That'll be all."

It takes a few more hours for Joe to be processed and released. Not only do they not charge him with anything, they offer police protection. But he's not worried about protection. The people he had discovered with Jacen have all been arrested and put in federal custody, and with the sort that they are, Joe doesn't figure they have many friends looking for vengeance when they could be watching out for their own collective asses.

After checking in with Lily, the first thing Joe does is drive to Jacen's home. There's a patrol car parked out front with an officer inside. He asks Joe about his business there, and the officer relays what Joe says to the officer stationed inside the building. A minute later, Joe gets the all-clear to go ahead.

His head buzzing with the new revelations about his employee, Joe climbs up to the third floor and knocks.

The second officer answers the door. Just the fact that Jacen is home is a balm to Joe's nerves. Trying to peer past the leery-looking cop, Joe distractedly explains why he's there.

"I, uh... I'm Joe. Jacen's employer. I was there today, and I need to see that he's all right."

With a backward glance, the officer asks someone out of sight, "This all right with you?"

Liam appears in the doorway, and Joe almost doesn't recognize him, he looks so different compared to the only other time they were face-to-face. Ragged with worry, dressed in a nondescript gray t-shirt and jeans, Liam seems unfocused and frantic as he pushes past the cop and joins Joe in the hall, asking under his breath for a minute of reprieve.

Once the door to the apartment is shut, and they're alone, Liam, scratching restlessly at his arm, blurts, "What happened?"

"What do you mean, what happened?"

"I mean, Jacen's not telling me anything," Liam tells him. "The cops asked us some questions but they weren't exactly forthcoming with information. I'm kind of going on rumors and hearsay at this point, so I'm asking you, what happened?"

"Why isn't Jacen telling you anything, and why isn't he in the damn hospital?" When Liam's expression only tightens with anxiousness in reply, Joe waves off the queries and takes a deep breath. "Well, okay. I don't know the whole story either, but I'll tell you what I do know."

He explains about Jacen being taken from the restaurant, and about how he could see Jacen's general location on his phone and used it to follow the black Lincoln, how he tracked it to the alley. Even with the benefit of the app showing Jacen's general whereabouts, it still took Joe a few minutes to find exactly where he was. Sparing Liam some of the gorier details of the state Jacen had been in at the time, Joe tells his part of it.

"I never remembered to follow up on that stupid phone app; with the whole gun argument, and the whole mess with the phone call with Ryan. But you—thank God for you and your protective instincts. I can't believe you shot them," Liam says with awe.

"Yeah," Joe sighs.

"But why? Why did you follow them? Why would you put yourself in danger like that?"

"Because I trust my daughter. She was really goddamned scared for that boy, and I knew if I didn't do something, no one was. I didn't want that on my conscience."

Liam searches Joe's face, realizing all at once how close he was to losing Jacen. "I might never have seen him again," he says almost to himself. "If you hadn't...."

He hugs Joe spontaneously, hissing, "Thank you! Thank you." Just as quickly, he steps back, apologizing, "Sorry, it's just that he's all I have. And we've been afraid of something like this happening for a while now." Liam doesn't meet his eyes when confessing the last part.

"You boys got mixed up in some bad business."

"You could say that." Flustered, he takes a deep breath and lets it out in a rush, then says, "All we wanted was to be left alone so we could have a normal life."

Joe analyzes Liam's expression, the blank glassiness of his eyes, and the dark circles around them, as well as the imbalanced mixture of relief and bubbling panic, over_aid with exhaustion. These boys have more than enough to worry about, and he's intruding, Joe knows, but he's not done. Not quite yet, at least.

"Can I see him?" Joe asks apologetically. "I can't explain it; I just need to *see* that he's okay."

"Yeah," Liam nods. "But, don't expect much from him."

The apartment is cozier and nicer than Joe expected, filled with personal touches and looking entirely lived-in but well-tended. Jacen is sitting at the counter in the kitchen, slumped over a mug that he has wrapped his hands around. He doesn't look around when the door opens and they enter.

"Travis," Joe calls.

That does it. Jacen turns. His face is bruised and stitched together in places, but he's no longer bloody, which is enough for Joe.

"Huh. So I guess it's true, then."

"Do you want some coffee?" Liam offers, trying to be useful, frantic energy still baking from him.

"No thanks. They gave me plenty down at the station. I'll probably be awake for days from all the damn caffeine."

Jacen watches Joe carefully, mistrusting, uncomprehending and guarded—more guarded than Joe has ever seen him before. The words "beaten" and "raped" ring in Joe's head, sounding sterile. Words like that don't have true meaning until you've seen the acts they encompass happening with your own eyes. Echoes of the horrors that Joe saw, and those he most likely prevented, flash red before him, washing out the duller shades of reality. And Jacen sees it happen, but not a shred of embarrassment or shame colors his features. It's like he dares Joe to judge him or his past.

"This is my fault," Joe starts, after a too-long silence.

"What?" Jacen blinks, moved to speak at last.

"I'm responsible for you when you're at work. They just... *took* you," Joe says in a soft voice, gesturing helplessly.

"They would have taken me from wherever I was. It had—it *has* nothing to do with you."

"Now it does," Joe challenges.

"You shouldn't have gotten involved."

"You don't mean that," Liam gasps. "If Joe hadn't followed you and been armed, who knows where you'd be right now!"

"But he did," Jacen argues sourly. "And now both he and Lily are a part of this, because of me."

"Hey," Joe frowns, "I wouldn't have done it any differently if I had the choice. Well, I might have tried to improve my aim."

"I had it under control," Jacen insists.

"Like hell you did!"

"I don't want anyone getting hurt because of me!" Jacen shouts.

"Tough shit," Joe says levelly, not backing down. "No man is an island. You aren't any different."

"He doesn't mean it," Liam says quietly to Joe. "He's been through a lot, and...."

Joe holds up a hand. "I understand."

"But you should know how grateful we are."

"I do. Trust me," Joe assures him. "Listen, I understand if you're not interested, but, after you have a couple weeks of paid vacation, I would like you to come back to work." At this, Jacen turns back to his coffee, bowing his head. "I'd be mad as hell if I lost my chef over this. The police have offered protection for the bistro until after they have this case wrapped, whether you're there or not, if it makes you feel better about it."

"Let me think it over," Jacen mutters.

Liam walks Joe to the door, taking them both slightly out of earshot of Jacen. When Liam appears on the verge of another out-pouring of gratitude, Joe deflects it. "You know I never met anyone with a real alias before."

"Why are you being so cool about this? You should be horrified, disgusted, *afraid*. Most people wouldn't want to have anything to do with us."

"I'm not most people. And the way I see it, when you save a life, you become responsible for that life. Jacen, or Travis, or whatever the hell his name is—I'm responsible for him now. I'll be in touch, whether he likes it or not." Joe turns, pulls the door open, and glances back over his shoulder at Liam's sincere expression, and warns, "Don't say it."

"Tough shit. Thank you, Mr. Barbara," Liam tells him.

"You're welcome, kid," Joe smiles.

Eventually it's just the two of them—Liam and Jacen, finally alone. Sure, the police officer is still stationed downstairs, but at least they don't have eyes on them anymore. Looking like he's gone twelve rounds with a prizefighter, Jacen finally gives in to exhaustion and admits defeat.

"Goin' to bed," he tells Liam who is standing by the window, scanning the street below. "Come with me."

It's not a request. Jacen is standing there, hands in his pockets, waiting for Liam and not meeting his eyes.

"I was going to call Val."

"Call tomorrow," Jacen says simply. The weight of the day hangs on him, slumping his shoulders, sagging his already haggard expression.

"Okay," Liam relents.

They get changed out of their clothes. Liam tries not to stare at the bruises on Jacen's body when he pulls his shirt off, or at his bandaged wrists, previously hidden by long sleeves, or let it show how much they upset him.

"Are we going to talk about this? I need you to talk to me about this," Liam pleads softly.

At first Jacen doesn't reply. He stands on his side of the bed, debating his response, or maybe just trying to have one. Maybe the horror of it all clouds out logic and normal thought.

"It could have been a lot worse," is what Jacen winds up saying. "They'd only gotten started with me. But it doesn't matter. You're okay. That's all I care about right now."

"Baby," Liam tsks, aching.

At last, Jacen meets his gaze. There is pain and regret and peace all mixed up there, Liam sees.

"I'm tired, Lee," Jacen says, beseeching with a look.

Liam gives in. He slides under the covers. Jacen joins him. Usually Liam sleeps on his back, and Jacen on his stomach, but Jacen slides close to Liam, lying on his side. He wraps Liam's body in an arm, pulling him close, turning him onto his side too. Spooning up against him, Jacen holds on, filling his lungs with the scent of Liam's skin and hair, getting lost in him.

Surprised, Liam eventually relaxes into the embrace, overlaying Jacen's arm with his own. There are long minutes of quiet where Liam feels Jacen breathing, his chest rising and falling, his exhales warm over the back of Liam's neck. It's nice. He uses it like an anchor to regain a feeling of steadiness with all of the chaos swirling around them. All day long, Liam has been trying to deal with the reality of Jacen's wounds, and the attack in general, something feared for so long. If he thinks too deeply about it, the sadness will consume him. But touching Jacen, being held so tightly by him, it helps a lot.

When he begins to wonder if Jacen has fallen asleep, Liam hears, very quietly, a hissed whisper, a mere movement of lips by his ear. "I thought I lost you today." Before Liam can find a way to respond, Jacen adds, "I was so scared that I'd really lost you."

"I'm right here. Not going anywhere," Liam tells him.

Jacen buries his face in his husband's neck, his scent, wracked with fear and relief all at once. Only a few minutes later, Liam is fast asleep. Despite his weariness, for hours Jacen fights to stay awake, savoring the rhythmic breaths of the man in his arms, swearing to God, the universe, and himself that he will do everything in his power to keep him safe.

Chapter 33
Nowhere to Hide

The day after the attack is a blur. It begins with Liam following through on his promise to call Valery and Yasha. The call doesn't last long, though. As soon as they get an inkling of what has happened, Valery and Yasha are hanging up, ready to drive up to San Luis Obispo from Los Angeles to check on Jacen. But before they can, Jacen takes the phone and recites a wish list of things from the hardware store for them to pick up on their way. Liam isn't surprised. He knows that Jacen would just go to the store himself if there were a chance in hell that his husband would let him set foot outside the door of the apartment.

When Yasha and Valery do arrive a few hours later, supplies in hand, they are eventually cleared by the cop still stationed downstairs to go ahead up to the apartment. Jacen, watching his friends' arrival from a window, is just as determined as he was the previous day to avoid heavy conversation, though he is glad to see them.

Valery, who is carrying the smaller of two bags, and therefore has her hands mostly free, grabs Jacen for a tight hug as soon as she is through the door. Patiently waiting his turn and taking the chance to survey Jacen's physical condition, Yasha sets down the larger bag from the hardware store. From over his wife's shoulder, he asks Jacen, "Are you okay?"

Valery examines Jacen's face with furious concern—the places where the skin is stitched together, the darkening bruises. He brushes her off, disentangling from her embrace, saying simply, "I'm fine."

Frowning with resentment at Jacen's dismissive attitude, she exclaims, "My ass! You don't look fine! What happened?!"

"Yeah, good luck getting an answer on that one," Liam mumbles, sipping coffee only a few feet away in the kitchen. He'd told Yasha and Valery the basics of the situation over the phone, but had spared them the more unsavory details.

Valery steps back to let Yasha have his turn, and goes to Liam to give him a hug next, as well as ask him how he's holding up.

"Seriously, I'm fine," Jacen tells Yasha levelly, knowing Yasha's scowl and what's behind it. Jacen had crossed his arms as soon as Valery broke their hug. His body language screams his desire not to be touched; his expression is blank and closed off, but Jacen does let Yasha give him a quick kiss on the lips. After a moment, Jacen softens enough to return Yasha's insistent but gentle hug. "But I do need you to give me a hand with this stuff."

What Yasha can read from Jacen tells him nothing about what the man's been through, but everything about Jacen's desire to spare Liam having to take part in his plans to make their home safer. Beseeching wordlessly, Jacen tries to get Yasha to follow him down the hall, away from the kitchen where Liam and Valery are quietly conversing.

"You're not *fine*," Yasha says, his feet firmly planted, refusing to humor Jacen's desire to deflect attention or discussion.

Jacen glances up as Liam who, wanting some privacy of his own, pulls Valery aside, farther into the living room as he explains more of the specifics about what's going on with the investigation. Once the two of them are settled on the couch on the far end of the room, Jacen turns his attention back to Yasha.

"What do you want me to say?"

Looking plainly insulted by this, Yasha mimics, "What do I want you to say? I want you to be honest—with yourself, and Liam, and us. You know better than this. All this is is reflex, and habit. Burying this shit," Yasha says severely, gesturing out at the world beyond the window, "instead of dealing with it isn't going to do you or Liam any good. It'll just fester and rot, and get you in even more trouble."

"I am dealing with it." Jacen points down at the bags brought from the hardware store on his instruction. "I'm being realistic. And it's done. Yes, they found us. So what? It was only a matter of time. And they didn't do anything to me that won't heal. They're locked up. It's out of our hands now and Liam wasn't hurt, that's all that matters."

"You matter," Yasha counters.

Jacen rolls his eyes. He sees Yasha and Liam exchange a heavy glance with each other from across the apartment.

"They know where we live," Jacen tells him, making sure his voice is lowered, though Liam knows as much anyway.

"Then maybe you shouldn't be here."

"And go where? This is our home now. I'm not giving up our home for these assholes. They've taken enough as it is."

"So you're not running?"

"I'm not running," Jacen agrees.

Yasha nods with some satisfaction. "You picked a hell of a time to stop."

"Yeah, well," Jacen shrugs. "I have my reasons."

A good part of the middle of the day is spent with Jacen and Yasha installing bars on the bedroom window, which leads out to the fire escape. After they're finished with that, they put new, thick deadbolts on the inside of the bedroom door and on the apartment's front door. In the meantime, Liam is able to talk to Valery, airing all of his fears and worries to her, including the ones he has hesitated voicing to Jacen just yet. They talk about every minute of the previous day, about The Company, and what it all means for Jacen and Liam's future. They talk about Jacen. They talk about Joe Barbara. They talk about the surveillance photos that had been found with Della and her goons; photos taken of Liam and the apartment building. The two of them gather all four of their phones and install the app that Joe used to track Jacen, just in case, and so that they will always be able to find one another.

They order an early dinner. The cop brings it up to them. The four of them sit around the kitchen table and play a few quiet rounds of poker as they eat.

Before Liam knows it, Yasha and Valery are leaving. Only a few things have changed. Liam has gotten input on some of his concerns. Yasha and Valery have seen the state of their friends' bodies and minds, and the apartment's security has been slightly improved. Jacen has even called a reputable security company to come and install cameras on the outside of the building to give them further peace of mind. It doesn't seem like enough. Danger lurks too closely.

Remembering how Jacen clung to him the night before, Liam anticipates it happening again, and it does. Jacen pulls him flush to his body, keeping him there with an arm and a leg, not letting go all night.

All week they sleep like that. Safe in their barricaded room, with the new bolts on the doors and bars on the thickly curtained window forbidding entry to anyone who might dare invade their sanctuary. Liam doesn't press Jacen to talk or for any hasty decisions on their future. They try to patiently wait for answers in regard to Jacen's abductors, but as things are being handled at a federal level, the information available to them is slow to come. All they know is that things have been very, very quiet. Even in L.A., Yasha and Valery don't hear any rumblings or rumors at all about Jacen, Liam or Della. It's like Della has vanished off the face of the Earth.

One week after Jacen is taken from the bistro by gun-wielding thugs, they get two pieces of news. The first comes from Clay, the second from the hospital. Clay, along with one of the federal agents, is able to tell them that charges have been officially filed against Della and her accomplices for conspiracy, prostitution, kidnapping and assault, as well as a laundry list of other offenses. Her lawyers are trying to work out a deal that would reduce her sentence in exchange for inside information on The Company. It appears she was working to track down Jacen and Liam, independently of the broader organization, in hopes of winning favor for recouping their investment in the two men. That's why no one in L.A. has gotten the faintest inkling of what's transpired, though that is soon to change. And given the United States government's interest in bringing down The Company, a deal with Della is likely.

The other piece of news is in the form of word from Jacen's doctors that all of his tests, his blood work and STD panels have come back clean. Jacen isn't surprised, since he knows things didn't really go far enough for there to be a valid concern, but he can see the huge relief the news stirs in Liam.

"I told you, I'm fine," is all Jacen says.

But if Liam thought that the news didn't affect Jacen at all, he learns otherwise that night. Like they have every night for seven days, they climb in bed together. Liam turns his back to Jacen, lying on his side, waiting for Jacen to move up close to him, shivering slightly at the intimate contact when he does. For a little while nothing happens, but Liam can sense Jacen's alertness. It's like an electric charge in the air around them. Sleep is a long way off. Staring into the dark, Liam waits to see what that alertness means, if Jacen is finally ready to talk about everything, or if something else is going on.

He doesn't have to wait long.

First, Jacen pulls away an inch or two, which is odd in and of itself. His breathing becomes marginally heavier, but it's almost too subtle a change for Liam to be sure. Then, almost reluctantly, Jacen presses close once more. And Liam can feel that he's hard. The thick line of him nudges from behind.

Understanding blooms. It's only because Liam knows his husband as well as he does that he notices the slight hesitancy when Jacen's right hand rubs down and over the right side of Liam's body. The caress skates over his hip and down around in front of his pelvis. He palms Liam's cock through his boxers, squeezing lightly.

It's Jacen asking permission. And there isn't a shred of doubt in Liam's mind of what his answer is. He responds with an act of his own, spreading his legs, opening them and planting his right foot on the bed, giving Jacen room. Liam inhales sharply and Jacen groans softly, the sound of it vibrating into Liam's body as Jacen slips his hand inside the boxers. He fondles and then gets impatient, pushing the underwear down and out of the way.

The need and quietly dark determination exuding from Jacen lights Liam up. His nerves tune in to each touch, his senses sharpen with anticipation. When Jacen gets the underwear past Liam's hips, Liam moves to help by kicking them off, but no sooner does he do so than he feels two of Jacen's fingers questing between his legs, finding and gently touching the center of his interest. Once contact has been made, Jacen exhales heavily with relief. He draws up onto an elbow to get more leverage to move. Skin pebbling with goose-bumps, heart beating quickly, Liam decides. He starts to roll onto his stomach, ready to get his knees under him, but Jacen grunts in nega-tion and turns him the other way, onto his back. Moving quickly, seeing Liam's nerves catching up with him and determined to beat them, Jacen lunges for a bottle of lube on the nightstand and gets in position, taking each of Liam's legs and guiding them up over his shoulders. Face-to-face, with Liam naked, and only a thin pair of boxers clothing him, Jacen bears down on him, pressing Liam's legs back toward his shoulders. A curtain of dark hair falls in Jacen's face, masking his predatory expression as he gets his fingers wet with lubricant and smears the fluid over Liam's clenched opening. Arching slightly at the touch as well as how helpless the position makes him feel, Liam holds his breath and closes his eyes.

Jacen's hair brushes Liam's cheek like a tickle of silk. Warm lips drag over Liam's jaw. The fingers trace, circling, rubbing around and then they enter him, slowly. Exhaling shakily through his nose, Liam tries to be quiet but when the fingers start to pump, going deeper, spreading apart, twisting, he can't. Lips parting around a moan, he flushes with heat of his own and begins to get hard.

He's been holding his thighs, just to have something to anchor himself to, so when Jacen says thickly, "Arms above your head. Keep 'em up there. Relax," Liam grunts, wriggling on the probing digits, but he complies.

"Jacen...."

"Look at me."

With effort, Liam opens his eyes. Jacen flips his hair back out of his face to clear his view. He withdraws his hand from Liam most of the way and immediately presses a third finger inside, deeply, adding to the stretch. The reaction paints across Liam's face, and Jacen feels it in the tension of Liam's thighs pressed against him, in the clench of his inner muscles. Holding his gaze, Jacen thrusts again, filling him up. Liam swallows a whine and almost turns his face away, but just manages to catch himself.

"I love you," Jacen tells him, scissoring his fingers apart, getting his lover ready for him. He's been looking for any of that old mistrust, that old hurt that had kept them apart for so long. It's not there though. The only things he can see behind Liam's expression are vulnerability and ordinary nervousness. Those are easy enough to understand. Liam has only bottomed for Jacen the one time in how many months, and besides that, he's still not become used to the feeling of someone else prepping him for sex. The prod and wriggle of strange fingers inside his body is foreign to him, and probably the most self-consciousness-inducing part of intimacy for him.

Liam's fingers curl and tense where they rest on the pillow his head rests upon. Jacen presses down on him, trapping him on the bed, pumping faster into him, making quick work of it without being rough. The tension doesn't leave Liam's body, but his breathing gets rougher. Lust blackens his eyes. Jacen dips in for a kiss and when his tongue enters the wet heat of Liam's mouth, Liam moans freely, giving into it. The kiss goes deeper, as Jacen sucks on Liam's lips, then opens him wide, licking back over his tongue, taking it all. Liam is so distracted, focusing only on kissing Jacen back, that he doesn't notice when Jacen pulls his fingers free so that he can get his boxers out of the way. He only surfaces when, a moment later, the fat, bulbous head of Jacen's cock is pressing demandingly at him and Jacen surges back down on him, folding Liam in half as he rocks down, entering him with an easy push.

Liam makes a small, desperate noise that Jacen devours with a growl, not relinquishing Liam's mouth, using it for all it's worth and kissing him dizzy. Once he's nestled safely inside his captive, Jacen's hand comes away from where it had been steadying his cock, and instead grabs Liam's thighs, both of his huge hands wrapping them as he rocks, working his way farther inside the snug vessel of Liam's body.

A slick sheen of sweat has broken out over Liam's skin. Jacen caresses through it. Then they are joined completely and Liam can't catch his breath. Jacen breaks the kiss and pauses his movements, letting him adjust. He even sits back on his heels a little to give Liam room to get air. Gasping and grunting, Liam's eyes close, feeling keenly observed and intimately possessed. He waits for Jacen to move and fuck and when he doesn't, Liam reaches between their bodies and down. He's fully erect and throbbing, needing relief. But before he can do much Jacen takes his hand and guides it back up above his head, lacing their fingers together and keeping him pinned. Liam curses and tests his range of movement, pressing down slightly onto the thick column impaling him, pulling futilely at his trapped arms. Breathing raggedly, Jacen watches the whole thing. He sees Liam pretend to fight, just as he sees his dick pulse pre-come when Jacen doesn't let go.

Itching to touch, Jacen guides Liam's hands up to the bars of the headboard, not letting go until he's grasping them. Then he caresses down each arm to Liam's chest, quickly finding the stiffened nubs of his pierced nipples. Pinching down on them and tugging gently, he moves at last, drawing back a few inches and pressing back in. It makes Liam moan, so he does it again, riding him at a smooth, unhurried pace, twisting his nipples until he's so worked up that he's fucking himself down on Jacen's every push, his dick an angry red as it bobs between them.

"You wanna touch yourself?" Jacen asks roughly. Adding a moment later, "Should I let you?"

The answer flashes like a spark behind Liam's green eyes, so Jacen bears down, releasing his nipples and holding his lover's wrists in place as he starts to fuck him harder and deeper. Liam cries out and takes it, his body looser now as he gives Jacen all the power and all of his trust. Each breath is ripped from him and Jacen's mouth hovers above Liam's own, kissing his abused lips gently as Jacen's hips twitch, thrust and slam into him. Every now and then, Liam surges up toward Jacen for more of a kiss but then Jacen just grinds into him that much harder, driving the breath from him along with another moan.

In a tease, Jacen dares to reach down between them with one hand, grazing it lightly over Liam's erection, feeling how wet and full it is before his fingers close around the piercing laced through the head, playing with it even as he holds Liam's hands to the headboard and continues to ride him. It causes Liam nearly to sob, he's so desperate to climax.

Shuddering with his own need, with Liam hugged around him

so perfectly, gripping even tighter as he wriggles and tries to buck against Jacen's hand to get off, Jacen gets close to release. Letting Liam's wrists go, he cups the side of his lover's face and gasps, racing toward his orgasm. Liam watches him come apart. Every care falls away. All that matters is the push and touch.

Jacen thrusts hard and holds, letting out a hard, shaky grunt as he empties himself into Liam. He's still recovering as he closes Liam's flesh in a firm grip and pumps it. Keening and rolling his hips up into the touch, Liam comes. A thick, milky jet of come arcs up from his cock onto his chest, neck and jaw. Grunting and groaning, his senses dull and blacken at the edges. The world falls out of focus and the only thing he can feel is the throb of his body around where Jacen is fitted inside it and the light tickle of the tip of Jacen's tongue and then the soft press of his lips as he cleans some of the come from his jaw.

Distantly, very distantly, an old, familiar voice in Liam's head tells him to go get cleaned up. He ignores it and drifts off. He's semi-conscious of Jacen pulling out and easing Liam's legs back down, then massaging some of the blood back into them. He's less conscious of Jacen curling up around him. Time slips by, but then Jacen's hand wraps the side of Liam's face. Jacen's leg is thrown over him where Liam is prone on the bed. His nose is buried in the short hair behind Liam's ear and Liam feels as much as hears Jacen's sharp intake of breath that holds and comes back out as a whine of pain.

"Jacen?" Liam's voice sounds foggy in his own ears.

Jacen sobs, trying to hold it in, even now fighting against it. But it won't be held. It all comes pouring out. So he clutches Liam as the hurt and terror of what he's been through, *everything* he's been through, is wrung violently out of him.

"Baby, it's okay." Liam tries. He's unable to move, Jacen has him gripped so tightly, as if, should he let go, he'll lose everything. Liam can't even turn toward Jacen. All he can do is hug with one arm around Jacen's head as he cries, caressing his arm with the other. "You're gonna be okay. It's over. Okay? It's all over and we're going to be okay. You and me. Together."

Jacen cries for a long time, with decades of unshed tears finally washing out of him, cleansing some of the soul-deep wounds scarring him. He cries until there are no tears left in him, and he's only hiccupping softly, holding to Liam as Liam holds to him, the both of them twined inextricably in one another, for better or worse.

Chapter 34
Reaping What You Sow

"You ready for this?"

Clay has pulled Liam aside outside of the same diner where they had their previous meetings about Liam's little project. Coincidentally, it's also the same place that Liam and Jacen met Clay when first coming to San Luis Obispo, since it's close to the precinct. At mid-afternoon, the place isn't busy, and through windows dappled with twisted reflections and shadows from the trees lining the street, he can see the forms of two people. One he knows, the other he doesn't.

Staring at them, feeling Clay's concerned, watchful gaze trying to read his expression, Liam is pulled out from under the weight of the recent events of his own life. It's astonishingly freeing, to for once be able to leave it all behind, to have something more pressing and, most of all, *positive*, to be focused on.

Of course, Clay sees the faint lines of wear and worry etching his friend's young face. It's taken its toll on Liam to endure what he has in trying to escape the life he was living, but having love and responsibility to anchor him once more has made him something like he used to be, yet wiser and stronger. He's Avery, all grown up.

Liam blinks and peers through ghosts and figments dancing in his memory, blinding him like sun through the trees.

"Yeah. 'Course I am. It's why I'm here, right? This is the whole point."

"Did you look at the file I sent you? With his profile and background history?"

There's a pause as Liam looks up at the figures through the window, but can't quite make them out. "Nah. I trust your judgment, and Valery's."

Clay sighs with aggravation, "Okay, that's great and all, but I really needed you to have a vague idea what you were walking in to here."

Liam hears him, but doesn't back down. He also doesn't apologize.

"Let's just go in. I'll know more when I get in there and see him for myself. Paper is just paper. It's meaningless to me."

"You're the boss," Clay relents, though not seeming too happy about it.

They walk up the ramp and through the diner's front doors. After a sharp left turn and a few steps, Liam sees the object of his curiosity seated across from Valery in a booth along the windows overlooking the parking lot.

Liam's breath catches. As real, true pain blooms in his chest, a small sound of soul-crushing despair emits from back in his throat. Clay grips Liam by the elbow to steady him, hissing under his breath at Liam's ear, "This is why you needed to be prepared for—"

"Shut up," Liam manages, sounding choked with emotion. "You don't know what I need."

Timothy was sandy-haired and the boy in the booth has raven-black hair, but Liam sees a resemblance despite the more obvious differences. It's not a matter of features or clothing, it goes deeper than that. They are both so desperately young, with an air of easily-shattered innocence and a more intangible, but no less noticeable, lack of something needed to know one has a future beyond the gutters and alleyways.

"You must be Aaron. I'm Liam," he says, extending a hand.

"Oh, hey, nice to meet you," Aaron says with a tentative glance to Valery and then Clay before giving Liam a crooked smile. "I mean... I should say thank you. Thank you, Liam."

"Not necessary. This is an agreement, right? We help each other out. That's how it works."

Liam sits and lets Clay slide in next to him. They place their food order.

Aaron was picked up for loitering a few weeks back, and, after asking around at the local shelters, Clay discovered the boy's homelessness. On closer investigation, and inquiries with some reliable sources, Clay learned Aaron's age—seventeen—and that he had begun to associate with a group of young men that were known by local police to prostitute themselves for cash and drugs. After learning this, Clay had a little one-on-one conversation with Aaron about where his life was headed. It was soon crystal clear that Aaron was a victim of circumstances, not a lack of common sense. He didn't want to become that which he was about to become; he simply saw no other options. Hunger was a real problem. The shelters were sometimes full, leaving him to the mercy of the streets nights on end. Without an address or clean clothes, he stood no chance of being employed. So, Clay, through Liam, gave Aaron an option.

Wanting to reach across the table and grab Aaron by the hands, to hold him there, a real incarnation of his own lost childhood and discarded dreams, Liam swallows his tears and his rage, and says, "Let me tell you a little about myself."

He starts at the beginning—his foster homes—and those people, essentially strangers, who gave him a bed and a real shot at life. They are something he will always be grateful for, but the system isn't perfect. It wasn't then and it isn't now. Eighteen-year-olds need help too. Liam tells Aaron about Timothy and himself, the paths to death and ruin that each of them took and why. If not for the silent screaming behind Liam's eyes, Aaron might not have believed Liam, but he sees, and he feels the yearning that comes through the story.

"This is the deal," Liam says earnestly. "You get a place of your own, your own apartment. I'll keep the kitchen stocked with groceries. And, in turn, you work for me, doing maintenance on the building and tending to the property. You'll still have plenty of time left over to get a job doing whatever it is that interests you, as long as it's legitimate. You'll have Valery, Clay and myself only a phone call away whenever you need to talk, for advice, or whatever. You get six months to lock down employment, and then we'll re-evaluate. The idea is to eventually get you established earning income, and stable enough to not need my help any more. But you've gotta play by the rules, or the deal's off. One of us will meet with you every week to see how you're getting along. You're not alone."

Valery is watching Liam intently, and he can sense that it would be bad to meet her eyes, lest his emotion bubble over again, as hers is about to. Aaron is focused on his hands as they pick at the wrapper of his straw. Their food arrives and the starvation Aaron has been suffering from lights his young face as a huge, heaping platter is set before him. Then he looks up at Liam. For a second there's vertigo. Aaron is Timothy. He's Liam too, and so many other boys that are now lost. Then he's just Aaron again.

"So, what do you think?"

Aaron pushes past the shame, the defiance born of naiveté and pride, the gnawing in his empty stomach, and the guilt at what he's been tempted to do. He pulls himself up in the seat, straightening. He clears his throat and extends his right hand over the table laden with steaming food. "I won't let you down. That's what I think. Just give me a chance."

"Okay," Liam smiles, shaking hands with him, trying to radiate strength and hope through the brief contact. "It's a deal."

When Liam returns to the apartment, he's surprised to see that Yasha isn't waiting with Jacen like he's supposed to be. Jacen is alone, sitting sideways on the couch by the window in the living room with one leg propped on the cushion, staring at his fingernails.

Before even bothering to say hello, his key still wedged in the door's bolt lock, Liam stands half-inside the apartment and frowns. "Where's Yasha?"

Jacen raises his head to look at his husband, and at first he doesn't say anything, just reflects resigned, dark restlessness. At least the stitches and the bruises are mostly gone, Liam thinks dully. "He's on his way home," Jacen mutters, then goes back to examining his nails. It's been so long now since he worked at the bistro that his nails are clean and neat once more, like when he was still a prostitute. He doesn't like it.

"Dammit, we talked about this! You shouldn't be on your own! The whole point of Yasha coming up here today was so that I could get this meeting handled without having a fucking coronary worrying about you!"

Jacen reaches for a nearby bottle of water on the coffee table, upends it and drinks. The bottle goes back on the coaster and he locks eyes with his husband. Calmly, softly, he asks, "You done? Because if you want to keep screaming at me, I'll wait."

With a scoff and a shake of his head, hurt and still carrying around a head full of memories of Timothy and homelessness, Liam hisses, "Fuck you." He yanks his keys from the door, drops them on a nearby chair and storms off to the bedroom, slamming it closed behind him.

Jacen rolls his eyes, at himself, at the situation, and watches the bedroom door, imagining Liam behind it, angry and closing off. The easiest out for Liam is always to run or hide, and when he's pushed, no matter how far he's come since L.A., that will be the course he instinctively takes. Jacen is actually a little proud of Liam for the 'fuck you.' Before, he wouldn't even have gotten that. Hell, before Jacen wouldn't have gotten the slightest hint Liam was angry, it would all be bottled, stored away under a careful facade.

The problem, for Jacen, is clear. The apartment isn't safe. Not anymore. And it will never be safe, no matter how many bars he installs on the windows or whatever fancy security system they rig up. The memories are what taint it, and those are impossible to dispel for good. But what do they do, he wonders? Run again? To what? From what? This is their home now. This is all they have.

Setting that train of thought aside, Jacen resolves to deal with it later. He wants to ask how the meeting went. It had clearly meant a lot to Liam, the idea of renting out the spare apartment to a gay youth in need but with the potential to make something of his life. They'd discussed it a few days earlier over a dinner Jacen carefully, lovingly, prepared for them both. Liam was bashful; Jacen adored every minute of it.

Despair and resentment, which he's been carrying around in spades since Della showed her sorry face in the bistro, anchor Jacen to the couch. Wanting so much to feel safe somehow, to be back at work, to apologize to Liam, Jacen just can't get past that mental wall.

His phone rings. Eyeing it mistrustfully, he waits for the caller I.D. then answers.

"Joe."

"You ready to come back to work yet? These idiots down here are giving me migraines with their impressive level of incompetence."

This makes Jacen smile. He loosens up a little bit. "I've been thinking about it, to tell you the truth. I'm bored out of my mind. But Liam...." The bedroom door is still closed tight. Jacen stares at it, weighing his options.

Hearing the heavy silence on the other end of the line, Joe breaks it with a reassuring, "Whenever you're ready. No rush. If things are still hairy over there, then...."

"No, it's just—" Jacen flounders. "I mean, they are. Hairy. I guess. The apartment doesn't exactly feel safe to us anymore, so that's the biggest obstacle for us right now. Maybe if we were somewhere where I don't have to worry about him being on his own all day, it would be different. They had pictures of him here. I don't know. I don't know anymore."

"Well that kind of brings me to the real reason I called," Joe says, sounding sheepish. It's unlike him. Jacen perks up, sits up straighter on the couch.

"What's going on?"

"Hmm. Let's see. Well, as a youngster yourself maybe you can commiserate a little, but when a girl works for her father at the family business, she gets kind of sick of him after spending day in and day out in his company. So the long and the short of it is that Lily's got her own place now, downtown near the bistro. Nice little condo. Small but fancy. Anyway, she had been living in the guesthouse adjacent to my home. I've always been a big fan of safety and peace of mind myself, so I live in a gated community. I wouldn't be able to afford it without the money from my inheritance. Damn impressive security going in and out, deluxe security system on the house itself, and the guest house...."

"Joe," Jacen tries to interrupt, sensing where this is going.

Joe barrels on anyway. When he does, Jacen stands and walks slowly over to the bedroom door. "It isn't a big place, but it's all set up and just waiting for someone to use it. You and Liam should move in there. I don't have anyone that might be visiting, it's just going to waste, and maybe if I knew you were in a safer place I'd get some damn sleep at night. And I know you're a man of pride—independent and all—and maybe it's because I'm the same way that I understand that so well. But let me do this for you. Please."

Taking hold of the bedroom door's knob, Jacen starts to give it a turn, waiting for the lock to catch, certain that Liam has locked him out. But it turns freely enough. He opens the door slowly, and when it's cracked an inch or two, what he sees makes his heart ache in his chest, his eyes pricking suddenly with tears. Liam is sitting, head bowed, on the side of the bed, the window with its new, thick bars, the curtains parted, casts stark shadows across his figure as he cries softly. Liam turns his head away, hiding his tear-streaked face from Jacen's sight, and crosses his arms over his chest like he's literally holding himself together.

Jacen wants to say no to Joe. He wants to do this on his own, and to not have to rely on anyone. Before, that's the way it always worked. Look out for number one and to hell with the rest. No one was going to give a shit about Jacen but him, so it made him selfish and pig-headed. Seeing Liam weeping despondently on their bed, precious, newfound hope draining rapidly from his bright eyes, Jacen is given a hard, painful look at what his responsibilities now encompass. Now is not the time to be selfish or stupid. Now is the time to man-up and act like a husband.

"Jacen? You still there? Damn phone connection."

"Yeah, Joe, I'm still here."

Liam is listening, Jacen sees, even if he can't raise his eyes or acknowledge his lover's presence.

"Okay," Jacen says, surrendering. Even saying the word, part of his heavy load is suddenly lifted from his shoulders. "Okay, I think we'll take you up on that. As, you know, a temporary solution. And you can take our rent from my checks."

"Rent?" Joe scoffs.

"Yeah, rent. And thank you. No one's done so much for me in my whole life as you have. I owe you, big time."

He chokes on the words, and wipes at his eyes. Distantly, he is aware of Liam standing and walking toward him, but it's washed-out and blurred. The phone is taken from his hand and he hears Liam say, "Joe, can we call you right back? Thanks."

And then Liam's arms wrap Jacen in a tender hug full of forgiveness and apology alike, in which hope is born anew.

Chapter 35
Rebirth's Reward

One season melts into the next, but since it's southern California, the differences are not very great. The air remains warm. The presence of rain in the winter versus the dryness of summer marks the passing of time most noticeably. For Liam and Jacen, however, the differences are many. Four months have slipped by, too full of activity and busywork to be marked in clearly delineated days and weeks.

After enduring the harrowing initial move from Los Angeles to the motel room in San Luis Obispo, and then the move to the apartment building, their third move is not as much of a trial. With plenty of experience under their belts, though many more possessions to box and cart across town, it goes smoothly. And since Jacen is around to help Liam with the packing, it doesn't take long at all.

Every truckload they transfer from the apartment to the guesthouse on Joe's property lightens any lingering worries about their own safety; though now they are comforted by the knowledge that those worries are largely unfounded—force of habit rather than born from logic. Della is securely behind bars—and her goons as well, while The Company, or any of its representatives would be beyond foolish to come anywhere near Jacen and Liam, given the heat the organization is under from the authorities, and the federal government's newfound familiarity with the two men. So, Jacen and Liam's remaining worries are more a psychological need, a yearning for rebirth.

They leave their tension and cares behind on the day they lock up their top floor apartment, ready to be leased out to a new tenant of Liam's choosing—someone with even more desperate need of it than they did. Aaron is already settled into the unit across the hall, and Liam and Jacen have just enough time to get him up to speed on the basics of building maintenance before taking their leave. With ample enthusiasm and a need to prove himself worthy of the generous trust Liam has bestowed upon him, Aaron seems to every one of them to be the perfect choice as the first candidate of Liam's social welfare project.

One month after Joe offers him the guesthouse, Jacen resumes work at the bistro. Some days he gets a ride in from Joe, or even Lily. The new security on the restaurant and Joe's reluctance to have Jacen venture out from the kitchen without acting as a personal bodyguard by his side works miracles on Jacen's confidence. Each day that passes boosts his comfort level a little more until he surpasses the joy it had initially given him to be gainfully employed and he achieves a satisfaction with his professional life that he has never before experienced. Joe and Lily notice the change. Yasha, Valery and Clay do, too. Jacen becomes the man he should have been, if his childhood traumas had never happened. And Liam believes it goes beyond that. Thanks to his many trials, Jacen carries a strength in him that is like iron, unbending, unshakable. The things he was most afraid of have stared him in the face, and he has survived them all. They don't have any power over him anymore. Not in the slightest.

And so Jacen *is* reborn. For so long he carried the burden of needing to be strong for Liam, or to be the provider, the protector, the martyr. With a new family, with support he never dreamed he could ever have—people who would risk their own lives without hesitation, for his sake alone, it renews his faith in the world, and what it might yet hold for them in the future.

There is no better way, in Liam's humble opinion, to wake up on a Sunday morning, than with a good, hard, slow, passionate fuck. The deliriously happy smile it puts on his face lasts all through his chores as he first does some laundry, then cleans the pool for Joe—

the pool's maintenance being just one of the many small ways that Liam contributes in order to not only express his continued gratitude for Joe's generosity, but as an extension of what has become an almost maniacal need to manage things with what some might say is an obscenely detailed eye.

Jacen once thought the management of their apartment building would be far too much for Liam to handle. But he was wrong. Not only has Liam flourished after witnessing the success of his outreach program for local gay youth, he has taken on the task of managing Joe's property in addition to their own. There are many things Joe Barbara would rather be doing than tending to his grounds and the buildings that stand upon them. Before he had such enthusiastic and multi-talented tenants, he would typically hire help to take care of what needed to be done. Now there's no need to even go that far, because there's hardly a task that could need doing that Liam wouldn't be willing to tackle. The pool, the landscaping, electrical and plumbing repairs, even a leak in the roof — that they did hire a roofing company to correct — are supervised by one Liam Timothy. Joe jokes to Jacen, when Liam is safely out of earshot, that this is what it must be like to have one of those battle-ax wives taking care of everything so he can spend his time off going hunting or sitting on his butt with a cold beer in hand. Jacen always laughs at this, noting the genuine respect and a little bit of healthy fear that Joe has developed for Liam.

It has been out of respect for Jacen's feelings that Liam has abandoned the idea of getting a gun of his own. However, Jacen has consented to Liam joining Joe at the firing range, getting some target practice in. Baby steps, Liam tells himself. There are some things that will always send Jacen into a panic, even given the newfound safety they find themselves enjoying, and Liam with a firearm strapped to his side is one of them. So he takes what he can get.

One sunny, fall, California morning, Jacen is out on a run, and Liam goes inside their house to straighten the kitchen once the pool is skimmed and the chlorine levels checked. With the bistro closed until much later that afternoon, Joe is off on a drive down to a local vineyard to sample some possible additions to their wine list. Everything is quiet. Liam surveys their little home, contented. It's just the right size for them, with most of the living space down-stairs — the living room and eat-in kitchen, a bedroom and adjoining bathroom. There's a small loft on the half-story above with some exercise equipment and a little office for Liam. Liam has painted the whole place from top to bottom in neutral but masculine tones, and has decorated it in a modern, classic, understated style. He's proud of it, and there is nowhere else he'd rather be.

But then the stifling quiet and niggling loneliness begins to have the effect on Liam that it usually does. He gets an idea and changes into the black kilt and combat boots that he knows well that Jacen favors, forgoing a shirt entirely. He rings his eyes with smoky black eyeliner and dampens his hair, tousling it and twisting the ends with gel. The finishing touch is a hint of plum lipstick — just enough to give his lips a bruised, used look.

He hears Jacen return. The iron gate clangs. Joe's huge mastiffs in the main house bark, and Jacen calls out to them in order to settle them back down. There's a loud splash as Jacen dives into the cooling waters of the in-ground pool. When he enters the guesthouse a few minutes later, he's already towel-dried off, with the towel wrapped around his waist.

Liam glances over a shoulder at his husband, rag in hand as he wipes off the counter in the kitchen, the morning light soft, hitting the house from the back, where the fewest windows are, so that most of it is in shadow. The expression on Jacen's face says every-thing. Liam represses a pleased grin and waits.

He doesn't have to wait long. Jacen crosses the living room, dropping the towel, peeling off his trunks. *To get a shower*, Liam tells himself. *He's going to shower.*

The towering, broad, solid, warm bulk of Jacen's body presses up against Liam's back. His breath skates over the side of Liam's neck.

"How was the run?" Liam asks innocently. "Hot? What is it, like ninety degrees today?"

Sounding like a man who has taken all of the power for himself, a man deadly serious, who's been pushed well past the limits of tolerance too many times to count, and is sick of it, Jacen growls a threat, "You're fucking with me. You think that's funny? Huh? You think it's cute?"

Liam feels all of the air get sucked from the room. Distantly, he wonders what time it is. The time is important, but it's hard to think clearly, because he can feel that Jacen is staring at him so hard his gaze leaves scorch marks everywhere it touches. The size difference between them has never been more noticeable and Liam feels small, even frail in comparison. Heart pounding, eyes mostly closed over as he stares at his hands on the counter, shaking slightly now with nervousness, Liam feels Jacen shift fractionally, heat radiating from him.

Liam moves, but slowly. He drops the rag and closes his eyes. He reaches down and lifts the back of the kilt, sliding his boot-clad feet into a marginally wider stance.

"Higher," Jacen barks. It sends goosebumps shivering out over Liam's skin, pulling it tight. He draws the kilt up even higher and quickly grabs the edge of the counter for purchase because Jacen doesn't waste time. He knows that Liam is still loose from taking his husband's cock earlier that morning. It's only once Jacen spreads Liam's cheeks and breaches him dry, pressing just the head of his dick through, then stopping, letting Liam feel the burn and shudder at the obscene way Jacen's girth stretches him wide, impaling him upon it, that Jacen spits thickly into his hand and rubs the saliva on his shaft. It's the only lube Liam gets. He white-knuckles the counter and Jacen grabs him by the back of the neck and by the hip, pulling him steadily back, millimeter-by-millimeter, onto him. A hard shudder rips through Liam's body and he gasps, the sound loud in the stillness.

When he's fully seated, his balls pressing flush against Liam's ass, Jacen sighs, then immediately withdraws. His crown catches on Liam's rim and he thrusts, hard, back in, eliciting a small cry. Liam's skin flushes pink all at once and he flinches slightly. Jacen soothes him with a downward caress, along his thigh. "That's my girl. My dirty, dirty girl... *Leah*..." Each word is punctuated by a hard thrust and Liam mewls softly, adjusting his angle as the force of Jacen's cock, driven into his body again and again, doesn't lessen one bit.

"Fuck," Liam hisses, gritting his teeth as Jacen holds him there and pistons his hips at a brutal pace, fucking him dizzy. Breathless, aching, Liam purrs as Jacen uses him, not touching him anywhere but to hold him down to take it. It goes on and on... and then it stops.

Panting, Jacen steadies himself by the root and pulls out. Liam hisses through his teeth, opening his eyes slightly, but knowing better than to turn and face Jacen. "Get in the bedroom. Now."

Liam walks in front. When they're inside the bedroom, he feels Jacen unfasten the buckle holding the kilt on his hips. It falls to the floor. "Lay on your back. Grab your knees."

A little embarrassed by how hard he is, Liam struggles onto the high bed, lies back and draws his legs up, holding them by the knees as instructed. Now he can see Jacen's face and his eyes are blown black with raging, unchained lust. His thickly muscled chest rises and falls with each heavy breath, and his cock is still huge and full.

With his ass hanging slightly off the edge of the bed, pulled open wide by his pose, Liam relaxes into it as Jacen holds him by the thighs and enters him again. Liam's mouth falls open around a moan as the position allows Jacen even deeper into his body.

"You can feel that, can't you?" Jacen says with a pleased, feral smirk. He gives Liam a long, deep dig and then again, hard enough to get him to make a small sobbing cry, his feet flexing and body tensing.

"Y-yeah," Liam answers, his voice hoarse and wavering.

Jacen bears down on him, and Liam's breathing chokes off completely in anticipation, tiny frown lines forming in his brow. The next thrust rakes right over his prostate and Liam spasms on the bed, swallowing the shout that wants to burst from his chest. But then Jacen does it again and again and coos, "Come on, baby girl."

Tears spring to Liam's eyes and his back bows, his hips bucking again, fucking blindly up into the air as Jacen triggers the bundle of nerves again and again. Liam cries out, roughly, and Jacen twists one of Liam's pierced nipples, praising him with, "That's it. Tell me what you want, Leah."

"*Fuck*," he cries shrilly, then composes himself with effort, his eyes rolling up into his head as he croaks, "More. Harder."

It's sweet torture to be used with such force and passion, his body throbbing, and with no promise of relief of his own. Jacen is careful not to touch anywhere near his husband's dick, leaving him painfully erect and weeping pre-come steadily. The cradle of Jacen's hips beats against the curve of Liam's ass and he's close now. Liam can tell, so he bears it and moments later, Jacen is gasping through his climax, pumping every drop deeply into Liam.

"Jesus," Jacen exhales, sweat and pool water alike dripping from the gently curling tendrils of his dark hair, hanging in his equally-darkened eyes, blue made black with lust. He thrusts in and tugs out more gently, more deliberately, and Liam knows what this is too. If Jacen thought his husband couldn't flush any pinker, he was wrong. Liam blushes fiercely and closes his eyes tightly. "Good. Stay still. Stay right there." Carefully, he frees his cock from Liam's ass and, with both hands, pulls Liam's cheeks apart. When he decides the come isn't leaking from him as quickly as he likes, Jacen inserts the first two fingers of his right hand, swipes them around and sweeps out some of the fluid. "Better." The spend he smears all around Liam's tender opening, into the slightly swollen rim, over his balls and the inside of his thighs.

"Jace...."

"Go on. Up on the bed," Jacen coaxes, like Liam should know better.

Liam glances at the clock.

"You heard me," Jacen says, sounding like that's the end of the discussion. Liam averts his eyes as he shifts up the bed to the headboard and obediently extends his arms to either side of the bed. He waits like that as Jacen moves around the bed and ties his wrists to each of the bed's posts, his head propped on a pillow. "Comfy?"

Lips pursed, his dick hard as granite, desperate for relief, knowing he's not getting any soon, Liam can't quite stop himself from glancing at the cabinet where they keep the sex toys. When Jacen notices and laughs, Liam grunts, "Shit."

Restless energy and anticipation screams through Liam's body, lighting it up like electric current as he plants his booted feet on the bed—he's naked except for those—and tucks his legs up snug to his sore hard-on. Jacen goes to root through the cabinet. A moment later, he turns with a thick, long purple dildo in his hand. Liam protests with a whine, "It's too big."

"Oh, I think I can make it fit," Jacen hums.

"*Jace.*"

"All right," Jacen sighs. He throws the dildo onto the bed. Liam scowls at it. Jacen turns back to the cabinet and finds something else. He takes it to the bed and doesn't let Liam see it, even though he tries to crane his neck to get a peek. Setting it down momentarily out of sight, Jacen sets to the task of unbuckling the boots. One by one he gets them off and puts them on the floor by the bed. Then he waits patiently and nods at Liam's legs. "Okay, come on."

Rolling his eyes, Liam curls his legs up against his chest, preferring that to going spread eagle. He bites his tongue and stays nice and still as Jacen presses a small, tapered plug into Liam's anus, then flicks on the switch. Immediately it begins to vibrate and Liam puts his feet back down.

"Straighten 'em. Flat to the bed," Jacen instructs.

"No."

Jacen raises his eyebrows at that. "I do have more rope, you know."

"Goddammit," Liam curses, straightening his legs. The toy's vibration sends jolts of white fire directly to his already painful erection, which bobs tightly, flushed dark red, up to his belly. After a moment's thought, Jacen returns with two metal clamps for Liam's nipples. He attaches them behind the piercings and Liam looks like he's drowning in the barrage of stimulation by the time Jacen gathers a pair of clean boxer briefs and takes them with him, along with his phone, into the adjoining bathroom to shower.

The first time Jacen tried this, leaving Liam to stew in his own juices, as it were, while he took his sweet old time getting cleaned up, he made the mistake of binding Liam's wrists together above his head rather than out to either side. When he came out of the bathroom, he found Liam quite satisfied and already asleep, having twisted around to his belly to rub off on the bed. Ever since then, the pre-bondage fucking Jacen gives Liam has been rougher, like he's still taking it out on Liam's ass that he had the gall to get himself off. But it has occurred to Jacen that that might have been the point all along, because Liam loves bringing out the animal in Jacen. That wild, clawing, possessive lust is the quickest way to turn Liam on, every time. All he ever wants is to feel like he belongs to Jacen, and no one else, and that Jacen would do anything to keep it that way. It's also the reason why he wears the kilt. It's been a long, long time since Liam has been able to wear it outside of their home, as Jacen usually has him bent over and ass-up before he gets anywhere near the door.

A few eternities pass as Jacen takes his shower. Liam tries everything to get comfortable, but each time he moves, the vibrating plug gets jostled inside his body, making it worse. At one point, the phone Jacen brought into the bathroom rings. There's a brief, muffled conversation then silence once more. By the time Jacen emerges, not only is he showered, but his hair is blown dry and Liam swears that his nails look freshly manicured as well.

Jacen tosses his used towel into the hamper, sets his phone on the dresser and Liam sobs, "Jace! *Please!*"

Holding up one finger, Jacen mutters, "Just a sec," before leaving the bedroom entirely.

"JACEN TIMOTHY!" Liam bellows.

"I love you too!" Jacen calls back.

"It's my own fault," Liam sighs, miserably, trying to curl up around his erection. "It's my own goddamned fault. Fucking kilt."

Chapter 36
Come Full Circle

It's no surprise at all when Liam hears the low rumble of a motorcycle from somewhere nearby, just outside their small house. The blood pounding in Liam's ears muffles the noise, though. Gutchurning, dizzying nervousness floods his system. His whole body begins to tremble, so he takes a deep, filling breath, holds it, and then lets it out.

In all of the varying spans of his life, all of the people he has been, the names he has used, the men he has been with, the person that now is Liam—belonging only to Jacen—has never been self-conscious about sex. He's had innumerable partners and been observed having sex with countless others. Privacy is a foreign concept. Even when he was very young, sex was an all-inclusive activity, not something secret or sacred

Somehow, though, sex has become something like that. Liam treasures his intimacy with Jacen, who knows him better than anyone ever has. Jacen loves Liam entirely, without judgment or conditions. Jacen understands what it is to become someone who gets paid for sex, who lives with that choice for years and, eventually, fights to move beyond it. Jacen understands, too, Liam's many-layered spirit and loves him for it in ways Timothy might never have. They have, each of them, known loss and survived it. They are stronger for their struggles.

Yasha, Liam knows, is just outside, with Jacen. His visit has been planned. The initial apprehension Yasha's presence stirred fades back as Liam reminds himself how completely he trusts Jacen. Jacen is safety, stability, freedom The excitement that comes from loving only him, with devotion and without reservation, is all of the thrill that Liam will ever need.

As his heartbeat slows to a more normal pace, a small thrill lingers in knowing that Yasha is nearby. It feels for Liam like he's getting away with something, and has tricked himself into, finally, enjoying a third, outside presence while he's submitting to Jacen's sexual whims. Jacen will keep Yasha from getting too close without Liam's permission, though Yasha might also suspect what's happening only feet away, in the bedroom where Liam is bound to the bed. It's not terrifying like it was with Claudia. Then, everything was out of Liam's control. The Company was pulling the strings. Claudia was a client. She called the shots. The danger in that is what caused Liam's panic. Now, Liam is in control, even while shackled and naked. *He* decides how far things go. No one can take from him what he's unwilling to give. This revelation infuses him with a heady sense of power and contentment. For possibly the first time in a life filled with sex, he's finally making choices not for money or out of a sense of obligation, but only for himself, and the man he loves. The satisfaction of finding happiness on his terms, freed of subjugation, is greater than he could have ever dreamed.

The bedroom door inches open. Jacen slips inside, closes the door behind him, and crosses to the bed. He leans down to press a soft, loving kiss to Liam's forehead. "He's outside by the pool."

"Okay," Liam mutters.

"I can tell him to take a drive for a while."

Knowing Jacen is giving him every chance to manage his own comfort, Liam shakes his head tightly, once.

A small smile curls one side of Jacen's mouth, twisting up his lips. "You look beautiful, Leah."

The gentle, pure affection in the words steals Liam's breath away. Aching with gratitude for Jacen and his tender, loving care, Liam yields readily to Jacen's kiss. Their lips touch too briefly. Then Jacen slinks down his lover's body, guiding Liam's legs apart and kneeling between them.

"What do you want? Hmm?" Jacen's voice is confident, roughened with arousal and readiness to please. "If you have a preference, tell me now."

It's not even a question. "Fingers," Liam blurts. "Take that fucking thing out of me."

"Yes, ma'am," Jacen says. He grips the plug by the flared base and starts to work it out of Liam's ass, twisting it sharply as he does, so that it rubs in a wide circle around his inner walls. Liam hisses and tilts his hips, Jacen guides the thickest part past his rim, letting him feel the stretch before pulling at his opening, prying him open with the tip before taking it all the way out.

"Thank Christ," Liam moans. Jacen swiftly stuffs two generously lubed fingers up his hole and Liam moans even louder. The fingers wriggle and twist. They stroke and feel and search. When Jacen begins to pump them in and out, Liam pushes his bottom down onto them on the in-stroke, greedy for more. "Deeper. Come on."

Jacen buries his hand to the hilt and asks, "Better?"

"Yeah," Liam sighs. "Add another."

Rocking his hips counter to Jacen's movements, Liam relaxes into the pillows and lets his eyes close. Jacen's hair tickles the inside of Liam's thighs as he lowers his mouth, opens it and suckles at the dripping-wet tip of Liam's cock.

"Oh *fuck* yes," Liam groans, trying to buck and bury himself in Jacen's mouth, but Jacen doesn't let him. He plants his free hand on Liam's pelvis, using the junction of his thumb and forefinger to steady his erection as he seals his lips around the jewelry of Liam's piercing and plays at it with his tongue, alternately flicking it and sucking forcefully on it. Liam hisses and writhes on the bed, surrendering to the pleasure being given to him, glad Jacen's not in a hurry to get on with it. It's so much better this way.

Jacen pulls off with a slurp, letting Liam fall wet to his belly, the piercing gleaming brightly with the added lubricant of saliva.

Sitting up, Jacen withdraws his fingers slowly. He rubs gently over Liam's opening, the engorged, reddened flesh. He pivots his wrist and taps it lightly before pressing four fingers back inside. The ring of muscle parts easily enough, hugging around the fingers.

Liam makes a needy grunt low in his throat, his whole body tingling from overstimulation. As Jacen bends down to lick a wet stripe up the underside of Liam's dick, Liam shudders, trying to rock and thrust against Jacen's tongue. Jacen licks over the piercing fed through the slit of Liam's cockhead, cleaning away fresh pre-come in the process, then tugs at the jewelry with his teeth. Jacen's hand pumps and strokes all the while.

For a while Jacen keeps playing at Liam like that, suckling at only the tip of his erection, not giving nearly enough to get him off, just to keep him going. Liam's attempts to fuck himself against Jacen's hand increase in desperation. When Liam begins to spill tears and choke on his breaths, as if sobs are quite close, Jacen growls in surrender.

Freeing his busy hand, planting both hands instead by Liam's head, Jacen looms over him and watches. Liam writhes, chasing up after Jacen, but knowing he's still too far away. His lower lip pouts unconsciously as Liam pleads almost too quietly to hear, "*Please.*"

Jacen nuzzles against Liam's neck, nipping and sucking a bruise there. Reaching down between their bodies with his left hand, he uses just the tips of his fingers to play and rub over and around the head of Liam's cock, ignoring the shaft completely. Liam hisses and Jacen moves to kiss his mouth. Thrusting deeply with his tongue, sucking and tasting him, Jacen moans. Trying to thrust against Jacen's hand, Liam whimpers into Jacen's mouth, needing more, unable to achieve orgasm with the fingering alone. But Jacen knows it'll be even better if Liam gets there like this, fighting for it, teased into it instead of pushed. Liam twists his face away, gasping, then he twists his body too, and violently, trying to somehow get closer to Jacen, begging, shamelessly, "Please."

Jacen drags his thumb in a broad, firm swipe under the ridge of Liam's crown, then again up through the divot. He holds Liam's eyes and caresses his cheek. Then, Liam shudders. His eyes roll, showing whites and Jacen grasps him in a tight fist, squeezing as hard as he dares in a long tug from root to tip. Liam bucks and holds like that, back arched off the bed and thick ropes of semen jet from Jacen's hand. Orgasming so hard, for a moment Jacen is truly concerned; Liam stops breathing, making no sound at all. Jacen jacks him through it and Liam twitches, slamming his hips into Jacen's hand repeatedly. Jacen kisses under Liam's ear and hears him whimper.

Once it's past, Jacen doesn't know if Liam is conscious or not, but he's wearing a peaceful expression and breathing evenly, so he takes his time untying the knots holding his wrists. Rubbing the places the ties held fast, Jacen soothes the skin and muscle.

After leaving to retrieve a wet washcloth, Jacen uses it to wipe Liam's face and neck. The cool touch rouses him. His green eyes flash, the dark lashes fluttering open and then shut.

"Take a nap, okay? That's an order."

"Is it?" Liam says with defiance

"Yeah. It is, actually," Jacen says levelly, already holding the huge purple dildo he'd threatened Liam with earlier. He picks up the lube on the nightstand and swiftly slicks some on.

"And what are you gonna do if I decide I'd rather take a bath instead?"

"What am I gonna *do*?" Jacen mimics. He takes Liam's left knee in hand, pressing it up against his chest, and aligns the end of the dildo with Liam's well-fucked opening. Applying steady pressure, he breaches him as Liam's eyes pop open and Jacen keeps on pressing. The wet toy slides in quick and deep, all the way to the hilt. Flinching against the sudden fullness and moaning against the violation, Liam frowns. His lips part softly. Jacen pulls the thick dildo halfway out and reinserts it.

"Dammit!" Liam cries.

"You gonna take a nap?"

"Yes," he says, giving up the fight.

"Good," Jacen smiles. Carefully, he twists the toy all the way out. Liam's mouth falls open around another moan.

"Evil fucker."

"Promise me."

"I promise. No bath."

Jacen drags a hand through the milky white drops splattered up the length of Liam's body, then sucks the salty taste from his thumb as he gets off the bed.

Liam smiles, drunk on pleasure and joy. He turns onto his side, curling up and getting comfortable.

Jacen stands there a moment, taking in the sight of Liam with a post-coital glow and a carefree, untroubled expression. Jacen gives Liam a small, honest grin that's so full of love that it would have knocked him over had he not already been laying down. "I'll be right outside if you need anything, okay?"

"Mm," Liam hums, already dozing off.

It's an hour and a half later when Liam reappears. Yasha and Jacen are seated in the shade of an umbrella around a table by the pool, with a few empty bottles of beer between them. They'd been talking about Yasha's current mission—a search for a modest home in the area, as he and Valery have decided to abandon L.A. for good and move to a less dramatic area. With the nasty business with The Company nearly resolved at last, they both itch to get away much as Liam and Jacen had.

Jacen asks, "Oh, did the guys at the gate give you any trouble this time?"

"Nah. I showed them the entry card thing you gave me and they only gave me the third degree for five minutes this time instead of twenty-five."

"Cool."

"Hey, at least they're doing their job."

"Mm," Jacen hums in agreement.

Both men look up from their half-finished beers, held in hand, their conversation halting abruptly as Liam emerges from the guesthouse. He's showered and wearing a tiny scrap of a bathing suit— white shorts that are so low they barely cover the crack of his ass, and cut so high that his butt cheeks pop out the bottom of the suit, his package stuffed and close to bursting from the front. The fabric is stretched so tightly that not only are his pierced nipples on full display but, for those looking, his Prince Albert can be seen rather clearly through the suit as well.

With a wicked grin and a low, "How's it goin?" he jogs past them and dives smoothly into the pool.

"God damn," Yasha says with awe. "Does he always go swimming in that?"

Jacen rolls his eyes, sipping deeply from his beer. He grunts, then says, "Of course he does. I have blue balls so bad, and so often,

I have to get a little payback now and then. Rough, kinky sex only seems to encourage him though. Go figure."

"It's... obscene," Yasha says, tilting his head to get a better look as Liam vaults out of the pool and sits neatly on the edge.

"Tell me about it," Jacen groans.

"Yeah, poor Jacen," Liam calls. "Boo hoo! He only gets to fuck his husband whenever the hell he likes to! What a hard life!"

Jacen hides his beaming, blissful smile behind his drink, but it shows in his eyes anyway. "It is! And you should know better, with an innocent young girl like Lily visiting so often. You're a bad influence!"

"Yeah, I can tell she really hates it when I go nude sunbathing. That must be why she tries to get someone to take over her shift on afternoons, so she can come over to Dad's and peep out the windows."

Jacen tries to look offended at this, but can't manage it as he bursts into laughter.

"Hey, you tell him yet?" Liam calls to Yasha.

His easy laughter gone is abruptly; Jacen feels his smile dying as well as he sits up and looks between the other two. "What? Tell me what?"

Yasha gives Liam a sharp look over his shoulder and sighs, averting his gaze from Jacen, who's suddenly on the edge of his seat. "No, actually. I hadn't."

"What... what's going on?" Jacen blurts. "What do you have to tell me?"

Liam smiles knowingly and dives back into the water.

"Yasha, what's going on?"

"I guess I deserved that, after checking out the free show and all," Yasha mutters, talking to himself.

Liam surfaces and folds his arms over the edge of the pool, watching them and listening.

"Yasha," Jacen says sharply.

"It's nothing," he sighs, wilting slightly. "I mean, it's not *nothing*, it's just not... you know... something that you need to be concerned about and, um... Val's pregnant."

"What?!" Jacen is out of his chair. It almost topples over as he springs to his feet. Liam laughs.

"It does happen, you know," Yasha frowns. "And that's why we're in a rush to move. We want to be up here and find something before she gets too far along."

"*I'm going to be an uncle?!*"

"Jesus Christ," Yasha groans, covering his face with both hands.

"I'm going to be an uncle!" Jacen nearly bounces with joy, it fills him so entirely, pouring from him and filling the air. "This is awesome news! Oh my god! Yasha! You're a daddy!"

"See, this is why I didn't want to tell him. He's going to be impossible now," Yasha grumbles to Liam, sipping his beer.

"Wait," Jacen says suddenly, his face clouding over. He holds out his hands like he isn't the only one on his feet and bursting with fevered excitement. "Wait a minute." He turns to his husband. "You KNEW?!"

"He knew before *I* knew," Yasha complains, pointing at Liam's satisfied, grinning face.

"How long have you known?!"

"Mm, 'bout a month and a half," Liam says.

"How long have *you* known," he asks next, turning to Yasha.

"A couple of weeks."

Jacen gasps, shocked. "You both suck!"

Yasha shrugs and drinks his beer. Liam pushes back off the wall and paddles water, but as Jacen slowly strips off his shirt and kicks off his sandals, Liam curses under his breath, "Oh fuck."

Bolting across the pavement, Jacen swan-dives into the water and barrels after the figure of his fleeing husband.

"How did we get here?" Liam asks, curled up on the couch, watching the sunset through the trees beyond the window of their living room.

"Through hell and high water?" Jacen offers.

Smiling at this, Liam tucks himself farther into Jacen's embrace. "No, really. It all seems like a dream, doesn't it? Some days I feel like I'm going to wake up on a dirty hotel bed with a John in the bathroom, and all of this is just going to evaporate. It seems too good to be true."

"No, it is true, and I'll tell you why," Jacen argues, his voice full of that iron that's always there now, beneath the surface. "We fought for it. Tooth and nail. We deserve this. We deserve to be this happy."

Liam thinks this over and then, after some time, nods. "Yeah. I just never expected it to actually happen."

"Me either," Jacen admits, holding on tight.

"So, you really think we'll be okay?"

The fragility he hears behind the question shakes Jacen a little. There's such pure hope in it, hope of the sort that Liam, born into hopelessness, never dared to strive for, that Jacen resolves anew to fight for it, no matter what, for however long he is destined to walk the Earth.

"Yes. We really will. I swear to it."

"Well, even if it doesn't last, I just want you to know that it was worth it, all of it, to have this with you. No matter if it's only for now."

And that's when Jacen knows. No matter how much time passes, or where they live or what they do, part of Liam, and part of himself will always be those scared little boys, doing terrible things because they can't see any other choice.

"Thank you for helping me get here," Liam says, with more honesty that he would ever have been capable of, as recently as a few months ago. "Seriously. Thank you."

He looks up into Jacen's eyes as he says it, and has a funny feeling he's talking not to Jacen, but to Travis as he says it. So Jacen holds the gaze as he replies, to Avery, "You're welcome. Thank you for coming with me. Thank you for trusting me."

A tear slides down Travis's cheek and Avery brushes it away.

"I love you."

If you enjoyed this story, you can sign up for a free membership at
ForbiddenFiction.com and discuss it with other readers and the author at
the *Whatever the Cost* story page at
http://forbiddenfiction.com/library/story/LK1-1.000005

We do our best to proof all our work, but if you spot a text error we
missed, please let us know via our website Contact Form at
http://forbiddenfiction.com/contact

Author's Notes

This story came together from as unlikely places as the characters within it. It began, first, as a naughty little birthday gift for a friend — a short story about a cowboy who seeks some company one night in the form of a handsome prostitute and overcomes some of his sexual hang-ups once that company arrives. I wrote the first draft and lived with it for a few weeks before sharing it with anyone. During that time, I became slowly more and more curious about the lonely cowboy's savior — the mysterious William, who came off so confidently at first but showed signs of vulnerability later. Who was William once he left Tucker behind in that hotel room? What kind of life did he go home to? What was at the heart of that flicker of improbable shyness?

William, the man, the complete person, flaws and all, began to blossom, but he had a counterpart — Jacen, someone who had some of the blind, impulsive courage that William lacked. Then, strangely, the story's timeline skipped ahead for me and all I kept envisioning were vivid scenes of those two men — friends hiding from the world, who were so used to being these living dolls for others to play with that they had forgotten what it was to live for their own sakes. I saw them trying, and failing, and finding themselves while the only thing keeping them sane was simple companionship.

As I worked backward, reveling in the promise of their twisted innocence before they listened to their hearts and ran, other pieces fell into place. Timothy, for one, was born of a song. The poignancy of music, its changeability, hope and the emotions it evokes have always been the key to his character for me. He became real before I even included him in the story, was whispering in my ear before he whispered in Liam's, and I couldn't have written this without him.

I took a lot of factual and geographical liberties with this book in my efforts to get the characters and story where they needed to go, and many thanks to my editors for steering things back onto a more probable track whenever there were bumps in the road. Though I knew clearly how things needed to progress and where the ending lay, at times I felt like I'd internalized these characters. Jacen was my muse, giving me ideas and taking charge; Timothy was my heart; Yasha was my devil's advocate; Valery was my sanctuary; Liam was my logic and emotion, striving to keep up and survive the journey. I struggled with the more painful passages, dreading the darkness and torment they would inflict, even though the light at the end was right there, burning brightly.

This book is dedicated to everyone out there that can relate to any of the horrors that the characters in this story endured, whether it is abuse, terminal illness, loneliness, hopelessness, homelessness or the things that those inflictions drive us to do out of self-preservation or for the sake of those we love. Be steadfast in your own journeys, pay the price that fate demands and use trust to guide you, as Liam and Jacen did. The only way out is through. I would also like to dedicate this book to my husband, who taught me how to trust, how to heal the heart with laughter and be brave enough to chase my dreams, wherever they may lead.

— Lynn Kelling

About the Author

Website: www.Lynn Kelling.com

Five years ago, **Lynn Kelling** spontaneously started writing and hasn't stopped since. It all started with the desire to take a closer look at behaviors and ideas lurking at the fringes of life — basically anything that people may hesitate to speak of in mixed company, but everyone wonders about anyway. She is drawn to that which some may consider to be taboo — the darker and wilder the better — in order to expose the humanity within it. Our most telling moments are conveyed through intimacy and that which makes us feel vulnerable, powerful, or both, and so what could be more intriguing? Lynn is an artist and lover of any form of creative self-expression that comes from a place of honesty and emotion, whether it's body art or opera. She works as a multimedia designer in the Philadelphia area where she lives with her husband and two children.

About the Publisher

ForbiddenFiction.com is a publisher devoted to writing that breaks the boundaries of original erotic fiction. Our stories combine intense sexuality with quality writing. Stories at Forbidden Fiction.com not only arouse readers through sensations, but also engage them emotionally and mentally through storytelling as well-crafted as the sex is hot.

ForbiddenFiction.com is also designed to be a social reading environment. You'll have fun even if just reading the latest post each day, yet you will have the chance for so much more. Readers and authors can be part of ongoing discussions of specific works and individual authors as well as more general topics.

Sign up for a FREE Membership at **ForbiddenFiction.com**